I0772385

ALSO BY LEE S. HANNON

COLIGO, Book One of the UNITAS Series
February 22, 2022

UNITAS, Book Two of the UNITAS Series
June 23, 2022

COGNATIO, A UNITAS Series Novella
June 23, 2022

REVIRESCO, Book Three of the UNITAS Series
November 29, 2022

UNIVERSUS, A UNITAS Series Novella
November 29, 2022

The Demon's Prometheus
Coming 2023

For more information, please visit:
www.leeshannonbooks.com

And be sure to follow Lee S. Hannon on social
(Instagram, TikTok, Twitter, and Facebook):
@LeeSHannonBooks

REVIRESCO

Book Three of the UNITAS Series

REVIRESCO

Re.ui̯ˈreːs.ko
verb
conjugation: 3rd conjugation

Definitions:
1. Grow green
2. Grow strong
3. Young again

BY

Lee S. Hannon

Idella Imprint
Publishing, LLC

First Edition, 2022

The Library of Congress has catalogued the hardcover edition as follows:
Names: Lee S. Hannon, author.
Title: REVIRESCO: Book #3, The UNITAS Series: a novel / Lee S. Hannon
Description: First edition. | Boston : Idella Imprint Publishing, LLC, 2022
Identifiers: LCCN 2022920362
ISBN 9798987044506 (hardcover)
ISBN 9798987044513 (paperback)
ISBN 9798987044520 (ebook)
Subjects: Fiction, Techno-Thriller | Science Fiction | Dystopian.

Our books may be purchased in bulk for promotional, educational, or business use. Please contact your local bookseller or Idella Imprint Publishing, LLC by email at: sleehannon@gmail.com.

www.leeshannonbooks.com
Follow on Instagram, Twitter and TikTok: @leeshannonbooks

For more information or inquiries, please reach out to Idella Imprint Publishing, LLC

10 9 8 7 6 5 4 3 2 1

To Dad,

For encouraging every single one of my dreams

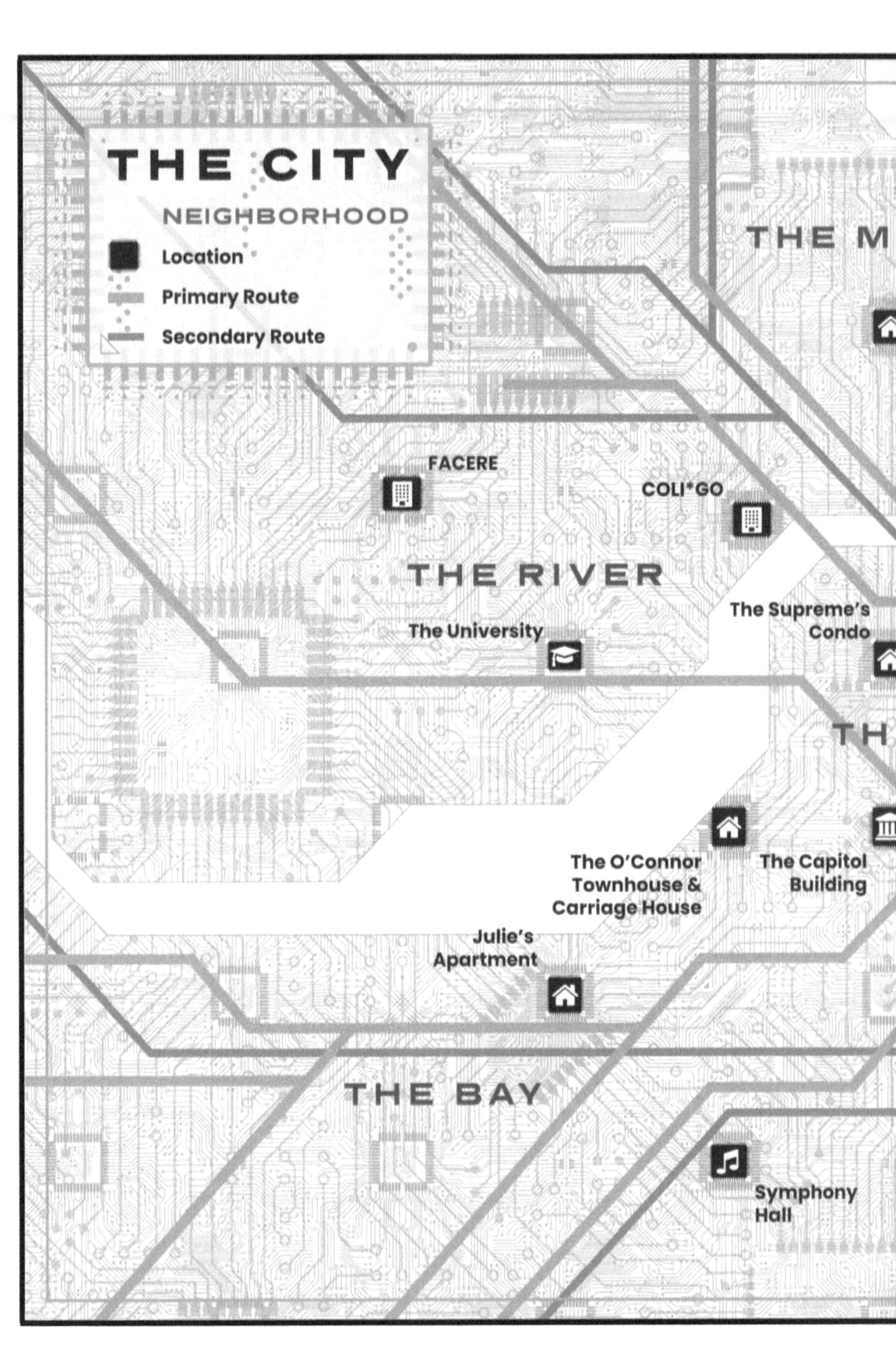

THE CITY
NEIGHBORHOOD
Location
Primary Route
Secondary Route
THE M
FACERE
COLI*GO
THE RIVER
The University
The Supreme's
Condo
THE
The O'Connor
Townhouse &
Carriage House
The Capitol
Building
Julie's
Apartment
THE BAY
Symphony
Hall

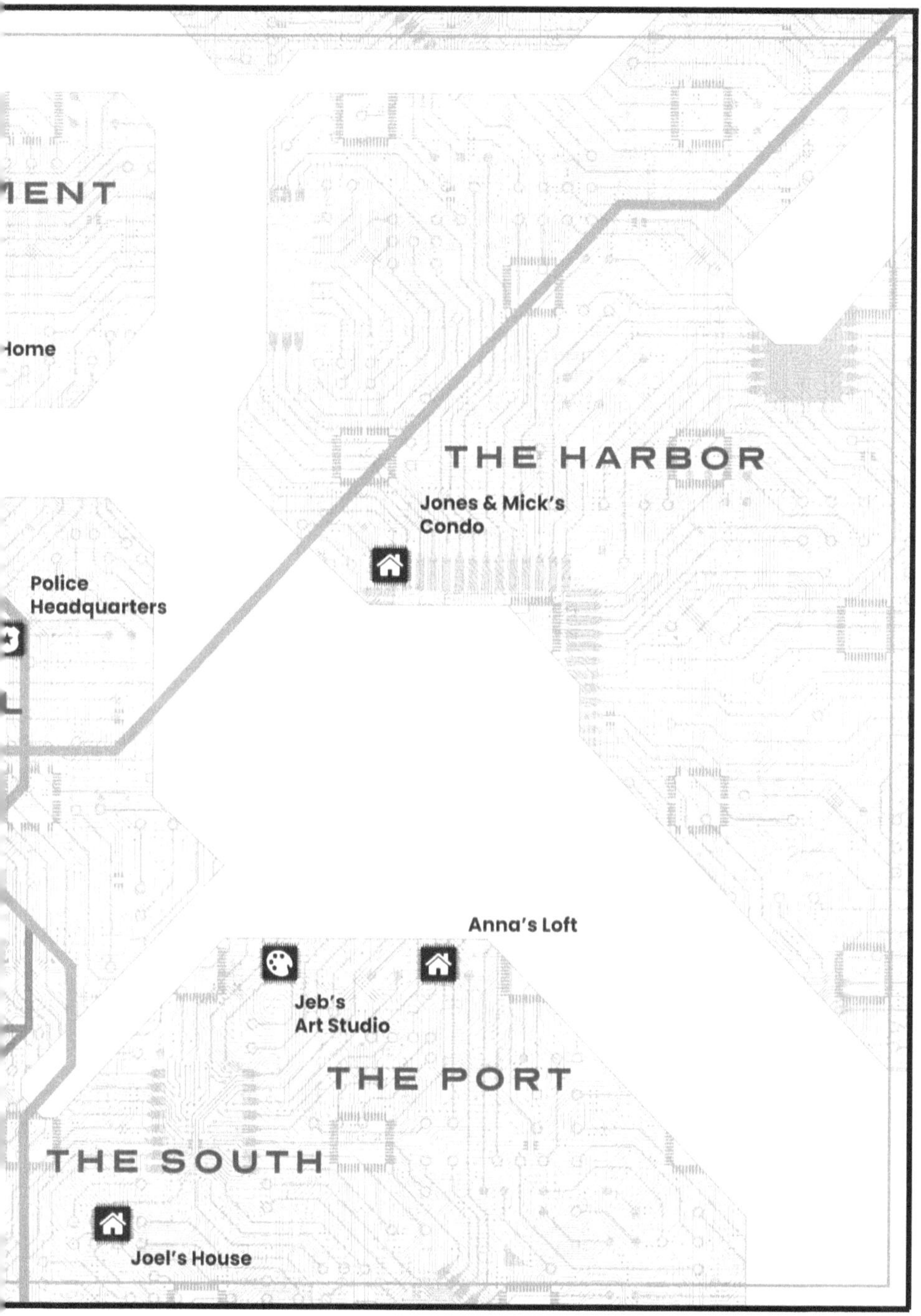

MENT
Home
THE HARBOR
Jones & Mick's
Condo
Police
Headquarters
Anna's Loft
Jeb's
Art Studio
THE PORT
THE SOUTH
Joel's House

OLD BLOODLINE FAMILY TREES

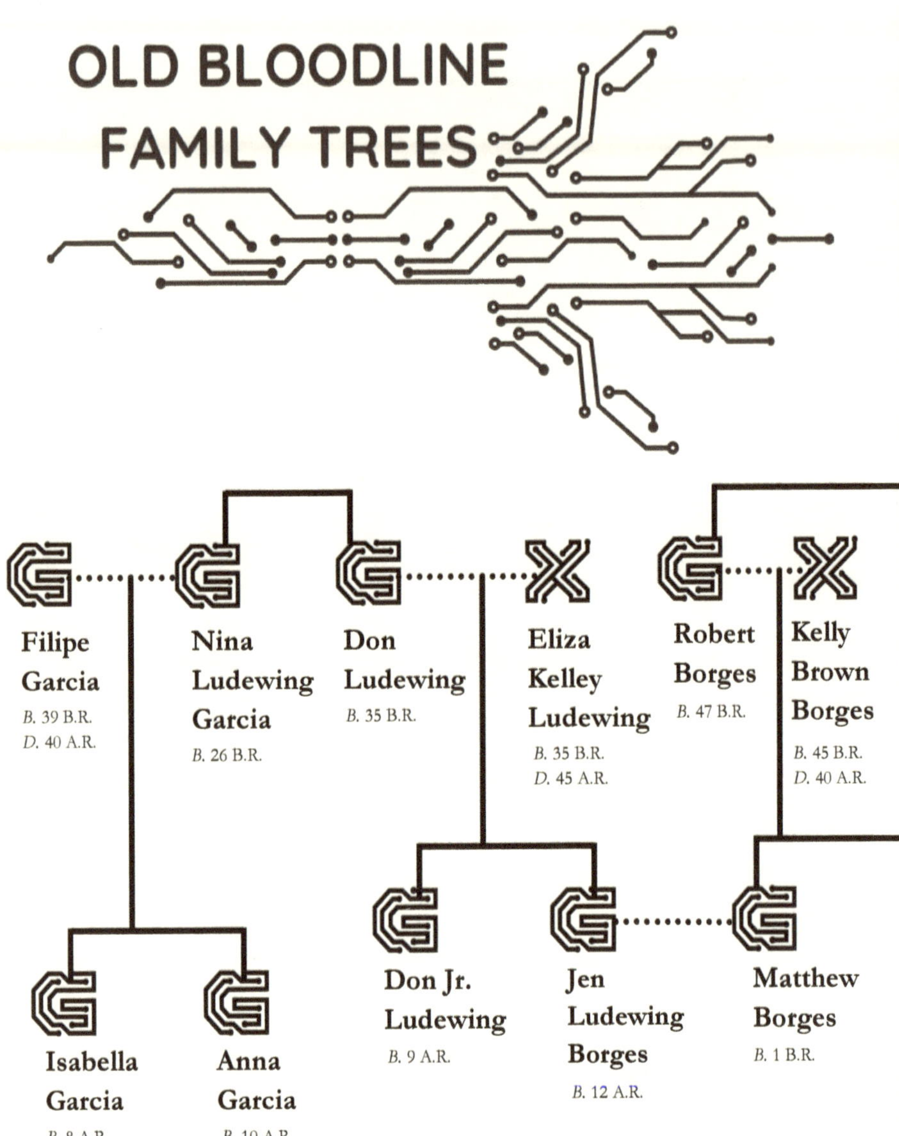

<u>Legend</u>

 Old Bloodline Lineage

 Nobody Lineage

·········· Marriage/Partnership

———— Blood Relation

B.R. = Years Before Resurgence

A.R. = Years After Resurgence

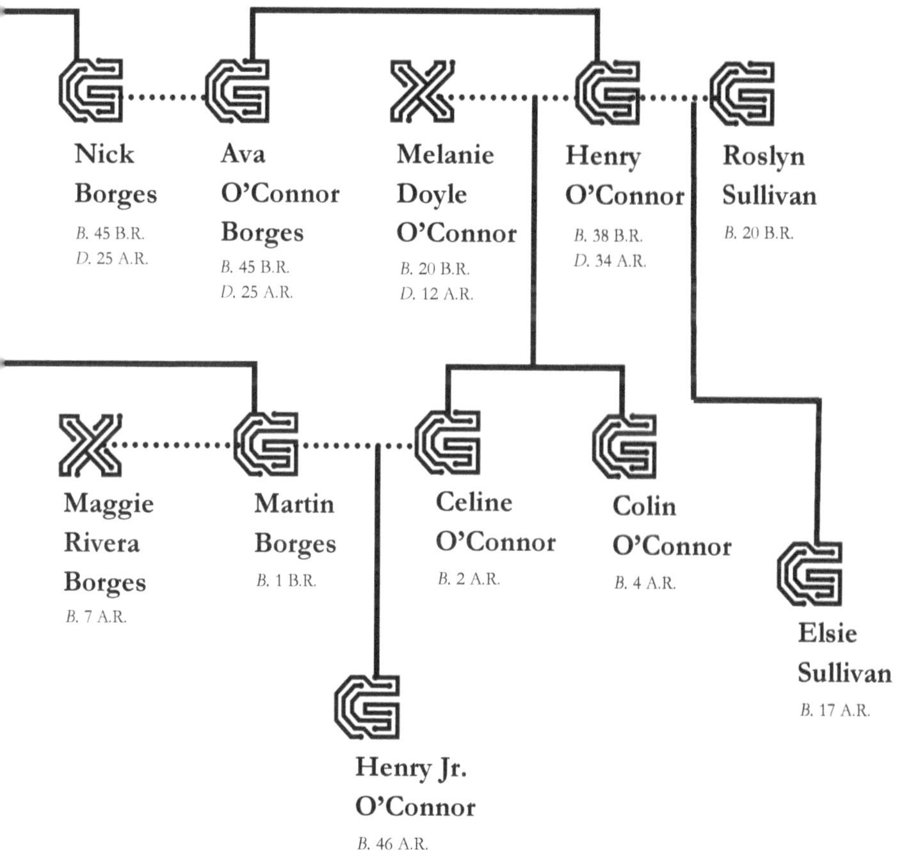

Nick Borges
B. 45 B.R.
D. 25 A.R.

Ava O'Connor Borges
B. 45 B.R.
D. 25 A.R.

Melanie Doyle O'Connor
B. 20 B.R.
D. 12 A.R.

Henry O'Connor
B. 38 B.R.
D. 34 A.R.

Roslyn Sullivan
B. 20 B.R.

Maggie Rivera Borges
B. 7 A.R.

Martin Borges
B. 1 B.R.

Celine O'Connor
B. 2 A.R.

Colin O'Connor
B. 4 A.R.

Elsie Sullivan
B. 17 A.R.

Henry Jr. O'Connor
B. 46 A.R.

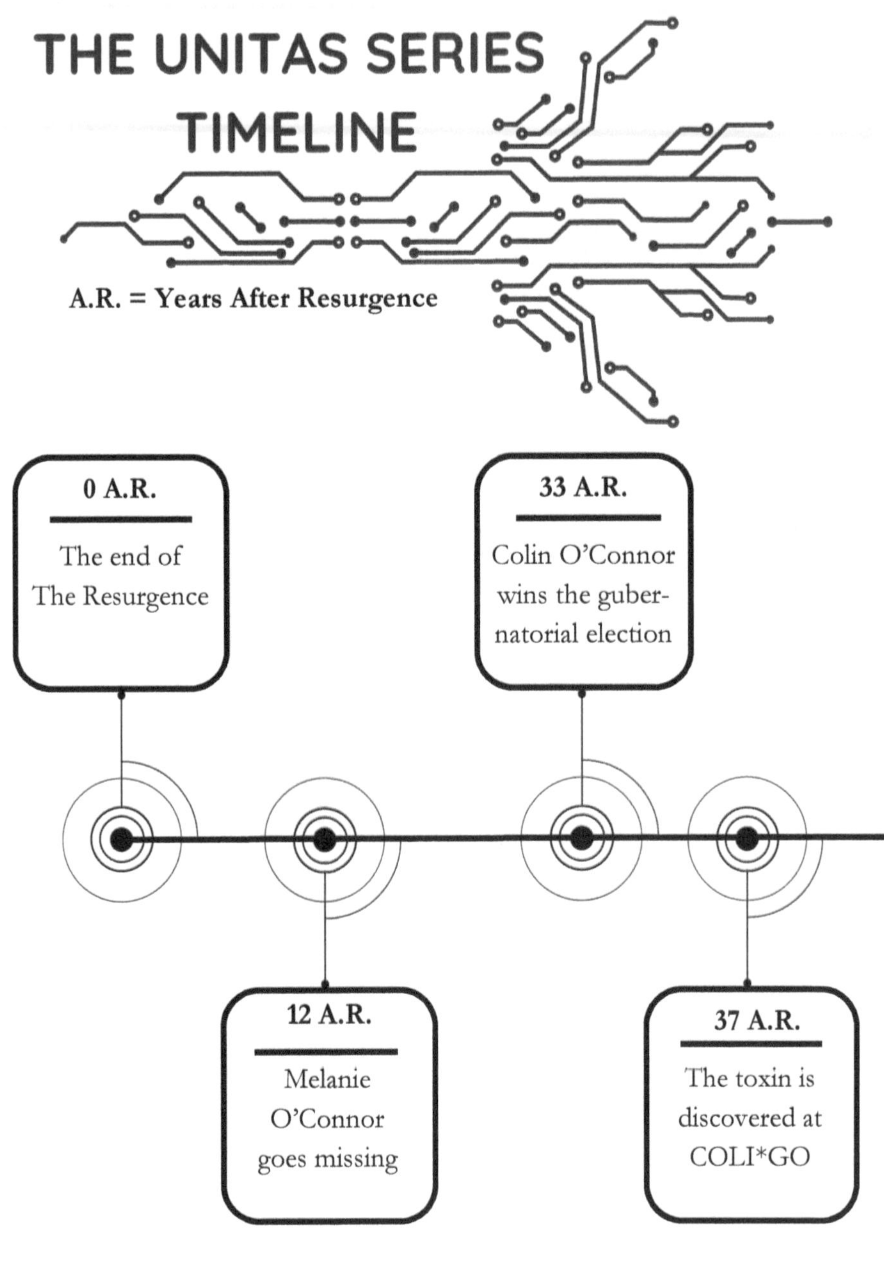

THE UNITAS SERIES TIMELINE
A.R. = Years After Resurgence
0 A.R.
The end of The Resurgence
33 A.R.
Colin O'Connor wins the gubernatorial election
12 A.R.
Melanie O'Connor goes missing
37 A.R.
The toxin is discovered at COLI*GO

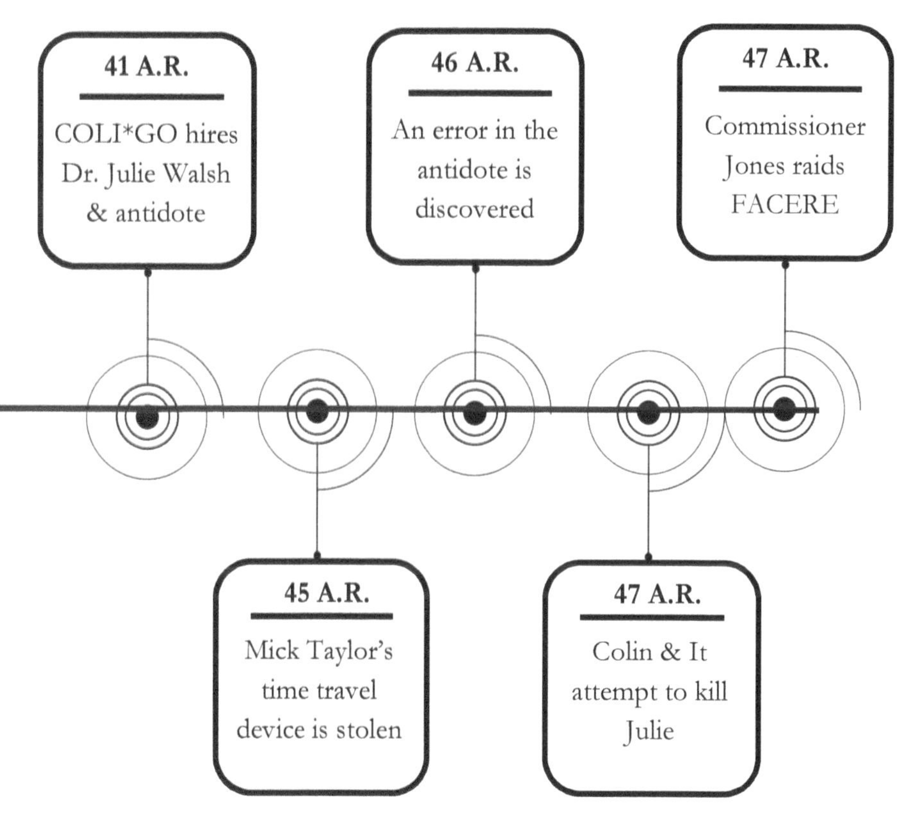

41 A.R.
COLI*GO hires Dr. Julie Walsh & antidote

46 A.R.
An error in the antidote is discovered

47 A.R.
Commissioner Jones raids FACERE

45 A.R.
Mick Taylor's time travel device is stolen

47 A.R.
Colin & It attempt to kill Julie

PART ONE

The Past

"There is a reason why all things are as they are."
—*Bram Stoker*

<u>Prologue</u>

<u>January 28th, 47 A.R. (A.R. = Years After Resurgence)</u>

The snow was cold against her ankles as she walked through the wooded trail in a summer dress. The ice crunched beneath her shoes, and a shiver rippled through her body, cascading goose-bumps across her fair and freckled skin. Gripping her cardigan tighter, she paused and observed her surroundings.

She recognized where she was—the emptiness in the dark midnight sky mixed with the whirling sounds of vehicles from the highway lingered in the distance. She wasn't far from The City.

Her home.

She traveled time before—this wasn't her first trip to the future. No one noticed her when she traveled to the summer of 45 A.R. The City was vastly different compared to decades ago.

The streets were cleaner, and optimism hung vivaciously in the air. People and androids coexisted with less strain, and there was more innovation with safer streets. Clean glass skyscrapers across in The River neighborhood and perfectly preserved historic brown-stones in The Hill neighborhood made her smile in remembrance.

The O'Connor townhouse in particular took the woman by surprise. She didn't linger too long with each visit but poked her head through the decorative black iron fence gate. A strange sense of belonging while walking the cobblestone streets back away from the townhouse and to the park coursed through her veins.

She had smiled wide walking past her favorite café. She couldn't order a coffee, for she was practically a ghost in the future—a reali-zation that at first shocked and terrified her. But she grew used to the loneliness. The large flat-screen device above the barista's head had played a news segment on Governor Colin O'Connor's popu-larity rating and his successful polling numbers in the upcoming election. People and androids loved him; the most optimistic governor The Constituency had ever elected.

An unjustified sense of pride filled the woman's chest, something she didn't deserve but cherished, anyway. Forty-five A.R. differed from right now. She could smell it in the air—the rotting, decaying embrace of darkness to come. By traveling to a date a year and a half later, an unexplainable and ominous presence surrounded her.

The bitterness clung to her with a sinister chill. But she believed in this nifty invention that had been gifted to her, this exquisite and maverick science experiment called time travel.

He told me this would all make sense once I got here, she thought, taking in the bareness of the trees surrounding her in this forest surrounding The City.

This spot was covered in snow, but a smile crept across her face. Her husband had proposed to her here. During that time of their lives, they were unencumbered with responsibilities. They were celebrating their last moments of freedom before his responsibilities in The Capitol Building.

They had ventured up the hiking trail, holding hands and laughing. When they reached the top, the skyline of The City poked through the bright baby blue sky and wispy white clouds. When she turned to him, he was down on one knee with a beautiful, classic emerald engagement ring outstretched in her direction.

But now, a gusty wind took the woman by surprise, rocking her back and forth to reality. She gripped the peculiar pair of glasses closer to her chest. The idea of time travel at first made her question her own sanity, even during the cherished moments watching from afar.

Now she was used to pain. She was used to heartbreak. She wondered if this was all some kind of mistake—a small decision that snowballed into a grave error.

These events and occurrences didn't add up. But nothing about the future made sense to Melanie O'Connor.

PART TWO

The Present

"The necessary knowledge is that of what to observe. Our player confines himself not at all; nor, because the game is the object, does he reject deductions from things external to the game."
—Edgar Allan Poe

<u>Chapter 1</u>
Julie

<u>June 23rd, 47 A.R.</u>

The black dress itched against Julie's skin like bugs creeping out of her pores, crawling and wiggling their way out to infest the world. Shadows cast along the walls of The Capitol Building, but Julie found a sense of stillness inside the walls of Governor Colin O'Connor's office.

Julie leaned back against his large leather chair and rubbed tears away from her eyes.

This wasn't part of the plan, she thought.

Rummaging through as many drawers in Colin's desk as she could, Julie looked for answers. The desk was mostly empty except for a few in-progress bills with Colin's comments scribbled across them, a half-empty bottle of expensive Scotch tucked in a dark corner wishing to remain unseen, and a small binder. Julie held the binder tightly in her hands and flipped through the pages.

Julie's heart dropped when she read its contents. Recognition quickly appeared across the pages staring back up at her: her research and pitch to the COLI*GO Board of Directors.

The charts, figures, and explanations of how the antidote she discovered could change the lives of those suffering from Alzheimer's made her smile, even years later. Colin had highlighted certain sections and made notes along the margins, all questions he eventually asked her at some point over the last few years when they worked together on the antidote's business plan.

Tears streamed down Julie's face, and a small wail escaped from her lips. Hugging the binder closer to her chest, she closed her eyes.

"Julie?" A strong but feminine whisper came from the doorway.

"Oh," Julie responded, wiping away her tears with the corners of her thumbs. "Elsie. I'm sorry. I didn't see you there."

"It's okay to cry," Elsie answered, closing the door behind her.

Elsie Sullivan was Colin's legislative aide and secretary. She was a tall woman with deep, chestnut hair that hung in loose curls around her shoulders. An intricate and beautiful tattoo of a serpent crept down her neck, sprouting from behind her earlobe. Julie and Elsie knew one another from high school but had only reunited when Elsie began working for Colin.

Elsie approached Julie with ease and sat in the chair opposite Colin's desk. "I can leave if you want me to, but I didn't like being out in the hallway by myself."

Julie nodded and grabbed Elsie's large hand with her delicate one. The day stretched out and moved at a blurred, slow pace since the morning. Earlier, Julie and Colin had stood outside The Capitol Building, and with a blink of an eye, everything changed. Two loud pops sounded in the air, and chaos erupted. Between holding a bleeding, dying Colin in her arms on the front steps and then the trip to the emergency room with a shocking discovery unearthed to her, so much swirled through Julie's mind.

Jones, Julie's best friend and The City's police commissioner, didn't have answers, but he held Julie's hand the whole way back to her studio apartment in The Bay and found her a change of clothes. Jones prepared Julie for the necessary duties following such a tragic event, snapping her back to reality when she wanted to get lost in her own sorrow and misery.

Julie had stood in her modern one-room apartment and couldn't peel her eyes away from her bed. She desperately wanted to wrap herself under the covers, close her eyes, and wake up from this nightmare. She would even take going back in time, opening her eyes, and being back in the wintertime woods, bleeding out in the snow.

Anything was better than this.

But Jones wouldn't let her. He picked through her closet, pulling out the dress she never expected. It wasn't anything overly special besides being a fashionable black dress.

The dress I wore to lunch with Isabella all those years ago, Julie had thought, staring at the ensemble ready to cry all over again. *The dress I wore the first time Colin and I admitted how we felt about each other.*

Tears erupted from her, but Jones didn't know the reason. He didn't even rush her along while all The Legislature waited for her here, back at The Capitol Building.

"When do I need to be in the Session room?" Julie asked Elsie, her head nodding toward the door.

"Soon," Elsie responded. She stopped at the chessboard on the side table opposite the governor's desk. Elsie stretched her arms out and grabbed it. Placing the board gently down between them, Elsie provided Julie with a soft smile. Two kings remained on the richly engraved wooden board, along with a few pawns, a queen, and a bishop.

"You know, Damiano's mate is one of the oldest methods of checkmating," Elsie said, pointing to the pieces set up perfectly for this particular maneuver. "It utilizes a queen and a bishop. It works by confining the king with the bishop and then uses the queen to execute the final blow."

Colin was an avid chess player and often shared fond memories of learning the game in his youth beside Emilia, the android leader who became known as The Supreme. The strong friendship between Colin and Emilia dissipated as they faced off in their eventual roles in politics. No matter how at opposite ends they were from one another, a deep and firmly rooted respect remained between the pair—one Julie found hard to understand and accept.

Elsie gently knocked the king down with the queen and looked up at Julie's emotionless facial expression. She placed the board back on the table and grabbed Julie's clasped hands in her own.

"I think it's time we leave for the ceremony."

"I don't want this, Elsie. There must be some other way?" Julie protested, her eyes shifting back to the chessboard and then down to her lap.

Elsie released Julie's hands, walked over to the floor-to-ceiling bookshelf, and grabbed a large, leather-bound volume containing The Constituency's Constitution. Carefully opening the book, Elsie flipped through the pages.

"In the event that the governor becomes incapacitated, falls ill, or cannot serve the rest of his or her term, the Session speaker takes the governor's place in the interim." Elsie looked up at Julie and shook her head. "Well, thank God Representative Joel Kennsington is dead."

Elsie's finger skimmed the lines, jumping to the next paragraph.

"If the Session speaker cannot fulfill the governor's place, the android holding supreme position shall appoint an interim governor from The Representatives of The People." Elsie paused and sighed. "And we don't have a supreme right now, either."

Elsie's eyes went back to the page when Julie didn't respond.

"In the event that a supreme cannot appoint a temporary replacement, the governor's spouse will serve. If the governor is un-married, his or her next of kin shall resume his or her place until a free and fair election can be held."

"And if the governor doesn't have any family?"

"That's it," Elsie said, closing the book with a thud. The noise echoed through the silent, hollow office. "There's nothing else written here, but that's irrelevant because Colin does have a legal spouse." Elsie placed the large volume back in its place on the shelf. "You. And the paperwork was filed back in November of 46 A.R. ratifying your marriage. I'm the one who notarized the license. If you two hadn't gotten married, then Celine is his next of kin. She would have served."

Julie wouldn't out Colin for the lie that she never signed a marriage license. She wasn't sure how Elsie notarized such a thing or how it was even possible. While she and Colin were secretly engaged for over a year, hearing him refer to Julie as his wife in front of the large crowd that morning confused her. Elsie had sent documents over a few days prior for Julie to sign, but they were a request from Colin that granted Julie the ability to claim the O'Connors' Oceanside estate as a legal residence.

Unless he used my signature from that document to place on a marriage license. But then he would have needed to travel back in time for Elsie to notarize it.

Colin never confided in Julie about using the time travel device—only his other personality, altered from his dissociative identity disorder, traveled time. It.

Was this part of It's plan or Colin's? And if this was part of It's plan, why did he keep this from me? Colin kept secrets, but It never would.

Julie grabbed the queen from the board, her thumb caressing the smooth wooden chess piece. Her fingers closed around it, and she placed it in her pocket.

"You're right," she said to Elsie. "We should go."

Elsie and Julie walked out of the governor's office and down the crowded halls of The Capitol Building. Whispers escaped from the figures with averting eyes—humans and androids alike. They paused and watched Julie with curiosity and uncertainty.

Julie was known in society for science and innovation. She acted as the interim CEO of COLI*GO, The City's largest and most prestigious biotech firm, while its founder—and Colin's sister—Celine O'Connor was out on maternity leave. Julie had developed the antidote and brought it through approval in an Alzheimer's indication. She was well known by the public and well-loved for her kindness and commitment to science and patients.

When she went missing back in the wintertime, The City cried in outroar. They demanded to know what happened to her, and the confessions of The Supreme transforming her into a posse hominem—a half-human half-android—placed a cumbersome fear in the hearts of many. Julie had her microchip removed by the surgeon responsible for its placement in the first place, and when she and Colin spoke to The City that morning, they embraced her regardless of which species she identified with.

Large wooden doors held open with iron posts led Julie and Elsie into the Session room. Inside, the ceiling soared high above their heads, and bright white columns stretched above them. The clawed pedestals rested at the bottom of the carpet's gold leaf pattern, intertwining with years of worn and weathered threads. Massive windows lingered along the walls and heavy maroon curtains cascaded down, only allowing small beams of the setting sunlight inside. The hue cast eerie shadows throughout the room.

One hundred desks of the same size and design aligned the room; the only difference between them was that half were painted blue and the other half were painted red. Each desk showcased a district number painted in gold on the front, and a list of names was engraved along the sides, indicating the representatives who served that district in the past. A haunting memory and a nod of gratitude.

Joel Kennsington's name was already carved into his desk with the dates he served The Constituency.

In the center of the room, a gold-edged casket rested atop a beautiful mahogany table. Colin's body wasn't inside but would be once the chief medical examiner finished her autopsy.

Celine O'Connor and Commissioner Jones stood beside the casket. Julie noted the leather-bound book in the crook of Jones's arm—a similar one to what Elsie read aloud from in Colin's office.

A small smile hesitated across Jones's scaly face as Julie approached. The full legislature stood from their desks as she walked down the aisle toward the center of the room. Julie stopped and looked from Jones to the high judge, another android dignitary, who sat in a seat off to the left. The high judge's shimmering blue scales flickered in almost a silver tone, and a sense of stillness momentarily calmed Julie.

Elsie stepped to the side and turned to face the rest of the room. When Julie finally made her way to Jones and Celine, the high judge nodded in her direction and stood.

"It is with great sadness that we swear in Dr. Julie Walsh as governor to The Constituency," he said, his scales vibrant alongside Jones's emerald ones.

Jones took the Constitution out and placed the book flat against his right hand. Both he and the high judge were the highest-ranking android officials now that there wasn't a supreme. Traditionally, the supreme swore in the governor alone. Jones nodded at Julie, and she took a deep breath, wishing for some of her friend's strength to pass over to her. She gulped and stepped closer.

Placing her left hand on the book's cover, the emerald stone in her engagement ring shone across the room. Eyes from the session floor followed the reflection before centering their focus back on Julie.

She looked down at the casket. It didn't matter that an emptiness filled the space or that Colin's body was in The City's morgue waiting on an official autopsy—tears pooled in the corners of Julie's eyes, and she blinked rapidly to keep them at bay.

Julie placed her right hand down on the richly stained wood, but her thoughts focused on It instead of Colin. She wondered if It felt the same pain as Colin at the very end and if Colin or It took the last breath.

Looking back up at the high judge and Jones, Julie granted them the silent permission they needed to continue with the swearing-in ceremony.

"Do you swear to uphold and defend all the laws in the Constitution of The Constituency?" Jones asked.

"I do," Julie answered with a bit more confidence than she anticipated.

"Do you swear to tirelessly persevere for the people you serve to protect and foster a safe, prosperous society for us all?"

"I do." Julie felt as if she were reciting the wedding vows she and Colin had never shared.

"Then make it known to all bearing witness on this day, June 23rd, 47 A.R. that I, Commissioner Jones, and High Judge Baxter hereby swear in The Constituency's one hundred and twenty-third governor, Governor Julie Walsh. She shall remain in office until the election committee sets a date for a gubernatorial election."

The room remained silent, and no applause followed. This wasn't a good day. Colin O'Connor was a beloved governor, one admired by both people and androids. Representatives from both sides of the room enjoyed working with Colin, and he loved all members of society, regardless of what type of species they were.

Julie removed her left hand from the leather book and placed it beside her right hand on Colin's casket. One by one, the representatives formed a line and approached her. Each clasped a white rose in their hand. The procession advanced in the silent room, and each representative placed their rose on the casket around Julie.

The last figure stilled before approaching. He stood just over six feet tall and possessed a chiseled, handsome face with dark features and welcoming large brown eyes. The man appeared to be in his late thirties with hardly any fine lines across his smooth skin. It took Julie a moment, but she recognized him. Don Ludewing Jr. paused and outstretched his white rose directly to Julie instead of placing it beside the others.

"My condolences, Dr. Walsh," he said in a deep, hushed voice.

Julie grabbed the rose's stem, and her fingertips brushed against

Don's. Her heart swelled and then raced when a thorn pierced her fingertip.

Don was the only representative to address her directly. Julie appreciated the rarity of the old bloodline man's sincerity.

Chapter 2
Commissioner Jones

<u>June 23rd, 47 A.R.</u>

The commissioner's office felt eerily silent, and even the streets outside—which normally buzzed with traffic and pedestrians—remained empty. Reporters and the media swarmed the lobby of the police headquarters, having followed Jones from Julie's swearing-in ceremony.

A slight knock on his office door drew his attention away from his device.

Dr. Anna Garcia, The City's chief medical examiner, stepped cautiously into Jones's office and took a seat. Her uneasiness spread across her dark hazel eyes, and she bowed her head down to look at her hands.

"I'm not sure I have the courage to do the . . . the autopsy alone."

Jones averted his gaze away from her, afraid when she looked up their eyes would meet. The thought of cutting into the governor's body caused a pulsating shiver across his scales. The scene of Governor Colin O'Connor's assassination violently replayed in Jones's processor. Colin and Julie had stood together outside The Capitol Building, and Jones lingered behind them. The couple addressed the crowd with enthusiasm and optimism.

But then there was a loud pop.

Jones watched in horror as Colin turned, his eyes shifting toward Julie before a second shot was fired. He crashed into Jones's best friend, his skull cracked and half-blown out. Colin's blood trickled down the stained, worn limestone steps, and all that remained were Julie's screams.

Closing his eyes, Jones shook the memory.

"I will be there with you every step of the way," he said, leaning forward and grasping her hands.

Quiet tears and sobs escaped his typically strong and brazen friend. Anna Garcia was not a woman Jones would ever describe as frail or delicate. She even hated the O'Connor family, driven equally by her distaste for Colin O'Connor's unruly demons in combination with the infamous old bloodline family feud between the O'Connors and the Garcias. But despite Colin's dark past, he was a beloved governor who cared about equality for humans and androids—and in the end, he championed a place in society for The Supreme's hybrid creations too.

"Did this really happen? I keep wondering when I'm going to wake up from this nightmare that we call a city. We were just healing from the pain and torment of uncertainty, and then this had to happen?" Anna rose from her seat and walked toward the window.

Peering beyond the blinds, she sighed. Members of the media loitered outside the police headquarters. They were relentless whenever a major tragedy was committed in The City and had been salivating at the chance of speaking to both the chief medical examiner and the commissioner about the governor's assassination. But nighttime threatened their persistence, darkness in The City's streets a newly emerged threat with a sniper out on the loose, desperate for blood and retribution.

At least the media had captured the swearing-in ceremony with class, Jones thought.

A few hours earlier, he watched as each representative, both androids and humans, approached Julie with hesitancy. Colin's shoes were not only enormous to fill but his looming shadow also cast a long, lingering haunting within the walls of The Capitol Building.

"I'm beginning to think The City will never know peace."

Anna looked back at Jones, and he shook his head. Without Anna Garcia, Jones would be lost. They formed a strong friendship a few years back when Jones began working as a detective for the android police force and arrived on the scene of an unusual, horrific murder case. He and Anna hunted down the serial killer—one who waited years in between his kills, but whose kills were gruesome and tragic. While it took them time to uncover the killer's identity, both Jones and Anna found the answer on their own. Jones wasn't sure what to do when he discovered Colin was a killer, knowing that if he turned Governor O'Connor in, instability and outrage would pour across The City, and that his best and only friend, Dr. Julie Walsh, would never recover. Anna also didn't take any action, knowing both Colin and The Supreme were up to no good. Instead, she quit her position and lay low until Jones was appointed commissioner.

It took begging and pleading for Anna to come back as the coroner, but he promised her justice and transparency in his new post, something the former commissioner never abided by because of his politically close relationship with The Supreme.

When The Supreme was arrested in February by The Legislature for treason and murder charges, the previous commissioner and all the other androids The Supreme had appointed stepped down from their roles. The Representatives of The Androids were quick to fill the empty positions—except for The Supreme's.

Peace and stability remained important staples in society, regardless of what type of being someone was. Maintaining that peace became Jones's number one priority. Typically, crime wasn't rampant in The City. Murders were a rare occurrence, and both humans and androids respected one another without too many disgruntled arguments or attacks. But with uncertainty after various terrorist attacks, the streets weren't safe anymore. The Supreme's arrest exposed her human-android hybrid creations, ones she called posse hominems. A sect of people called Humanizers, who believed androids were second-class citizens, flooded the streets in numbers. They set a vicious manhunt against posse hominems, murdering them in the streets and ensuing chaos.

Jones had finally helped settle the streets, having raided FACERE, the android manufacturing facility. He and Governor O'Connor's legislative aide, Elsie Sullivan, discovered the leaders of this movement—FACERE's finance lead, Paul McGuire, and Representative Joel Kennsington—and stormed the company. They rescued Julie in the process and helped The Supreme escape. Governor O'Connor and Julie's remarks this morning were supposed to bring peace and joy, not bullets.

"We have to figure out who was behind this," Jones said with a strong current of poise lacing his voice, "or The City will never forgive me."

***

The steel walls and cold tile floors in the morgue made the room feel as if it were ten degrees cooler than it actually was. A white noise hummed in Jones's ears as they stepped farther inside. A gurney with a body bag sat untouched in the center of the room.

Even with Governor O'Connor's body inside, the whole situation didn't feel real. Images of Colin's skull exploding around Julie—his skin, his bones, and his blood—flickered before Jones's vision repeatedly. He heard the screaming. He heard her scream.

Jones closed his eyes. Anna stood still and looked down at the black body bag. Jones couldn't see inside, but he wondered what kind of fear Anna felt knowing she would have to unzip Colin out of his confinement and perform an ungodly task. Her body shook, and Jones placed his hand on her shoulder.

I must remain strong. I must be the rock that Julie needs. I must help Anna with this gruesome endeavor. Jones's scales flashed a deep hunter green. He fiddled with his sleeves even though Anna knew that he could feel more emotions than what was legally allowed for androids.

He was only allowed to feel and understand up to 20 percent of human emotions. Feeling and understanding human emotions were distinctly different. The Constituency feared that between their logic and knowledge, if androids also understood everything a human felt, they would have an unfair advantage in the world. When Jones was in high school, he convinced Julie to remove the microchip from his processor and adjust the code, allowing him to not only understand 60 percent of human emotions but also experience them. She warned him that the code was a continuous learning model and that, with time, he might acquire more understanding and more emotional intelligence. Each time Jones experienced a feeling, his scales gave him away, illuminating brightly and changing colors.

Before Julie modified the microchip in his processor, Jones only understood about 13 percent of human emotions but only experienced half that amount. Feeling an emotion was painful for androids. The sensation cascaded through their scales on their bodies, making the hues change and vibrate in various colors. Jones normally possessed green scales, but when he felt an emotion, his scales shifted from muted shades to vibrant emeralds. In the trick of the light, sometimes his scales appeared neon or brighter.

As time went on and he aged, Jones was surprised to feel the sensation in his scales more frequently, and the database that was essentially his brain stored more and more information. He cataloged everything—whether or not he wanted to.

He wasn't exactly sure the percentage of feelings he now understood and felt, but he guessed it to be somewhere close to 80 percent.

"It's time," Anna said and handed Jones a pair of latex gloves. She hastily unzipped the body bag, and Jones helped her move Colin over to the examiner's table.

The smell of dried, rotting blood filled Jones's nose, and he held his breath, stepped back, and let out a loud cough. Anna maintained a flat expression while Jones worked more diligently to compose himself. Jones and Anna carefully removed Colin's clothes: a navy suit and an off-white dress shirt now painted vibrantly with his blood, a beautiful deep green tie symbolizing a color of importance to his old bloodline family, and his intricate and stylish brown dress shoes.

Anna's gloved fingers pressed down on Colin's chest, and she looked up at Jones with a wide stare.

"His body still feels warm."

There was no doubt in Jones's processor that Colin was dead. No one could survive two gunshot wounds to the head like this, and the man didn't have a pulse. But considering Colin's body had been left in a chilly morgue, in a temperature-controlled room, Jones also found this unsettling.

Colin is a time traveler, or at least he and It traveled time, Jones thought with curiosity. *And this is the first time anyone held a dead time traveler's body in their presence.*

"Fucking Mick," Jones muttered under his breath.

His relationship with Mick Taylor was strained, one that made little sense even to Jones's logical android nature. Jones loved Mick and still did; he couldn't deny that fact any longer. But Mick and Jones broke off their relationship back in the winter, when Jones learned that Mick helped The Supreme in her madness, feeding her with information about the past and the future so that she could develop her creatures and plot her attack to control The Constituency while unleashing her full retribution against humans.

Time travel remained a bit of a mystery to Jones, but he had helped Mick initially with his research at The University. Mick utilized the proteins in blood as the mechanism that propelled a human forward or backward in time. Blood held all the answers to a person's life, a unique identifying biomarker that allowed a traveler to journey to the beginning or end of their life—or anywhere in-between. Where time travel went awry was when Mick began traveling on other people's blood. The side effects were jarring: premature aging, amnesia, fine lines, dry skin, and not to mention Mick's constant emotional swings.

Mick only created a certain number of devices, and both Colin and Julie possessed some. The journal Mick kept with his notes and observations of time travel wasn't entirely reliable, but there were some truths to his ambiguous assumptions, including that a time traveler was invincible to death in most situations, unless they were killed by another time traveler.

So, Colin was killed by another time traveler.

He looked back down at Colin. He was an attractive man in his early forties with a strong jaw and slight stubble, large steel-gray eyes, dark hair barely peppered with gray, and an extremely tall build that was muscular but approachable. His legs and feet hung off the edge of the table, his olive skin appearing paler in the harsh lights of the morgue, and the fine lines peeking out from the corners of his eyes seemed more pronounced than the last time Jones thought to look.

Was Colin traveling time on someone else's blood? Or is this just some consequence of human skin in death?

Jones was so lost in his thoughts that he hadn't realized Anna had walked away until her petite frame loomed over Colin's still body. She held a surgical knife in her right hand and pulled down her protective visor guard. Almost in slow motion, the knife closed in on Colin—an odd sight considering the nature of Colin's own kills. Stab wounds, a shiny knife piercing the skin of so many women . . . so many connected women in politics and at COLI*GO.

Julie's frantic scribbles in Mick's journal appeared in Jones's line of vision. She had been the last keeper of the journal. Unlike Mick, Julie's entries focused on her work with the antidote and the toxin—suggesting that she was finally close to scientific break-through. Her second to last entry depicted a quest for Jones, for him to truly understand what happened to a time traveler when they died. Julie defied many time travel "rules" that Mick lay forth in his research of the advancement, but her entry was dated from June 23rd.

She warned me of Colin's assassination. A large pit of horror filled him at his core.

"Wait!"

Anna paused and looked up at Jones with an arched brow.

"What if this is different?" Jones asked. "What if something is very different about this because of time travel?"

"Are you telling me," Anna said with a firm huff, "that Colin O'Connor traveled time?"

Jones nodded slowly.

The clank of the steel surgical knife colliding with the metal tray of tools beside Anna burst inside the room. Anna paced back and forth with her hands on her hips, shaking her head and stopping every few moments to speak but somehow finding no words.

"Maybe we're all just a little bit shaken from what happened this morning. And knowing that someone was willing to go to this length to continue the chaos in The City might have both you and me second-guessing ourselves." Anna's words were grounded and strong. Logical.

Jones wanted her to be right. He wanted this all to be nerves and nerves alone. But as much as Jones wished he were a human, he wasn't. He was an android. He did not have "nerves." Sensibility and facts coursed through his man-made body. He couldn't deny that there was something different about Colin, about his lifeless-ness. This wasn't a trick of the mind because Jones didn't have a mind to trick.

"Jones," Anna said, "are you telling me that the man with no pulse, the man with no heartbeat, isn't dead?"

"I don't know. I don't think it's that simple."

"Then why would cutting into his body change any of that?" Anna's voice erupted inside the morgue, and her flailing arms pointed in Colin's direction. "He's missing half his head!"

Jones closed his eyes. He couldn't shake knowing that Anna wasn't wrong, but something about defiling Colin's body bothered him.

"We can't put this off, Jones," she said, finding a seat on the stool she normally kept beside the examiner's table. "The Legislature won't allow it. We need to find the assassin."

"We know what happened. We don't need to cut into his body."

"Are you asking me to lie on my autopsy report?" Anna walked closer to Colin's body and peered down.

Jones shook his head, but Anna wasn't having any of it.

"Yes, you are," she accused him. "But let me play along with your strange aversion to this autopsy for a moment and try to understand why your processor is so freaked out about this. We know that the first bullet entered through his forehead here." Anna pointed and tilted Colin's face to the side. "And exited here in the back of his head. The weapon was powerful; it blasted his skull out."

"That's correct. I'd go as far to say it was some kind of hunting rifle. Not anything that my sniper team would ever use."

"And the second bullet entered through the side of his head and exited out the other side." She pointed to what little remained of Colin's face. "Slicing right through his brain."

"Yes, well, he was shot first in the front, and between the forcefulness of the bullet and probably his body's shock, he turned. He turned and faced Julie, who was standing to his right. That's why the second shot ended up in the side of his head, not the front, like intended."

"And that's what you want me to write in the report?" Anna asked, her eyes glancing back and forth from her surgical tools to Jones.

"Well, that's what happened. And we collected the bullets. None of them are lodged."

"Should I also mention that the commissioner asked me to not run a full analysis?"

"Isn't your job to determine the cause of death?"

"Yes, but it is also for me to tell the detectives who work this case what else was going on underneath the skin. That might help them uncover his killer. Was Colin O'Connor addicted to any illegal drugs and, therefore, a drug dealer and his gang went after him? Was Colin O'Connor filled with cancerous cells that were already killing him? Did Colin O'Connor have any kind of medical conditions that affected him?"

Jones gulped, and the two looked at one another with her lingering threat.

"But I can see all of that, Anna. With my new eyes. The new technology from FACERE. The technology that Maggie Rivera upgraded me with. You don't have to cut through Colin's body. I can answer all of that right now."

Anna's eyes blinked rapidly, and she took a loud breath. "But I promised I'd never do this again."

Jones leaned his head to the side, unsure what her comment insinuated.

"Promise me you will reveal everything. No secrets."

"Are you saying you don't trust me?" Jones asked. "After everything we've been through?"

Anna rolled her eyes, aware of her jaded and unfair accusation. Jones looked back down at Colin's body and allowed his eyes to scan him. All of Colin's vitals—his pulse rate, blood pressure— showed up blank, but the technology did work in providing toxicology reporting and body temperature, which was still too high, running at ninety-eight degrees Fahrenheit. A great reprise of other biometrics marked themselves in the report within Jones's processor.

"The governor wasn't high on any drugs, but there is a slight bit of alcohol in his veins. We all know he had a fondness for Scotch. He smoked a cigar within twenty-four hours of his death. No cancerous cells are in his body, at least nothing active or threatening." Jones closed his eyes. "But yes, you're right, his dendrites appear slightly damaged, so the cortex of his brain is a bit shrunken. Not significantly, but patients who suffer from Alzheimer's, dementia, and certain psychological conditions have smaller cortexes compared to their healthy human peers. And I do have confidential information about the governor's medical conditions—he was taking Julie's drug, COL23 for a period of time, but I don't see any of it in his body now."

Anna pulled off her gloves with force. An annoyed and slightly angered sneer crossed her face. She walked over to the camera that was required to record her autopsies and pulled the battery out, throwing it to the ground. The crunch of it underneath her booted foot made Jones cringe.

"Fine, I will trust you won't fuck me over on this one, Commissioner Jones," Anna said with agitation, "but we cannot let anyone know I didn't perform the full autopsy. You must sign off as the witness on this, and our story is that we thought the camera was on and recording but, apparently, the battery was never charged."

"Understood."

"And now you'll help me dress him and we'll deliver him to the cemetery tomorrow morning . . . where he will be buried for good, along with our lies."

Chapter 3
Celine

The townhouse was quiet when Celine returned from the ceremony at The Capitol Building. She watched as Julie Walsh was sworn in as governor, how the girl blotted back tears that still escaped the corners of her eyes, no matter how much she blinked to keep them away.

Her brother was dead. Gone from this world, or at least, this dimension. He was a time traveler, and knowing how Julie made her way back into their lives gave Celine a sense of hope that this wasn't the last time she would see Colin.

Celine and Colin had a plan, and now she didn't know what to believe. Between Colin's assassination and the news of his marriage to Dr. Julie Walsh, a million thoughts turned inside Celine's mind. No one knew Julie and Colin were married—Celine didn't even know the two snuck behind her back last fall to officiate and legalize their scandalous affair. Instead, her brother followed in their father's footsteps—marrying a "nobody" in society and further diluting their old bloodline. And now that "nobody" held all of the power for the people in The Constituency.

And they love her, Celine thought, annoyed by Julie's popularity in the court of public opinion for humans, androids, and hybrids. There would be no easy way to usurp Julie Walsh from her new role without an outroar.

Celine sighed and, with a trembling hand, reached for the bottle of vodka in the back of the cabinet, pouring it with a heavy hand into her glass.

"Take it easy there." Emilia's smooth voice echoed from behind Celine.

Celine smiled coyly and turned around. The Supreme was an inch taller than her but stood stiffly, like most androids. She donned beautiful amber scales, and when they shimmered with emotion, a deep golden hue emulated in an autumn fashion. Emilia was The Supreme's given name, one that no one used anymore except for Celine. Emilia took her position as the android leader with the utmost importance and allowed it to consume her entire identity.

After Colin exposed Emilia for treason and her creation of hybrids to The Legislature, her fate remained in limbo. The high judge allowed FACERE to take possession of The Supreme and study her processor. Maggie Rivera, the former head of FACERE, had other plans for The Supreme, but her brother and Commissioner Jones helped Emilia escape. Nobody knew where Emilia hid now—right under their noses in the O'Connor family townhouse—but someone was bound to discover her eventually, especially with the sizeable bounty on her head.

Celine and Emilia were close growing up. She lived with the O'Connor family, and the friendship forged between the young girls was a bond deeper than Celine had ever formed with anyone. She loved Emilia and feared that, at FACERE, Emilia lost her ability to understand and feel emotion and that she would lose her memory. Androids could only indulge in a certain number of human feelings, but the former supreme had programmed Emilia to understand them all even if she could only physically experience a small percentage of them.

While Julie left a distaste in Celine's mouth, she couldn't hate the young scientist. She saved Emilia at FACERE and reprogrammed her processor. And for some reason, her brother loved Julie. Celine might not like their relationship, but she respected Colin.

"My brother was assassinated less than eight hours ago. I think I'm entitled to as much vodka as I'd like." Celine walked past Emilia and headed for the living room.

The O'Connor townhouse was elegant and classic, a multilevel brick brownstone with a large roof deck overlooking the views of The Hill and even a small stretch of The River. Colin used the townhouse as his primary residence. As the only male heir in the family, most assets were left in his possession when their father passed away. It didn't matter that Celine was older than him. She lacked the equipment between her legs that she needed to claim what was rightfully hers.

The couch engulfed Celine's body, and she closed her eyes and allowed herself to sink in deeper.

"He'll come back, won't he? He promised."

Emilia didn't respond to Celine's comment, and a sense of doom settled in on the couch next to her. After several moments of silence, Emilia's scaly fingers ran through Celine's chestnut hair, a calming and appreciated gesture. The sounds of Henry Jr., Celine's baby boy, wailed through the corridors of the townhouse. She stirred from Emilia's grip and looked up the stairs. As quickly as his crying began, it stopped.

"I'm trying to understand grief, but this is a new emotion for me and I'm not sure what to think," said Emilia.

Emilia and Colin had been close too—and even when they were serving opposite ends of The Legislature, they always worked together. They appreciated how fiercely they both played their metaphorical games of chess.

"The thing about grief is, it's different for everyone. There are a million thoughts I'm experiencing, and several of them, I don't understand myself."

Celine looked up at Emilia before grabbing her face and kissing her. Urgency spread through Celine, the need for distraction both raw and forceful. She grasped for The Supreme's hands and led them to the places that yearned for release. Straddling Emilia on the couch, Celine moaned softly into her mouth.

Their love was forbidden, an indulgence that must remain a secret and a behind-closed-doors affair. Androids and humans were not allowed to mix their relations beyond friendship—romantic partnerships were against the law and strictly forbidden in The Constituency. Fear that a species-mixed couple would become too knowledgeable and powerful being the only antiquated reason.

But these restrictions didn't stop Celine and The Supreme from expressing their desires now that Emilia was out of the public eye. A fire spread through Celine while Emilia's fingers explored her. Celine took hold of Emilia's wrist, and Emilia bit down on Celine's lower lip before retreating.

"I'm sorry, I shouldn't," The Supreme said with shameful, averted eyes.

Pulling Emilia into a warm embrace, Celine said, "Don't apologize for anything."

They sat on the couch together in silence. A sense of stillness brought them together, allowing them to forget about the pains of this day.

"Unfortunately," Emilia said, a flicker of her enchanting scales distracting Celine's attention, "these grave events have exposed how the pieces have fallen on the board. We need to discuss our next move."

Celine sighed. This frustratingly android tendency of logic deeply rooted in Emilia would never truly subside. Logic trumped passion. Logic always outweighed spearheading forward with emotion.

"You're right," Celine said, shifting off Emilia and putting her head between her hands. "And we need to figure it out quickly."

"Now that we know Julie's microchip was removed, I'll need a different host." Emilia's eerie words reminded Celine of their original, sinister plan.

Emilia created hybrids in COLI*GO's lower lab. All hybrids started out as humans first before an android microchip was implanted into their brains. Emilia explained the process to Celine, how each person was taken and how each microchip was different. A control device tracked all the microchips, keeping biometrics and tabs on her creations.

When Emilia suggested planting a blank microchip into Dr. Julie Walsh, Celine agreed it was a glorious idea. The blank microchip contained Bluetooth technology and acted as a space saver—a place silently awaiting The Supreme's own code.

Julie would be the perfect host. She rose as the apple of the public's eye, and Colin trusted her explicitly. The original plan included introducing hybrids to The Legislature and lighting the match of turmoil. Celine knew her brother was an idealist at heart—he would die on his own sword to request hybrids receive the same rights as people and androids in the government. And Emilia believed there would only be room for one leader in The Legislature, because three would simply be disastrous.

As a hybrid and not an old bloodline appreciated by androids and humans, Julie stood the best chance of winning a free and fair election. She'd easily receive the popular vote from all three species with the backing of Celine from COLI*GO and Colin on behalf of The Legislature.

Once Julie won, Celine would upload Emilia's microchip code into the blank one lodged into Julie's brain with the control panel device she kept in her condo. Then The Supreme would live inside Julie's body.

A small sense of regret waded through Celine. She hid this plan from Colin—his ignorance paramount to its success. And Celine had never concealed a secret this large from her brother.

"We'll have to be thoughtful on this one," Celine said with a small sense of distress. "I have the control device back at my condo."

Chapter 4
Elsie

<u>June 23rd, 47 A.R.</u>

Colin's quiet office at The Capitol Building provided no comfort to Elsie. She hadn't figured out her feelings about her half-brother's assassination happening only hours before. But she was glad Colin confided in her—that he told her the truth about her father.

After thirty years of believing her father was a nobody, she realized he was a man from one of the most notorious old bloodline patriarchs, which unsettled her. Elsie hadn't confronted her mother on the issue, wondering if she placed the pieces correctly on the board, she might lead her mother to reveal the truth on her own. But Elsie's tactics were rooted in complete innocence when the little devil pin pricking inside her mind demanded otherwise.

Roslyn Sullivan was a poised woman. She came from an old bloodline family but was cast out when she became pregnant out of wedlock with Elsie. Roslyn wasn't married, the oldest child, or the one to inherit the majority of her family's trust and legacy. They were a "lesser" old bloodline family. Roslyn was independent and fierce—she kept her career in politics, easily getting reelected each cycle as a representative of The People until her early retirement. Representing The Monument neighborhood, a district deeply invested in loyalty and hard-working families, Roslyn looked out for her community, and they looked out for her.

Elsie turned on a single light in the office and paced toward Colin's desk. Julie had looked particularly tiny seated in his large worn leather chair, but Elsie didn't feel as inadequate here. She sunk into the seat and closed her eyes. With outstretched hands grasping the arms of the chair, Elsie imagined how different her life would have been growing up the way Colin had.

As an O'Connor.

The best schools. The best tutors. The best restaurants and symphonies. The family retreats to The Oceanside. It all sounded like a fantastical fairy tale.

The O'Connors lived ostentatiously but somehow garnered the respect of normal, everyday people. The Sullivans had enough money, but the family drained their trust instead of reinvesting into it, while old bloodline families like the O'Connors capitalized on their long-term wealth with continuous business and political ventures.

Would I be more than just a legislative aide and secretary? Would I be sitting in this seat? she wondered, opening her eyes and allowing the dusky sunset to soothe her pounding heart.

But Colin had a distaste for the man who raised him, and Elsie wanted to know why. To the outside world, Henry O'Connor was a legend. He helped bring a sense of security back to The Constituency after a tumultuous rise of violence from The Resurgence. He worked with androids even though he believed humans held more sway as their creators. Henry was noted as more somber after his wife's death, but he still vivaciously supplied the people he served with meaningful change.

A sharp sting sliced through Elsie's head, but the moment passed, the threat of something similar to a migraine leaving as strongly as it had arrived. The microchip in her brain still puzzled her and the full effects of what and why still a concern.

Elsie was a rambunctious child, acting out in hopes of gaining her mother's attention and affection. She had a wild side but never considered herself dangerous or violent. After discovering something went terribly wrong at Celine and Martin's party—the night she referred to as her transformation—anger festered uncontrollably inside her. Headaches plagued Elsie, and dry, itchy rashes flashed across her skin.

Then she met the infamous artist who was supposed to be dead.

Commissioner Jones shot Jeb Taylor in the courtroom after he was put on trial for Kathleen Murphy's murder. But there he was—Jeb Taylor—sitting on her couch, waiting for her to return home after a night of letting loose. His hands had shaken as if he were afraid of her, and he handed her two letters.

"They come from The Supreme," Jeb had said. He instructed

Elsie to open the first letter after he left and the second to be opened on June 23rd, 47 A.R. Jeb had confessed to Elsie the process—that he had kidnapped her at Celine's party and taken her to COLI*GO for the operation that transformed her into a posse hominem. Learning that a microchip resided in her brain infuriated Elsie to no end. She'd smashed most of her glassware, a powerful rage crashing through her as she searched for the imperfection on her neck. A tiny silver scar—barely noticeable.

The serpent tattoo on Elsie's skin itched in response to her memory. She lightly touched the ink, the most valuable piece of information that only a few knew about: Julie, Colin, Commissioner Jones, and Peter Schneider.

The first letter Jeb gave her was typed crisply in the logical but riddle-filled ramblings of The Supreme, and she kept it in her condo in The Monument.

Elsie kicked up her feet on Colin's desk in a similar fashion to what he constantly used to do, especially when contemplating a challenging piece of legislation. Elsie had only worked for Colin for a few months, but they grew close in their time together. Even before knowing her true identity, Colin always acted like a protective older brother.

The sealed envelope of Jeb Taylor's second letter burned in Elsie's hand, the paper on fire between her fingertips. She paused several times with her fingernail tucked into the corner flap— seconds away from ripping it open.

The events of the day caught back up with Elsie. Colin's assassination wasn't part of the plan, and knowing that The Supreme gave her this letter and wanted her to open it on this particular day gave Elsie an incredibly haunting chill.

Was it The Supreme who shot Colin? Why would she? He had just saved her. But nothing else made any sense. No one else made any sense.

The rip echoed loudly in the governor's office, and Elsie stared at the envelope one last time before pulling out the note she had been instructed to read today. The paper was folded in threes, thin and translucent, similar to the first letter. Elsie expected another neatly typed confession: a confession for the truth behind Colin's death.

But a sloppy, familiar, loopy handwriting consumed only a few lines on the page.

Dear Elsie,

I desperately need your help. Peter cannot be trusted—please remind me of this. He has acquired a new pharmaceutical asset. It is more dangerous than the toxin, and he is going to play off this drug as new research from my trials with the antidote. I'm not sure how he came into its possession, but please, I need you to provide me with this information so I don't use his new molecule in my research.

Best,
Julie

Elsie's heart fluttered in her chest as the thin parchment slipped out of her grasp. Floating down, it landed soundlessly on the marble floors. Julie and Elsie had become fast friends in the last few months. Both were strong, ambitious women often portrayed as underdogs. The bond cemented between them when Julie time traveled and couldn't let anyone know that she never died that winter night in the woods outside The City or of her true location.

But if Julie sent me this letter, does that mean she's now working with The Supreme?

It wasn't until Elsie heard the clicking sound of heels that she scrambled out of Colin's chair and scooped up her treasured letter.

"Elsie?" a feminine voice called out.

"What do you want, Mom?" Elsie asked like a deer frozen in headlights.

"I just want to see how you're holding up." A small, solemn smile inked across Roslyn's face, and the graceful woman approached her daughter with outstretched arms.

"I'm okay." Elsie's words were harsher than she intended. She feared appearing vulnerable to anyone, especially her mother.

The two stood in awkward silence before Roslyn cleared her throat, a cue for Elsie to say something, to say anything.

"I know," Elsie said with large eyes. "I know Colin is my

brother. That you and Henry had an affair and that I'm the product of that stupidity."

Roslyn had always refused Elsie the truth about her father, no matter how much Elsie begged. Elsie developed a resentment for the mysterious man, and that reflected in her own utter lack of respect for men in general. Knowing the truth caused conflict. Colin happened upon the information from an off-handed comment Roslyn made. *Did Henry even know about his illegitimate daughter?* was one of the hundreds of questions rapidly firing off in Elsie's mind when Colin offered to publicly accept Elsie as a member of the O'Connor family. She didn't jump on the opportunity, telling Colin she needed more time to think about it. Now she feared no one would believe her.

Roslyn stepped away from her daughter and hung her head in shame. "It wasn't stupid. We loved each other at one point."

Elsie crossed her arms, challenging her mother's rebuttal.

"You think he loved you?" Elsie asked with a snort.

"It sounds like you're getting a one-sided story of him—a perspective from Colin? You weren't there, Elsie. And neither was Colin half of the time. You wouldn't know."

"But Henry wasn't there either. He was never there for me. Henry isn't the O'Connor who accepted me, who welcomed me, who believed in me," Elsie said, approaching her mother with tears stinging from the corners of her eyes. "But that doesn't matter. Whatever it was, you continued obsessing over him even after he died. You were probably so thrilled to hold the affections of an established old bloodline man. What did he threaten you with for your silence?"

Roslyn's eyes shifted away, guilt and shame filling her brow.

"Right," Elsie responded in a huff. "No answers, like always."

"I'm sure the minute Colin told you the truth about your father's identity you hoped he would accept you as an O'Connor and welcome you to their family. Even after all I've done for you, you would drop the Sullivans in an instant." Her mother's lips trembled, and an indescribable shock wavered through Roslyn's tiny body.

"You're right, and he did. I'm glad Colin accepted me. And I will use the O'Connors; I will use the father who never loved me. And you can't stop me."

Chapter 5
Peter

<u>June 23rd, 47 A.R.</u>

Peter's hands gripped the handles of the heavy metal box. He approached 15 Beacon Street in a near stumble, the weight of his container a hindrance to his normal smooth, steady strides. The instructions he received days before were clear but didn't specify the timing.

The abandoned streets wouldn't have bothered him if it was deep into the evening, but the sun had only recently disappeared from across the horizon. Bright orange and pink colors still mesmerized the sky on such a tragic, unforgettable day.

Peter had woken up earlier in the morning and lay in bed for a couple of hours. He paced around his one-bedroom apartment in The Bay before turning on the large device in his living room.

The ceramic mug in his hand collided with the stone floor, shattering into dozens of pieces around his feet that he would need to vacuum later.

Someone assassinated Governor Colin O'Connor in bright daylight. The news channel played the horrific clip of Colin O'Connor's assassination over and over again. The image zoomed in and focused mostly on Julie, avoiding as much of Colin's blown-out head, the gore more splattered across Julie's face while she held the governor in her arms.

Julie appeared in public for the first time in months after time traveling. They were infatuated with her. No one knew she time traveled, except for a select few. Instead, Commissioner Jones crafted a mythical lie about her being kidnapped and held captive inside FACERE.

Clever, Peter had thought later, after the shock of the rest of the events subsided.

Peter never cared for Governor O'Connor, but seeing his death and the impact of two bullets striking skin and bones made Peter pause. And the heartbreak on Julie's face—he could see the shock, confusion, anger, and disbelief even on the screen. Peter decided it was then time to do his bidding before someone came after him. No one was safe anymore, or at least, no one who time traveled.

He had an inkling of what was inside the metal briefcase without having to open it and look. The various vials locked up in the contraption were meant to keep the contents slightly cooler than room temperature. Peter had traveled to the past—he successfully straddled two alliances. One with Celine O'Connor and one with the Garcia family.

Now was his time to choose the side to pledge his loyalty to.

"The future can always change" was what Julie had once told him. Peter believed her words—the future was not a constant variable. And this explained why Julie defied all logical aspects of time travel, to which there were a complicated few. Her admission that the date on the device changed when she dropped her blood into it later was confirmation enough for Peter.

Julie was supposed to die that night, but something happened. Something prevented her death—and it wasn't just Mick Taylor alone.

The building ahead loomed lowly compared to the massive Capitol Building across the street. A small coffee shop occupied the first level of 15 Beacon Street, but Peter didn't enter for an evening espresso. No one was inside the shop anyways, no barista, no patrons. The Hill was an abandoned ghost town.

He walked through the café and headed toward the back, making his way up the narrow staircase. The building had been constructed hundreds of years ago, during a much different time—a time when androids didn't even exist. It was hard to conceptualize what society looked like back then, without the liberties of today's landscape. Even with the disorganized chaos of late, The City historically never stayed quiet, always rioted: the birthplace of freedom.

When Peter arrived at the second level, he stopped in front of a light eggshell-colored door. His knuckles collided with the wood. The golden circular handle jiggled moments after his knock and the door swung open.

Anna Garcia stood in the nearly empty, abandoned apartment.

Anna resembled the traditional characteristics of her old bloodline family, the Garcias. She had a short and petite frame with dark features. Anna held a bit of muscle in her arms and kept her hair stylishly shorter than her older sister, Isabella. The older Garcia sister stood beside Anna. She was truly stunning, with dark brown hair cascading down in large curls around her face, highlighting her sharp, angled cheekbones and button-sized nose. Faint crow's feet erupted from the corners of Isabella's eyes.

Time travel, Peter thought with a rush of adrenaline coursing through his veins.

Peter traveled time, and until now, he was under the impression very few others had the means to do so. Celine originally presented him with the device back in the winter, asking him to use the technology to locate Julie. Celine needed the beloved scientist to save her brother, Colin. And Peter needed Julie to save the antidote and COLI*GO's entire operation.

Everything spiraled out of control when Peter learned that his nemesis and colleague, Mick Taylor, was the inventor of time travel. During Peter's first trip to the past, he ran into Mick and Colin O'Connor—another time traveler—and the list continued growing when Celine threw herself into the mix. But Peter hadn't identified who possessed the last missing time travel device.

Until now.

"Anna. Isabella," he said their names in a whisper, hoping with a blink of his eye that they would disappear.

Peter stepped farther inside the apartment. A kitchen with old-fashioned white appliances and faded black checkered linoleum floors left the space feeling dated and unsettling. Someone once called this home—but not for a long time. A barely used, cheap-looking loveseat touched the right wall, and a flimsy door sat slightly ajar, leading toward a small bedroom. The window in the living space was ajar with black dust on the windowsill, and a slight burning smell lingered in the room.

"I'm glad you're here," Anna said, stepping closer to him.

Peter trusted Anna. After he hired her to help him uncover who aided The Supreme in the lower lab at COLI*GO, they formed a friendship. Investigating the various COLI*GO board members and interviewing posse hominems led to the shocking discovery Peter subconsciously knew but never wanted to admit: Celine O'Connor was aware of the lower lab project in more detail than she initially led everyone to believe, and Isabella was the one who performed the surgeries for her and The Supreme. The news shook Anna, and both she and Peter had yet to confirm their next step. His friendship with the chief medical examiner was more than a working relationship. Peter grew fond of her sarcastic retort and her charming abilities. He even looked for Anna's father—which was her advice—while he time traveled to the past.

Dr. Filipe Garcia was a renowned psychologist who hoped to change The Constituency for the better through the power of medicine and therapy. He was passionate like Isabella and fierce like Anna. His youngest daughter held on to his notes and shocking discoveries he left behind after his death. He understood the brain like no one else, and Peter appreciated his input when he handed over Julie's toxin for evaluation.

Peter closed the door and placed the metal box on the kitchen table with more emphasis and noise than necessary. His mind spiraled with many questions: Why was Anna here? Did Isabella allow her sister to use the time travel device too? Was Isabella the assassin from earlier in the day? Or did she know anything about her previous partner's death? Did Anna also work with The Supreme and Isabella and play him for a fool in front of COLI*GO?

"Is this what I think it is?" Peter asked, unlatching the metal box and pulling out a glass vial filled with a mysterious liquid—a subcutaneous drug.

He studied the samples with a keen eye, a small silver tinge inside the otherwise clear liquid. This wasn't the toxin or the antidote.

Anna snatched the container from Peter and gazed upon the pharmaceutical for herself. Her lips turned upward, and she cradled the single glass tube with affection. Standing on her tiptoes, she wrapped her arms around Peter's neck and hugged him.

"This is it, Peter. This is the answer to your problems with the antidote," Anna said with a gleaming smile. "This is something better. It's what COLI*GO refused to invest in. It's what he left behind with his notebook."

"Don't get ahead of yourself, Anna." It was Isabella's voice that broke across the room, sounding as smooth as honey.

Anna stepped away from Peter and looked out toward the perfect view of the front steps of The Capitol Building across the street. A disturbing feeling shifted around the apartment. Peter's first experience with time travel flashed in his memory: the chrome box asking him to select his destination, the past or the future. The past provided various options all the way to the year of his birth.

Mick Taylor, the inventor of time travel, must have gauged the curiosity levels of people using this technology, especially about how far into the future they could go. Future date selection did not appear unless the user selected the future button twice. If the traveler didn't select twice after providing their blood sample, they would never know how far they could go.

But Peter contained very little self-control. He selected the future and nearly dropped the glasses to the floor when he could only travel to October 47 A.R.

A short amount of life left to live.

And that was when Peter decided he didn't care. He would be self-serving; he would act and relish in the consequences since they wouldn't last long, anyway. But another variable, according to Mick's notes and answered by Julie, showed that if a time traveler died on their journey, their physical being returned to the place of their death. The sensation acted as a rebirth, an option to relive what they shouldn't be able to. The only caveat was if the time travelers killed each other.

Then it was truly lights out—goodbye for good.

Watching the governor's death on live television should have shaken Peter to his core and made him feel sick to his stomach. One of the time travelers was out for blood—but who? The knowledge that Colin O'Connor was truly dead was too satisfying. Colin couldn't cheat death—and that meant no one could. Julie defied death through Mick Taylor's rescue. Someone could rescue Peter too, if he played his cards right. If he aligned with the correct time traveler. The confirmation that Isabella held a device provided a deep sense of satisfaction.

No one came back to rescue Colin, he thought. But why would they? He was a murderer. He thought because he was an old bloodline he could do as he pleased under the guise of vigilantism with no repercussions.

"Peter," Isabella said, closing in with a grin as wide as a Cheshire cat's. "What if this is the answer? You have to destroy the antidote. Julie so easily discovered its toxin, and the toxin . . ." The elegant woman looked away.

Peter gulped. His mixed feelings toward the Garcia women maneuvered wildly throughout his mind. They were a complicated family. Isabella was kindhearted, and her involvement in Celine's lower lab experiment puzzled him. But the O'Connors were also intoxicating, especially Elsie. He suspected her true lineage after their tryst together. His pull toward the vengeful and fearsome woman was unlike anything he ever experienced. Simply the thought of her made him shiver.

"It's time that the O'Connors step back. They're causing more harm than good for society," Anna said, glancing down at the metal box filled with perilous liquid.

"And you think I can change that?" Peter challenged, hiding his fear. He was ashamed of his terror, ashamed of how willingly he would fall into the traps of all these false players just to save himself from death.

"Yes, with this, you could."

PART THREE
The Past

"I've always been under the impression that death is a one-time, encompassing event."
"Why would you ever think that?"
—Grace Draven

Chapter 6
Julie

The waves crashed violently against the cliffs at The Oceanside. A winter storm threatened the coast, promising to trap her here if she didn't use time travel as her vehicle. The O'Connor family estate was empty, and Julie turned on some lamps in the large living space at the back of the house. The walls were a series of glass French doors, and large sticky snowflakes slipped down the glass. Flashes of lightning cast a lavender hue in the dark mansion.

Instinct guided Julie through the darkness and toward the study. Green marble floors greeted her as she explored the space. Julie spent many summer days here with Colin before everything terrible happened, before he tried killing her, and before he forced her to hide through time travel. But she never spent time in the study in the present. Colin also rarely used it, refusing to take too much of his work here with him.

But in their travels to the past, Julie often found herself in this room, mulling over her lab notes when something didn't align, when results were inconsistent. She had a difficult time sleeping when she traveled to the past, odd nightmares threatening any kind of rest.

Peter had sent Julie a frantic message a month before about the toxin's formulation going missing. Julie hadn't fretted much—she kept a secret log of her dangerous drug in Mick's time travel journal for this specific reason. There were other more urgent matters to orchestrate over those weeks: the raid of FACERE.

What concerned Julie was who took the toxin, especially with so few players in the game who had even known that such a pharmaceutical existed: Peter, Celine, and herself. Elsie was also aware, but she didn't travel time—her ability to delete the work at COLI*GO was nearly impossible. While Celine would stop at nothing for power and control, she stressed that Julie's success would mean a cure for her brother. With her faults, Celine cared about Colin, and Julie couldn't hate the otherwise cold woman for that. But there was something about the way Peter's fingers fidgeted whenever she talked about the potent drug that made her leery of his intentions.

Why would he want to jeopardize the toxin? It isn't like we planned to ever use the drug, only to help aid us in figuring out the inverse, in correcting the anti- dote.

Julie's hands shook, and she looked in the darkness for the notes she left behind in the desk. Her body froze when she saw the shimmer of a metal blade in the study drawer. With clear and slow intentions, Julie reached inside.

"I keep the knife in the bottom left drawer," he had said—It had said—to her on one of their trips to 37 A.R.

It provided Julie this knowledge when she confided in him that she felt unsafe.

How I wish that level of discomfort was all I felt now. She closed her eyes. After watching chunks of Colin's skull tangle in her strawberry blonde hair, Julie desperately appreciated this memory of It wanting to protect her and that she did need this weapon now. When Julie reached inside the drawer, she clasped on to an old-fashioned and intricately carved letter opener.

The knife isn't here, she reminded herself. *The knife is in the lower left drawer in his study at the townhouse.*

Julie looked around the room once more, her fingers trailing across the deep mahogany wood. A notepad and old-fashioned ink fountain pen were positioned perfectly on the placemat beside a stack of envelopes, and she thought about resting the letter opener beside the iconic set.

The house was empty, and the sound of The Oceanside's fa- mous waves cascaded an eerie but serene setting. Even during the summer height of tourism, the O'Connor estate sat up on the cliffs, isolated from the town center. This was the best of both worlds— equally secluded with the option for interaction.

I came here because this is the only place I truly feel safe. This feels like home.

The sound of a door opening down the hall made Julie halt in place. Her nerves got the better of her. Her constant fight or flight reverberated through her body, a triggered response occurring far too frequently these last few months.

A dark shadow swiftly passed the front of the room, and without hesitation, Julie gripped the letter opener in her hand and advanced forward.

A flicker of lightning struck outside, revealing Colin's chiseled face in its wake. His sharp, square jawline was filled with a couple of days' worth of stubble. He wore a casual outfit of a white T-shirt and dark denim, a look most wouldn't recognize him in.

The glow of pleasant surprise at the letter opener in Julie's hand gave away his true identity. This wasn't solely Colin. As much as both Colin and Julie didn't like to admit it, It and Colin were one and the same.

Julie might have been nimble and swift with her small frame, but It was stronger and more experienced with danger and threats. He anticipated her move, and his large hand tightly gripped her tiny wrist. The feeling of a bruise blossomed beneath her skin, threatening to emerge later if he didn't relax his grip soon.

To be fair, I almost stabbed him with a letter opener.

"What are you doing here, Julie? Are you trying to kill me?" he asked, a devilish grin creeping out of the corners of his lips.

Julie stammered. After the swearing-in ceremony, she lay in their bed at the townhouse with no hope for sleep. Every time Julie closed her eyes, the scene from earlier in the day replayed disturbingly in her brain. To Jones's dismay, she insisted on heading to her own apartment at two thirty in the morning and didn't want to be alone.

Time travel felt like the only option—and science always distracted her, always provided her with a sense of calmness. She needed to consume herself entirely in her work, or her grief might push her over the edge instead. By coming back to 37 A.R., Julie yearned for the release of finding her notes on the toxin and continuing her work on the antidote.

It grinned at her silence. Hurt and sorrow primarily erupted through Julie but there were other emotions like rage and suspicion rippling through her—a lingering inclination she couldn't stop obsessing over: that Colin knew all along that he'd be assassinated, yet he did nothing to prevent it.

She was angry at Colin. At It. At herself.

I also came here to confront him.

It loosened his grasp on her wrist but remained firm in holding her, submerging her delicate fingers with the powerful hold of his large hand. His skin was warm to the touch, an unexpected but pleasant surprise. He slowly guided her hand and the letter opener up to his throat.

The blade rested delicately against his slightly tanned skin, paler than normal from a lack of time spent in the sun. He never broke his gaze from her.

Colin O'Connor was a handsome man. Standing at about six and a half feet, he towered over Julie even though she wasn't a short woman. His steely gray-blue eyes captured her gaze, which slowed in observation across his broad shoulders and strong arms.

Julie concentrated with more strain to keep her shaking hands from slicing his skin with jagged lines. The letter opener was dull compared to his true weapon of choice and probably wouldn't break the skin. If this had been his knife—the one in the study at the townhouse—the blade would have nicked him by now.

"Well?" It asked, his cold eyes large and round with curiosity.

Julie released her hold on the letter opener, and he moved back, allowing the metal to crash to the floor in between them. The clanking sound pierced the room, but neither Julie nor It watched the knife. They focused solely on one another.

Another flash of lightning shimmered outside, illuminating and exposing the man Julie loved—the confusion and hurt across his eyes made her lean into him.

Only a split second passed before he bent down and kissed her.

A flood of adrenaline coursed through Julie's veins as the feel of his lips collided with hers. The passion ignited her already rapidly beating heart. When his large warm hands lingered from her back and around the front of her stomach, a shiver passed through her body.

It's fingers lightly traced the scars on her skin underneath her shirt, tickling her, but a delightful sensation took over after the

the initial intrusion. His movements were slow and purposeful, rubbing in soothing, slow circles. A smile formed on his lips against her own when he reached her lower abdomen. There was a pause, and then he pulled his lips away.

Recognition passed between them. Without sharing any words, It sensed where the Julie in front of him came from, exactly where in the future she traveled from to find him. The small distance felt too significant to Julie, and she pushed closer to him. It resumed kissing her, but this time, he was gentle and loving, his tongue deep and satisfying against hers.

His response to caressing her scars normally came from a strange satisfaction of the wounds being his own doing—something that was an anomalous affection Julie allowed him to indulge in. This shift in him differed with acknowledgment of what lay beneath her skin, and his reaction to her and her body provided Julie with a sense of optimism mixed with sorrow in a blurred cloud of vast emotions.

It pulled away from their embrace, and his hands left a fierce warmth that spread across her stomach before disappearing. Julie's own hands trailed to where his hands once were.

"I would never kill you."

Julie wanted to share the news she had just discovered shortly ago in the future, to confide in her excitement, confusion, and doubts—her scared happiness.

"I never doubted you for a second." It's lips curled into a genuine smile and tears escaped the corners of Julie's eyes. He softly wiped them away with his thumbs. "Don't cry, Julie."

"I can't do this without you." The words raced out of her, her darkest fear and confession exposed to the man she trusted above anyone else. Even more than Colin.

So much had happened to Julie in the hours after his death in the present. She didn't know what to do, and she felt alone. She wanted him alive, to feel his heart beating beneath his chest, to feel his rough hands on her smooth skin. Julie missed the excitement that once lived in his eyes, a fierce resident resisting any kind of eviction. She yearned for his smile, a smile he kept hidden from the rest of the world most of the time. Something he saved for only her.

But the only way she could have these unrealistic desires now was through time travel. That wasn't sustainable—the risks were too high. This was her last time with him.

"Yes, you can. And you do." He kissed her forehead and ran his fingers through her hair, pulling her into his chest.

"This isn't fair to you."

"Fair isn't always an option. Don't feel like I'm cheated out of this. You gave me everything, Julie. Love. Empathy. Understanding. Purpose. And life."

"So you do know?" The question hung in the air as she clenched her stomach and backed away from his embrace. "And did you know that someone would assassinate you too?"

It looked away and hung his head low. He grabbed her hands in his and provided a comforting squeeze.

"Yes, I was warned. This wasn't what I originally planned. I didn't realize a time traveler fatally killed another time traveler. I thought from my experience with you, that time travelers were immune to death. I always planned on coming back."

Julie stilled, realizing Colin or It never read Mick's journal. He didn't know the rules and was a rogue time traveler, figuring them out along the way.

Mick started keeping a physical written journal when he began time traveling. He claimed it secured any of his observations and research from being distorted through different dimensions of time. Julie possessed the journal herself, finding it hidden in her apartment in The Bay when she made her way home after that terrifying night of her attempted murder. When Julie began time traveling back to fix the antidote—and coddle in her and It's illicit relationship—she wrote in the journal, addressing her entries to Colin, hoping someday he would read them. Julie made several confessions in the diary, admitting that she had played with the past on a few occasions when she knew she shouldn't.

I never warned him. The color drained from her face. *I never thought to warn him.*

"But you didn't try to change the course of events? Even knowing what you know?" Julie's voice trembled.

It hid nothing from Julie in the months they had spent together.

She treasured how open and honest It was compared to Colin, feeling guilty that she might even love him more in this way. For how hated It was by most in Colin's life, Julie and he had a special bond, and this was the first time they collided with unspoken truths.

"The choice wasn't easy, but because I was warned, I was able to adjust, to prepare. To make sure everything was planned for you and our baby in the case that I couldn't beat death. I wanted our bond to stay safe, and I wanted to help you in any way I could. It wasn't until later that I discovered there was no way for me to cheat death, nothing I could control. I didn't want to leave you alone. I planned on coming back, but I can't get to the future."

A wail escaped Julie, and It's large arms brought her into his body. The anger bubbled up as an ache that pained her limbs. Her palms slapped his broad chest, again and again, and she crumpled her hands into loose fists and lightly pounded against him. It allowed her to scream, lightly hit him, and cry into his embrace for what felt like an eternity. Standing firm and strong, he was the rock she needed in her outburst of spiraling mourning.

He understood her anger. He was the only one who ever could.

Exhaustion stole Julie's thunder, and she collapsed into the steady hold of his arms. Lifting her, he walked them out of the study.

The O'Connor estate was quiet as he strode across the expansive space while securely holding Julie. Climbing the elegant staircase in the darkness didn't physically strain It and he knew his way around the house with an uncanny sense of accuracy.

She didn't remember falling asleep in his embrace, but when she opened her eyes, a warm, thick blanket protected them in the bed, a fire burned in the large brick fireplace, and his arms were curled around her. She heard his deep labored breaths—his peaceful slumber soothing her. The last time they'd been this close, he'd died in her arms. She squeezed her eyes shut, trying her best to shake the memory and enjoy him now while she had him.

The storm rolled through the evening, but by morning, a misty sun shone across the snow-dusted lawn. Julie rolled closer into his hold, and he brushed away the hair from her face.

"Have you changed the past? Is that why you asked why I chose not to?" he asked, his voice low but comforting.

Julie shook her head yes against his chest. "Are you disappointed in me?"

"No. But why did you tinker with the past?" he asked, grabbing Julie's jaw in his large hand. He tilted her head tenderly so that their eyes met. "Tell me."

Julie squinted and pondered how to reveal the answer to his question. "I suppose I'm not as honest and noble as everyone believes. I guess there is a dark side to me too."

He smirked and guided her face closer to his. Their lips nearly touched, a buzzing vibration passing between their bodies. He loosened his grip on her.

"I like your dark side," he cooed.

And I'm terrified to admit that I like your dark side, too, Colin. She shuddered, acknowledging in her mind for the first time that Colin and It would forever be the same—even if he didn't want to believe this.

It pulled her on top of his body, and his hands wandered down her back, stopping at her hips. Julie grabbed his face in her palms and traced the outlines and small imperfections on his skin. The lines spreading from the corners of his eyes weren't deep. It hadn't traveled to the future on someone else's blood, or if he had, he had only taken one or two journeys. The thought calmed her.

"And what are you going to do with all this power you now hold in the future . . . in the present?" he asked, his grip firm against her skin.

Julie smiled, and her eyes sparkled with delight.

"Rip out every weed in The Legislature, every thorn at FACERE and COLI*GO. I'm going to make those who threaten stability pay for their crimes. Everyone who thinks they can use nobodies like me for their own game. I'm going to bring balance back to society. For you. For me. For us."

"Good," he replied before hungrily kissing her.

***

Julie's coping mechanism wasn't healthy. All she wanted was to go back to The Oceanside and indulge herself. She wanted all of Colin, physically and emotionally. She longed to kiss him tenderly and fiercely, to shiver as his breath lingered on her, to consume the heat of his skin with her own, and to feel him beside her.

Julie believed in the carefulness and rawness of their relationship. She cradled the sense of intimacy that wasn't physical but emotional—something unspoken and unknown bonding them further together.

Acceptance.

But I'm so close to him, to all of this. Am I so close that I'm not grasping the truth?

They couldn't continue this way. There were important obstacles to overcome, a great burden they carried in making sure others were safe. She could not visit him again through time travel, and she needed to continue the plan they had carefully laid out by herself. There was a greater responsibility for her to look after now.

Julie sat on the lab stool at COLI*GO with wide dreary eyes and the sound of Peter's pacing behind her droned on. Peter didn't know which Julie sat here in the room with him. He assumed this was the time traveling Julie from before Colin's death.

He rattled off concerns about their progress on the antidote from Celine, and Julie couldn't help but roll her eyes. Celine didn't understand the way they conducted drug discovery, how the process of adjusting molecules and studying reactions took time. Julie shouldn't have come to the laboratory now that she had her notes. She should have returned to the present and the exhausting burdens that faced her there.

I'm the governor of The Constituency.

Being the interim CEO of COLI*GO was a prestigious role at such a young age but did not prepare her for this new massive responsibility. Julie embraced her time at COLI*GO, enthralled by the technological challenges presented to her.

As governor, Julie was lost. She promised It she would pluck out the weeds, but a tightness filled her chest at the idea that she might mistake a weed for a flower.

The lab was her element, her safe space, and something she desperately missed when she moved into a managerial leadership position from her coveted role as a lead scientist on the COL23 asset. In the present, the antidote failed. Julie unsuccessfully attempted to treat Colin with her drug, but It still prevailed. Some answers came to her when she traveled back to the lower lab and worked endless hours on the antidote. Without the development of a single-dose injection, there was no hope for this drug, a reality she didn't want to admit to herself.

In her quest to remedy the antidote, Julie accidentally created the toxin—a pharmaceutical that threatened to enhance the damaged receptors latching to the dendrites, a part of the brain that received information from other neurons and transmitted electrical stimulation. The toxin, if injected into Colin, could allow It to fully take over his mind.

"What I don't understand is how easy it was for you to develop the toxin." Peter's harsh words brought Julie back to reality.

Peter and Julie had a complicated friendship. They once dated off-and-on again for a couple of years after she graduated from The University. Their relationship ended when he was requested to take a role at an affiliate office that required relocation and Julie wouldn't join him. After some time, they reconnected. Peter had a brilliant mind, one that understood all the consequences and took caution in moving forward. She hired him to lead her antidote's clinical studies, but now he acted as the interim CEO while she was missing.

*I'd rather be at COLI*GO than in The Capitol Building.*

The Legislature wasn't where Julie belonged, no matter how much Colin thought she'd make a good leader. The role as governor was better suited for someone else, someone more affiliated to old bloodline families. Julie fit at COLI*GO; that's where the true innovation and transformation for The City lived. There were thorns to discover and cut off to make sure nothing infectious infiltrated the gilded glass walls of the biotech company, but COLI*GO's vision held the answers, not The Legislature.

Colin's sister was a sore spot for Julie. They disagreed but respected the drive they both possessed—a drive that festered from their desires to prove everyone wrong. But Celine was also part of the problem. Nothing would change if Celine remained in power—it didn't matter that Julie was an acting CEO; Celine still ran the show from her extended maternity leave. Celine's shadow lingered in Julie's office, and she never intended to stay away for too long.

"Shut up, Peter." The words left Julie's mouth before she could stop them.

Her pettiness ignited a large flame. Julie was tired, and she was exhausted mentally from Colin's assassination, the new responsibility that loomed over her regarding The Legislature, and the news that she was pregnant.

Peter furrowed his brows, waiting for her to continue after speaking those mistaken words.

"You of all people should know that drug discovery isn't that simple," Julie protested. "I'll figure out the correct antidote, but until then, get out of my way and let me drown myself."

Peter's eyes blinked rapidly, and he hesitantly nodded.

"We'll work in silos, then. I'll figure this out before you."

Peter's retort was immature and ridiculous—he felt the pressures from The Board of Directors, but she didn't excuse him from being rude. They were supposed to be friends, colleagues, and allies. Friends didn't hit below the belt, and if they did, they apologized.

Julie bowed her head and closed her eyes. Shame filled her chest, but when she looked at Peter, he didn't appear bothered by their disagreement. A glimmer of overconfidence and cockiness flickered across his face. She didn't recognize this new power-hungry monster.

Her breath slowed, but her eyes hardened. *Why? Why is he trying to distract me?*

Chapter 7
Mick

<u>January 28th, 3 A.R.</u>

The O'Connor townhouse glistened in the snow-covered streets of The Hill. The warm morning hue of yellow gas lamps lining the streets provided a soft view of Melanie O'Connor holding her baby while puttering around the living room. Henry O'Connor barreled down the stairs and kissed his wife, and his large hand affectionately supported baby Celine's head before he placed his gentle lips on her forehead.

Mick envied the beautiful family. Colin looked much like his father, the uncanny resemblance chilling Mick to the bone. While Melanie was much taller, fairer, and blonder than his friend Julie, Mick allowed his mind to wander into the unwelcome thoughts of pretending this was them.

What they could be if I hadn't invented time travel.

Guilt was a fickle friend of Mick's but also his only comfort in his life of loneliness.

Mick continued watching the pair from the carriage house, an abandoned small structure resting on top of a historic garage. A small fire crackled in the fireplace in the open front room. The Supreme had acquired this space for him. He needed a place to hide when traveling to the past or the future. The small converted carriage house sat directly behind the O'Connor townhouse, providing the perfect viewing of the prestigious old bloodline family's lives.

His friend Julie also used the carriage house in the future as a hiding spot. She spent countless hours burying herself in the worn leather sofa with a dark glass of Cabernet in her hands. Julie's obsession concentrated on Colin—a man she loved—and his other personality, It. Another complicated pairing.

Mick admired Julie's perseverance for the truth. She was a

scientist and researcher by training with a keen eye for observation. Her affection and passion for helping those she loved drove her mad—perfectionism would be the death of his thoughtful friend if she weren't more careful.

After Henry's vehicle left the garage, Mick exited down the steps from the carriage house. He approached the front door of the townhouse but took a step back before lifting the large knocker that replaced the need for a doorbell. Mick hesitated in many areas of his life, from his professional pursuits to his expression of love for his boyfriend Jones, but he grew accustomed to the ups and downs of time travel and the decisions he committed to when traveling.

Something about Melanie O'Connor's bright smile made him pause. The thought that this moment was incredibly important in cementing the time loop society needed.

When she opened the door, she cocked her head to the right and looked down at the man standing before her.

Time travel did a number on Mick's body. He made a grave error in traveling on other people's blood—from Julie's, Colin's, and even his uncle's. If he stuck to his own blood, the side effects would lessen. Deep lines spread across his forehead, and crow's feet littered the corners of his eyes.

Prior to his experiments, Mick possessed lovely ebony skin—smooth and soft. Now, the flakiness flickered off him like severe dandruff. He lost a significant amount of weight, no matter how much food he shoveled into his mouth.

There were many complications to time travel, logs, and entries littering his research journal. Another notable infraction included invincibility that time travelers experienced while on journeys to the past or future. Time travelers escaped death unless another time traveler killed them. If they did experience death, their eyes ripped open in a new location—the location of their actual death. Mick's journal revealed this truth, but to his knowledge, only he, Julie, and Jones possessed the information. His journal remained hidden in the floorboards of the carriage house, and eventually, when he found a lockbox for the treasure, he kept the contents hidden there.

Julie and Jones left entries in his diary—Julie with her own time travel observations and Jones with grave warnings of the impacts of time travel.

"Can I help you?" Melanie's voice was as sweet as Mick remembered. This wasn't his first time visiting her on a time travel adventure, but he'd never addressed her before.

"This might sound strange, but I need to speak with you about an important manner involving your family. I'm the one who sends you the letters."

Melanie's eyes opened wider, and she stepped aside to open the door for Mick. He entered the townhouse with a pause. Colin kept the townhouse similarly decorated as his parents had. Family heirlooms lined the walls in the form of paintings; the only difference between how the townhouse looked now and in the future was modernized furniture and the fireplace. Sometime in the future, Colin had it painted white, but here the expansive brick heater showcased deep reds and dusty browns.

Mick couldn't simply knock on the O'Connor's front door and expect the governor's wife to let him saunter inside their home. He carefully crafted a letter to introduce himself without sounding crazy. The only time the tactic of plainly spelling out his time travel abilities worked was with Supreme Edward, the former supreme before Emilia.

He had allowed Mick to enter The Capitol Building and listen to the tales of the future and the need for Emilia to understand 100 percent of human emotions. Androids were driven by logic, seeking reason and sensibility in any problem presented to them.

Melanie was a warm woman, but she would presume Mick a madman, crazy and irrational. The letters started out as admirable and fanlike. She came from a nobody lineage, marrying herself into an old bloodline with wealth and fame. A gentle and thoughtful woman, Melanie used her kindness to connect with Henry's constituents, and the public adored her.

After a few letters, she eventually responded, and their communication formed a sense of familiarity where Mick finally felt he could approach her in real life. Melanie was lonely in a society of unknowns. Her husband was the newly elected governor and faced several uphill battles in stabilizing a tumultuous Constituency. The Resurgence ended a few years prior, leaving a wake of newness to android freedoms. Previously, androids had no representation in the government and were created by the quasi-government organization FACERE for use within The Constituency. Androids were created to maintain fairness in certain jobs and aid humans in life. They were treated as second-class citizens, a modern version of a slave.

Edward rallied other androids, and The Legislature was caught off guard. They didn't understand how their own creations became so powerful and so self-aware. But somewhere along the line, Mick suspected dark web coders pushed for this—upgrading the microchip in android processors to understand and feel more human emotions. And with more emotions, androids acted more human-like.

Melanie was lonely in her glass bubble of a townhouse. Her husband didn't want her to leave, and she seemed out of her element. Melanie grew up in a poorer neighborhood of The City, and her meeting the esteemed O'Connor heir came by chance when she volunteered for his political campaign.

Marrying outside of old bloodline families, particularly for the first-born son, was normally an atrocity by societal standards. But Melanie's kindness won the hearts of people, and with a change in freedoms granted to androids, the nobodies in society realized they, too, held power in shifting public opinion.

Forming a friendship with Melanie became a simple task for Mick, and he genuinely enjoyed their letters. *I should glue them into the journal,* he often thought, but parting with these flimsy little treasures kept him from committing to the act.

"Would you like a glass of water? Tea?" Melanie asked, walking into the large kitchen. She turned on the kettle sitting atop the stove.

A small whimper interrupted her. Baby Celine looked up at Mick from her highchair with the infamous O'Connor large steely gray eyes. Melanie attentively approached her child and smiled at her, soothing the wails before they began.

"You don't need to trouble yourself," Mick protested, already uncomfortable in a home that seemed welcoming.

"Nonsense, it's freezing out there."

Mick took a seat at the kitchen island, his left foot still planted firmly on the floor and his body half seated on the barstool.

The time travel device burned in his pockets. The contraption consisted of two pieces, a pair of glasses and a small chrome box. Mick hand-crafted each time travel device, unwilling to hand over the exact specifications to The Supreme when he worked for her as a consultant. He took great pride in his craft, carving intricate designs into the black metal frames of each pair. No pair was the same, a secret way for him to pay tribute to the time travelers using his device.

This particular pair of glasses showcased a Greek creature, the Mantikhoras. Mick enjoyed these fantastical myths and legends when he was attending The University, living in the confines of Uncle Jeb's apartment. At the time, Mick didn't know Uncle Jeb was really a time travel version of himself. He assumed the troubled man took too many hallucinogenics to inspire his artwork, and when Jeb was tripping and high, Mick lost himself in the stories and legends of heroes.

With a human-like face, the Mantikhoras had three rows of ferocious teeth and a strong tail like a scorpion's. They guarded the gates of the underworld, promising to inflict pain upon any trespasser.

Another favorite design of Mick's was a phoenix, a lovely creature with beautiful wings and scales. The creature represented an immortal bird that continuously regenerates and becomes born again. Colin held this time travel device—the symbolism of his lover's immortality and the lack of his own.

"It's nice to meet you in person," Melanie said with a genuine and warm smile. A whistle from the kettle sounded loudly in the kitchen, and she poured the steaming water into a mug.

"I have something for you." Mick gently placed the time travel contraption on the granite countertop.

Melanie picked up the device with a raised brow and an upturn in her lip. She leaned her elbows on the countertop, her face now only inches away from Mick's.

"I won't lie; I didn't believe you when you finally revealed that you're a time traveler." Her admission didn't surprise Mick, but a small bout of disappointment butterflied through his stomach at her revelation.

"I don't recommend time traveling much. But you'll need to make a few trips." Mick shifted in his seat, sweat pooling under his arms. "I've given you a few samples of blood to place into the slide here." Mick gestured toward the center of the device, a small spot between the frames. "These are blood samples from your son."

Melanie stilled, and her eyes shifted from Mick to her daughter.

"Your future son," Mick said, placing his scabby hand on top of her gentle skin. "I've written the instruction in the note taped to the underside of the chrome box of which dates to travel to and when you should."

Melanie's gaze upon his contraption mirrored that of a curious child rummaging through small treasures of seashells collected at the beach. Time travel was novel, unique, and fascinating.

I don't blame people for their inquisitive nature when given a device.

Curiosity was dangerous. Life-threatening. He needed Melanie to travel to understand her situation and was instructing her to travel time to the day of her death. But on Colin's blood, he needed her to see the future—to travel to January 28th and distract It from doing something that would crash the time loop and close off the dimension he traveled from.

"I understand your wanderlust with this innovation," Mick cautioned, "but please promise me you won't use this while you're pregnant."

Mick eyed her belly, empty for now. Melanie wasn't pregnant yet, but soon, Colin would occupy the space. Mick contemplated how much to stress this importance to Melanie. She could ruin and unfold everything if she traveled time while pregnant with Colin.

The mystery of Julie Walsh's inconsistencies with experiencing death during her time travel clouded Mick with confusion and frustration. She evaded death and the typical rules of time travel. Julie traveled back in time and pushed herself off a cliff—triggering the rule of a time traveler killing another time traveler. For an unexplainable reason, Julie ended up back in the woods on January 28th, 47 A.R. But Mick had saved her there—that was where she was supposed to die but didn't.

At first, Mick pondered on the reasoning why. She had once been considered a posse hominem, but the microchip in her brain was turned off and didn't affect her biologically the same way as other posse hominems with powered technology.

When a future version of Julie traveled back and confronted him on the snowy hillside forest outside The City, dread had filled his core. That Julie was pregnant. And she traveled time.

Time travel operated through blood—a biological component that affected every human. When someone traveled time, the proteins in their blood forever responded differently after a journey to the past or future. The baby inside her not only had a combination of two time travelers' blood genomes—Julie's and Colin's—but also traveled time itself with its vehicle being Julie.

The two beings were now tied together in life and death.

Julie couldn't die where she was supposed to because her baby was conceived during time travel. Julie's body needed to live long enough to provide the capability. Mick couldn't test his theory with exact certainty unless he traveled to the future and obtained her child's blood. He pondered the idea often, but the child was born after his death. The journey would be challenging, and he would need the correct blood. Colin's wouldn't take him there, although Julie's would.

But Mick couldn't allow himself to trespass the trust he was attempting to reestablish with Julie with such egregious intentions.

If Melanie time traveled while pregnant with Colin, Mick couldn't promise the same outcome—Henry was not a time traveler—but he didn't want to risk the possibility of rippling an already complicated web of abnormalities.

"Would it hurt my future baby?" Melanie asked, carefully placing the glasses and chrome box into her small bag.

Mick looked up at the beautiful woman before him with wide eyes. Feeding her a half-lie, an unknown and unverified truth didn't sit well with him, but he couldn't risk this. Melanie had an integral and important part to play in the fate of the world. He took a sip of his tea and placed the warm mug back down with shaky hands.

"Yes," he finally answered.

Chapter 8
Isabella

<u>April 16th, 46 A.R.</u>

Isabella didn't like the lower lab very much, but it oddly reminded her of her time in medical school, a stage of her life where she actually lived freely. After she graduated, there were expectations: her family, her philanthropy, and her continuing advancement and prosperity for the Garcia bloodline. Isabella said goodbye to a life of autonomous decisions, a life of wanting to settle down with an adorable no-named hematologist she met in residency.

She would never get used to referring to the brain that lay before her as Lexi. Isabella fondly remembered her as Alexandra.

Alexandra gossiped with her in the kitchen on The Island as she prepared dinner for Isabella's mother, Nina. Memories of the Alexandra who snuck out of the property at night for a few hours to meet her boyfriend—a young man who worked at the renewable energy plant on the other side of the fourteen-mile island—and giggled when Isabella asked her where she'd been.

Alexandra was so much more to Isabella than Lexi could ever be.

The Supreme's choice in selecting Alexandra as a prototype for their experiments felt like a cruel and targeted attack to keep Isabella from straying away—a thought the surgeon-turned-philanthropist had more often than she'd like to admit.

Thinking back to all the surgeries performed to date made Isabella lightheaded. Each time she recounted a patient, her tiny bony fingers gripped the edge of a chair with the strength of a thousand warriors. The longer and longer Isabella continued down this quest, the more and more the sheer volume of patients startled her.

After just over a year, Isabella had successfully produced over a thousand creations. A mix of astonishment and terror filled her, but no one would better suit this role. When Isabella looked at the first posse hominem on her operating table, everything cemented into place.

Isabella hadn't chosen the specialty of a surgeon so much as it chose her. Her hands were small and delicate, quick and smooth in their movements. She remained calm under pressure, believing in herself through each step of surgery, no matter what went wrong in the process. Isabella was never afraid of blood or organs, gore that typically scared her father.

Her sister Anna was much like him in that sense. As a child, Anna cried at the sight of blood bubbling to the skin from small cuts.

I'm not sure how she survived The University, Isabella thought, *except out of sheer perseverance to compete against me.*

Anna's sick, twisted obsession with her proved a point of no return. Anna's professional choice to pursue a career as a medical examiner instead of a practicing surgeon suited her. The mechanics were the same, but there were no repercussions for a slight mistake, no added stresses when slicing through the body and adding multiple incisions.

Anna's patients were already dead. The point of no return.

Isabella had requested The Supreme help Anna get her job back—her sister quit without warning and in a grand, obnoxious fashion that could have embarrassed the Garcia family. The android leader was fierce and intimidating, but her gratitude to Isabella out-shined her normal snarky demeanor.

Proudness poured through Isabella as she held her head high and demanded her terms. Her father would have been delighted. Both of his daughters fulfilled their bloodline legacy of medical profession-als. Isabella satisfied her father's own dreams of becoming a sur-geon, but with his constant lightheadedness and uneasiness, Filipe became a psychologist. He was respected deeply as an advocate for those with psychological disorders and new wave treatment and management plans before his death.

Nolan, the android helping her and studying with her, cleaned up their workstation with meticulous care and enthusiasm.

He will make a good surgeon one day but needs more practice. She smiled in his direction. His purple scales shimmered briefly under the harsh overhead lights.

Isabella's device vibrated against the metal desk, and The Supreme sauntered over to the large device with all the microchip tracking numbers. Keeping track of biometrics had been Isabella's idea, a way for her to ensure her patients weren't experiencing dangerous side effects from their surgeries. But The Supreme used the mechanism differently—she liked keeping tabs and collecting personal data on these creations.

Kathleen Murphy's tracking number appeared in large bold letters on the screen. Isabella hadn't been overly thrilled about performing the operation on Colin's legislative aide and secretary but secretly wasn't bothered by The Supreme's request. Kathleen and Isabella never saw eye-to-eye on much of anything. It didn't matter how many times Isabella kindly offered to grab a coffee or stop by The Capitol Building with lunch; Kathleen refused to warm up to her.

Her loyalty to Colin, Isabella realized. *She kept all his secrets. Hid his affairs.*

Isabella's love for Colin didn't make any logical sense. Deep down she suspected Colin had strayed from her before. They'd been courting for over a decade, and he refused to marry her. His lack of urgency made sense at first with their family feud, but even after her father's death, Colin never knelt down on one knee or bestowed any O'Connor family jewelry to her.

The beginning of their relationship felt pretty magical, with grand, romantic gestures, before rummaging into a routine partnership. Isabella found him charming and attractive. He fit the exact image of what any old bloodline woman longed for in a societally approved partner. The danger and mystery behind her father's hatred for the O'Connor family provided a forbidden allure to the tall, dark, and handsome, if not broody at times, O'Connor heir.

Colin's fascination with Dr. Julie Walsh unsettled Isabella from the very beginning, but it wasn't until recently that Isabella sensed a shift and a difference. Julie's name appeared more on his device, and he was recluse about his whereabouts. Colin didn't ask to visit Isabella on The Island with her family and never inquired when she left for long periods of time. And then he stopped touching her. A couple of months could count as a coincidence, but now it'd been over a year since he'd even kissed her romantically.

True, I did tell him I needed space last summer, Isabella recalled. *But that was so I had space for this—time without worrying about him and keeping this hidden. We both have our secrets.*

A stinging hurt rippled her veins, but Isabella was a strong woman—she wouldn't let anyone, even Colin O'Connor, make her feel inferior.

"What is it?" The Supreme asked.

"Well, Kathleen's fine but dehydrated," Isabella's words rushed out of her, covering up the true reason for the furrow in her eyes. "I think the placement of the microchip might be slightly off; she's experiencing extreme migraines almost daily. That is an awful side effect."

"Do you think it has to do with Kathleen being left-handed?"

Isabella crossed her arms and leaned against the back of her chair.

"I hadn't thought about that. I don't believe if we put the microchip in the other side of her brain that it would make a difference." Isabella's eyes darted across the screen, scanning through various electronic records. No other abnormalities appeared on Kathleen's chart. "Her organs are all doing their jobs, and her eyesight is still clear."

One of Isabella's larger concerns was the body rejecting the microchip. This risk escalated whenever a foreign object was placed inside a human. The exact materials used for the microchips had been her first objection to The Supreme's initial plan, delaying the start of creating these new creatures by nearly six months.

"Good," The Supreme responded. "Let's look at the others now, shall we?"

Isabella clicked on the microchip-tracking dashboard, and they skimmed through logs of all the posse hominems they had created. Nothing alarming drew concern from Isabella, and her body eased as The Supreme wandered away from her desk.

"I do have one more request," The Supreme said quietly from behind her.

She pulled out a small sealed bag from her pocket and handed it over. Isabella took the delicate microchip and tilted her head to the side. Upon inspection, this microchip was identical to the others Isabella had surgically implanted in all her patients.

"This one isn't activated," The Supreme said, sensing Isabella's confusion.

"I'm not sure I understand."

"I'll activate it remotely when the time is ready. Remote activation is a new technology I'd like to test out. Please use this on your next patient and leave as little of a scar as possible. I don't care how you do it, but make sure it's nearly invisible. Then you can hand off all your operations to Nolan if you choose. You don't have to make that decision right now."

Isabella nodded, placing the microchip inside a desk drawer and locking it with a scan of her thumb. The Supreme had walked over to the far wall, a clear motion she wouldn't answer any more of Isabella's questions.

Who is my next patient? When will he or she be delivered to this chamber? Why are they so important in not only testing out remote activation but also remaining a secret?

Isabella made her way to The Supreme but paused. The metal wall beckoned her, the shiny metal drawers a sickening but enticing pull. Her hands danced across the large drawers, stopping briefly over the ones occupied with a sleeping body inside. She paused at the glass tube that housed Alexandra's fascinatingly preserved brain. Her pointer finger tapped the glass with the lightest touch, and her stomach threatened an unease that could pour up her body. Isabella backed away and grabbed the small table behind her to steady her balance. The plastic storage cubbies housed all the personal effects of her patients, including necklaces, watches, wedding bands and engagement rings, and glasses. The items told personal stories that Isabella found comfort in.

Her eyes gravitated to Kathleen's plastic cubby. It was completely empty. The color drained from Isabella's face.

She distinctly remembered removing Kathleen's family earrings from her attached lobes and placing them aside. Kathleen was married but never wore a ring, and beyond that one pair of earrings, there was nothing else for Isabella to remove.

Her mind darted to the laundry room at Colin's townhouse. Isabella shouldn't have been snooping all those years ago, but she had spilled red wine on a crème silk blouse and didn't want the stain to set. Frantic and hurried, she pulled open as many random drawers as possible looking for bleach and stain remover. Her hands violently trembled when jewelry she didn't recognize rattled around inside a small compartment. Isabella didn't know who the pieces belonged to, with the exception of Amanda MacDonald's silver key necklace. Amanda's body had been found outside the dumpsters behind The Capitol Building only a few months prior.

Isabella's soul had left her body, accusations she wanted to yell in Colin's direction bubbling to the surface. But her legs wouldn't move. Isabella stood there for so long that her absence had been noted. The sound of Colin clearing his throat finally shook her out of her stunned state.

"What is this?" she asked, dangling the silver key necklace out only inches from his face.

Colin's strong but sturdy hands gently gripped her shoulders and led her out of the laundry room. Isabella appreciated Colin's ability to stay calm regardless of the situation. Something she longed to one day learn from her partner.

"We should talk about It" were his last words before she learned about a completely secret part of his life. A part of the man she thought she loved at that time for over four years.

Isabella's father had diagnosed Colin at a young age with dissociative identity disorder, a psychological diagnosis in the family realm of bipolar conditions. When Colin confided in her, she wasn't sure how to respond. Logic told her to leave him. But his honesty and truthfulness, mixed with his shame and apparent discomfort, changed her mind.

Accepting Colin for his true self didn't come easy. Their relationship strained from that moment—Isabella pushed down the admission and pretended It didn't exist. Colin yearned for her acceptance of him, exuberating extreme trust by never threatening her, by never hurting her. Promising her he never would.

And he never did.

I don't think I ever truly accepted him.

The tic of stealing his victim's jewelry didn't make sense, but rationalizing his irrational mind was an exhausting effort.

"Are you all right, Dr. Garcia? You look a bit faint." The Supreme's steady, sound voice snapped Isabella out of her memory.

She looked away from the plastic cubbies and back at The Supreme. "Yes, I'm sorry. I think it's the lack of natural light down here."

The Supreme's eyes narrowed, trying to follow which cubby Isabella's stare had been fixated on.

"Make sure you're back here in the lower lab first thing in the morning when you return to The City on Monday. Your next patient will be waiting for you."

***

Nolan's robotic voice reminded Isabella that she was late. Her flight from The Island had been delayed by springtime fog, but tardiness was something The Supreme had no patience for.

Isabella snuck through a back entrance at COLI*GO and took several flights of stairs down to the lower lab. The wait was finally over—she'd get to meet this incredibly important specimen. She'd spent her week on The Island with her mother, pushing as much of the unsettling requests coming from The Supreme lately out of her mind. The saltiness of the air there was warmer, and flowers were budding and blooming.

Her mother seemed in great spirits. Nina Garcia was a beautiful woman with an impeccable pedigree. She was technically a Ludewing by birth and a Garcia by marriage, the younger sister of Don Ludewing. She'd fallen fast and furious for Filipe Garcia, and her marriage to him heightened the Garcias' to the closed ranks of the Ludewings, Borgeses, and O'Connors.

Nina was pleased that her eldest daughter helped her youngest and was committed to not only restoring but also differentiating the Garcia family in The City.

Isabella walked through the sterilizing machine and removed her outer layer of clothing before reaching for her white coat. Nolan stood over an operating table, small feminine feet dangling off the edge. His scales were tamed, drifting from lilac around his fingers to deep violet.

"Good morning, Nolan," Isabella said, approaching him quickly, knowing she'd need a few minutes to take a deep breath or she'd rush through this important operation.

She jumped back nearly several feet as her purple android counterpart lifted the surgical sheet away from the patient's face and rested it above her breasts.

Julie Walsh's unmissable freckled face and red hair looked up tauntingly at Isabella.

"How did . . . how did Dr. Walsh get down here?" Isabella asked Nolan.

He shrugged before responding. "The Supreme drugged her coffee with a sedative. She told me Dr. Walsh must be returned to her office before the end of the workday."

"What?" Isabella stammered. "Is she out of her mind? She wants us to perform the surgery and check her vitals and send her off on her way within the course of"—Isabella looked down at the delicate gold watch on her left wrist—"seven hours?"

"It would have been nine, had you not been late."

Isabella rolled her eyes and took a deep breath. Her hands trembled uncontrollably, something she couldn't allow if she were to leave no trace of a scar on Julie's pale skin. A difficult task to begin with. Isabella shook her head in frustration.

"The surgery only takes forty-five minutes."

"But it's the recovery that takes time," Isabella protested.

Nolan shrugged again and gestured toward the surgical tools on the tray.

Isabella closed her eyes, willing her body's nerves to calm themselves. After a moment, she nodded in Nolan's direction, indicating she was ready to perform the horrid task.

The idea of slicing into Colin's lover should have provided an immoral sense of delight, but Isabella found herself fighting back tears. She had always wanted to hate Dr. Walsh but never found the strength. She admired Julie's ambition and her ability to remain strong in the swaying wind of politics at COLI*GO. A woman of science, a woman who wanted to leave her own mark on the world—something Isabella wanted for herself.

The tangy, metallic smell of Julie's blood stained Isabella's blue plastic gloves. Her nose wrinkled in response, but Nolan didn't seem bothered. He handed her the special microchip with ease, and with the tiniest tools, Isabella secured the technology's placement into Julie's brain. Nolan threaded Isabella's small incision with dissolvable stitches the same color as Julie's skin.

Isabella threw her surgical tools on the table and let out a scream. Her outburst was safe in the soundproof lower lab, but she secretly hoped someone had heard her.

"Did you know Dr. Walsh?" Nolan asked. His curiosity was a strange trait for an android.

Ripping off her plastic gloves, Isabella allowed the tears to release from her eyes.

"Yes."

Nolan bent down to Isabella's crouched position and placed a scaly hand on her shoulder.

"I'll finish setting her up on the IV and start tracking her vitals. Why don't you take a seat in the office?"

Isabella nodded, appreciating his logical approach to a wild situation. The quiet, dark room provided little solace. Numerous questions crossed her mind: Why had The Supreme wanted to remotely activate Julie? Was she trying to hurt Colin? First Kathleen, now Julie.

A loud crash startled Isabella out of her seat. She rushed out of the office and turned the corner. Nolan's arm shot upward, holding a syringe with a clear tranquilizing liquid. Julie's naked body convulsed underneath him, her screams loud and sharp. In Julie's hand was a scalpel—a weapon she acquired from the unattended surgical table to protect herself. After a moment, her body went limp, and Nolan lifted her off the ground. He placed her gently back on the operating table.

Blood droplets from Julie's ripped IV splattered across the white tiled floors. Isabella raced to Julie, inspecting her scar, hoping the stitches hadn't ripped loose. They appeared perfectly intact, and Isabella's shoulders dropped in relief.

"You say nothing of this," Isabella said, pointing a finger in Nolan's face. "Do you hear me?"

"Yes, Dr. Garcia."

Chapter 9
It

It felt Julie's warm fingertips against his bare shoulders. He smiled, looking at the large flames crackling in the fireplace before turning around to face her.

The infamous O'Connor emerald engagement ring shimmered on Julie's left hand, and It smiled at the sight of her. She was dressed in a pair of black leggings and a large cable-knit sweater, one side hanging loosely off her shoulder. Her strawberry hair waved down along her face, the strands darker from time spent indoors, neglecting the needed sunlight to illuminate them.

It stood from the couch and leaned over the back of it to kiss her. She tasted sweet on his lips, and he savored each embrace. They didn't have much time together.

Placing his hands on the small of Julie's waist, It lifted her with ease over the back of the couch and placed her on the beige cushions. He deepened his kiss, his urgency for her matching her own urgency for him while his hands explored under her sweater. Kissing down her neck, he traced the jagged silver scar with his tongue, taking a moment to affectionately suck on the base of the reminder that The Supreme tried using Julie—but that Julie prevailed.

Continuing down her shoulders, It allowed her oversized sweater to loosen off the side of her body and reveal how she wore nothing underneath. He loved her skin, he loved her physique, and he loved her passion, her commitment, her intelligence, and her mind. It could get lost in Julie forever. She was made for him, the right kind of woman—fierce and independent, fiery and unafraid. Julie accepted him and his darkness. She enjoyed her time with him, aware he wasn't exactly Colin and never questioning It. Julie made It warm.

She provided hope that It wasn't all evil, that there was good inside him too. That maybe, just maybe, he was a better choice than Colin.

"I missed you." Her words were a soft whisper.

It looked up at Julie's warm ocean blue eyes. They resembled the waves outside, crashing along the cliffs during a thunderstorm. A winter storm roared outside now, the snow hitting the ground and dusting the windows with low visibility to the surrounding beautiful landscape of the seaside town.

"I missed you too," It said. He'd seen Julie only yesterday—but that was a different version of her. That version of Julie time traveled after Colin's death and that version of Julie was pregnant with It's child.

Our child.

The thought created a large grin across his chiseled face. The thought of such a glorious reality made him ravenous. The thought made him insatiable for her.

Goosebumps flushed across Julie's skin as he continued discovering her with his tongue, fingers and lips. Gripping her rear, he picked up her naked body and carried her across the estate.

No one came to the O'Connors' Oceanside home during this time of year except for the occasional housekeeper to tidy up any odd-ended visits. The refrigerator had been empty when It traveled here a couple of days ago, forcing him to take a trip to the small quaint downtown area that was about a leisurely twenty-minute walk. He bought coffee and milk, her favorite produce—apples and blueberries—and then the ingredients to make them a hearty pasta meal for this evening.

They'd stay here the night, then Julie would head up to The City and spend a full day at COLI*GO. She'd come back to The Oceanside to sleep if she needed more time in this year, more time to work on her antidote.

And the toxin, It thought with a smirk.

But It wouldn't stay. He'd head back to The City and then make his way back to the future. He spent too much time wandering these halls, waiting for different versions of Julie.

After climbing the stairs with Julie tightly in his arms, It reached the oversized master bedroom. The room had a large balcony, a white brick fireplace, and lush green marble flooring. The bed faced the floor-to-ceiling windows and French doors overlooking the estate's grounds and vivacious Oceanside cliffs with crashing waves.

It placed Julie on the bed and walked over to the fireplace, igniting a flame to keep them warm while they slept. But sleep was far away from them, and shadows erupted in the otherwise dim room while the fire grew. The scars on Julie's stomach hissed in his line of vision, the scars he was partly responsible for, even if it wasn't his mind that enacted the blows.

It approached Julie slowly, stalking back to her and the large bed with a deep hunger in his eyes. Her hands gripped the sides of It's face, pulling him back in to her. He broke from her embrace and tucked a loose strand of hair behind her ear.

"I love you," It said, his eyes never leaving hers.

"I love you too."

His kiss silenced any other words.

They made love—messy, uninterrupted, passionate love. Julie and Colin had adoring, zealous, and exciting sex, but with It, their lovemaking was soul-crushing. He didn't hold back. He was never careful. She pushed boundaries with him. She was never afraid. They felt whatever they wanted to feel. They allowed themselves to fully embrace the other, fully embrace all their emotions. Together, Julie and It opened up and accepted each other.

It held Julie, tracing the scars along her stomach. Brushing his slightly calloused fingers against the imperfections on her silky, smooth skin brought an odd sense of comfort to him. He thought back to the night of their reunion, how somewhere in the future she watched him for weeks on end before climbing the fire escape and sneaking into the window of Colin's study.

Julie initiated this, It realized, stroking her hair. *She knew who I was. And she came to me, anyway.*

That night, he had fervently taken her on top of Colin's desk and in Colin's leather chair. He claimed her in Colin's bedroom, on the floor, and in the bed. He would have made her his on every inch and on every surface of the townhouse if time and energy allowed.

"You've always been mine, not his," he had whispered in her ear before initially burying himself between her legs. An act of not only defiance but also a warning to Colin that he was a force to be reckoned with. That It would prevail. She tasted so good then, that very first time—but she tasted even better now.

It felt Julie's heart beating erratically against his chest, the heat of their bodies keeping them warm under the thick covers. Wrapping his large arms around her, he drew Julie in tighter to him.

"We should stop doing this," Julie said into the darkness.

It's heart sunk, and his breathing slowed.

She doesn't mean those words.

"Why?" he probed, leaning into her neck and gently kissing the base of her scar.

"I'm afraid you'll fully corrupt me," Julie said but still allowing her body to collide closer to his.

Knowing what she became in the future, It laughed at her statement. His chuckle was deep-rooted but honest, and he looked into her dewy eyes. It's fingertips danced along the curve of Julie's hip.

"Are you telling me," he said, pulling away from her lips, "that I'm growing on you? That you're starting to like me more?"

Julie placed an urgency in her kiss, afraid of the words that he felt lingering on her luscious lips: *I do love you more.*

She didn't need to say this out loud. It never doubted Julie, and he understood how hard her decisions would be in the future.

Yet I hope she still chooses me.

***

It picked up his pace, climbing the cobblestone sidewalks of The Hill. The wind whipped fiercely from the river, a chill so vivid he felt the rawness of his exposed skin shiver. The O'Connor townhouse was located on the lower side of The Hill, nearing the public garden and neighboring The Bay. Passing The Capitol Building, It walked toward the other side of his neighborhood, in the direction of the police headquarters.

The Supreme buzzed him into her building, and It climbed the first set of stairs to her condo. While he'd known her practically his whole life, he'd never been inside her home. They kept the extent of their friendship at bay, separating the reality of how much like brother and sister they were to each other. There never was, and there never would be, any kind of attraction between The Supreme and It, but even anything perceived as a close friendship could hinder Colin's reputation.

Emilia's golden scales shimmered underneath her white sweater, and she kept her hair pulled up in a large bun. A decade made her appear younger than he remembered her, although androids didn't age the same way as humans. Android scales did sag on their faces, but wrinkles were nonexistent. What It noticed was a spirited energy in Emilia's eyes—the last time he saw her, she looked tired.

"I didn't expect to see you, my friend," The Supreme said, walking over to her stove top and turning on the kettle.

It relaxed his shoulders and took a seat in her front sitting room, making himself comfortable inside her home. He didn't plan on leaving anytime soon.

"Your appearance is more distinguished than the last time we met," The Supreme said, walking toward him with a warm mug filled with honey and tea. "But you look happy."

Emilia was skilled in the art of observation—her comment insinuated a curiosity of an answer for why he appeared older than he truly was.

"I never understood happiness until recently." The words slipped out of his mouth. It scolded himself for his liberal attitude toward the younger version of Emilia. He needed to remain careful.

Emilia nodded, taking an elegant, long sip out of her porcelain teacup. Her bright green eyes never left him. While she studied It, he observed her home. She kept it minimalist, but instead of cool, bright tones, the walls were painted in dark colors. Mauve purples in the kitchen, and deep reds and rich chocolate wooden paneling engulfed the living room. The lack of artwork and other décor fitted Emilia's aloof personality. The only decorative piece was a beautiful-ly engraved wooden chess set on her coffee table.

It leaned forward and moved a pawn out while eyeing Emilia. She placed her teacup down on its saucer and followed suit with the chess pieces. The silence in her home didn't bother either of them. An occasional honking noise from outside on the street below inter-rupted the peacefulness between them but no words were spoken, no arguments exchanged.

"Why are you here, my friend?" Emilia asked, moving her bishop over towards It's knight, stealing the piece and placing it gently on her side of the coffee table.

"Honestly?" It asked with an ominous smirk. "I wanted to remember a time when we didn't hate each other."

Emilia concentrated on the board, unwilling to look at her opponent head-on. A physical stiffness spread across her shoulders.

"Time travel is real."

"You know?" It advanced his queen on the board, his fingers delicately holding the crown, suspending the piece in the air for a moment before placing it back down.

"Edward told me. There's an inventor of time travel whom I must invest in when the time is right. He said I'll know, that the time traveler will come to me. Is that you?"

It chuckled. He wished he could take the claim to fame for discovering this wicked technology. It admired Emilia. She was an excellent player, keeping all her moves close to her chest, only revealing her uncertainties when the threat of the unknown was greater.

"I am not the inventor, no."

Emilia smirked, the corners of her mouth stretching across her scales. "I didn't think so."

They continued their game, The Supreme's brow upturned as It contemplated his next move. He feared she caught him in one of her traps. A skilled player, Emilia always provided a challenging and vigorous match and only a few pieces remained on the board.

It held his queen and king, and one spare knight. The players were all outlined right there. It envisioned them with vivid accuracy.

Julie's freckled face and bright strawberry hair. Mick's ebony skin, dried and marked with the sketches of too much time travel.

Time travel—an addiction all on its own.

Elsie with the bright black ink of her tattoo. Celine and her high cheekbones, resembling the perfect mixture of both his mother and father. Commissioner Jones, the emerald colors of his scales symbolizing more importance with each flicker of emotion coursing through his processor.

But it didn't matter. It saw the next move in his mind before Emilia's golden hands shimmered over the board, grabbing her queen and lightly tapping It's king three times.

Thump. Thump. Thump.

"Checkmate."

Chapter 10
Peter

<u>February 8th, 38 A.R.</u>

The lower lab was quiet without Julie. Peter hadn't seen her familiar smiling face since December 37 A.R., back when the rift between him and Julie started.

Amanda MacDonald, Celine's chief of staff at COLI*GO, typed furiously on her device. Her wide smile shone across her snow-pale skin, and she wore her blonde hair in a stylish braid. The woman was beyond charming and alluring—she held a special, flirtatious delight that was just as bright as her red lipstick.

Celine O'Connor was a fool to think no one suspected her relationship with Amanda was strictly professional. Peter saw the spark between them: two hungry women wanting to burn down the authoritarianism of the world for their own power and control. But Amanda didn't have the means to do so—only Celine did.

Amanda threatened to expose COL2120, believing that if Celine wouldn't listen to her, Colin would. Peter held back his laughter that a man like Colin O'Connor would care what someone as insignificant as Amanda had to offer him, but he tried not to dwell on her too much—he knew the future, he knew she would die at the hands of The City's infamous serial killer. But Amanda was Peter's gatekeeper in the past, allowing or denying access to the lower lab to the outside world.

Peter was more concerned about Dr. Filipe Garcia than the hasty blonde who used her attractiveness to climb society's ladder. A loyalty to Anna Garcia surged through Peter. She believed so much in what her father tried to accomplish—similar to what Julie wished to do with the antidote.

When Celine founded COLI*GO, she'd initially wanted the psychologist's investment in her company, but he ultimately denied her. Rumors spread from him that Celine's company was dammed, proposing mad science experiments over sound, thoughtful, and life-changing technologies. But there was more to the story, and after a couple of glasses of wine, Amanda let the unsavory truths escape her full cherry-painted lips.

Dr. Filipe Garcia was very interested in COLI*GO when Celine was trying to secure funding and investments. Martin Borges, who evaluated the science behind all business propositions, and Dr. Garcia spoke at length in the beginning. One of Garcia's conditions for loaning money for the start-up was that Martin needed to prioritize Garcia's proposed assets. He was interested in developing only neurological and psychological drugs that targeted neuro-receptors in the brain—similar to the asset COL2120.

Martin believed in partnering with academic institutions as the right path for an asset like this. He didn't think the laboratory or staff would be ready for such a project upfront. Martin argued that COLI*GO needed to establish trust and respect within The City and The Legislature by taking over the production and perfecting pharmaceutical assets that couldn't be trusted with other biotech-nology firms. Martin believed this was COLI*GO's moral and ethical responsibility to society since so much of the company was funded through The Legislature and government subsidies. In the beginning, COLI*GO needed to right the wrongs of greedy compa-nies before investing in their own aggressive and lucrative assets.

Celine wasn't married to Martin yet, and during those funding years, he was married to Maggie Rivera. If gossip was true, Celine and Martin's affair had already begun. Celine was courting the man for many reasons: business, pleasure, and societal desire. She was pitted against receiving more funding from the Garcia family—a family that the O'Connors publicly hated—or staying true to the man she wanted to someday marry. She chose the latter.

"I do wish that this could help many patients, but I don't think it will. I think it will hurt them," Dr. Filipe Garcia said, turning from the screen containing more simulations produced by the toxin. He reached into his pocket and pulled out a small vial. The liquid inside was clear like the antidote and the toxin, but a small metallic tinge shadowed the edges of the tube.

Peter grabbed the bottle from Filipe's hands and held it up to the light, further inspecting the contents. He hadn't expected that Filipe had produced a physical drug. Filipe smiled at Peter and pulled his glasses off his face.

Dr. Filipe Garcia's dark skin shimmered against the metal table, and his frail but solid voice soothed Peter. Filipe was a shorter man, and Peter secretly enjoyed physically intimidating the old bloodline patriarch with his height and gangly, broad shoulders.

"What is this?" Peter asked.

"I encountered a peculiar case nearly twenty-five years ago. A boy who spoke oddly about another person living in his brain. How he witnessed this other voice claiming to be from the future, asking him to do unspeakable things. How this voice was the same man who killed his mother. He was otherwise a quiet child. Smart, thoughtful, even caring. The normal standard of care didn't calm his spells or outbursts. I knew I needed to try harder."

Filipe placed his head in his hands and let out a deep sigh that Peter nearly mistook for a sob. "I promised his father, who was a near and dear friend of mine. I created a biologic that would help release his otherwise restricted dendrites, the part of the brain affected by these conditions. I believed if I could enlarge it to mirror a normal, healthy person's, then the standard of care would work better. That's why I fear your drug."

Peter extracted some contents from the vial and placed it inside a tube. The device attached began its evaluation, reports appearing on the screen.

"The mechanism is slightly different but very similar to what you have proposed with this asset," Filipe said while the toxin flurried across the screen beside his drug. The evil concoction Julie created was indeed similar—but hers only required one dose of treatment. Filipe's needed chronic management.

"My drug didn't work. I tried telling his father. He wouldn't listen to me." Filipe pointed to the screen. "I understand why your researcher pursued this mechanism of action. The science and the data point in this direction, but a single dose isn't the answer."

"Do you mind if I take this?" Peter asked, gesturing toward Dr. Garcia's homemade pharmaceutical. "I want to investigate it, study it. See if there is something here."

Dr. Garcia looked up at Peter and nodded.

"It's all yours."

The toxin's ability to grab hold of the disease would eject one of Colin's personalities out of his mind—but the wrong one. And no matter how hard they tried, the antidote continued failing. Ripping apart the antidote and reengineering it again and again strained Julie, and it strained Peter too. The process exhausted them, and Peter needed a shortcut.

Filipe's drug might spark a new wave of thinking. But I'm afraid Julie will never give up on her antidote, on her toxin, and that she won't take kindly to this.

"As a psychologist, I know evil lives inside all of us," Filipe said with a heavy sigh. "But when we can't distinguish which part of ourselves is truly evil and which is really good, that's when monsters are born. You are trying to cure a monster. Instead, this drug creates one."

Amanda grabbed Dr. Garcia's hand and squeezed him tightly. A soft whimper escaped Filipe's lips, and he leaned into the pretty blonde almost too easily.

"I promise I won't let anyone else be hurt by this."

***

Amanda pulled Peter aside into the built-in office of the lower lab.

"Your associate, Dr. Walsh," Amanda said with a glitter in her eyes, "she warned me of some of COL2120's faults. Do you think maybe COLI*GO isn't ready to venture into neurological assets?"

COL2120 was a complicated but important gene therapy for COLI*GO. Peter had worked on the molecule during his PhD program at The University with his lab partner, Jonathan Riles. Jonathan didn't want to hand over his prized possession to COLI*GO before graduation for fear that they would start working on the development and research without him.

Martin Borges visited The University laboratory daily, watching as Peter helped his friend to no avail. Peter didn't know that, at the time, COLI*GO was struggling to catch its footing. When Martin offered to lend a hand, Peter felt awestruck.

Martin was a celebrity of sorts in the scientific field. He came from a family of scientists, his father having made most of his money in drug development for other pharmaceutical companies in The City prior to The Legislature cleaning up many of the organizations and instituting new laws and regulations in drug making. Martin was also from one of the most prestigious old bloodline families.

Peter nearly handed COL2120 over to Martin without question. This act put him in good graces with the young executives, Celine O'Connor being one of them. He was offered a higher salary, able to climb the political business ranks of the organization with ease compared to his colleagues. The only other person who surpassed him in those efforts was Julie Walsh. But that wasn't until much later.

COL2120 was never perfect. Many researchers spent years studying the drug after The Legislature had approved it. Perfecting the asset became a top priority for COLI*GO. Julie called out the ridiculous quest to perfect a near-perfect drug. Peter couldn't allow Amanda to question too much of COL2120. He felt an odd fury at Julie for potentially causing such a strife through time travel, and he felt it was his obligation to set the record straight with Celine before Amanda went running to Colin O'Connor for help. If the COL2120 project failed at COLI*GO, Julie would never have gotten a job and had the chance to use the innovative technology COLI*GO owned to work on her antidote.

"COL2120 will be fine. We just need to keep our funding so we can continue researching it. Dr. Walsh doesn't know what she's talking about."

Amanda tilted her head and frowned. Even her frown was charming, and the slumped posture in her chair accentuated her voluptuous figure.

"I haven't seen her in a while," Amanda noted. "Is she okay?"

"Why do you care so much about Dr. Walsh, Amanda?" A voice from the lower lab's entrance traveled toward them.

Celine O'Connor's heels clicked against the gray floors, and she pushed a strand of chestnut hair behind her ears. She appeared tired with bags under her eyes. Celine time traveled, albeit infrequently.

But something about her appearance here startled Peter more so than Amanda.

"She's nice," Amanda answered quietly. "She made me wish we were friends."

Celine strode into the office and stood behind Amanda's chair. She gripped Amanda's shoulders firmly, rubbing small circles with her thumbs. Amanda eyed Peter quickly, but he knew. He knew how much his boss had loved this ridiculous woman. Clearly, she still held Celine's heart in the future for Celine to act this way while traveling to the past.

"Friends?"

"Yes, and I used to see her here all the time. Now it's been a month or so. I just wanted to make sure nothing bad has happened to her." Amanda relaxed into Celine's embrace.

"Dr. Walsh is fine. She's taking some time away from the lab. She's a very busy woman," Celine said, eyeing Peter.

Peter took the hint and shuffled out of his seat. Amanda's device sat on the edge of the bench and pondered on the possibility for a moment. With stealth fingers and the right swing in his lab coat, Peter snagged Amanda's device.

Once in the stairwell, he pulled the sleek device out of his pocket. He typed the transgressions of his boss's lover with flying fingers, hastily spilling all of Amanda's worries, her plans to reach out to Colin O'Connor and urge him to whip votes against COL2120.

Guilt consumed Peter as he made his way back up the building. The elevator was packed with other scientists, colleagues he recognized, and he kept his head low to avoid meeting their gaze. He approached Amanda's desk and plopped the device on the corner near her leather bag.

Peter couldn't consider himself a bystander in this game for control in The City. He was a player now too.

PART FOUR

The Present

"But are the dreams of poets and the tales of travelers notoriously false?"
—H. P. Lovecraft

Chapter 11
Celine

The O'Connor family lawyer, Jeffries, shifted uncomfortably in his seat. He was an android and his scales throbbed an uncanny maroon color under the harsh lights of his office in The Hill.

Jeffries had served as the O'Connor's attorney since Henry ran for office. Jeffries's sponsor had handed down the business to him. Androids didn't have families in the same ways as humans. They couldn't produce their own offspring naturally—it was anatomically impossible, for they lacked the ammunition but not the equipment. After an android left FACERE at a young age to attend public school, they were placed with a sponsor android family that raised them like a family unit.

"I have Mr. O'Connor's will here," Jeffries stammered, his scales flickering quickly before calming down.

Dr. Julie Walsh sat beside Celine, and she looked over at her before glancing back at Jeffries. The scientist sat rigid and straight in her chair and wore a conservative full-sleeved black dress despite the heat. Her hair was pulled tautly into a ponytail, and the bruises on her face cast a ghostly yellow shadow on her freckled skin.

Celine smoothed out her deep midnight-colored skirt and tucked a lock of hair behind her ear. She'd let her bob-styled cut grow out and desperately needed a visit to her hairdresser.

"All right, let's get started," Jeffries said into the silent room, flipping through the pages on his device. "We'll begin with property and estates. Mr. O'Connor left the family townhouse in the care of the family trust, a home he requested by used by his wife, any children they may have, as well as his sister and her family. In his words, 'The townhouse is to remain an equal asset, meant for O'Connors.'"

Jeffries coughed and looked up at Celine and Julie. Neither

woman indicated their true thoughts.

He continued, "The Oceanside estate is left solely to Dr. Julie Walsh, but she must grant visiting rights to Ms. Celine O'Connor."

Celine sucked in a sharp breath. Julie's glare glanced at the sound, and a question of concern shadowed in her warm blue eyes.

"Really?" Celine asked, leaning over the table with piped curiosity. She contained her anger, for now.

"That is what Mr. O'Connor wished, yes," Jeffries answered in the monotone, logical android fashion. He tilted the device in Celine's direction so that she could see the words on the screen. "He wrote, 'It is my wish to leave The Oceanside estate to my wife, Dr. Julie Walsh. The fond memories we have together in that home were all thanks to her. It is there, with Dr. Walsh, that I learned acceptance. That I learned what love truly means.'"

Celine fought the urge to roll her eyes at her brother's uncharacteristically flowery words. She didn't visit The Oceanside estate often, avoiding the area of The Constituency altogether. But it was the place she had spent much of her childhood summers, the place where their mother disappeared. Celine silently vowed to fight for what was rightfully meant for the O'Connors—especially if her brother was cast under the foolish enough spell to give any more of the family fortune away to a nobody.

Jeffries pinched and zoomed in on his device, clearly bothered by Celine's uncomfortable breaths, poking, and prodding.

"There were two boats," he said plainly.

"Two? No, there's only one."

"According to Mr. O'Connor's will, there are two boats. One kept primarily docked in The Port Yacht Club with a secondary slip in The Oceanside. The second boat is docked at The Harbor Boating Club." Jeffries's scales vibrated, and an amusing grin crossed his scaly face. "He left the larger yacht, Emerald, to Celine and the smaller vessel, Blade Runner, to a Miss Elsie Sullivan."

A small noise escaped Julie's lips, and Celine glanced at her with scolding eyes. Elsie Sullivan was Colin's legislative aide but had only been appointed into the role a few months prior. Neither Celine nor Colin had any reason to concern themselves with Elsie Sullivan even if she was part of the Sullivan old bloodline family. Elsie was a bastard, knocking her mother Roslyn down a few pegs in the social standings of society.

Colin recently updated his will, Celine realized. A heavy pit of agony grew deep in her stomach with an eerie sense of impending doom.

"When did Colin last notarize his will?"

Jeffries looked down at his device and back up at both women with wide eyes. He stuttered, a small beat of sweat excreting from his scales. Fear was an emotion Jeffries was programmed to understand and feel—his flippant display of the emotion rampant across his face.

"Jeffries, it's okay," Julie said, leaning across the table and placing her hands on top of his shaking ones.

He closed his eyes before answering, "June 22nd. At nine a.m."

The room grew silent and the air thicker around them.

"Did Colin know?" The words came from Julie, a sharp shiver cascading through her body. "I'd like to think that he didn't," Celine answered with a stern but crisp tone.

"There is additional paperwork regarding Miss Elsie Sullivan." Jeffries reached into his briefcase and pulled out a notarized letter.

The heavy cardstock nearly sliced Celine's fragile skin as she ripped open the seal. The color drained from her face, and a small gagging noise tickled in her throat. Julie leaned over, peering at the words on the letter. Celine shook her head and slid the paperwork over to Julie, unable to speak.

There wasn't any way for Celine to deny the fact that Elsie Sullivan was her half-sister, no matter how desperately she wanted to. The evidence was apparent: The words spelled out the DNA matches, linking Elsie as a half-sibling to Colin, her paternal lineage shared.

"Who else knows about this?" Celine asked through gritted teeth.

"Elsie and Roslyn. I'm not inclined to believe anyone else does." Jeffries's monotone voice didn't provide a reassuring answer to Celine's inquiry about her father's indiscretions.

"You're not to say anything to anyone until we figure out this public relations nightmare. Do you understand?" Celine's sharp eyes glared over at Julie.

"It's not my business to tell."

"Mr. O'Connor did express the interest in publicly accepting Elsie into the family if and when she chooses to do so. You cannot go against those already promised wishes, Ms. O'Connor."

Fire engine red flushed across Celine's cheeks, and she counted to ten before looking back at Jeffries.

"I'd like to move on from this, for now. I need time to process this information."

Jeffries shrugged, the feeling not something he clearly understood or experienced himself.

"Mr. O'Connor left his vehicle to Dr. Walsh. The title is in his home study at the townhouse. Next, I'll move on to investments and trusts." Jeffries paused and took a sip of water from the glass placed beside him. "Regarding investments, Mr. O'Connor named his beneficiary for all his COLI*GO stock as Dr. Julie Walsh. His other stock portfolios he asked be divested and added to his part of the family's trust. As you know, Celine, the family trust is split three-quarters to Colin and one-quarter to you. Colin left 50 percent of his portion to Dr. Walsh and the other 50 percent to Henry Jr., only to be abridged in the event that he and Dr. Walsh have children, in which he specified, the other 50 percent would be placed in a separate trust equally amongst his children."

Celine didn't need Colin's portion of the trust, but a small sharp jab thrust through her body knowing that Colin willingly left so much money to a nobody—someone who didn't deserve the prestigious, hard-earned assets. As a nobody, Julie didn't need that kind of money to live a comfortable life. Celine paid Julie's salary at COLI*GO—the young scientist was quite the pricey and expensive investment.

Sure, it would be different if they had children, but at least my brother didn't foil that up. A soft smile spread across Celine's lips as she thought about her own son. *Colin was always fond of Henry Jr., who should be the rightful and only heir to the O'Connor bloodline legacy.*

Colin's gesture of leaving her son a large part of the trust warmed her heart.

"I'll have you set up an account for Henry Jr., and you can transfer the funds," Celine said earnestly, tapping her fingers on the metal table. "Dr. Walsh, I suggest you work with Jeffries to create an account for yourself with the other half of Colin's money and his COLI*GO stock if you decide to sell it back, which I would recommend you do. I don't think the board will take too kindly to you owning more of the company than me." Celine watched Julie roll her eyes, and the arrogant, young woman lit a match inside her grieving soul. "Since you're a nobody, I'm sure you have never dealt with this amount of wealth and that no one in your family has taught you to manage money properly. Jeffries works with the best investors and can make sure the funds continue growing."

Celine was harsh, but her flippant remark spoke her own truth. She questioned Julie's composed silence, and that the scientist didn't offer any snide remarks of her own.

The banter over the last few years between them was something Celine secretly enjoyed about Julie.

What more does Julie know? Why isn't she surprised by any of this? Celine wondered with a troubling feeling that scheming between Colin and Julie took place without Celine's knowledge.

"The remainder of Mr. O'Connor's assets are all listed out here, in section twenty. They appear to be part of the properties, and he wished they remained as such." Jeffries looked back and forth between Julie and Celine. "I know this is a difficult time, and there might be something we discussed here that doesn't sit well with you later. If either of you wishes to contest anything in Mr. O'Connor's will, I ask that you do so within a week. Please contact me directly so we can privately speak on the matter."

Don't fret, Jeffries, you'll be hearing from me shortly.

Chapter 12
Elsie

<u>July 7th, 47 A.R.</u>

Elsie glanced at Don Ludewing Jr. as his sculpted naked body left her bed. He looked over his shoulder and slyly grinned his charming, brilliant smile. Reaching out, Elsie's fingertips trailed down his smooth sepia skin. Goosebumps flashed across his abdomen, blossoming from where she touched him and spreading like spilled wine.

"You're nothing but trouble, Elsie Sullivan." Don laughed and changed his mind, crawling back under the covers beside her.

"That's easy for you to say," Elsie replied while he kissed the edge of her serpent tattoo. "You only started paying attention to me to bother Colin, and now I'm fairly certain you're only using me to get in Governor Walsh's good graces."

Don's large heavy hand gripped her upper thigh, holding her against the bed. The risky grin on his face grew even wider. He pulled Elsie into his chest and kissed her forehead, an odd but affectionate gesture.

In any other circumstance, Elsie's mother would have been ecstatic that her daughter chose another old bloodline member, especially a Ludewing—one of the highest-ranking old bloodline families in The Constituency. But what she and Don shared wasn't traditional, and Elsie was anything but a conventional woman.

When their affair first started, Don insisted they keep it under the radar to avoid speculation. She was the governor's legislative aide and secretary, and he was a member of The Representatives of The People. This was a scandal waiting to happen.

And Colin never liked the man, either.

Elsie was no fool—Don used her, and she used him. A physical relationship was all this would ever be even if he was fascinating and even if she wanted more with him.

"Dr. Walsh is a curious creature for sure, but in any regard, the last time I checked, you were having your own fun with COLI*GO's CEO." Don accused Elsie of straying, but she could equally blame him of the same. There were rumors of his fondness toward androids—which made her chuckle because he didn't know she was partly one herself.

"Peter's fun to toy with," Elsie said, shoving the top sheet on her bed away from her body. She pulled the cotton fabric off and ran her fingers through her hair. Thoughts of Peter Schneider filled Elsie's mind. She didn't even feel guilty about the betrayal— something amiss in her mind . . . something amiss due to the micro- chip that remained lodged inside her. Elsie acted more selfish lately, more impulsively than before, but she couldn't stop herself and did- n't want to stop herself. "But Dr. Julie Walsh is not someone to try to trick with your charming ways."

"I have no intentions of trying to seduce a widow," Don Jr. said with a chuckle, hinting at a sense of sarcasm that Elsie didn't appreciate. "I did hear from one of my legislative aides that Julie is pregnant."

Elsie stilled. Elsie never played at gossip in The Legislature, most being a fabrication of small truths. The accusation made little sense—Julie had been "trapped at FACERE" as far as anyone else was concerned, and if that was the lie they were all forging toward, a pregnancy wouldn't make sense. Elsie knew the truth of where Julie truly was during the last five months. She spent her days at former Representative Joel Kennsington's home, a prisoner within his walls.

Julie traveled time, going back to meet with Peter and work on fixing her antidote. Colin also traveled time, Elsie wouldn't deny the suspicion, and now she wondered if her new boss and her former one conspired together through time travel.

Elsie squinted in Don's direction with no intentions of disputing his claims. Regardless, Don Jr. could seduce a widow if it pleased him and added to his own personal and professional gain.

"Okay, well, it's just a rumor and one I don't believe. Maybe I would charm her but not right away. It's tacky—Colin was only just assassinated. I suppose I owe him a little respect." Don's tone was slightly threatening, a bit unsettling in Elsie's accurate accusation against his true nature. "But all I really want from Dr. Walsh is an alliance. I don't want drama. I don't want rumors. I've had too many of those in my career. Julie's unaware of this, but her influence and loyalty are highly respected and highly coveted. Whoever runs for governor will surely need her endorsement if she chooses not to run herself."

Don's eyes gazed upon Elsie's, looking for an answer to his unasked question: if Julie would throw her name in the special gubernatorial election. Elsie looked away from Don and huffed.

"Well, then," he said, inching away from her. "I'm not above seducing the widow if it will make you jealous. I find this oddly invigorating."

Elsie laughed, the sound deep and verbose.

Julie was incredibly brilliant—Elsie and she had formed an odd but close bond while Julie traveled time, and now all they had in The Capitol Building was one another. But Dr. Walsh had an attractiveness to her that everyone seemed to admire. There wasn't anything traditionally beautiful about Julie, but her full pink lips, long limbs, and elegant neck made her pulchritudinous enough.

Colin O'Connor, a man of power with classically handsome looks and wealth, risked everything for Julie, including the societal prized possession of Dr. Isabella Garcia, Elsie thought. *There isn't a more stunningly attractive woman and kind soul in The Constituency than Isabella. But now these other rumors about Julie . . . Is that why they got married?*

"Do you think she'll decide to run?" Don asked, sitting on the edge of Elsie's bed. His sudden movement and absence of touch brought the humid warmth in Elsie's room to the forefront of her mind.

The condo Elsie owned in The Monument was simple, but that was how she preferred to keep her living quarters. It was a one-bedroom with a yellow kitchen and thick crown molding. Her home barely looked lived in even though she'd owned it for several years.

Elsie sighed with more gusto than required. Julie had made herself clear—she didn't want this role as governor. She wanted to be back at COLI*GO. Elsie imagined the scientist in the lower lab of the prestigious glass skyscraper working on her antidote: Julie belonged on the side of science, not the side of politics. Politics were a necessary evil to Julie, not a full plan for her career ambitions.

But I'm not so sure that Don Jr. deserves this tidbit of insider information.

"I don't think so. I think with everything being so fresh, Julie hasn't decided her next move."

Elsie raced out from under her sheets and walked into the adjoining bathroom. She turned her shower on and impatiently placed her hand under the stream of running water. After a few moments, it was almost warm enough to warrant the cooler tinge and submergence of her overheated body. The muggy, unbearable weather for the beginning of July indicated that The City's summer season was in full bloom.

"Are you thinking of running?" Elsie asked, a flirtatious grin spreading across her face when Don sauntered into the bathroom beside her.

Don kissed her longingly, his fingers trailing her chin and his sticky, sweaty body colliding slickly against hers.

"I'm kicking around the idea," he said, breaking away from their embrace and placing his hand under the showerhead to test the water temperature for himself. "I'm not sure I actually want to deal with all the responsibilities. It'll all depend on who throws themselves into the running, but I would be just as happy if I was appointed Session speaker instead."

Elsie peered at Don, taking the bait he dangled delicately in front of her.

"I would love the responsibilities of the governor," Elsie responded, deflecting the favor Don sought from her. "Being a representative seems more taxing from my experience."

Elsie ripped open the shower curtain and stepped inside, relaxing into the hot water pressure. Don quickly joined her.

"I'd be terrified if you were ever the governor," he teased. "While Governor Sullivan has a nice ring to it, you're too ferocious. You wouldn't ever let representatives like me get anything done. You remind me of The Supreme in that way. A governor needs a gentle touch."

Don grazed Elsie's tattoo again with light fingers, and a shiver shot through her body. Elsie hated how he did this to her—how attractive she found him despite how shallow he was.

"I can be gentle," Elsie said in response, grabbing Don's chin with a firm but tender grip.

Don laughed a deep-rooted chuckle, his voice baritone and whimsical. For a moment, Elsie felt like her old self—the person she used to be before the microchip.

The sensation invigorated her.

Chapter 13
Commissioner Jones

Jones's device constantly rang. There wasn't an hour that passed without a reporter asking for an update on the investigation into former Governor O'Connor's death. Jones wanted a better answer and longed for the truth, but the riddle laughed at him, the photos on his corkboard in his office tormenting his processor with every peering glare.

Jones held an affinity to Colin he didn't like admitting. The former governor was a charming man, one who eased words into the correct sentences, whose positivity and confidence created a lush garden, one sprouting optimism and promise.

I believed in him, he sought my friendship, and he tried to be my confidant. Even with his transgressions, they felt . . . logical even if impractical.

Strange habits hindered Jones lately, habits similar to when Julie went missing in January. When his best friend was untraceable, he went as far as renting the apartment across the street so that he could dutifully watch her place—hoping she would emerge in his line of vision one night.

Similar to Jones's desire to find Julie, he wished to know what truly happened to Colin. Sitting opposite Colin's grave every night wouldn't provide any new answers, and the lack of powering down his processor for a full eight hours each night weighed heavily on his handling times. And when he wasn't there, he watched the footage from a surveillance device placed in the cemetery. But that didn't replace the strangely soothing sensation that calmed his scales when he sat in the grass some twenty feet opposite the headstone engraved with Colin's name.

But Colin never rose from his grave. He was truly dead—as dead as anyone who didn't travel time would be if they were also shot twice in the head.

Jones would wait until Julie was sound asleep and sneak out for an hour or two. He'd spent the nights since the assassination by Julie's side. She often woke from nightmares but only when she was in a heavy REM cycle. Jones could guess when that would occur with the new technology embedded in his eyes—Julie's vitals were as clear to him as her physical being was.

Jones found an odd sense of peace observing the vitals of her foreign body. A baby grew inside her—a whole other being, one he watched with a careful eye. One that made his scaly android face beam in delight.

Only a time traveler can kill another time traveler were the words Jones once read in Mick's journal. The commissioner longed to find solace in this fact, but that meant a small pool of suspects. Twisty, uncomfortable accusations. Jones kept their names written in crisp block letters, and their photos were mismatched between candid and professional shots.

Jones's corkboard resembled the work of a madman, but it was the only way he could make sense of all the puzzle pieces. On the far left of the board was Dr. Julie Walsh.

Almost completely unlikely. Almost.

Counting Julie out of the equation entirely was impossible—that would mean Jones wasn't looking at the case with an objective, traditionally android-trained eye. But based on her reaction, based on the entries she wrote in the journal, Colin's brutal death blind-sided her too. Colin might have attempted to kill Julie and revenge was a sticky, sweet high, but Colin really hadn't intended death when Julie became his victim. She was aware of this; they had made amends . . . The baby was convincing enough.

Beside her photograph hung one of Mick Taylor.

Another complicated defendant.

Jones and Mick had a colored past, one filled with illicit intimacy, longing, and understanding. Jones understood love—or most of the required feelings associated with the word—but Mick was the one who showed him how to act on those feelings. Jones ended their relationship after discovering Mick used his invention of time travel to help The Supreme. Mick had the motive to kill Colin: He worked for Colin's arch-nemesis. But Mick also desperately wanted to reunite with Julie and rekindle his relationship with Jones, going as far as neglecting The Supreme when she needed him most. Mick could never fully recover from his atrocious betrayals, but if he was Colin's killer, Julie nor Jones would ever forgive him.

Dr. Peter Schneider's photograph appeared distinguished beside Mick's frantic one. It was a professional headshot, one taken right after Peter was thrust into Julie's former role as interim CEO of COLI*GO.

A legitimate concern. The scientist and researcher turned business-man made his opinion well known that Colin O'Connor wasn't his favorite person. *But is that enough to kill the man?*

On the right side of the board was Celine O'Connor. Jones's fingers paused on her glossy photograph. A graceful woman, one with so much influence in The City that made Jones uncomfortable. Celine would gain heavily from her brother's death: She'd inherit the O'Connor legacy and would have even become the new governor if Colin hadn't been married to Julie.

But does Celine have the capabilities to pull off a stunt so violent and extreme?

Jones walked over to the far end of the board and paused. Last on his list was Isabella Garcia. Her stunning picture illuminated back at him with bright white teeth, a generous smile, and smooth, silky skin. Her chestnut curls bounced past her shoulders, and her mani-cured nails were painted a cherry red.

It is odd that she never acted like a scorned lover—especially being of a rival old bloodline family.

Isabella's motive was strong, but Jones carried the same question of Isabella that he had of Celine: if she was expert enough to be that good of a shot.

Jones sighed. Whoever the killer was, they were skilled. He pon-dered the idea of a hired marksman, but if the shot wasn't fired by the time traveler themselves, the laws of time travel applied. The intent wasn't strong enough—the killer had to be one of them.

Unless there's another time traveler, Jones thought.

Celine and The Supreme touted only six time travel devices—but the images of Mick's office in their condo in The Harbor flashed before Jones's eyes.

A large question mark loomed over a photograph of Elsie Sullivan. Jones couldn't prove that the posse hominem traveled time, but something about Colin's legislative aide bothered him. She'd been standing on the podium beside Jones when Colin and Julie spoke to the crowd, but if another version of her time traveled, Jones couldn't put the possibility completely out of his mind. Elsie's motive remained fuzzy, but she was loyal to Colin—if he asked her to kill him, he believed Elsie would pull the trigger on his command.

I need to find Mick.

***

Jones hadn't been to his and Mick's condo located in The Harbor in several months. After confronting Mick in January, Jones moved in with Anna Garcia for a couple of weeks until he secured his own apartment in The Bay.

A thick coating of dust layered the coffee table and the faded wooden floors needed a mopping, but the condo was lived in. Bags of groceries lined the kitchen countertops, and a blanket on the couch was left unfolded. The smell of their home consumed Jones—the smell of Mick.

The floorboards creaked under the weight of Jones's feet as he peered down the hallway. To the right was a small bedroom, one that Mick used as his office. The room was cluttered like the work of any madman, with small tools and metal pieces thrown across the multiple tabletops. Various glass slides for the blood samples were stacked up on the middle of the desk: some stained, some new, and never used.

The primary bedroom was to the left, farther down the hall and past the bathroom. Jones let out a large sigh when he opened the door and found that the sheets and comforter on the bed were haphazardly thrown around. Jones was a stickler for a perfect and neatly made bed but Mick never seemed to care.

He is still here, Jones thought with a bit of optimism.

Wandering back to the living room and kitchen, Jones sat on the outdated couch. His scaly palm rested against the cushions, and he closed his eyes, hoping to find some peace and relaxation.

The sound of Mick's raspy breathing alerted Jones and his lip trembled slightly at the ghastly man standing in the doorway of their home. Time travel made Mick lose weight, his limbs poking out like a gangly holiday tree and his aged skin crackling against the masked shadows of The City's sunset.

"Jones," Mick spoke with a wobbly voice. They stared at one another in awe.

Jones's reaction was instantaneous, oddly primal for a being that was anything but. Jones leaped from the couch and raced to Mick, embracing him in a consuming hold. Mick was fragile in Jones's arms, breakable with just the slightest twist, the wrong pinch to the left or right.

"I thought you hated me. I thought you never wanted to speak to me again," Mick said the words, but Jones refused to listen to them.

He had essentially told Mick they were through, especially after Mick provided the cryptic and grave warning about something terrible happening in The City—an event he claimed he couldn't prevent, one he wouldn't tell Jones about.

Colin's death weighs heavily on us all, Jones realized, thinking about how it affected each player differently.

"I think Colin's death has taught me something about forgiveness," Jones said. "He was the one who taught me what the feeling conflict meant—it's only right that he introduced me to this feeling too. I've not completely forgiven all your transgressions, especially those against Julie. But I couldn't live with myself if I never spoke to you again. If you weren't part of my life in some way. You mean so much to me."

Mick's body relaxed into Jones's chest, and they stood like this for a long time. As darkness cast deep shadows across the messy condo, Jones released Mick and grabbed his hands.

Mick's vitals vibrated across Jones's vision with insanity. Spiking blood pressure, a rapidly beating heart thumping inside his chest, trying to pump the blood through his body, and the organs slowing themselves down, waiting for release of their essential functions. Jones had to subside this power he possessed, or he wouldn't be able to concentrate, to speak with Mick.

"I'm sorry I couldn't tell you about Colin's murder. If I did, you would have done everything in your power to stop it. And then that would have ruined everything. We cannot change what fate has in store for us, no matter how much we desire to. I hope you understand that while I have played with the past and tinkered with the future, I have never touched death except for Julie. And the repercussions of interfering with someone's death require a high price. One I can't afford to make again."

Jones stepped back and took in Mick's words. They weren't what Jones expected—he thought vengeance and defensiveness would pour out of Mick's mouth. This confession was honest, mournful, and sorrowful. Sadness brushed the dark eyes behind Mick's large square glasses.

"I wouldn't have been so angry with you if you were honest. If you communicated. If you didn't keep everything so hidden." Jones hoped for Mick's own forgiveness of him, especially of how he acted out the last few months.

"You're right. We shouldn't keep any secrets from each other." Mick stepped toward the living room and took a seat on the couch. He patted the empty cushion beside him before speaking. "You might want to sit down for this next confession."

Jones approached Mick slowly and crossed his arms, hoping to provide some distance between them. He was afraid if he didn't place a physical boundary, he would subside to any emotionally driven advances Mick made. They were both raw and vulnerable, and they both still loved one another. This confusion clouded Jones's processor unlike anything else ever had before.

Jones reached for his bag and pulled out Mick's leather journal. The soft cover soothed Jones, but the contents inside haunted him. The first time he read through the entries, Mick tasked him on a mission to save The City and discover the identity of the infamous serial killer. By doing so, a string of events exploded in Jones's wake, and he wondered if this quest for truth sparked the decision Colin made in trying to kill Julie. After he promised to never involve himself again with Mick's life choices, the journal reappeared in Jones's possession. But instead of Mick's chicken scratch, Julie's messy script scribbled throughout the pages inside.

Most of her entries were addressed to Colin, and some held answers to her research on the antidote and a toxin she discovered along the way. In entry sixteen, Julie asked Jones if he trusted Mick. His best friend and the man he loved were trying to make amends, but after all his betrayals, Julie hesitated.

Should I continue to hesitate too?

Julie traveled on June 23rd and went back in time to write this message. She begged for Jones's help in discovering why Peter couldn't be trusted, who truly stole the toxin's recipe, and what happened to a time traveler's body after they died since her experience was an abnormality.

Julie's grief might have clouded her judgment.

Jones noted that the death of her husband stained her heart in unimaginable ways. But she still wrote to him.

Jones sat beside Mick and extended the journal to him. Mick glanced away from the journal in shame before grabbing it between his shaking hands.

"Who gave this to you?"

"Julie," Jones answered. "I originally thought it was you, but then I read the entries."

Mick flipped through the pages and slowed once he reached Julie's unrecognizable words on the yellowed, aged pages. After reading her entries, Mick closed the journal and placed it on top of the coffee table.

"You want me to give this to Colin."

Jones didn't respond and placed his head in his hands.

I do, he thought, unable to say the words aloud. *And I can't because I can't travel time.*

"Do you want to know what happens to a time traveler after they die?" Mick asked, taking his glasses off his face and rubbing his eyes.

Jones stilled. He wanted to be as far away from this madness as possible, but the magic of it drew him in. Jones was in the thick of it now; there was no way out, not without severe consequences.

"Yes."

"Good. Then I think it's time for you to learn that you quasi-killed me, and that's proof that non-time travelers cannot truly kill a time traveler."

Jones pushed himself back against the arm of the couch, increasing the distance between him and his former boyfriend.

"What?"

"Well," Mick said with a clarifying cough, "you didn't really kill me. You're not the demise I face in the end. But you did still kill a time traveling version of me."

"I don't understand."

"Jeb." The singular name silenced the room, and the outside traffic seemed to halt in response to Mick's admission. "I took over his identity. Jeb was a time traveling version of me. I was Jeb, in the end."

"That can't be true," Jones said, standing and pacing around the living room. "I watched the casket get buried into the ground with a body in it. I scanned his eyes."

"I understand why this is difficult for you to believe—" Mick started, but Jones interrupted him.

"Mick, that isn't logical. You can't speak in riddles and expect me to understand. Is this your strange way of telling me that Colin O'Connor isn't really dead?"

Jones stepped away from Mick and sat in the armchair opposite the couch. He disliked the extra space distancing them, but his sharpness needed room.

"No," Mick answered, "Colin O'Connor is really dead. A time traveler killed him. And you're right to believe that there are more time travelers than you think. The situation is getting very out of hand."

Jones relaxed into the confines of the chair. Conflict filled his chest.

The irony, but at least I'm on the right path.

Colin not being dead would cause severe complications to his investigation. It would also require a public relations disaster plan if Colin was ever found roaming the streets. The public didn't know about the invention of time travel. When Colin admitted to killing his previous legislative aide and secretary, Kathleen Murphy—the same woman who Jeb Taylor or Mick was falsely arrested for murder—he revealed the secret of posse hominems to The

Legislature, and the knowledge eventually leaked to society.

Time travel remained safe, a tight-knit secret amongst society's largest and most influential strategists. But there was a part of Jones that longed to hear Colin's deep chuckle again, wished to see the smile on Julie's face that he knew Colin was responsible for.

And I would want to see him hold their child. Jones brushed the thought away. He wouldn't reveal Julie's secret, although it was naïve for him to think Mick wasn't aware. *How could he not be? He's been to the future.*

"Then why was Colin's body so . . . warm?"

Mick grunted, showcasing his own frustration.

"I'm not sure. My body was warm before it dissipated into thin air. That's when I woke back up. But a time traveler shot him. He must be truly dead."

"And I assume you can't tell me who it was?" Jones asked, annoyance cutting sharply through his tone. Mick's eyes glistened at Jones's with apology. "I know you cannot tell me, and I understand why. I know that means you believe in me, that I'll uncover the truth. But I'm so tired, Mick. I'm exhausted."

Mick approached Jones, their matched height providing a perfect gaze, and he leaned into his ear. He whispered so quietly that Jones almost didn't hear the admission that escaped Mick's lips.

They looked into one another's eyes before Mick's lips met Jones's tentatively. Jones relaxed into the familiarity they shared for so long, his scales shimmering brightly in happiness.

"I still love you." The words were said but not returned. A pang exploded in Jones's chest—a feeling he was all too familiar with: heartbreak.

Mick stepped back and looked toward the front door.

"You know where to find me," he said to Jones, a small smile breaking across his face. "But you should get back to Julie. She needs you now more than ever."

Chapter 14
The Supreme

<u>July 15th, 47 A.R.</u>

The Supreme sat in Colin O'Connor's study with her feet planted firmly on the ground, slowly sipping some of his expensive Scotch from a crystal highball glass. Her eyes never left the window, her gaze locked on the carriage house across the courtyard.

Mick Taylor hadn't appeared as he promised.

Emilia's new understanding of feelings surged through her processor like an unwelcome house guest overstaying their welcome. She now felt anticipation in the pit of her stomach growing and contrasting in a painful blossom.

The townhouse carried a foreign air to it without the presence of Colin. Julie passed through the home, but her awkwardness cascaded around her like a fierce riptide. Celine made her presence known like a dog marking its territory, reminding Julie that the house was not distinctly hers.

Celine's visits during the day didn't last long, a small relief from Emilia's loneliness and constant fussing and stress over their next move—which game pieces to sacrifice and which to advance becoming more complicated with the evolution of their personal relationship.

The Supreme wanted to feel heartbroken from Celine rushing back to the odd, eccentric man she married more than a decade ago. She even heard Martin Borges downstairs from her hidden post on the third floor.

Celine and Martin seemed like a perfect couple to the outside world, but they were anything but. Emilia recalled Celine's wedding day with a clear and accurate uncanniness. The wintertime affair with Celine's white lace dress, the countless number of small silk buttons blending into the fabric burst out into Emilia's processor. Colin had walked his sister down the aisle, his eyes oddly warm pinned on the man he felt indifferent toward as he gave his sister away.

Henry O'Connor had only passed away a month prior to the wedding. The rushed celebration did its job: Society stopped asking questions about the truth behind Henry's illness and death and focused on their favorite socialite's wedding instead.

Emilia and Celine shared a deep bond—one of friendship and understanding. Both women were driven and conniving at times, but they were so much more than the nasty, ruthless women others gossiped about. Emilia admired Celine's confident fierceness and how she didn't hide behind any walls. Celine appreciated Emilia's strategic mind, thinking about each move with precision. Together, they pushed one another and helped restrain when appropriate.

She had a different relationship with Colin but considered him an ally all the same. Both O'Connor children mirrored and exposed the other's faults. Colin and Celine were pitted against one another from the day their mother went missing, but no one else understood their pains, the tragedy and grief that ripped through them like a gushing waterfall. They only had each other.

Until me. And especially once I told Celine that I understood, until she realized I'm not just an android. I'm much more.

The Supreme bit down and puckered her lips. She hated the taste of whiskey and Scotch, no matter how appealing, sophisticated, and powerful the amber liquid looked inside the glass. She longed to fit in with the old boys' club, and drinking this toxin ignited a great homage to the friend she carried many regrets over. The man she had no right to call her friend.

I did play a hand in all the downfalls and suffering in Colin's life, Emilia thought as she placed her glass down on the O'Connor heirloom mahogany desk. *I'm the reason his mother is dead. I'm the reason he didn't trust anyone. And when I gave him Julie, I ripped her away from him too.*

The scientist was a snarky pest, ruining her grand plans with stealth and agility—as if Julie anticipated Emilia's next move without even knowing what it would be. The microchip was the perfect idea. Isabella questioned the blank technology she had surgically placed in Julie's brain. The control panel Celine kept not only tracked all posse hominem microchips but also possessed the ability to make remote updates. One of those updates was transferring information—and The Supreme planned on transferring her own microchip contents into Julie's new one.

The Supreme carefully crafted Julie's public image. She played a large role in how beloved the scientist was by society, trusted by her colleagues at COLI*GO, and her relationship with Colin extended a sense of compassion from The Legislature. Emilia nudged Celine and Martin into making Julie the interim CEO while Celine took her maternity leave. They had other more qualified candidates to consider over the young woman deeply involved in all their lives, thanks to Colin.

Colin's assassination wasn't calculated into The Supreme's original plan, but that didn't matter anymore. She always planned for Julie's presence to linger in The Capitol Building. Joel Kennsington was a useless pawn in Emilia's game, but he did his job by placing doubts about the O'Connors and their old bloodline lineage, expressing interest in more leaders like himself within the gilded golden dome housing The Legislature. His promise of power and excitement fell as lackluster and unclear to the scientist, but it was only a matter of time before she wanted more after rising so quickly at COLI*GO.

Celine taught me that humans always want more power.

But without the microchip in her brain, The Supreme needed a new host. And quickly.

She was the most wanted being in The Constituency, with a hefty bounty upwards of five billion dollars. Celine promised The Supreme shelter and safe haven in the O'Connor townhouse, and now that its inhabitants were inconsistent, that reality was vastly turning into a fantasy.

A slight knock on the sturdy study door perked Emilia's ears. She hadn't sensed another presence in the townhouse, but Elsie Sullivan stared back at her with piercing brown eyes.

Elsie's tall and lanky frame outlined in hard-earned muscle tone from countless logged hours inside the boxing ring made Emilia pause in her examination of the posse hominem. Elsie wasn't a typical beauty, but her high cheekbones and silky hair showcased a softness to the otherwise intimidating young woman.

"Madam Supreme," Elsie said with a breathless ease and settled into the seat opposite her. Elsie didn't ask before pouring herself a glass of Colin's best Scotch and swirled the liquid around in her clear glass, transfixed on the contents.

"You might want some ice for that."

"No," Elsie said and took a generous sip. "I like it better at room temperature. More of a bite."

The two sat in silence, and Emilia practiced holding control of her emotions. When she experienced them, her scales painfully swelled, excreting a vibrant flash of golden hues: a vulnerability that she wasn't used to.

"We should talk about Colin," Elsie said with a squinted glare.

Does she suspect me as the assassin? Emilia wondered. No matter how fitting of a narrative it would be if The Supreme were Colin's killer, the task was completely impossible in The Supreme's hands. Her android body didn't travel time, even if she desperately wished to.

"I'm tired of talking about Colin." The words slipped out of Emilia's mouth liberally. Regret didn't course through her body even with the rapid blinking of Elsie's eyes in response to her harshness.

"Then let's talk about Celine."

The Supreme groaned and eyed her half-empty glass. "Why?"

"I know she can't possibly be happy to know that we're related."

"You wouldn't be incorrect in that statement," The Supreme said, recalling how Celine had come back from meeting with Jeffries over Colin's will. Throwing her device against the wall and screaming, Celine's rage extended beyond just learning she had a half-sister. Colin had left as much as he could to Julie—and Celine had planned on the O'Connor empire being hers and only hers after her brother's death.

"And I imagine she won't be happy to learn that I plan on embracing that Henry O'Connor was my father."

The Supreme stilled, and a salacious smile spread across her scaly face. The colors of her body flickered as an alluring reflection in Elsie's eyes—a sharp, beautiful gold emulating against deep red ambers. Emilia resembled a mystical fall foliage, a time of the year that she enjoyed here in The City. A time of year when the crispness promised a silent rebirth.

"But my allegiance falls with Dr. Walsh. Not Celine O'Connor." Elsie took a long gulp from her glass, draining it.

"I ventured that was the case," Emilia replied, having noted the odd friendship between Julie and Colin's legislative aide. "But Julie won't run in the gubernatorial election."

Elsie sat incredibly still, and The Supreme appreciated how willing the young woman was to hold this secret—her knowledge that politics wasn't for Julie—close to her chest.

"Are you afraid that Celine is going to run? And that you will have to support her?" Emilia asked, slowly sipping her drink and savoring the smoky flavors she despised.

Elsie scoffed, her chuckle verbose and intoxicating. "Are you afraid of what she'll do with you?"

The Supreme smiled wickedly at Elsie's astute observation.

"Whatever are you insinuating Miss Sullivan?"

"Don't forget that I was here the day of the FACERE raid. I saw the way you two looked at each other. Your reunion meant everything."

A part of Emilia wanted Elsie's accusation to be correct, but another part of her processor mocked her. Celine might love you, but she will always love herself more.

Elsie's narrow and long fingers drummed along the arm of her chair as she watched The Supreme with a fierce gaze. Elsie fascinated Emilia, and that was why she chose her as a specimen for the posse hominem project. Being half an O'Connor only added to Elsie's allure—she was the dirty stain that Henry forgot to clean up. But the lack of Henry's efforts made Elsie so brazen and independent. She was quick-witted and fierce at her core: a dangerous force to be reckoned with. The gift of providing Colin with someone who understood his demons, someone who would hate his father just as much as he had, and someone who was willing to do the devious acts that It deemed necessary.

The Supreme reached into her pocket. Her scaly fingers rubbed against the piece of technology she longed to use—one that she couldn't because no blood ran through her veins.

"You're one to judge. Sure, do I care for Celine? Yes. But we're all victims of the O'Connors," The Supreme said with a sarcastic laugh. "You idolize your half-brother when you shouldn't."

Elsie squinted. "I don't idolize Colin."

"But don't you?" Emilia challenged, pulling out the intricate time travel device and laying it on the desk between her and Elsie. "Do you really know how Colin enacted change when The Legislature wouldn't listen? Do you really know what went on inside his brain? How cruel he truly was? How bloodthirsty?"

Elsie's breathing slowed, and her face paled.

Yes, The Supreme thought with a sickening enthusiasm, *you do know or at least you suspect. You were so willing to kill Paul McGuire. And that wasn't something you felt you could admit until Colin entered your life.*

"What is this?" Elsie asked, her large hands reaching for the edge of Mick's device, unwilling to answer Emilia's accurate accusation.

"This is the time travel device."

Elsie eyed The Supreme with suspicion before picking it up. She examined the glasses with a strange peril in her eyes, her fingers rubbing slowly against the intricate design Mick Taylor carved into the device. This design included a depiction of Cerberus, the king of the underworld's famed three-headed dog. This was Celine's device—Celine had ridiculously given The Supreme's to Peter Schneider back in the winter.

"Can I use this?" Elsie looked up at Emilia with large curious eyes. "Can a posse hominem travel time?"

The Supreme pondered Elsie's question. Mick successfully brought Julie somewhere in the dimensions of time while she still possessed a microchip in her brain—even if the microchip wasn't active. He never tested his technology explicitly, but blood was the qualifier for time travel. And posse hominems didn't contain any silver android liquid—they were initially humans with human blood.

I don't see why Elsie couldn't time travel.

"Yes. And aren't you interested in knowing how Colin secured Don Jr.'s win into The Legislature? Or to learn about the truth behind Kathleen Murphy's death?"

"Colin helped Don?" Elsie asked with curiosity, a tinge of

intrigue on her pink lips. Elsie's desire for the horrid Ludewing man wasn't a surprise to The Supreme. She had logged every interaction on the control panel Celine kept. Watching Elsie's rollercoaster of emotions flying up and down at the charming whims of Don Jr. made The Supreme question if Isabella implanted the correct microchip into Elsie's brain. She was far more infatuated with the representative than he was with her, but Emilia didn't blame Elsie—Don Jr. was attractive, intelligent, and while he used Elsie for his own games, Elsie learned quickly of his intentions and outsmarted him.

"I thought Jeb Taylor killed Kathleen Murphy."

The Supreme couldn't help but chuckle at the young woman's ignorance. Elsie's curious nature bothered Emilia—adding to the anomaly of her as a posse hominem.

"Jeb Taylor was never The City's true serial killer."

Elsie stood from her chair and paced the room. "Are you suggesting Colin O'Connor killed all of those women?"

"What I'm suggesting is that you spend some time in 35 A.R. first and make your way back to the present if you really want to decide on pledging your allegiance to Colin and Julie over myself and Celine," Emilia said with a small smile slicing across her scaly face. "I selected the code for your microchip. I modeled it off something that intrigued me about Colin."

Her scales showcased an alluring gleam of rose gold against her typical amber hue. Elsie's eyes darted back and forth across the display on The Supreme's body, but she remained silent.

"Are you afraid, Elsie?"

Elsie gripped the time travel device and reached for the other component of the technology—the chrome box. Recognition flashed in her fawn-brown eyes. "No."

Elsie backed away toward the door, but Emilia interrupted her otherwise eerie departure.

"Colin isn't who you think he is half of the time," The Supreme warned.

Elsie shook her head. "Maybe Colin is all I needed him to be. And maybe Julie is too."

The Supreme inhaled deeply. She liked Elsie Sullivan for more reasons than she dare admit.

Chapter 15
Julie

<u>July 16th, 47 A.R.</u>

Julie sat in the front of the Session room and watched all human and android eyes glaring up at her. This was her first time leading a Session, and nervousness pooled in a slight sweat under her arms. The black nylon dress itched against her pale skin, and Julie straightened in the chair that was too large for her.

Elsie sat at a desk a bit further away but close enough to gesture toward Julie if need be. Her face was the only welcoming one in the room, but Julie didn't want to depend on Elsie too much—when she was the interim CEO at COLI*GO, she had needed to gain trust and establish control in front of The Legislature on merit. She wanted their respect—the same kind of respect they held for Colin.

Most likely an impossible task.

No one spoke as they settled into their seats. The androids pulled out their devices with a rigid sense of duty while awkwardness lingered across their human counterparts.

Don Ludewing Jr. sat at his desk and looked over at Joel Kennsington's empty one for a moment too long. Don Jr. intrigued Julie. He was one of the younger representatives and known to break away from his father's conservative sense of politics, similarly to how Colin differed from Henry.

Julie knew little else about Don, and when she inquired with Elsie earlier in the morning, her legislative aide wiggled at her desk with an empty promise to review bios and briefings with her to prepare for the afternoon's meetings.

"Good afternoon, Representatives," Julie spoke out into the room, mustering as much confidence as she could.

"Good afternoon, Governor . . ." one android representative responded but stopped himself.

"Should we refer to you as Governor O'Connor? As Governor Walsh?" a different android representative asked from the back of the room.

Hushed murmurs erupted around him—a question they all had but none were brazened enough to ask until now.

"I think she prefers her formal title, Dr. Walsh." Don spoke out into the crowd, throwing Julie a small but warm smile and nodding in her direction. "Is that correct?"

"That's correct, Representative Ludewing," Julie said and took her large flat device out of her bag. "Regardless, call me as you wish. I will respond to either Dr. Walsh or Governor Walsh, but enough of that. We have quite the agenda today. First, we must elect a new Session speaker to replace former Representative Kennsington."

Eyes awkwardly darted around the large domed ceiling room. Julie paused, waiting for everyone to settle before continuing. "We must also determine the next steps in selecting a new supreme, and I have an appointment for Maggie Rivera's former role as head of FACERE that I seek your approval on."

"You have a selection for the leader of FACERE?" an android representative called out.

"Yes. I've done an extensive vetting process over the last two weeks, and I don't want the position vacant for too long. I urge us to move quickly on this one."

A tiny smile formed on the corners of Julie's lips. The high she felt in this room reminded her of her time at COLI*GO. She'd been thoughtful in her decision process for the new head of FACERE. This nomination would prove to her if The Legislature stood behind her and supported her or if she faced a large, uphill battle.

"I propose Dr. Isabella Garcia fill the role, effective immediately."

Don Jr. nearly jumped out of his seat and stumbled to pick up his dropped device. Other representatives eyed him suspiciously, waiting for Isabella's cousin to sit back and steady himself.

"Do you have an objection, Representative Ludewing?" Julie asked coyly.

Don chuckled and shook his head. "No, my cousin is highly qualified. Her education speaks for itself, and her kindness is well known and appreciated throughout The Constituency."

"Then why are you so shocked by my nomination?"

"That's fairly obvious, isn't it?" Don asked, pushing his words with a tender playfulness. His deep brown eyes hinted at a special liveliness. "Given the circumstance, I simply didn't expect you of all people to have any kind of affinity for Isabella Garcia. I simply want to ensure you're making a logical decision not shadowed by guilt and emotion . . . guilt about any overlap or indiscretions."

What a peculiar thing to say, Julie thought. *What kind of working relationship did you have with my former husband?*

"I'm not sure what you're insinuating, Representative."

At COLI*GO, Julie rarely faced this level of skepticism. Her formal training as a researcher and scientist, along with the trust of her colleagues, provided her with a false sense of confidence that she shouldn't have thought to possess inside The Capitol Building. But she hoped her brazen self-assurance would grant her points with these politicians.

"Well, a good Session speaker challenges the governor. It's their responsibility. But we don't have one right now, so I've taken it upon myself to remain sure that role isn't forgotten." Don smiled as he spoke, leaning back in his chair and crossing his arms.

His attractive grin showcased a row of pearly white teeth, and his defined shoulders protruded against his white button-down shirt and silk vest. Don's intentions clicked inside Julie's mind; he was cunning and sharp as a whip. He would push her buttons, but she didn't mind. She actually reveled in the notion.

"Is that so?" Julie's lips parted slightly, and she found herself chuckling for the first time in over two weeks. The sound felt foreign but delightful in her ears.

Several representatives, both people and androids, stood and clapped. Don bowed his head slightly in defeat but smiled up at Julie. His wink cemented he wanted her as an ally, a friend. That he wanted to work with her so that he could benefit too.

Julie's gaze drifted toward Elsie. An attractive blush appeared on her face, and her eyes focused on her device while she quickly typed. A vibration coursed through Julie's palm. She looked down at her device and read Elsie's message on her screen:

Don could be a great ally to your office as the Session speaker. He's a better candidate than any other fool. It also keeps his arrogant ass from trying to run for governor.

Julie nodded at Elsie and looked back out at the crowd.

"Well, we need a formal vote, but I don't oppose your self-nomination for Session speaker, Representative Ludewing. But I also need the representatives to approve my appointment for Dr. Isabella Garcia before I officially sign your nomination."

Everyone in the room quieted down, understanding the move their new governor played on the board. Strategy wasn't foreign to Julie. She knew how to play the game.

Almost too well.

***

Dr. Peter Schneider stood in a fitted three-piece suit underneath an open white lab coat. His bloodshot, ghastly eyes revealed torment and a lack of sleep. Peter was a good-looking man and his tall, lean muscular body had slightly thinned since Julie saw him the last time they time traveled together. Peter's beard was peppered with a few stray gray hairs, making him appear more mature. Always a fidgety man, Peter seemed even more unnerved today than Julie had ever seen him.

His eyes stared too long at Elsie, and he leaned away from her, treating her like a rattlesnake ready to strike. Elsie took her time in allowing the premeditated intentions of those surrounding her with the opportunity to marinate in the uncertainty.

That's not Elsie's style, or at least that's not how I've ever seen her.

Only a couple of weeks had passed since June 23rd, and avoiding her woes with ridiculous busywork was her only solace. These moments of pure stillness happened more and more frequently, and with them, an astonishing rage followed. Agitation, malice, and vivacity consumed Julie, and certain distractions that once helped ease and calm these demons did nothing for her anymore. This all seethed through her, and she felt herself aiming to crawl out of her own skin and release herself through the revolting satisfaction festering hungrily inside all her desires.

I promised Colin. I promised It. I will succeed.

Peter looked at Julie like she was the enemy and she wanted to slap him, but all she could think about was how much she'd enjoy making him think he still had her trust and friendship. In reality, he was a vessel for her to get to her ultimate destination.

"Julie, I'm sorry for your loss and want to extend my condolences."

She still dressed in all black and likely would for the unforeseeable future. Mourning periods for old bloodline families could last months, and while Julie wasn't of old bloodline origin herself, she now needed the respect from the community of her husband's upbringing. She needed to follow their rules.

As both the governor and The City's most influential man, Colin O'Connor would linger in all their lives for a long time. And Julie loved him.

Her emerald ring glistened in Peter's bright office lights. Her bright office lights.

The CEO office had been hers before she went missing, and by the looks of it, Peter made himself very comfortable here. His belongings spread across the desk and in the odds and ends of the built-in shelves throughout the room. Being here felt like extreme déjà vu.

"I apologize for the urgency in our meeting, especially in your time of mourning, but we need to discuss the antidote."

Julie noticed Elsie's clenched fist. A desirable smile spread across her face, and Julie couldn't tell if Elsie wanted to reach across the table and punch Peter or rip his clothes off. Peter looked away from Julie's intense stare and squinted his eyes toward Elsie. Julie felt like an outsider with them—a third wheel. She almost chuckled at the thought.

She glanced over at her legislative aide with thick lashes, and a warning passed between them. Elsie took her queue and grabbed her device from her bag to take notes. Elsie didn't possess a scientific background but provided sage advice—and Julie had written various communications to Elsie while she time traveled and worked on the antidote and toxin. A major reason why Julie waited so long to reconnect with Colin was because of her diligent work in perfecting her drug—a lifesaving therapeutic promising a cure for patients suffering from various conditions ranging from Alzheimer's to psychological conditions.

"What about the antidote?"

"I've been working on creating a new version even with the toxin formulation missing. I think I have something valuable and want the board to pursue it."

Julie stiffened in her chair and readjusted the hem of her dress.

"I've shown the preliminary findings to Martin Borges," Peter said. Elsie let out an audible sigh, but Julie continued focusing on Peter. "He still wants your input, Dr. Walsh. I suppose he doesn't trust only mine because this asset takes us back to a scheduled once-a-week dosing regimen."

"The toxin promises us a better chance at success. It's the backbone for the drug discovery for a single-dose antidote asset. I would hesitate to redirect our energy at this point—"

"No," Peter interrupted, "not until we find the original reports. While we eventually need to know who stole the toxin's formulation, this is all about timing. We're running out of it, and if we have to cut corners to get ourselves an approved asset from The Legislature for these patients, then we will."

"As the governor, I will not allow The Legislature to approve anything that was founded on 'cutting corners.'"

Silence sliced through the room and weighed heavily on Julie's chest. Julie had no one she could depend on now that Colin was dead, especially in the manner of politics and the quasi-government secrets of COLI*GO. But she did have authority, and she held public opinion.

"Then I'll be forced to involve another researcher to help you and me in this endeavor. To ensure that you don't purposefully delay or compromise it."

"Lies can never cloud the truth of science."

Julie rose from her seat, and Elsie followed her. They walked down the hallway of the 101st, floor of COLI*GO and entered another office. This room appeared abandoned, with only a desk, a large screen, and a small seating area.

Julie's fingers affectionately trailed along the edge of the chrome desk, and she opened a drawer. The hologram device lit up quickly in her hands, and at the push of a button, a small photograph of her and Colin against the backdrop of The Oceanside appeared.

"He rarely used this office," Julie said to Elsie. "I suppose it's mine now."

The fury in her warm blue eyes calmed, and Elsie tilted her head to the side.

"Who else knows that there even is a toxin?" Elsie asked Julie, her question hanging like ripe fruit dangling off the lowest branches of a tree.

"Me, you, Peter, Martin, Celine, and Colin." Julie eyed Elsie with an upturned brow.

"Fuck Peter," Elsie said the words with a vicarious hint of annoyance. She leaned into her bag and pulled out a piece of paper and handed it over to Julie.

"What is this?" Julie asked, her own handwriting hauntingly staring back at her. A slight tremor moved through her hand as she realized she wrote this note to Elsie—or at least some past, present, or future version of herself did.

"Jeb Taylor gave me this letter some time ago. He told me to open it and read it on June 23rd, 47 A.R."

Julie rested her head in her hands and let out a whimper of frustration.

"Peter is up to something," Julie admitted. "I traveled back in time to confront Colin and then I went to COLI*GO. Something about Peter was different in that visit. This confirms my suspicions."

"The real question is: Where did he get this new drug?"

"He couldn't have created this on his own, and I know I didn't help him," Julie said, pulling the report Peter had shared earlier on her screen.

This was the first time Julie was seeing this new asset. The mechanism of action differed from the antidote and the toxin. It was an entirely different drug.

"An antidote derived from our knowledge of the toxin is the correct answer, not this. The initial risks identified from the antidote would still apply here. Peter's messing with my drug discovery. Colin was right to distrust Peter so much."

A slight growl vibrated from the bottom of Elsie's throat. "You saw Colin?"

"Yes," Julie admitted. "But you can't tell anyone, even Jones. I know I shouldn't have visited Colin in the past. It was selfish of me, and it isn't the right way to deal with my grief. But I needed to see him. I needed to know if this was all part of his plan."

"Colin knew?" Elsie asked, leaning forward, shaking her head, and rolling her eyes. "He knew he was going to die and did nothing?"

Julie bit her bottom lip and nodded slowly. A look of pure exhaustion passed across her otherwise delicate, stoic face.

"Did he tell you whom?"

"No."

"I can't stand how stubborn men are," Elsie nearly whispered the angry words.

Julie's eyes gazed at the door leading to the hallway of executive offices. "We need to talk to Martin. He knows something."

Elsie shook her head and sighed in annoyance.

"I really fucking hate men."

Chapter 16
Isabella

Don Jr. warned Isabella that she'd be summoned by the new governor but not until after he spent an alarming thirty minutes bragging about his new post as the Session speaker.

Isabella and her cousin were indifferent to one another. He was a man of politics, something Isabella loathed, and while there were fond memories of their youthful and rambunctious childhoods, they had since grown apart.

Don Jr. started out as a policy researcher for Colin after graduating from The University, and an odd strain pulled between Isabella and Colin after Don unexpectedly quit. Colin never wanted to hire Don Jr. even though the two shared a political ideology, siding with the Sympathizers. Don was more extreme than Colin, but the shift in these young men away from the staunch, old-fashioned views of their fathers eventually brought them back together when Don ran for The Legislature. Colin enthusiastically endorsed Don in his initial run for the seat representing The Hill neighborhood, and Don owed the former governor for his glowing recommendation.

Other than their family connection and Colin's close working proximity, Isabella and Don hadn't spent much time together lately. With her constant worry and care for her mother and her work as a philanthropist—and then taking a side turn to work as a surgeon for The Supreme—Isabella rarely had time for extended family affairs. But her cousin's tone threatened something delightfully sinister. His lips had curled into an attractive grin on the video call, and his eyes sparkled with hunger.

It only took a matter of a few weeks, but The Legislature is back to its usual, conniving ways, Isabella thought. *How distasteful.*

Isabella needed Don's support moving forward, especially if the rumor was true that Julie would appoint her to a government post, but family affairs between the Garcias and Ludewings were tricky.

Much as the Garcias and O'Connors feuded, the Garcia family and Ludewings suffered from similar strife when Isabella's parents endorsed Colin O'Connor in his initial bid for governor. Isabella held a large role in that decision, having pushed her parents in that direction for her own societal ladder-climbing games. Nina Garcia, Isabella's mother, was born a Ludewing and a younger sister to Don Sr. He ran against Colin, and when his niece cozied up to the aspiring, young politician, he had threatened his sister. Nina, a strong and fierce woman, believed in people and morals over trivial alliances and family allegiance. Don Sr. was a severe Humanizer, a point of contention between himself and the more liberal ways of the Garcia family. A shift was forming within old bloodlines, and tensions bubbled. Isabella predicted an eruption on the horizon—but where and when still a hazy unknown.

Her own family was fraying at the threads. The morning before Colin's death, Anna confronted Isabella. She knew her sister was behind aiding The Supreme in COLI*GO's lower lab. Anna's knowledge made an unnerving large pit grow in her stomach—Peter Schneider remained an unknown threat to Isabella's safety.

Isabella and Anna bargained over the situation, and Isabella agreed to support her sister in her quest to take down the O'Connors. But if Julie Walsh was going to offer Isabella a prestigious and adventitious opportunity, Isabella was willing to listen.

The scientist appeared a bit brighter today, a little burst of invigorated energy in her otherwise solemn demeanor. She still wore all black—a dress with a small embroidered gray collar and nearly sheer tights with patent black Mary Jane shoes. Isabella was also expected to mourn, but her societal requirements were less stringent. While she and Colin spent over a decade together, they hadn't been romantically involved for quite some time now. She didn't want to compete with the beloved scientist and switched her ensembles to deep navy blues and dark mauve after the first week.

A small part of Isabella still ached for Colin's affection, though she hadn't held it for nearly three years. There were plenty of times they could have given up on one another, and Isabella felt a pang of guilt bouncing around her chest, knowing she never allowed Colin to be his true self with her. Fear stopped her.

My father had an answer much sooner than Julie—I regret not pursuing it, not pushing for this. Maybe Anna is right about bringing back his drug.

Isabella smiled at Julie and delicately crossed her ankles while relaxing into the rich leather chair. Julie hadn't touched anything in Colin's former office; it felt like the two women were secretly meeting behind their lover's back.

They were an odd pair, Julie and Isabella, and an unspoken awkwardness always lingered between them, no matter how earnestly they tried snubbing it out. Yet, a bond formed between them through time travel—particularly with how forthcoming and honest Isabella was with Julie after removing the microchip in her brain. They were never one for pleasantries, except in the beginning when they tiptoed around each other. It was the way they were, and any other inclination caused pause.

"I've appointed you as the new head of FACERE, effective immediately," Julie said with the corners of her pale pink lips upturned.

Isabella's eyes blinked rapidly.

"I'm sorry . . . You did what?" she asked, leaning forward in her seat.

Julie was an independent and intelligent woman, one who led successful programs at COLI*GO, but was still young and inexperienced at the delicate dance needed in this upper ring of society.

She's so green, Isabella thought with trembling hands. *She didn't even ask me if that's what I wanted.*

Denying the position would be a disaster for Isabella's public image, and she wondered if Julie understood this too. If so, Julie tested a power move on the larger board. Isabella leaned back into her seat and allowed her hands to dangle off the ledge of the armchair. She tapped her nails against the decorative metal buttons and cocked her head to the side.

"You told me you wanted something that was yours," Julie started, retreating to show a small sense of vulnerability. "You cared about your creations."

"They aren't creations; they're patients," Isabella interjected.

"Exactly." Julie smiled, and her eyes grew glossy. "Androids are patients at FACERE. They deserve the same dignity. What I saw Maggie Rivera do during my time there was—unimaginable. You would never allow that kind of atrocity."

Julie's intentions for Isabella's nomination did showcase her true art of persuasion in The Legislature, but they weren't as trite as Isabella initially anticipated. Julie believed in the equality of androids and put a small gesture of faith into Isabella to prove their allegiance.

"So I don't owe you any favors for this prominent role you're bestowing upon me?" Isabella raised a brow. She was used to the backstabbing deals and political ruthlessness that occurred in this office, from Colin's stories to her upbringing in an old bloodline family. An O'Connor did not grant a gift without the hint of a debt owed.

But Julie isn't an O'Connor, Isabella reminded herself.

Julie's lips pressed in a tight line, and she peered out toward the lush courtyard. An android gardener puttered around the large group of blooming lilies, his turquoise scales glistening in the sun. His watering pail provided relief to the overheated flowers, promising a chance at rebirth. Julie's eyes faltered back toward Isabella and away from the outside distractions.

"No."

Isabella grinned and reached across the governor's desk to shake Julie's hand.

***

The décor of FACERE needed to change—that would be the first thing Isabella would add to the building enhancement budget. After Commissioner Jones raided the facility, none of the damages had been properly attended to. While the blood and carnage no longer stained the tiled floors, bullet holes in the walls and doors barely hanging on by their loose hinges littered the building.

The building resembled an outdated hospital with large leafy palms and an odd odor. COLI*GO had a much sleeker design in comparison, but both campuses were massive. FACERE contained five labs in the main part of the building and an additional three on the west side. All prototypes were grown in the main building, but there were individual laboratories dedicated to different components that made up androids. One lab focused on microchip improvements, one dedicated to the processor, one concentrated on scale development, a lab specializing in organic organ matter, and one considered strictly experimental.

The experimental lab suffered the most damage in the commissioner's raid, and the androids that had been created there now stayed in the housing development of FACERE's campus. Isabella needed to speak with these androids—she needed a plan for them. Most were not capable of roaming the streets, the public unknowing what truly happened behind these walls.

Few of the original staff remained. Casualties were low in the incident, but injuries were high. Jones's police force was expertly trained to not aim deadly shots, but in moments of life and death and chaos, mistakes were made. The staff that was not present for the event provided resignation immediately, afraid to return to work. Some retired android police officers and a few humans from The Legislature's security detail replaced them for the time being.

Isabella's car arrived at the front of the building, and an android with yellow scales greeted her. His comforting smile was peculiar for an android, but for some reason, she felt like he was an old friend.

He showed Isabella up several stories to her new office. Maggie Rivera's things had mostly been removed except for a bar cart in the corner with expensive liquors and an array of neglected, half-dead plants. Isabella hardly knew Maggie Rivera. She only interacted with the woman while she was married to Martin Borges. Martin was a society favorite—kind, thoughtful, slightly eccentric, but consider-ate. Much like Isabella in his demeanor. Maggie had seduced the Borges man with ease, but Celine was swifter. Maggie was a nobody in society, but her intelligence gained power and influence after at-tending The University on a scholarship and securing a prestigious internship at FACERE.

Colin spoke indifferently about her, fidgeting whenever her name was brought up in conversation. But the woman couldn't have been so terrible. She attempted to reach out to Colin and Celine after their father's death, even with the strain of Celine and Martin's affair on her marriage. Celine was never a welcoming woman—she refused any friendship advances Isabella made, keeping her demeanor cold and distant. But Isabella tried to remain indifferent to the scorned O'Connor woman. Anyone who stood in her way seemed to experience an unkind fate. Maggie now faced spending the rest of her life in prison for her crimes at FACERE against The Constituency, and Isabella sensed Celine O'Connor had a hand in this somehow.

How quickly the act of falling truly is.

Part of her wished to say no to Julie's appointment. She could have spent the rest of her days on The Island helping her mother, and part ways from her philanthropic ventures that she spent years establishing. But a sense of duty, guilt, and shame washed through Isabella with a stronger current than her desire for an early retirement. The threat of exposure made Isabella vulnerable, and Julie providing a very public opportunity to shine a bright, kind light on Isabella's true nature was an opportunity she couldn't turn down.

Isabella was in over her head with The Supreme when she transformed thousands of humans into posse hominems. The Supreme pushed Isabella's buttons with Lexi Pvadinish, then Kathleen Murphy, and finally with Julie. Leaving seemed like the right decision at the time, but now Isabella regretted her harsh departure. Righting all her wrongs would be an impossible quest, but she wouldn't stop trying.

The yellow android nodded at Isabella and left her alone in her new office. She walked toward the windows and drew back the blinds. Sunlight flooded through, casting yellow hues across the warm beige tones of the building.

Isabella emptied the contents of her purse onto the chrome desk, and her eyes gravitated to her time travel device. The intricate design Mick carved into the glasses made specifically for her was beautiful. Each had a unique design, but she appreciated the indentations and coarse feeling across her thumb. The staff of Asclepius peeked through the corners, and the singular serpent's scales cascaded around the circular parts of the frame. There was something oddly satisfying and meaningful in the design choice

Mick made for Isabella's device—especially knowing his device showcased the grisly depiction of Medusa, the mythological monster representing danger and deterring evil by repelling evil.

Mick adored Isabella's commitment to the field of medicine, to her desire to save beings in any way she could. Isabella proved him correct in her successful extraction of Julie's microchip and in saving the scientist's life. Julie should have died that evening. While her stab wounds were shallow, the sheer number was extreme and promised the kiss of death.

Isabella's fingers brushed against the desk, and she settled into the oversized chair. Her device flickered to life, and she worked her way through Commissioner Jones's reports. Inventory of androids and copious notes about the horrors and inspections occurring in the experimental lab filled the documentation and notes.

She hadn't spent much time practicing with patients of android descent, but she was trained in the rare instances that an android would require surgery. Androids were mostly organic matter, made similar in the eye of their beholder. But their silver liquid version of blood didn't coagulate the same way. It glided through the android body, to power and regenerate the charge of their processor and microchip. Android blood was still susceptible to its own types of infections and, if not properly treated, threatened to permanently shut off their processors.

The Supreme longed for blood. Mick's time travel capabilities only extended to the proteins inside human blood, and androids were never tested after initial discovery and simulations warned of a malfunction in the silver liquid.

But if Isabella could harness more organic matter into androids, the possibilities were endless. Maggie Rivera never considered testing a new android blood. She focused primarily on the processor, the eyes, and the physical traits of androids. Her experiments were wretched, but they were also profound in creating strong, fast, and agile creatures outside of traditional androids.

The Supreme's experiments on humans aimed at creating creatures out of a host. Maggie was much the same monster as The Supreme, but instead of appreciating androids, she despised them.

No, Isabella corrected herself. *Maggie enjoyed the idea of control and power. She wanted a sense of authority and treated androids like second-class citizens. She aligned herself to the likes of Humanizers to allow for her own sick, twisted test in power.*

Isabella drafted a quick memo on her device. The Legislature expected her to shut down the experimental lab, to bury any of the atrocities performed there by her predecessor.

*But that's just the same as what they did with the lower lab at COLI*GO. And Julie put me in this role to push back against the status quo.*

The letters on her screen crisply stared back at her.

Dear Representatives,

The experimental lab in FACERE will remain in use until further notice. The previous purpose of the experimental lab focused on developing new features and creatures for The Legislature at the expense of android health and safety. All new experiments will focus on android improvements with the goal of long prosperous lives through advancements in medicine.

Progress will be measured by prioritizing high-functioning beings and closing the divide between humans and androids.

No androids will be experimented on in this laboratory.

I look forward to presenting FACERE's innovation roadmap at the next Session.

Sincerely,
Dr. Isabella Garcia

Isabella sat back in her seat and grinned. The sent notification appeared on her device screen, and she flickered through her contact list and called the first number on her screen.

"Hello?"

"Give your two weeks' notice," Isabella said into her device, red tones flushing to her cheeks as her heart rate increased. "I have a job for you."

Chapter 17
The Supreme

<u>July 17th, 47 A.R.</u>

Emilia smelled Celine's perfume before actually seeing the woman she loved, her partner in crime for eternity. She inherently trusted Celine—something an android shouldn't understand or appreciate. But with all these new emotions scourging through her gut, Emilia wasn't sure how to react in nuanced social situations.

Celine puttered around in the kitchen while Emilia left the living room and sought her escape on the roof deck. Being trapped in the O'Connor townhouse was nearly the same as being locked away in her jail cell. Emilia longed to stretch her legs along the halls of The Capitol Building. She wished for a furious debate with her representatives, her disagreements with Colin in his pristine, historic office.

The Supreme and Celine's metaphorical game of chicken ignited. Celine wished for Emilia to roam to her, and consequently, Emilia longed for the O'Connor woman to venture out into the nighttime darkness. They both wanted the same things but used different means to obtain them.

Celine seeks gratification and gain, and I seek security and predictability.

Emilia had watched Celine love her from afar and had observed how she loved others. Celine obsessed over her former chief of staff, Amanda MacDonald. Their affair nearly matched the intensity and passion of Colin's and Julie's relationship. But Celine's love story never stuck. Instead, she encountered endless nights filled with tears and sobbing after Colin killed her mistress.

And then there was Martin Borges. Celine returned to him with bloodshot eyes. That moment marked an interesting bond between them—forgiveness. Martin embraced the importance of Amanda in Celine's life and allowed his wife to honor that part of herself. Each year he hosted an anniversary of Amanda's death. Celine claimed she didn't love Martin, but that wasn't the case—she probably loved him the most. She sought comfort in the man who provided her with a family and companionship. Celine cared for him, and he cared for her.

Emilia resented their relationship, feeling as if Celine would never detach from Martin and this would take away some of Emilia's only happiness.

Which is odd. I'm the android, yet all I want is Celine's commitment, her understanding. I want to be the only one she loves, but she isn't built that way. I have to accept this, or it will ruin what we do have.

The feel of Celine's sturdy but sounding fingers against Emilia's shoulders brought her back to reality. Her eyes shot wide open, and she smiled—she won this round.

"I'm sorry I've been all over the place," Celine said in her typically soothing tone, her lips brushing against the scales on Emilia's ear.

The Supreme only nodded, unwilling to provide a verbal confirmation of Celine's indiscretions. She was technically still on maternity leave for one more week before having to return to her position as CEO of COLI*GO. How Celine planned to discard Peter Schneider, The Supreme wasn't quite sure, but she suspected Celine formulated an intricate plan.

"I'm angry with Colin. He left so much to Julie."

Emilia wanted to laugh at Celine's insinuation of Julie's unimportance but couldn't bring herself to reveal so much. Celine was unaware of Julie's many secrets, components of Julie and Colin's life together that Emilia doubted her lover even deserved to know.

"Why?" she asked, playing along with Celine's game. Being coy never bothered Emilia—while she was in The Legislature, it served her well.

"Because he's a man and men are generally idiots," Celine huffed, but her paused movement indicated she didn't fully believe her own accusation.

Celine wandered to the other chaise lounge chair and looked up at the stars. Emilia liked the roof deck even if she was only allowed up here at nighttime. There was plenty of privacy, but any risk that someone might spot them was too high. The Hill neighborhood was the perfect spot for a 360-degree view of The City's skylines. Tall glass skyscrapers over in The River shimmered with the reflection of water and bright lights, and a golden hue from The Capitol Building held its own allure in the evening sky.

"He updated his will the day before he was killed, and he had all these clauses about a future family, future children. It was oddly suspicious."

"Sometimes timing and coincidences are nearly the same," The Supreme responded, wanting Celine to come to her own realizations about her brother on her own terms. Telling Celine the truth only forced a miserable attitude.

If Celine guesses the results of Colin's—or more likely, It's—sloppiness, then I don't think there's anything I can do to stop whatever warpath she charges on.

"Do you think they were trying? Is Colin really dead? And if he's not, why hasn't he come back to tell me? To see me?"

The accusations hung in the air, the silence threatening to reveal both Emilia's and Celine's game plans.

Fuck, Celine is too smart for her own good.

"Please tell me if my brother is really dead or not, Emilia. Please tell me if I'm missing something in this odd equation. Because none of this is adding up."

An odd sense of loyalty to Colin acted like an instinctive reflex, making Emilia unable to physically form the words she needed to say. Julie was a fantastic piece on the game board, one that Emilia didn't want to give up. Julie was Colin's weakness, but she was also a player in her own right—strong and independent on her own. Colin ruined himself by trying to protect his queen—a character trait that The Supreme wouldn't expect from him if it were any other woman, including Isabella Garcia, whom he held a platonic fondness and loyalty to.

Julie was a different game piece altogether—the woman of nobody origin determined to earn her way to the top, from her time at The University to pitching her lifelong work to COLI*GO. Julie struggled for recognition, and The Supreme was an instrumental part in strategically placing Julie in the right light. In Julie's first years after The University, The Supreme tested Julie's perseverance and commitment to the overall organization by placing her on the company's most important asset—COL2120—rather than allowing her to work straightaway on her antidote. Julie passed the test, using only her personal time to commit to her beloved drug.

When The Supreme guided her into another role not associated with the scientist's beloved antidote, Emilia fluttered in intrigue as she watched Julie pursue Governor Colin O'Connor's assistance in making noise for her. Colin fell for the scientist easily. She was different—forbidden. The same reasons his father fell for Melanie Doyle. Melanie was a woman below Henry's class but still a forgiving woman who wanted to change society for the better, promising revival in a dreary, unstable City.

History repeats itself. And Emilia salivated over this fact.

Julie was also forgiving. Colin would relive killing her again and again, much like he relived killing his mother. But Julie came back tougher with each remembrance—haunting him. This should have broken them, but the pair were twisted in their own ways. And together, they became too strong. The Supreme couldn't allow for them to be reunited too long.

This was the first reason Emilia selected Julie for her experiments. It wasn't until she began experimenting with the different versions of microchips that another idea sparked through her processor. She and Celine planned for ways Emilia could surmount society. How she could continue on as a leader for The Constituency. The blank microchip allowed this, and what better person to digitally transfer the contents of her own microchip to than Dr. Julie Walsh?

The move on the board was flawless, knocking out Julie and Colin simultaneously. The two largest threats in Emilia's planned victory.

She never expected Mick Taylor, her puppet, to betray her. He went back and interfered. He brought her somewhere—to that extent, The Supreme was unaware—and someone removed her microchip. Isabella Garcia was the top candidate, although the jagged, twisted scar cascading down Julie's neck strayed from Isabella's normally graceful moving technique. Isabella was a kind woman who lingered in the shadows behind the other pieces on the board.

The moments of Julie's recovery and reversion back to a human were cloudy to The Supreme. She needed to clear this part of the story; she needed answers. And with Mick Taylor conveniently missing in action, the only one she would learn the truth from was Julie herself. She needed favor from the scientist.

"I won't lie to you," Emilia said, caressing the side of Celine's cheek with calming motions, "but my knowledge is an intrusion. One I didn't ask for."

The Supreme leaned into Celine with worry and need for comfort. Celine wasn't lashing out this time, but she knew what she was doing—pitting Emilia into a corner because she suspected Emilia knew the answers and would then expose the dirty truth.

"My eyes," The Supreme responded and pointed to them. "You can thank Maggie Rivera for that. I can see every vital of yours if I want."

Maggie experimented on androids with little repercussion during her time at FACERE. One of her projects included tricking The Legislature into supporting a change in the android eye-scanning technology. Androids had the capability to scan and know a human's identity. Now, androids with this update had access to a human's biometrics, everything from vitals to even making a fairly accurate diagnosis.

The moment Julie Walsh walked into the experimental laboratory at the insistence of former Representative Joel Kennsington, all was revealed. The Supreme suspected she knew about the pregnancy before Julie did. Her biometrics had buzzed across Emilia's line of vision like a wild painting similar to the works created by Jeb Taylor. Emilia didn't enjoy this newfound talent, nor the exposed dissatisfaction that the all-important microchip no longer was lodged in Julie's brain.

Celine's device buzzed, and her eyes grew wide staring down at the screen. Emilia's eyebrow lifted the moment the sleek screen slipped between Celine's fingers and crashed on the wooden decking. Celine's fingers twitched.

"Julie contested the will. Is the baby even Colin's?" The anger rose like a bubbling, sticky-sweet, sugary coating in Celine's mouth.

"Of course the baby is Colin's."

"But he was always so careful. He craved control, structure, and planning."

She is right about that. Celine's observation struck a chord with The Supreme. Colin thrived on dotting his I's and crossing his T's. And he hadn't known when she asked him to share a celebratory cigar the day of the raid.

Colin and It never shared anything, but Emilia now believed they did share Julie. It shielded Colin's lover from The Supreme even when they were allies—a realization she came to during her trial at The Capitol Building months before.

And Julie's newfound harshness, her ruthless actions of late, all point to It. Colin didn't know the woman he loved carried his child, but It did. I'm sure of this.

Celine plopped back down on the lounge chair and pulled at her hair. "Why?" was the only word Celine said, one that asked more than one question.

"Are you asking why I didn't tell you?" The Supreme asked, but Celine couldn't look her in the eyes. Pain settled in her beautiful human face, along with confusion and tears.

No, she's asking why Colin betrayed her. Why he outplayed her. Especially since he always doted on his sister. Their competition was fierce, but his loyalty to Celine was always stronger.

"Can you blame him?" The Supreme questioned, hoping to defuse the tense situation. "They were married, apparently. He was in his forties. If he wanted a family, he needed to start sooner rather than later. All the same reasons you had Henry Jr."

Celine wheezed, a nervous laugh vibrating against The Supreme's rapidly changing scales.

"Men have a much greater luxury of time than women."

"What do you want, Celine?" Emilia asked, agitation seeping into her tone. "He was also my friend. He didn't even know about Julie's pregnancy. He was completely oblivious to my innuendo."

"Then why did he write his will the way he did? As if he knew Julie carried his child? Did he time travel? Is he really not dead?" Fear crept in Celine's tone, not grief. And it made The Supreme uncomfortable. She stiffened herself away from Celine and sighed.

"That I don't know." While Celine wept, guilt coursed through

The Supreme's processor. She grabbed Celine's hands in her own and gave a gentle squeeze. The Supreme had granted It a time travel device. The possibility that Colin's other personality knew was a strong contender. This strange condition of Colin's always logically made sense to Emilia. While Colin and It were the same, they were also different. It didn't always know what Colin was up to, and Colin wasn't always aware of the tricks the other occupant in his brain played.

"I cannot change the past. And while you can through time travel, you shouldn't. There will be much larger implications if you try to do so. We have to stick the course. We're already too far down this path."

Celine wiped away her tears and nodded. Taking deep breaths and placing her hands on her hips, Celine turned back to Emilia with wet eyes.

"How far along is she?"

The Supreme sighed. This felt like trite gossip—something a woman as immaculate as Celine wouldn't typically engage in. Emilia hated the capabilities of her eyes more than ever.

"Just shy of two months. So, if you're wondering, then yes, I would assume Colin and Julie were traveling time during the last few months, plotting and planning their own strategy."

"What is it about her?" Celine shook her head.

Emilia lifted herself out of the chair and walked toward the railing. A cooling breeze rustled against her scales, a sensation she welcomed. The heat wave in The City was too consuming, too demanding. She couldn't breathe; she needed an escape.

"He loved her. She still loves him. If you can't see that, Celine O'Connor, then you're a larger fool than I ever expected. It'd do you good to befriend Julie Walsh even if it's just a façade. Then at least, you could see yourself coming on top. You could use her, piggyback off whatever plan she and Colin were conspiring on together. I say this as a being who has spent their whole life in the political arena: Don't fight public opinion."

"I'm an O'Connor. I won't succumb to a nobody."

"Then you'll find yourself alone in The City." The Supreme's words were sharp and poignant, but she no longer cared—Celine needed a solid kick in the ass, something to remind her that old bloodline families might have wealth but they were slowly losing power.

"What could Julie do to help me?"

Emilia's gaze shifted over from the tall skyscraper of COLI*GO to The Capitol Building. An idea formed inside her processor. She didn't need to physically occupy the marble-floored building with large, multiple-story-tall windows. She could still win the seat if she played the pieces just right.

I haven't lost the game yet.

"Think about it," Emilia said with a scandalous grin. "You own a majority of COLI*GO, especially in combination with Martin's shares. That's power, but imagine if you also sat in the governor's seat."

Emilia no longer needed Julie in The Legislature to continue her puppet-master games. She no longer possessed the necessary microchip in her brain. She needed Julie to be as far away from the seat as possible. And she needed a different piece sitting in Colin's chair so that she could essentially occupy it.

Celine's sinister smile brightened the dark sky around them—the gears in her mind turning, the options of power and control endless in her eyes. A family legacy completed and a slap in the face to the men in her life who held her back.

"And," The Supreme interrupted Celine's devilish composure before she could say anything, "if you have Julie's endorsement, you won't even have to work for the seat. It'll be an easy win."

"You don't think Julie will run? That she isn't power-hungry for the governor's seat?" Celine asked, leaning her head onto Emilia's shoulder. With her brilliantly shiny, scaly fingers, Emilia brushed Celine's deep, overgrown chestnut hair.

"Julie is not after supremacy the same way we are. And she'll not run, especially if you offer her something she can't say no to."

Celine's breath stilled, and Emilia tenderly kissed the soft spot of skin between Celine's neck and earlobe. Celine hummed, her eyes flickering closed as she inhaled heavily with relaxation.

The Supreme smiled. Her vigor and her thirst were back.

PART FIVE

The Past

In the desert
I saw a creature, naked, bestial,
Who, squatting upon the ground,
Held his heart in his hands,
And ate of it.
I said, "Is it good, friend?"
"It is bitter—bitter," he answered;
"But I like it
"Because it is bitter,
"And because it is my heart."
—*Stephen Crane*, In the Desert

Chapter 18
Melanie

<u>August 10th, 4 A.R.</u>

The waves crashed against the cliffs on the backside of the estate. Melanie smiled, basking in the warmth of the summer sun that The Oceanside provided.

She heard Henry's feet swishing through the lawn, which needed a cutting. Celine yelped from Henry's shoulders and giggled the innocent sounds of a toddler's laughter. The infant in Melanie's hands stirred at the noise but didn't cry out.

"And how are my lovely wife and handsome son?" Henry asked, kissing Melanie's forehead before removing his daughter from his shoulders.

"She's too young for that," Melanie scolded, her eyes rolling. Celine was two and a half years old and already plenty rambunctious. Henry's encouragement of her adventurous spirit worried but excited Melanie.

He was a wonderful father, a wonderful husband. She never suspected him of any foul behavior while she spent the full summers here at The Oceanside estate. He came each weekend, leaving early on Friday mornings and staying until the last possible second on Monday to head back to The Capitol Building in The City. They could barely stand to be apart, and she looked forward to seeing his smile on her device when he video called her each night to wish both her and the children peaceful dreams before bed.

They met when she worked on his gubernatorial campaign. Melanie had finished high school and spent almost two years working as a secretary for a young android attorney named Jeffries who practiced in The Hill neighborhood. He had just taken over the business from his android sponsor, his father figure in the android way. Melanie's parents swooned over what they considered a prestigious role, but really, Melanie arranged his calendar and answered his requests. The commute was a pleasant change for her—she had rarely left The South neighborhood and wanted to explore, but with the violence across The City, she usually stayed home.

The Resurgence rocked any sense of safety on the streets. Graduating in the midst of turbulent times left few choices. She was a thoughtful student but belonged to a poor family. There were no hopes for Melanie to attend The University. Even a scholarship wouldn't have been feasible. Her parents could hardly afford to put enough food on the table for her and her siblings.

When the android leader Edward rebelled, he forced his way into a half-burned Capitol Building, throwing the current governor behind bars. He was later found guilty of horrific experimentation on androids and of authoritarian legislature.

Representative Henry O'Connor had walked into her boss's office shortly after The Legislature announced they would honor a special election for a new leader. She knew the O'Connors were important clients of the android attorney, so she barely spoke a word when the tall, broad-shouldered man entered the room. She meekly pointed toward a chair before he grinned, strode past her, and walked right into Jeffries's office.

His charismatic laugh boomed with optimism as he sought Jeffries's legal advice on running a campaign.

"You'll need some man and potentially android power to help you," Jeffries had advised.

"The Murphys helped me get elected to The Legislature. I know I have their support."

Melanie knew the Murphy family. They lived in the duplex across the street from her. She was friends with the Murphys' eldest daughter, Anabella, who was expecting a baby girl in the next few months. Their families watched out for one another—if they believed so strongly in this man's ability to bring some peace to The Constituency and stand up for the constituents' rights, she believed it too.

"I'll help you with your campaign." The words raced out of Melanie's mouth before she could stop them.

Henry grinned at her and extended his hand. She took it in hers. He was self-aware of his strength and build—his handshake was firm but gentle enough against her freckled skin.

"Welcome to the team, Mrs. . ."

"Miss," Melanie corrected him. "Miss Melanie Doyle."

The pull toward Henry O'Connor was strong, and it had been in that moment she knew she wanted more of him. She never suspected a man from one of the most prestigious old bloodline families would ever want her. But after long nights of working on the campaign, everything fell into place.

They had been on the campaign trail for several weeks at that point and were only days away from the election. Henry was neck-in-neck with his competitor, Don Ludewing, in the polls. He slumped in his chair at the campaign headquarters in The Hill and shared his fears. He wanted to quit. Melanie had gripped his shoulders tightly.

"You can't. Don Ludewing isn't strong enough to lead us out of this depression, to help us smooth things out with the androids. You can. We need you. I need you."

And then he had kissed her.

Melanie still smiled at the memory of their first encounters. He genuinely loved her, and she couldn't imagine her life without him. He didn't care that his advisors told him his relationship with a nobody would ruin his chances at the governor's seat, so he embraced Melanie in his life without hesitation. And he had proven them all wrong.

Henry sat behind Melanie on the lawn, his long legs stretching out on either side of her body as she scotched back into his chest. Celine grabbed the teddy bear on the picnic blanket and gripped the stuffed animal tightly.

"I think The Legislature might complete the summer Session early. We should finish the agenda mid-next week as long as Edward doesn't filibuster any legislation." Henry whispered the next words in Melanie's ear. "That means I could come here and stay for the rest of the summer." The gentle brush of his lips, the source of a tingling sensation, chilled her sun-drenched body.

Colin smiled the beautiful grin babies often provided, and the newness of fresh skin cascaded in a lovely scent while Melanie held him against her chest. He let out a soft giggle.

"I think we'd all like that," she said, looking from her baby to her husband.

Henry spent the rest of the weekend with them, venturing to their favorite cafe in the quaint downtown, grilling out on the back deck, and reading the children bedtime stories. The sound of his vehicle's tires crunching against the seashell driveway Monday morning left a small tinge of disappointment that she still had a few days to wait to see if Henry's lofty promise would come to fruition.

Celine and the baby were settled down for a nap, so Melanie wandered from the bedroom to the patio. She pulled the strange contraption belonging to the man who claimed he was a time traveler. He warned her a year and a half ago not to use the device while pregnant. She hadn't been at the time, but she and Henry were trying for another child—a son, something so important to old bloodline families—so she hid the device away and never tempted its use. In the excitement of her pregnancy and the birth of their baby boy, she nearly forgot about the device. Until now.

Melanie found herself getting lost in the design etched into the glasses for hours. The intricacies were perfect and artistic. Beautiful and enchanting. The sleek box that accompanied the glasses didn't belong.

Pulling the slide out of the middle of the glasses, Melanie looked back into the house, wondering if her children were still asleep. Silence confirmed they were.

She slipped the glasses on and looked at the words glowing on the chrome box. The question from the unknown blood sample asked if she wanted to travel to the past or the future. The past tempted Melanie, a Pandora's Box of secrets taunting her with promises of alluring secrets she couldn't ask of her husband. Fear rose in her throat when the blood sample showed it could only bring her to June 23rd, 47 A.R. While Melanie chose to travel to the future instead of the past, that date unsettled her too much. She didn't want to witness death. June 23rd was decidedly important, but Melanie chose a much closer year, one less intimidating for her first dangerous dance with the unknown. The date appeared on the screen: June 23rd, 12 A.R.

***

A harsh sensation coursed through Melanie's body as she made her way eight years into the future.

She found herself walking along the gardens in the back of the O'Connor estate at The Oceanside. The sun shone brightly for a June day, the temperature warm and the air salty from the spray of the ocean's waves. Meandering downtown, Melanie appreciated the scenery of the place she felt most comfortable, most at home.

Large mansions and estates sprawled across the landscape in front of Melanie, but the lights remained mostly off. A few twinkled against the early morning sky, but sleep seemed to captivate the inhabitants of The Oceanside. Peaceful. Still. The sun was threatening to awake, orange and pale pinks painting across the sky in one large messy brushstroke.

The town square came into view. A vacation destination for old bloodline families, The Oceanside was home to fancy restaurants, charming cafes and a large yacht club with various boats docked along the harbor. Most of the shops were empty now, and the cobblestone roads were quiet. The hustle and bustle of summertime visitors would soon welcome the dreary-eyed shop owners and workers.

A few people and androids mulled around a bakery and coffee shop. Melanie adored this place and knew all the baristas by name. As she stepped inside, the cascading smell of ground coffee beans filled the air. A patron standing by the door smiled wide at Melanie—recognizing the governor's wife instantly.

Melanie worked twice as hard for the affections of the public. She wasn't born into an old bloodline family, and change sparked a fear in people. But allowing her husband's constituents to know her beyond just his wife helped her over the years. Melanie never missed a charity event, hosted plenty of her own, and put a concerted effort into shaking every person and android's hand when outside the confines of an O'Connor estate.

The barista's face instantly lit up with recognition as she approached the counter.

"Mrs. O'Connor! I'm so glad to see you. Might I add you look beautiful?" she said with rosy cheeks.

Melanie never got used to being treated as a celebrity. She fiddled with her thumbs and replied a small thank you with rambunctious laughter before ordering her normal double-shot espresso.

Gripping the warm cup, Melanie turned toward the rest of the shop.

The sound of chatter drowned out any specific words or conversations, and Melanie moved through the crowded coffee shop. A flickering light in the corner caught Melanie's attention, and her eyes nearly fell out of her head at the sight of a young woman seated by herself. No one noticed the strange strawberry blonde who looked out of place.

Melanie looked down at her hand, the emerald ring Henry had given her matching the exact same ring on this woman's left hand.

Impossible.

Her lips parted, and the color drained from her face. A man with wiry hair and a grim smile blocked Melanie's sight of the mysterious woman.

This isn't right. I need to get out of here. Instinct took over.

Melanie darted out of the café, nearly spilling her coffee on the ground. She rushed back up the streets, trying to avoid the eyes of those around her as the streets began to crowd. Making her way back to the O'Connor estate, Melanie had no game plan.

The purpose of this visit alluded her, her own curiosity a detriment to her sanity. The large blossoming garden made her nerves quiet down, and she finally felt relaxed.

"I don't understand." The words came from a voice that sounded like her own.

Melanie paused, leaning against the large elm tree to hide from her future self. The sound of Henry's voice followed.

"I must run in the next election. The people need me."

"Your family needs you. We have plenty. I'd rather us spend our time here year-round. We can go to The City to visit friends. I don't see what the issue is."

Melanie didn't like the sound of their argument. A hurt she recognized, one she kept buried in the present, crept through her future self's voice. She held on to the bark of the tree, steadying her hands.

"What we really need to do is try for another baby."

"Why? Celine and Colin are wonderful children."

"Celine is rambunctious. She'll never find her way in an old bloodline circle if she doesn't acquire some temperance. And Colin . . . Colin is too quiet. You coddle him too much."

"He's intelligent. Sure, a bit introverted, but he's still so young. Not to mention, Edward cast Emilia on to us, and we're raising her like our own. I don't think I could handle four children, especially if you're still in the governor's office. You'd need to retire. You'd need to help me."

"We can hire a nanny, I told you this already. I need you by my side in The City. You're my wife, you're my best friend." Henry's retort sounded genuine, but Melanie wasn't sure what to make of this intense argument. She and Henry rarely fought in the present time she came from, but this future seemed gloomy, unimaginable.

"Then stop drinking so much! Be present. This role as governor is eating you alive from the inside. Please, finish out your term and then stay here."

Melanie's attention from the argument ripped away when she felt a tug on the hem of her dress. A little boy stood by her side, looking up at her with recognition and awe in his eyes.

"Mom?"

Melanie's heart stopped beating in her chest, and tension stilled her body. She'd been caught; she'd been distracted. Her eyes glanced over toward the argument still happening between Henry and the future Melanie before she looked back down at the little boy, at Colin.

"Let's get away from here," she said in a trembling voice, one she tried to portray as playful. Excitement flickered across his eyes, and he grinned wide.

"I bet you can't beat me to the cliffs!"

Confusion crept in Melanie's brow for a moment too long as the boy raced away from her toward the edge of the estate. The cliffs were beautiful, but they were dangerous, especially for the clumsy feet of someone so young.

Wait! she wanted to call out while danger threatened, but she covered her own mouth, pushing down the word. She didn't want to draw attention to Henry or Melanie, and by shouting, she would. But she didn't have to. Her future persona caught sight of a sprinting Colin in her peripheral vision and yelped.

"Colin!"

"Colin!" Henry's voice boomed after Melanie's. "Come back! I promise, I didn't mean it!"

The pair took off after the boy, and Melanie backed away from the side of the tree. She took off in the other direction, afraid of what would unfold if she stayed. Her knowledge that this was truly her last day on this earth caused bile to rise in her throat as the shadowy figures leaped toward the sides of the cliffs.

Oh, God . . . I did this to myself.

Melanie fumbled with the glasses in her pocket, ripping the edge of the fabric while hastily pulling out the chrome box. Everything around her stilled, and harsh pain ripped through her body. The sensation brought her to her knees.

The time traveler she recognized peered over the edge of the cliffs. He was younger here, a confusing thought that didn't process logically in her mind. How could he be younger when nine years prior he was sitting in her kitchen, giving her this powerful, life-changing device?

The sharp pain occurred again, and Melanie gripped her stomach. When she looked across the field, a tall figure stalked through the high grass. She did not recognize this man, but he looked oddly familiar, oddly enough like Henry. It wasn't Henry, she had just seen him, and this man was slightly taller and his hair not quite as dark.

Who are you? Melanie was mesmerized by the confusing experience occurring around her.

She fell to the ground as a third sting raced through her body, her arms and legs trembling in pain. This time, the young woman with strawberry hair from the coffee shop appeared in the clearing. She acted as confused as Melanie felt, and instead of heading in the direction of the others, he raced toward the meadow.

Melanie gripped the glasses, unable to get up from the severe pain coursing through her. She dropped a speckle of her own blood onto the glass slide and inserted it into the device.

A final bang pounded through her body. Looking out toward the field again, the time traveler she recognized reappeared. He was older, more lines crept from the corners of his eyes, and he had significantly speckled gray in his hair.

Fear crippled her, and Melanie swore she would never come back to this date. Her curiosity already imprinted a terrible reaction from this selfish visit to the future. She punched the date she came from into the chrome box and slipped the glasses back over her eyes.

Chapter 19
Mick

<u>November 6th, 46 A.R.</u>

Elsie's apartment fitted her personality perfectly. In the living room, there was a love seat, a chair, and a beaten-up coffee table that had seen better days. A sleek, modern device hung mounted on the wall, and a faded area rug tied the mishmash room together.

Mick's thumbs rubbed across his knuckles, his left leg bounced against the floor, and his heart beat rapidly in his chest. The last time he had seen Elsie, he drugged her and carried her off to the lower lab at COLI*GO. After a few hours, Mick returned to Dr. Isabella Garcia and brought Elsie's unconscious body back here.

He didn't know she was an O'Connor at that time but discovered the coveted secret on another trip to the past. Remembering how many, or which one, proved challenging. But the memory rang through him with extreme heartache; he placed his hand on his chest to steady himself just thinking about it. The future was constantly changing, but lineage was always finalized.

Seeing a distraught Roslyn Sullivan in the O'Connor townhouse weeping in front of Henry O'Connor made him shiver. Mick hid in the carriage house across the street—his secret hiding place whenever he time traveled. The only times he risked another inhabitant were when Filipe and Henry locked Colin up there in their youth or when Julie used the place to watch the man she loved work through his grief in the early spring of 47 A.R.

By Roslyn's tears, she might have expected a different reaction from Henry O'Connor when she told him she carried his child. She loved the man, and to some extent, he loved her too. But he would never plan on raising another child; he never wanted the responsibilities when he already felt like a failure with his son.

"You want me to do what?" she had asked him before slapping his face. Henry never hit her back but instead hung his head low and turned away from his secret lover.

"You'd rather be outcast by society?" he had asked.

Women of old bloodline lineage wouldn't birth bastards. They were supposed to marry—they were supposed to have class. Henry wouldn't admit to his affair with Roslyn. He cared for the young woman he charmed, but even she knew better than to threaten an O'Connor.

"We could be together. What's so wrong with that? The City doesn't expect you to mourn Melanie forever."

Those were the wrong words. And those were the last words Roslyn would ever speak to Henry O'Connor. Mick's eyes gazed across the room and stopped at the clock above the stovetop in Elsie's kitchen.

Elsie's transformation didn't sit well with her. Like in her youth, Elsie took to the only coping mechanism she knew—rebellion. She did the bare minimum to perform well enough at her job. She went out with a group of friends she hadn't interacted with since her youth. She drank, forgot to eat, and spent hours in front of a punching bag.

Sweat exacerbated her symptoms. Moisturizer helped a bit.

She had no idea who he was. To her, he looked like Jeb Taylor. But Jeb Taylor was supposed to be dead. Mick admitted he didn't handle the last appearance at The Courthouse very well. He held in his emotions as long as he could, but that was his breaking point— the realization he needed to know that The Supreme would always backstab him. That he was never safe and her promises were gilded. She didn't really care about equality for androids. She was after revenge and retribution.

Mick couldn't condone that. So he tried to expose her as his Jeb persona. But that didn't work.

The courthouse screamed and yelled at him. He'd killed the beloved Kathleen Murphy. And while Jeb wasn't formally put on trial for all those other deaths, the media accused him of doing so.

The eerie look of Jones—Mick's lover, his boyfriend, his best friend—pointing the gun in his direction, in Jeb's direction, and firing when he wouldn't drop the knife in his hands . . . The memory was almost too much for Mick to bear.

The shot ricocheted through his body, and he felt the gushing effects of his blood barreling through his chest. His eyes had closed, but he could still see everything. The bailiff grabbed his bleeding body, and an ambulance rushed him to the emergency room. The android nurses, those who didn't have an emotional response to if they were trying to save a criminal or not, attempted their best, but his heart had already given out.

But not his brain.

Mick watched them zip him into a black body bag and carry him off to the morgue.

Anna Garcia took one look at him and shook her head, waving her hands at the android assistants who then carried him away to a cheaply made wooden casket. They didn't even clean off his blood-soaked skin. They didn't change his sodden clothes.

They placed him inside the chamber and dropped him harshly into the ground.

After that exhausting adventure, Mick's vision blurred, and his body burst around him. The only way Mick could describe the sensation was by relating it to a type of disintegration. His body evaporated, bones and ligaments dissipating around him. When clarity finally reached him, he was back in the place of his actual death.

Mick had died several times while traveling time. Each time, whether he accidentally killed himself or was killed by a non-time traveler, he ended up in the location of his actual death. A chance to live again and change his fate.

To an extent.

The sound of an old-fashioned key slipping into the front door distracted Mick from his thoughts. Elsie returned home and now he had to face her.

She was a tall woman, and while he was still taller than her, her heavy footsteps provided nearly nonexistent stealth.

Or she's drunk, which is highly likely.

"Woah," Elsie said, pausing in front of Mick. "I know you."

"Yes, you do." Mick stood with his hands securely in his pockets. He felt the two envelopes against the pad of his thumb and caressed the sharp edges.

"You're fucking Jeb Taylor," Elsie said with slurred words and a pointer finger in his direction. "You're supposed to be dead."

"Surprise," Mick answered half-heartedly. "I come bearing two messages."

He revealed the letters to Elsie, who grabbed them with hesitancy. She scooted far away from him, afraid of what was an illusion and what was reality.

"Do you want to know the truth behind why you feel so ill?" Mick asked her.

Elsie nodded, her silence indicative of how little she trusted him.

Mick explained the posse hominem experiment to her. While Elsie didn't need to believe any of the stories he shared, his consistent narrative seemed to soothe her.

Gripping his fist into a tight ball, Mick grunted in frustration. Hatred for himself found its way back into his heart. He kidnapped so many people for The Supreme and Isabella, bringing back hundreds upon hundreds of men and women, old and young, rich and poor, for their lofty experiments. Each time he placed a new posse hominem back in their bed, tears escaped the corners of his eyes, and he affectionately rubbed a circle on their cheeks with his flaky thumb.

The first few times, Mick didn't mind the task. *Disgusting,* he thought. But Mick was used to performing unsavory acts for both The Supreme and his Jeb Taylor persona. Jeb Taylor made his money off drug sales. The rich and old bloodline members of society purchased party drugs off him, ones he obtained from The Supreme. Presumably from her connections to the drug manufacturers and The Legislature. Whenever someone made a purchase, they selected some of his artwork. This served two purposes: one, art was subjective in price, and he covered the costs of his labor and the costs of the drugs with an extra percentage for himself and The Supreme to pocket. Second, it served the purpose of his art hanging in the most prestigious homes across The City. This was a lucrative business even if distasteful.

"Open this first letter now. Open the second letter on June 23rd, 47 A.R.," Mick instructed, his eyes averting from Elsie.

Her fingers trembled as they ripped through the envelope.

"Dear Elsie," she said out loud, holding both sides of the paper with her left and right hands. "You are probably angry with what I've made you. With what you've become. But you need to realize, you have become more than a game piece on my chessboard. Do not give up on yourself. Do not allow confusion, sorrow, and anger to ruin the chances you have in this life. Continue striving toward your goals. One day, you'll be the governor's right-hand man. You will help lead him toward the truth. One day, you'll run yourself. You'll strive to make meaningful, impactful changes for the people in The Constituency. They will need you. You are the only one who could represent both humans and androids. You are both. Do not forget that part of yourself. Work each day and focus your rebellion on the microchip in your brain—not the rebellion of those surrounding you. Befriend Commissioner Jones. You must work closely together, or all will fail for societal equality. Sincerely, The Supreme."

Elsie folded the paper in threes and placed it in her lap. Her eyes squinted, and she shook her head in confusion.

"What does this mean? Rebel from the microchip in my brain? Who is Commissioner Jones? How would I ever work for Governor O'Connor?"

Mick placed his head in his hands. He wished he'd read the letter himself before delivering it.

"I never understood Emilia's riddles," Mick whispered, "and I never understood Jones's, either."

Elsie raced to the kitchen sink and ran the faucet. Cool water hit her face, sending goosebumps across her arms.

"Are you going to tell me anything?"

Mick stood and walked toward the door.

"Julie Walsh," he said and turned to face her once more, "she's the only human you can trust."

***

The cool, crisp fall air of The City hit Mick in the face. He had one more task in this trip to the past. One much more excruciating than visiting Elsie Sullivan.

He felt bad for her because he was also confused by The Supreme's cryptic note. She never got to the point of her stories. The Supreme thrived on having the upper hand. If she didn't, she demanded a rematch. Mick had watched this behavior of hers her whole life, through first-hand experience and through the experience of time travel.

Mick wandered down into the subway and scanned his metal chip card. The ancient beast roared, nearing the platform with a startling presence. The car was crowded this evening, the rancid smells of humans and androids stiff in the air. He didn't stay on the subway long, waiting for a few stops until he crossed the waterway that separated The Monument neighborhood from downtown.

Walking the rest of the way, he ventured along The City's picturesque cobblestone streets and gas lamp lights. People and androids strolled on the streets, heading home from bars and restaurants.

The carriage house greeted Mick with a quiet hello. Not much of the space changed since the last time he visited—which felt like so long ago.

Mick's fingers trailed along the coffee table, and he sunk into the old, lifeless couch. He pulled the blanket hanging off the cushions and wrapped himself in the warm embrace. Sleep threatened Mick, his eyes closed, and the crackling warmth of the fireplace lulled him into a light slumber.

A creek in the floorboards alerted him, his left eye opening before his right to look for an intruder.

Governor Colin O'Connor was a tall overpowering man. He had broad shoulders, defined arms, and a large square jaw. His steely gray eyes and dark brown hair cast a gloomy shadow. He was not dressed in a suit, the way Mick normally saw him. Colin wore a pair of jeans and a T-shirt, which was more casual than his typical attire. A few tiny wrinkles sprouted from the corners of his eyes. Colin—or It; Mick had a difficult time telling the difference even after all these years—time traveled. Mick assumed if he walked across the courtyard to the O'Connor townhouse that he would find another physical Colin inside, one wrapped up with his best friend, Julie.

Mick only felt unsafe with a few others, time travelers, Colin included. They were the only ones who could kill him. He had to keep reminding himself that he knew the truth about his death. Colin was not responsible for it.

But the man's stare was still predatory, the wolf slowly closing in on the deer rustling by the bushes. Mick took a deep breath and stood. He was shorter than Colin but still tall enough that the other man needed more to intimidate him than just his height.

"Mick." His voice was gruff as he gestured back to the tiny living room area. Both men sat opposite each other, and Colin leaned over, his elbows resting on his thighs. Mick lowered his back onto the loveseat and reached for his duffle bag.

"I want to start by saying I don't believe in warning time travelers of the future. You have the ability to change it." Mick continued fumbling in his bag before gripping one of his most prized possessions. "But I'm making an exception for you because you won't try to avert your true death. From everything I've learned about you—for all the hatred and confusion a man like you has made me feel, all the rage—you didn't change the time loop you yourself created. You could have, but you didn't. That was the ultimate test. Your mother travels time, so a time traveler needed to be her demise. And I believe you deserve another opportunity outside of June 23rd to speak to her."

Colin shifted in the chair that was slightly too small for him. Mick expected a lashing, an eruption of anger, but Colin remained still.

"You're cruel to yourself," Mick continued, "but I will trust you with this warning I'm going to provide because of what you've shown me. Not because of Julie. That needs to be clear. I know you respect the game, and I think you've realized you aren't the winner."

Colin's eyes darkened, and he pressed his lips tightly together. Admitting defeat wasn't a comfortable notion for the governor. He had always won each match. Colin surpassed his sister, stole his father's seat in the governor's office, and convinced the woman he loved that the most sinister side of himself would prevail without her intervention.

Mick handed over his journal, the one Jones gave him in the

present. This version of the journal contained Julie's warnings, her admissions, and her truths.

If this was truly Colin sitting in front of him, then Julie's words would break his heart. But Colin needed to read them. Colin needed to know.

"Julie loves all of you."

"And I love her." Colin's voice trembled, and he grabbed the journal from Mick's grasp. "She's accepted me. I didn't realize that then . . . I mean, now."

Colin's eyes gazed out the window toward the townhouse. Shadowed figures moved behind the curtains, one at his height, the other hers.

"So, you are time traveling?"

"Yes," he answered, looking back at Mick. "I'm not from too far in the future. Only six months or so. But I like to come back here sometimes. It gives me peace."

Mick nodded, an odd sense of comradery he shared with the governor. "Then you know about the assassination."

"I'm aware," Colin said, with his chin now resting in his hand. "It is difficult to not ponder on the last date of travel when your blood hits the microscope."

Mick agreed—one's death was accessible through the chrome box, but that knowledge was an intended savory warning, a dish often served cold.

"You might not be the winner of the game, but you can set up Julie for success," Mick cautioned.

He debated in his mind how much to reveal, how much to confide in Colin. If he gave away the future, he'd effectively change it. There'd be no way that Colin wouldn't alter the course of the dimension, even without intending to. But if Mick didn't share enough insight, The Supreme would win. And she would destroy everything—using all of Colin's pieces against him, stealing them all off the board. A sparkle danced across Colin's eyes and his lips turned slightly upward in a half-grin.

"She's highly capable on her own."

"Of course she is," Mick said, shifting back in his seat. "But your sister is a wild card. And she has more experience."

Colin's face turned stone cold, and his breath stilled.

"I doubt Celine would hurt Julie."

"No, she wouldn't dirty her hands of that," Mick said. "She believes Julie isn't worthy, that she's a nobody and essentially doesn't matter. But she would hurt your child. And The Supreme would help her."

Colin's eyes grew wide, and he swiftly stood from his chair. His large stride brought him to the window in one step, and he placed his palm flat against the glass, leaning close to the windowpanes. Mick sensed an urgency in Colin, in It. He possessed the tenacity of an unleashed tiger roaming the jungle, hot on the scent of its prey.

"We need you. Your child's existence results from time travel. Without yours and Julie's baby, I fear that this reality would simply be the largest time loop, and all of this would have been for nothing."

Chapter 20
The Governor

<u>May 1ˢᵗ, 47 A.R.</u>

Elsie complicated the situation at FACERE by killing Paul McGuire, but Colin provided her with the means to do so. Introducing her to his ways of killing—grooming her, in a sense—was the right decision. She was an O'Connor, and while Colin had to keep this secret close to his chest a little longer, other plans were at play.

He gripped the steering wheel of his vehicle and looked up at her condo in The Monument. Jones fidgeted in the seat beside Colin, his scales blinking like a stoplight, the greens vibrant and distracting.

"You didn't tell Elsie that Julie's microchip was removed."

Colin had tasked his new legislative aide to work directly with Jones on the FACERE case, to help uncover the terrorist network of humans who were locating posse hominems and killing them in the streets. Jones and Elsie concluded that Paul McGuire was the ringleader, with Maggie Rivera and Representative Joel Kennsington funneling information.

"You didn't tell me you stopped taking the antidote." Jones's words were harsh—slicing open a healing wound and letting the festering blood ooze out with a sting.

Colin sighed and turned on the self-driving vehicle. The roads in The Monument were mostly one-ways but not in the configuration of a grid. The City was old, and the people who lived here before androids were fiercely independent and liberal but hated changing anything that reminded them of their historic city. The only vehicles on the road were parked and abandoned for the evening, their owners tucked in the confines of their homes in time for the curfew Commissioner Jones enacted to protect them.

Taking the antidote conflicted Colin. A part of him wanted to get rid of It—to relieve himself of the torment of a struggling mind constantly at ends with itself. But It was an important part of him too. He'd been there from the very beginning, taking the time to listen when his father wouldn't.

And the antidote isn't guaranteed to work.

Julie worked endlessly to perfect her drug, but Colin didn't think perfection was attainable. While he admired her for trying, her youth stood in the way. She needed to step back at this point, or she'd get lost inside her scientific madness—and that would negatively consume her, making her desperate.

"The antidote doesn't work," Colin said.

"Is that what Julie told you?" Jones asked, a hint of optimism straining in his voice.

"I haven't seen or spoken to Julie."

Jones bent his head down, and Colin waited for him to admit he was in communication with her. This was an ultimate test of friendship, of loyalty. Earlier in the evening, Elsie confided in Colin that she and Jones found Julie and communicated with her. Julie was a captive to Joel fucking Kennsington but traveled time, working on her antidote in the past to fix the errors.

"I have." Jones spoke the words so softly that Colin almost didn't hear them. He looked over at the commissioner, his head in his hands. Instead of bright, colorful and vibrant green, his scales muted in sorrow. "I don't know how I feel about Elsie."

Jones's admission sparked a slight flinch in Colin.

"Why?"

"I think she travels time."

Colin looked out the vehicle's front window. They passed the police headquarters on the right, taking a sharp turn to head to the side of The Hill that abutted The River. They were inching closer to his townhouse.

"We were able to get Julie a new device with the assistance of an android prison guard that Elsie claims to have known for a long time, from back during her days at The Record Department. I've scoped him out myself because I am thorough."

No, Jones, Colin wanted to say, *you're cautious—you don't trust very many people. And rightfully so—we haven't given you any reasons why you should.*

"The android claimed he's done work for Elsie before in the past and was confused why I didn't seem to know who he was. That he'd done odd jobs for me and Elsie before. But he never called her by her name."

"What did he call her?"

"Madam."

Colin's body shifted, and he placed his large hand on Jones's shoulder. The salutation was old-fashioned, something a youthful woman like Elsie would never insist upon. Colin found the formal greeting strange whenever someone used it when addressing The Supreme. He hated calling Emilia "Madam Supreme" and held back from rolling his eyes each time he did.

The Supreme was a touchy subject. Colin wanted to save her—what they were doing to her at FACERE was wrong, and he wished he'd been more present in the dealings of the quasi-government android manufacturing company. He couldn't believe in his heart that Emilia was out to get him or that she planned on playing him all the way to the end.

"I have a feeling time travel will get out of control with the more people using the glasses. It's the main reason I was afraid of Mick's invention. With so many going backward and forward, the ripple effects are endless and the implications awful. Mick said before it's hard to understand which version he is of himself." Jones finally looked up at Colin with his large eyes. The quick glance up and down indicated he scanned him, trying to unearth any strangeness in the man before him. "Does It ever feel that way when traveling time?"

Colin chuckled. He appreciated Jones respecting the two personalities that occupied his mind, distinguishing his knowledge that It traveled time, not Colin, but that they shared the same vessel. Time travel was complicated enough, and so was It. Mixing two elements that made Colin unsure who he was or what he was convoluted everything lately. He always felt that way with It. It was never a figment of his imagination—It was always real, physically standing beside him because of time travel.

Except for that one time, when I took Julie into the woods.

"Constantly," he answered Jones.

They sat in silence for the next few minutes, the charming and quaint streets in The Hill neighborhood welcoming them. Jones didn't come inside the townhouse and instead opted to walk back to his apartment in The Bay.

Colin turned on the hallway light and found a note from his sister, Celine, taped to the fridge. She wouldn't be home this evening—opting to stay with her husband and the baby at her own home. She and Baby Henry had been living with Colin since the horrid day in the park when a group of Humanizers openly killed a posse hominem woman. But she still felt an affiliation with her husband, and as much as Celine told Colin that she didn't love the man, she did. Martin accepted his sister, accepted her faults.

Martin could have left her, especially after finding out about Amanda. But he didn't. He loves her too much.

The townhouse was his and his alone for the evening. An odd quietness lingered through the halls. Colin smiled, placing the note on the kitchen island.

While his hands hadn't committed the kill this evening, he felt a nudge to perform his ritual. Colin took out a hoppy beer from the refrigerator and popped off the top. The fizzy foam coated his mouth with temptation while he strode to the laundry room. He stripped himself of his clothes and placed them inside the machine. There was no trinket in his pocket to place alongside the others in the drawers in the counter.

Climbing the stairs, Colin paused when he made it to the third floor. He continued guzzling down the beer in his hand and walked into the master bedroom. The sight of Julie's college sweatshirt broke the trance of his routine. Rummaging through the dresser on the far wall, Colin put on a pair of gym shorts.

The ritual was important to him, more than It. He needed a sense of control. And now he'd lost it—because of her.

Grief, fury, and anger swept through Colin like a tornado, and with the swipe of his large hand, he pushed all the contents off his nightstand in one large swoop. The photographs and case with his watches crashed onto the hardwood floors.

Pacing with his hands on his hips, Colin exited the bedroom and raced for his study. He barged inside and rummaged through the drawers. The time travel device and his knife sat on the bottom left, and beside them was a secret stash of pills. Fumbling with the cap, Colin placed the demon capsule in his mouth and reached for a bottle of Scotch on the cabinet beside his desk. He took a long swig of the amber liquid and relaxed in the confines of his large leather chair.

Darkness occupied his line of vision as he closed his eyes, the high coursing through his veins.

***

He dreamt of Julie again. He dreamt she came to him, sneaking through the window of his study, that he held her in a passionate embrace. Colin imagined the plans he and Julie made—how they would reunite at FACERE, and in the meantime, she would work on perfecting the drug that could finally free his mind, provide a sense of unrestrictive welcome in their lives. And once all this madness was finished, they'd escape this hell, this dimension. They wanted to leave the world in the right hands before departing off into the sunset of their fantasy, their fairytale ending.

Then they could find solace in the place that meant so much to them. But this was just a dream, his imagination running wild from alcohol and drug consumption. The impact of stress on his brain knowing that Paul McGuire was dead because of him but not feeling the relief of the knife piercing skin didn't help either.

Dreams weren't reality, no matter how real her voice sounded, how welcoming her embrace was, how she tasted on his lips. Lies, woven together with a desire for a happy ending—and happy endings didn't exist in this city.

Flipping onto his side, Colin almost felt Julie in the confines of his bed, almost felt her snuggle into his chest. When he woke, he nearly didn't believe his own eyes.

"Julie?" he asked, reaching out toward her naked body. His fingers traced her shape through the light darkness peering through the curtains.

She froze in place, and he took her hall in. Colin's mouth remained ajar while he noted the flushness of her skin, the small marks and light bruises from intimacy across her collarbone and snaking up her inner thighs. Shooting up from the bed, he clenched the sheets.

This wasn't a dream. She's real. We're real.

Julie cupped the sides of Colin's face with a softness, and he pulled her body closer to his. An overwhelming feeling escaped his body as he felt for the first time with Julie that they were one. He loved her with all his mind, and she allowed him. She trusted him.

We will win this twisted game.

"I can't stay," she whispered in his ear. "I'll come back, I promise. There are a few things I need to do before I let The City know I'm still here."

"What do you need to do?" he asked, hoping her answer would finally confirm that the plans they made actually happened and weren't something he made up inside his head.

"I'm fixing the antidote. That doesn't mean you have to take the antidote once it's fixed. I'll always leave that decision up to you."

A large grin spread across Colin's face, hidden mostly by the darkness.

This is all real.

***

There were a few more components to his and Julie's plan that he needed to cement before the future occurred. He wished he could simply retire, but The City needed a strong leader. Society also needed a new android leader who would rule justly instead of a machine like The Supreme whose thirst for power matched that of a predatory lion.

Celine sat on the other side of the dining room table with a questioning glare. She took a long sip from her wine glass.

Family dinners were a tradition of theirs, like many old bloodline families. They aimed to sit down together once a week before she moved back to the townhouse to keep each other abreast of what was going on in The Capitol Building and at COLI*GO.

"What are the next steps for Emilia?" Celine asked him.

"She's at FACERE now, where they will run tests and

evaluations on her processor. There are talks of upgrading her processor to the newest model configurations, but they won't take out her microchip unless it's approved by The Legislature."

"And what happens when they take out her microchip?"

Colin gulped, placing his utensils beside his plate and reaching for his glass of water. What Maggie Rivera and FACERE wanted to do with Emilia's microchip was a violation, no matter how corrupted the android leader truly was. She was a sentient being, and while the FACERE researchers claimed they could "program out" pain from an android, Colin didn't believe this to be true. He'd seen the way Jones acted; he'd experienced how in tune Emilia was when they grew up together.

How can humans decide what pain feels like for other species?

"I'm not sure," Colin answered, picking his fork and knife back up and cutting into his steak. The meat wasn't cooked quite to his liking—he'd let the steak sit too long. "That's why I'm stalling The Legislature."

This wasn't the full truth, but Celine didn't need to know the details of Paul McGuire and Elsie Sullivan. His sister couldn't handle the information—not yet.

Colin usually trusted Celine. They had their ups and downs, but they were always there for one another. She released him from the binds in the carriage house when Filipe Garcia used Colin as a science experiment, and she squeezed Colin's hand tightly under the dining room table whenever their father chastised him for not being "normal" enough.

When their father died, Colin contemplated telling her the truth about the progression of Henry's Alzheimer's. Colin had injected him with an overdose of a drug used to calm him during his uncontrollable fits. An odd, full circle moment. Emilia advised against this, casting doubt in his mind about just how close he and Celine were. While all they had growing up was each other, bonds could always be severed.

It pained Colin to know that Julie felt at ends with his sister at COLI*GO, especially in the confines of scientific morality. Celine's selfishness and brazen spirit were her detriments, and Julie's stubbornness was hers. He needed to play the part of puppet master with them.

When Colin broached Celine in his plans, she didn't question him. He doubted she would—his sister wanted the O'Connor legacy. Celine craved a sense of command that she could never have because of her brother, because of him.

Colin preferred to learn this lesson from his father, from the way the pieces fell into place now in his own life. Time travelers experienced a sense of immortality, able to avoid the limitations of death. Death provided a chance for a do-over, an opportunity to reset with new, valuable information. A spare move to make with the pawns on the board.

Colin couldn't tell Julie this part of his plan—she would try to prevent him from killing himself. But he knew what happened—she was living proof. She came back, received a second chance. And so would he.

"I'm going to push off The Legislature's vote on Emilia's microchip for as long as I can," Colin finally revealed, cutting more aggressively into the overcooked steak. "But there is something else."

Celine stopped chewing, and they were silent while Henry Jr. giggled in his highchair. Colin smiled toward his nephew.

"I promised you we'd stay on the same page."

"Of course," Celine said, worry furrowing across her brows.

When Celine and Colin made amends, they promised to not keep secrets, to get back to the relationship they used to have: one where they shared their plans and helped fill in the missing pieces or potential cracks.

"Julie time traveled. She killed herself and came back."

Celine's eyes widened, but she remained silent, not looking away from Colin while still rubbing her son's cheek.

"That creates a time loop. And we need to create another one to prevent the chaos the inventor of time travel has instilled."

"How do we accomplish that?" Celine asked the question, but it sounded more like a statement as if she already knew what Colin was about to say.

"With a disruption. Something to jolt society back into reality and reevaluate how to move forward together as one. Calm the chaos," Colin answered, finally giving up on his terrible steak and placing his knife down loudly on the long dining room table.

"And how do you plan to do that?" Celine asked, an alarmed tone emulating from her voice.

"I'm going to kill myself."

Chapter 21
Elsie

<u>April 2nd, 34 A.R.</u>

When Elsie used the time travel device, an odd sensation filled her core. A migraine swept through her head, a side effect caused by the microchip lodged into her brain.

The temptation to see Colin in action broke her down after days of contemplation. Elsie didn't trust The Supreme nor her advice, but following down the path and watching Colin kill was an oddly satisfying, if not enlightening, experience.

Elsie expected to find him alone in his killings, but he never was. A double of him showed, a copy of himself—a physical doppelgänger.

A time traveler.

Others might have thought Colin was indeed a madman—and maybe he was to a certain extent—but the realization that a future version of himself had planned these killings, had traveled back in time to the correct dates and times, and established all these intricate time loops fascinated Elsie.

The genius behind this power is what made Colin seem so untouchable for so long.

Elsie could play this game. And she was on a warpath, particularly after Don Jr.'s betrayals. He used her feelings against her, tricked her into helping him secure the Session speaker seat he longed for.

Being part-posse hominem should have prevented emotional mistakes, but clearly, something was amiss with the microchip Isabella implanted in her brain. Confirmation from Julie that she was indeed pregnant changed everything. When Don Jr.'s accusation about the other woman slipped from his mouth, Elsie didn't care.

But when his legislative aide began spreading rumors, that's when it all spiraled in her mind.

The desire for a real family—even if that only included Julie now—struck a fierce, protective chord in Elsie's approach. Understanding the true nature of her brother served for a larger purpose in Elsie's plan to advance herself and get the scum out of The Legislature.

Julie is too kind. She isn't ruthless enough. I could do this job. I could enact real change with the representatives.

The O'Connor townhouse was empty when Elsie arrived. Isabella was off with her philanthropic adventures, and Colin was busy at The Capitol Building. Colin was a man of habit, and privilege proved to be his downfall. He never changed his home codes, and after punching in the number and hearing the soft un-locking click, Elsie smiled.

Figures.

Elsie headed straight toward the laundry room on the second-floor landing. It was small compared to the grand nature of the townhouse, but a full-sized washer and dryer occupied the space. A small table on the opposite wall for folding clothes had a large basin sink, and beside it was a small table with three drawers.

Her fingers trembled as she pulled open the top drawer.

A couple of trinkets and jewelry lay inside. With a gloved hand, Elsie pulled up a gold chain bracelet with pearl beads. A bit of blood stained the pearls, and a shiver ran down Elsie's spine. Placing the bracelet inside a clear bag and closing the drawer, Elsie was unable to look at the jewelry that belonged to Colin's other victims.

While Elsie had killed before, there was something different about her methods than Colin's. Colin was calculated and ritualistic. Elsie was vengeful and reactive. Neither was right, and while she liked to think the instances were isolated, Elsie almost physically felt the handle of Colin's blade wrapped inside her palm. She couldn't explain the odd memory—something that wasn't supposed to belong inside her brain. Memories and dreams often convoluted Elsie of late, another side effect of time travel, according to Julie.

Backing out of the laundry room, a movement brushed down the hall. Elsie stilled, holding her breath to hopefully not give away her presence to whoever else intruded upon the townhouse.

The sight of Isabella Garcia's short stature made Elsie audibly gasp. Isabella turned to Elsie with a raised brow. She looked exactly as the last time Elsie saw her in the present.

What are you doing here? Why are you also traveling time?

Elsie hadn't felt Isabella's abilities. The few times she did travel, she noticed Colin coming back in time. A sharp pain coursed through the pit of her stomach each time he did so.

"So posse hominems with active microchips can travel time."

Elsie tucked the clear bag behind her back, hoping Isabella hadn't noticed the contents inside.

"What are you doing coming back here?" Elsie asked her, moving adjacent to Isabella.

"I'd ask you the same thing, but I suspect you're going to play some sick mind trick on my cousin?"

Isabella is smarter than I thought. Elsie relaxed her arms and allowed them to hang loosely beside her body.

"He's spreading lies."

Isabella nodded. "All men lie. All women lie too."

Their stand continued as neither moved nor spoke.

"What did Mick promise you with time travel?" Isabella finally asked, glancing away from Elsie and out the window. She eyed the carriage house across the courtyard.

"Mick didn't give me a time travel device. The Supreme did."

Isabella stopped breathing and wheezed loudly. "Elsie—"

"No," Elsie interrupted. "You do not get to scold me. You're also traveling back for your own selfish reasons."

Isabella shrugged, her long hair wavering with her movement. An elegance and an air of sophistication still surrounded the philanthropist even in her sinister acts of time travel.

"The difference is," Isabella said, smoothing out the wrinkles of her perfectly fitted maroon dress, "I'm after Colin's blood. I need it for experimental purposes in the present."

Elsie didn't know what to make with this information, but she felt a powerful urge to tell Julie.

"Don't follow Colin's footsteps too closely, Elsie," Isabella said with a voice filled with regret. "I know you seek familiarity. I know you want answers. But those aren't the right ones."

"That's for me to decide," Elsie responded, shifting toward the back door.

Isabella hung her head low and nodded. "Good luck, Elsie."

"Good luck to you too, Isabella. I hope we don't cross paths time traveling again."

"Oh." Isabella chuckled. "Don't worry. We will."

***

Elsie found her way to The Courthouse. Not much of the decor changed from 34 A.R. to the last time she'd been inside it in 47 A.R. Murals of android judges lined the shadowy walls, and the deep wooden panels cascaded a subdued feeling with the lights dimmed.

"Madam," a voice interrupted.

Damn, I need to get better at hiding when I travel time, Elsie scolded herself.

She turned around and found a bright android with rainbow yellow scales. He looked pleasantly surprised to see her. She knew him—his name was Jimmy, and he worked at The Courthouse and at the prison. He shouldn't have known her now. Elsie was only seventeen in 34 A.R. She had yet to get her job working for the high judge, let alone finish school.

But Jimmy approached her like a long-lost friend and embraced her in a formal yet comfortable hug. His hug was an odd gesture for an android. "I'm glad to see you are doing well."

"Jimmy?" she asked, stepping out of his embrace.

"Yes. It's been a while. I'm so happy to see you again."

Elsie tilted her head to the side and ushered him with her farther down the hall. Being out in the open made her nerves twitch, and she felt like a schoolgirl caught with a forbidden piece of candy in her locker.

They made their way to The Records Department. The hallways weren't as grand as those in The Capitol Building because the courthouse was newer. Brighter lights lined the halls, and the carpet running through the middle of the floor showed exposed tiles to the left and right sides. Outside of a large office and a meeting room was a collection of scattered notary desks that lined the walls and an array of office supplies.

Elsie once worked at the desk directly to her left. A mural of the high judge hung above the desks, and his soft muted silver-blue scales illuminated in the bright lights. Placing her palm flat against the manufactured wood, Elsie felt a surge spark through her at a memory of her first interaction with Colin.

His presence was overwhelming even in the late hour. Elsie was on after-hours duty that particular day, agitated that she drew the short straw again for the task that was supposed to be shared equally among all junior notaries. Her tattoo itched, freshly blended into her skin only days before by her tattoo artist to cover up the tiny scar, the barely noticeable imperfection. When Colin reached her desk, she instantly stumbled. Elsie didn't recall having an appointment scheduled for the governor.

And surely, he'd have an appointment.

Colin had pulled out his device and placed it on the sharing drive. Elsie's eyes grew wide, but she tried to hide her shocked emotion from him. The document scanned on her screen was a marriage license to that famous scientist she went to high school with: Julie Walsh. Elsie counted to five in her head before grabbing her notary stamp and pressing down to solidify the pages.

Colin time traveled with that document, Elsie realized, remembering Julie's confusion on June 23rd. *Colin asked me to obtain Julie's signature for a different legal document. Then he must have lifted it and placed it here.* The former governor's stealth and illicit acts fascinated Elsie. He moved with a sliver, a bright ease with such a fierce amount of confidence. *The repercussions for him never even crossed his mind.*

Elsie looked over at Jimmy, his vibrant scales bright and beautiful. They mesmerized her for a moment, and she forgot why she even came to The Records Department.

"Have I visited you before?" she asked. Elsie was new to time travel, unaware of all the ins and outs. But something in Jimmy's casual response and blind willingness to follow her around provided her with the insight she needed without asking the question.

"Oh yes," Jimmy said with a smile and a shimmer of neon across his enchanting scales. "Several times."

Elsie looked away, almost forgetting that she came here for a specific purpose: to creep into the Ludewings' legal records and see if she could find any leverage to hand over to Don Jr. in the future so that he'd stop bullying Julie and his legislative aide would settle down.

"How are you doing?" Jimmy asked when Elsie didn't respond. "And how is Commissioner Jones?"

Elsie stiffened at the mention of the commissioner's name. She and Jones worked closely together and she considered him an ally, but the casualty of Jimmy's question made her feel faint.

"Commissioner Jones is doing well," Elsie said, her mind racing as a sinister idea popped inside it. "Can I ask a favor?"

Jimmy chuckled, clasping his hands together. "You always do."

"Oh." Elsie's cheeks flushed bright red. "I'm sorry."

"Don't apologize. I'll always be loyal to you."

Elsie couldn't understand why, but she would take any supporter she could get. She grabbed a piece of cardstock and a pen from the table. Pulling the bracelet out of her bag, she carefully wrapped it in tissue and secured the contents inside a small cardboard box.

"I need you to deliver this to Don Jr. Ludewing as soon as possible."

Jimmy's sparkling yellow scales took the box from Elsie, and his scaly lips turned upward into a menacing smile.

"Anything for you, Madam."

PART SIX

The Present

"Knowledge is dangerous. Once you know something, you can't get rid of it. You have to carry it. Always."
—Samantha Shannon

Chapter 22
Mick

The COLI*GO office building bustled with scrambling researchers and hasty business executives. Excitement filled the air with a heavy sense of optimism: The woman that the company employees believed in, admired, and cared for now sat in a coveted seat in The Legislature.

Mick picked up his pace in the laboratory, desiring the confines and silence of his cubicle. His reprise was short lived as the towering sight of Dr. Peter Schneider turned the corner. Mick hung his head, hoping to avoid his boss's gaze. Peter and Mick always butted heads in the research lab back when Peter managed the clinical trials. Mick hated the man because he knew the future—he knew of Peter's betrayals, his weakness, and his desire for success. He never trusted Peter after his journeys to the future, and he didn't care how aggravated Peter grew toward him.

Mick's grip on the tiny transfer device tightened in his pocket. A few weeks ago, Peter showed Mick the plans for a high-performing single-dose injection of the antidote. And he also showed him another version of the molecule: one with a greater success rate. Mick had listened as Peter tried passing off this version as another of the antidote.

He really thinks I'm stupid. Mick shook his head at the thought. Peter had shown Mick the antidote and the toxin. *And the toxin is better.*

The inverse of Julie's dream drug shimmered like glistening magic on the screen.

"Look how it binds," Mick had said to Peter. It was perfect. The drug didn't need any modifications—the mechanism of action worked flawlessly as a subcutaneous compound.

But the single-dose aspect was a frightening permanent solution to everlasting evil.

Stealing the contents of Julie's hard work bothered Mick, but he didn't trust Peter with Julie's invention, especially after all the back-and-forth communication between him and the Garcias. Mick needed Julie to suspect Peter and his wrongdoings to fully expose him.

Hanging back in the laboratory that evening, Peter waited until the lights dimmed and the prestigious scientists and researchers went home. He had access to the 101st floor, something most weren't granted. Peter's password-protected device was easy enough to hack into. Mick initially debated deleting everything instead of stealing it. Julie kept all her documentation elsewhere—she was meticulous and careful. Peter was the one who had grown sloppy in his years on the business side of COLI*GO. The scientist in him faded away little by little each day. But he needed proof that his intentions here were valid, that they were honest. Mick transferred the files onto his drive and then deleted them from Peter's machine, the device now free of the toxin and its taboo magic.

Ever since, Mick avoided Peter like the plague.

"Taylor!" Peter shouted—a nickname Mick loathed. Something felt grimy about the insinuation that he was part of the club, a member of Peter's inner circle, when in reality, Peter set Mick up for failure multiple times at COLI*GO.

Mick halted and slowly turned around. There was no point in hiding or pretending he didn't hear Peter's booming voice.

Peter was an attractive man, and the overconfidence he portrayed indicated his knowledge of the power of persuasion. He stood about six feet tall with the muscular, lean frame of a runner. Mick matched him in height, but time travel wore him ragged. With bony limbs protruding awkwardly from his body, his frail arms wavered with no sense of physical strength.

"Yes?"

Peter clasped his hand on Mick's shoulder, squeezing roughly. Mick's eyes squinted shut in slight pain. Peter's face had hollowed out during the last couple of weeks. His hair appeared slightly thinner, and a shimmer of gray freckled his otherwise dirty blonde hair.

Fine lines spread across Peter's forehead—a premonition of future time travel.

"I want you to lead the team for the new antidote. And I would like to employ your help on recreating the asset with Dr. Walsh with the following formulation." Peter transferred an unfamiliar file from his device to Mick's.

Mick's eyes widened. He and Julie mostly communicated through time travel, and the last time they interacted in the present had been a trip to The Island. Mick insisted on visiting Dr. Isabella Garcia—an unlikely ally of his.

Over the last few months, he noticed a stark difference in himself. Along with his dry skin and wrinkles, jitters ripped through him. When the shaking started, Mick couldn't control his physical actions with any level of certainty, the episodes lasting anywhere from thirty seconds to five minutes. Time travel posed nasty side effects on the body, but these recent intrusions differentiated from the norm. He wondered if a microchip was placed inside his brain— an intrusion from the future. Mick traveled to the past and the future so often that he lost track. He no longer logged the number of trips in his journal. His addiction grew worse with each venture.

"You showed me two single-dose candidates. What happened to those? The one looked nearly perfect, if I'm recalling correctly. Why would we need this incorporated?"

Peter's grip tightened on Mick's shoulder before releasing.

"This has more data and is actually formulated," he said, fidgeting. "It just needs some final touching up. Julie will help you."

Mick pushed his glasses up the bridge of his nose and studied Peter further. He desperately wanted to make amends with Julie, and they at least worked toward that in the last few months. But he doubted he would receive a warm welcome from the woman he once considered his best friend. She wasn't immune to Mick's extensive knowledge of the past and the future. Withholding the truth of Colin's assassination would only ruffle her feathers further. Mick avoided Julie since June 23rd even though she needed friends and love more than silence. The thought of lying to her, the thought of knowing who pulled the trigger but being unable to reveal the truth, strained Mick.

"We must keep this under wraps. The governor shouldn't be spending too much time at COLI*GO; she should be solely at The Capitol Building."

"Okay, when would you like for me to start?"

"As soon as possible, but I need you to report any time Julie pushes you to revert to the original antidote formulation."

Mick's eyebrow raised at the informality Peter showed the woman he once cared about, the woman who shared the peculiarities of time travel with him. Julie was a good friend—too forgiving, too kind.

And that is what will truly kill her in the end if she's not careful, Mick thought, images of It looming over Julie's dying body in the wintertime woods a vivid, horrible memory. *If she doesn't escape this dimension.*

***

A message from Isabella appeared on Mick's slightly outdated device. Her request for him to stop by FACERE at the end of the day created a bit of suspicion, but Mick trusted the surgeon.

When he entered FACERE, he wandered for a few minutes before heading to the check-in security desk. The building was mostly empty, except for a small crew of androids re-painting the walls and polishing the floors. His footsteps echoed loudly in the large ceiling lobby, but the greeter at the desk smiled politely in Mick's direction.

"Are you Mr. Mick Taylor?" she asked in an even tone.

"Yes."

"Dr. Isabella Garcia is ready to see you. The elevators are around the corner. Once you get in, press the L button. That will take you to the laboratory spaces. Dr. Garcia will meet you by the doors." She handed Mick a visitor badge. Mick's shaky hands clasped the plastic card with as much strength as he could muster. He felt one of his jittery attacks developing and took a deep breath—counting to ten with closed eyes before stepping through to the elevators.

When the elevator doors opened, a familiar but unexpected face greeted him.

"Hello, Mick."

"Anna."

She shushed a small giggle and straightened to compose herself. Dr. Anna Garcia looked like her sister but held a stockier pose and a shorter hairstyle. Both Garcia women studied surgery at young ages while attending The University, but Anna skipped grades and completed classes at a faster pace than her sister. Isabella never ended up practicing, but Anna took a role at The City's morgue as the chief medical examiner immediately after her schooling.

Mick never expected to find her at a place like FACERE.

The last time he and Anna spoke, he'd nearly shoved her into an elevator at COLI*GO. Anna had been tasked by Peter to uncover the identity of the person aiding The Supreme in the creation of posse hominems.

Mick was a terrible liar—he knew about Isabella's involvement intimately and didn't want to risk slipping any information to her nifty, quick-witted sister.

"Don't worry, Isabella will meet us inside."

Mick followed the younger Garcia sister down the hall and took in the surroundings. The tiled floor resembled that of a hospital, and large double doors with the words "Restricted Access" in bright red letters shadowed the walls.

Commissioner Jones and The City's police force raided FACERE at the end of June, but by the looks of the building, Mick felt far removed from the aftermath. No blood or silver liquid stained the floors, the doors, or the walls. No broken windows or chipped paint.

A large set of heavy doors automatically opened when Anna swiped her badge. The room's ceiling extended several stories, and big empty tubes lined the enormous space.

Mick stopped walking and turned around in a full circle to fully consume his surroundings. Dr. Isabella Garcia was perched over a workbench in the opposite direction. Her head peeked out beside the device she was intently staring at moments ago.

"I'm glad you made it, Mick," she said in her enchanting, smooth voice.

Isabella was both striking and intriguing. Her presence entranced Mick each time he was in it. Her small frame added to her attractiveness. Even with his skinny body, Mick towered over her. A bright red shade painted Isabella's lips, and her long luminous eyelashes flickered against her tanned skin.

Mick looked at her device and the contraption beside it. The machine consisted of various tubes, and both a red substance and a silver one coursed through the various lines jetting in and out. A sinking feeling coursed through Mick's stomach: This was human blood and android blood.

With light fingers, Mick tapped the glass containers. Isabella smiled while Anna smirked at his curiosity.

"I was curious when you asked for my assistance," Mick said, looking over at Isabella.

She smiled a large white grin.

"I've been thinking . . . All your notes on time travel and the effects on the human body really fascinate me." She moved closer to Mick and peered inside the machine he previously observed. "I wondered if there was a way to create unique androids through blood."

"Unique androids?"

Anna approached Mick on the other side. For the first time in their interactions together, he didn't feel animosity or annoyance. Concern replaced those previous feelings.

"When I was looking into the lower lab at COLI*GO and investigating the posse hominem project, I discovered something horrifying."

Mick pushed his glasses back up his face.

"Time travel works for humans because blood is unique and it possesses our DNA," Anna continued.

Mick nodded—he had spent his entire academic and professional career, most of his life, studying blood. He knew nearly everything about the concocting liquid that coursed through his veins.

"Well," Anna said, looking up at him with large bright eyes, "androids are uniquely identified through their microchip in their processor. Otherwise, their organs, the silver viscous that runs through their veins to keep their body functioning, and even their scales, are not uniquely identifiable."

"Exactly," Mick interrupted, "which is why they cannot use the time travel device."

"So, the only thing stopping an android from taking out their microchip and inserting it into a new android—a new host—is that someone would need to perform the action for them if it couldn't be done remotely. But if it couldn't be done remotely . . . why does Celine O'Connor possess a dashboard of all posse hominems in her home?"

Fear that Mick kept buried deep in his chest exploded. He had never pondered this possibility before. His mind raced to where he assumed Anna would go next: The Supreme.

She was interested in time travel for her own strategic reasons. Learning about the future and the past exhilarated the android leader. But Mick assumed she pursued her mission of posse hominems not in the hopes to "unite" society as she claimed—rather, The Supreme wanted to create a species of androids that could travel time. He never imagined that the microchips in the body of humans could ever be replaced with android microchips.

"Are you saying that The Supreme planned on taking microchips from androids and implanting them into human hosts?" An odd sense of relief left his body by expelling the words out loud.

Isabella nodded slowly.

"She had me insert a blank microchip into Julie's brain. The Supreme told me it was because she wanted to test out Bluetooth technology." Isabella clasped her hands together and let out a large sigh. "But now I wonder . . . Did she plan on migrating her microchip to Julie's remotely? Did she desire to assume Julie's identity? And what is to stop her from doing that to another posse hominem? Or another android?"

Mick's eyes grew wider, and he gripped the edge of the table beside him tightly to steady himself.

"What are you suggesting?" he asked, unsure whom to point the question toward.

"Well," Isabella said, her manicured fingers tapping against the glass tubes in front of her, "if androids have more unique identifiers, then that would solve the problem. The issue is, human blood typically is ridiculed with various components that don't work well with the silver liquid required. The silver liquid cleans out android organs, making androids last longer than humans if we program as such. But time travelers, their blood has a unique binding. That's what makes us all so invincible to everyone else. I'm trying to harness that advancement into new android blood technology, linking their blood to their microchip. And while testing the equation on my own blood is great, I need more subjects. I need to validate this."

Isabella turned and faced Mick with a serious glare.

"I need the original time traveler's blood."

Chapter 23
Commissioner Jones

<u>July 23rd, 47 A.R.</u>

The corkboard now looked like madness. Various color strings pinned from pictures to notes in a nonsensical fashion. This puzzle reminded Jones of when he first started investigating The City's infamous serial killer nearly five years ago.

A large red "X" wavered across Mick's face. Mick had not assassinated Governor Colin O'Connor. While time travel muddled alibies, Mick was not at the scene of the crime. He had been too busy playing with the past and visiting Melanie O'Connor, a secret in which Mick confided to Jones in the darkness of their home.

Jones shook his head, toying with his own feelings of disappointment and uncertainty. He loved Mick. He admitted so to him. And Mick was trying . . . He wanted to make a difference. Jones longed for the good in humans, looking for it at every corner and with every chance he had.

Another "X" also marked Julie's face. She'd been beside Colin, and regardless of her ability to travel time, Mick reassured him he could trust his best friend. Julie was more ruthless than she let on, but killing wasn't in her nature.

Peter's photo remained untouched, along with Elsie's, Celine's, and Isabella's. Jones didn't like the idea of Celine or Isabella killing Colin. Elsie still confused him. Peter made sense.

But wouldn't that be too easy? Jones wondered.

He sat at his desk and reviewed his notes before typing a quick message to Anna. He was losing her again. She handed in her two-week notice without being able to look Jones in the eyes. When he pressed her for reasoning, she shook her head.

"I can't do this anymore, Jones. Death consumes me too

frequently. I feel its essence growing on my skin, infecting my heart, and morphing my thoughts," she had said.

The shooter's location was easily found the next morning after scouting the area around The Capitol Building and using recording devices from the local area. A coffee shop occupied the first floor, and on the next few levels were various abandoned apartments. A developer had recently purchased the building and planned on renovating the outdated living quarters into something more modern. Now the builder would be stuck with a "ruined" unit, one that would draw attention from true crime chasers and conspiracy fanatics.

The remnants from the weapon coated the windowsill, and the two bullet casings rested neatly on the floor. The shooter took no time to clean up after themselves but wore the correct equipment, leaving nothing identifying behind. No hair, no traceable DNA.

"Commissioner Jones." An android with violet scales knocked on his door. Jones looked up from his desk with a raised brow. "Ballistics found a hit on the weapon."

The scraping of his metal chair sounded loudly as he stood. Jones met the detective halfway across the room and grabbed the slender device containing the results. He scrunched his face as he read the words on the screen and looked up at his detective with a rapidly shaking head. The detective averted his eyes and nodded.

"This is correct. We believe the gun belonged to Governor Colin O'Connor."

"What?" Jones placed the report down more forcefully than he intended, nicking the corner of the device. His eyes scanned the page for a third time, capturing all the information into his processor.

An antique rifle was used in the shooting, a hunting weapon. There were only a few of its kind left in circulation: one in a museum, two out in The Countryside registered to a prominent farmer, and one of which belonged to Colin O'Connor.

The report included a list of all of Governor O'Connor's weapons. Most were antiques, inherited from his father and his father's father before that. Ammunition had never been purchased by the governor, but his father secured rounds over twenty years ago for his hunting weapons. Jones absorbed the notes in more detail: Colin had the guns moved to his address in The City ten years ago, and previously, the guns resided at the O'Connors' Oceanside address.

"Do we know for a fact that the others weren't used?" Jones asked, referring to The Countryside farmer and the museum owner.

The detective nodded. "Both check out and claimed that they don't use these weapons anymore. The farmer said his are considered family heirlooms at this point. The one on display at the museum in The Bay is still there, still intact. It hasn't been moved in nearly fifteen years."

Jones felt his breathing slow, and he gripped the edge of his desk to steady himself.

Time travelers were invincible when killing themselves. Julie was living proof of this, and Mick had ventured into those waters too. The memories of this in-depth, dark admission shook Jones's processor, and he blinked rapidly to push them aside and concentrate on the task in front of him.

"Thank you, Detective," Jones said and ushered the android out of his office. Jones grabbed his red marker and walked over to the board, drawing a large circle before backing away.

***

Celine O'Connor's eyes darkened at the sight of Jones on the doorstep of the townhouse. She looked down the street twice before letting him inside. He was used to Julie's warm embrace when Jones was here, not this cold, unwelcoming presence.

"Commissioner?" Celine asked, closing the door behind them. "Can I help you? Julie isn't here. She's in some meetings at The Capitol Building."

"I'm sorry to come over unannounced, but I have a lead on your brother's assassination," Jones said, eyeing to see if Julie really was hiding somewhere in the charming, historic home. He let out a sigh of relief, knowing she wasn't truly here. "The weapon used was registered in your brother's name."

Celine tilted her head to the side and let in a sharp breath.

"I'm not sure how that's possible."

Jones contemplated how abrupt and curt he should be with Celine. He barely knew her and took a step away from her, capturing all of her in his line of vision. Her biometrics were elevated, her heart beating a bit faster than normal, so he had caught her off guard.

"Colin traveled time," Jones started, and Celine's eyes grew wide. "I know about time travel, Ms. O'Connor. That's why I came alone, without any other detectives."

Silence suffocated them, and Celine shifted her weight from one side of her foot to the other.

"Are you saying my brother killed himself?"

"I'm not ruling it out. What I need to do is confiscate the firearm from the home and test it for fingerprints."

Celine nodded, and her eyes shot over to the grand wooden staircase.

"Okay, I'll show you where he kept them."

Jones and Celine walked up three flights of stairs, pausing between the floors in uncomfortable quietness. The layout of the home was familiar to Jones. He often slept on the large chaise lounge in the master bedroom while Julie slumbered, curled up in a ball, in the large king sized bed. She couldn't stand being alone in the house, insisting that, if no one was home, Jones come over or her security detail bring her to her tiny studio apartment in The Bay. None of the android guards liked this option—the space was too small for all of them.

"Which weapon was it? Colin inherited all our father's guns when he passed away," Celine said, breaking their silence as they approached the third floor.

"A hunting rifle," Jones answered casually, not wanting to confirm the specific weapon with her. According to the report, Colin was the unlucky owner of several hunting rifles that once belonged to his father.

"I see . . ."

They reached Colin's study, and Celine opened the door. The room was pristine and neat, the way Colin always kept it. A large bookcase filled the circular corners of the room, and an elegant mahogany desk with a large leather chair was situated on the one end with a window behind them. Jones peered out the window to a perfect view of the carriage house. On the other side, a large wooden case with golden engraved leaf patterns was positioned stately against the wall.

Celine walked over to the case, looking at Jones for a suspecting moment, and then punched in a security code.

The doors clicked and popped open slightly. Celine pulled back the doors and stepped aside.

Inside the gun safe, various vintage weapons lined the walls. One spot lay bare, the hunting rifle Jones was looking for clearly missing.

How convenient. Jones rested his hands on his hips in disappointment.

"Who knows the code to the safe?"

Tears burst from the corners of Celine's eyes. She walked over to Colin's desk, grabbed a tissue, and dotted her face with light pressure.

"I'm sorry," she muttered softly before answering, "myself, Colin, The Supreme, and Isabella. I'm not sure if Julie knew the code or not. There's a lot about her relationship with Colin that I was left in the dark about until recently."

Jones took out his device and tried ignoring Celine's tasteless comment about Julie. He captured photographs of the barren spot inside the gun safe and considered the other weapons and ammunition. The log was lengthy, taking him a bit of time to read. Celine stood patiently, small sniffling sounds resonating behind Jones as he worked.

"Can I share something with you, Commissioner?" Celine asked while Jones finished up his accounts.

"Of course."

Celine walked toward the door and poked her head out into the hallway. She shifted back and closed the door, walking back and forth between Colin's desk and the gun cabinet.

"I'm sorry, it's just that Emilia—I mean, The Supreme—is down the hall, as you know."

Jones nodded, another secret he didn't enjoy keeping from The City and his detectives. The Legislature had a hefty reward out for The Supreme's location, and she endangered all of them by staying in The City: Jones, Celine, Julie, and Elsie.

"Well." Celine paused, gripping the edge of Colin's desk. "The Supreme invited Dr. Peter Schneider over the morning of Colin's assassination. They met in private, here, in the study, to talk about the pharmaceutical asset he and Dr. Walsh were investigating at COLI*GO."

Jones's eyebrows lifted at this new piece of information. He pondered Celine's admission. She hadn't mentioned this before in the statement she provided him right after Colin's death when she met him and Julie in the emergency room.

Peter hated Colin . . . I'm sure Celine knew this. And The Supreme is always after some sick sense of control. I can't figure out how The Supreme plans to execute her win, but she's still plotting it, I'm sure of that.

Jones eyed Celine. Her biometrics revealed a quickening pulse thumping through her veins, and her gaze refused to focus in on one place. Jones quickly looked away—he didn't want her catching on that he had these abilities with his eyes. The Supreme had the same skill after her time at FACERE, and his nights here led him to believe the android leader and the O'Connor woman were more entangled than either was willing to formally admit.

What game is Celine playing? And whose side is she on?

"Thank you for that information," Jones said, nodding toward the door. "I'll bring Peter in for questioning. I think once I've found the weapon, we'll have more answers."

"Thank you," Celine said, letting out a large sigh. She opened the door and ushered Jones down to the main floor. "Do you think you're getting close?"

Jones pulled at the corners of his long sleeves. It was too hot to wear them, but he was glad he did—his scales shimmered an emerald green similar to the color of Julie's engagement ring.

"Very."

***

The cemetery provided a sense of calm, with the bright pink and orange vivaciously looming in the sky. The lawn was recently cut, sharp blades of green grass providing a crisp scent in the air. Jones slowed his pace, and his eyes rested on the gravestones.

Colin's name was carved elegantly with his birth year and death below, 4 A.R. to 47 A.R. Forty-three years of age. The words "Esteemed Governor—the one who fought for justice and equality until the end" stared back at Jones. No mention of his family, his wife, or his friends.

Jones continued walking. As tempting as it was to stand there and wait for nothing to happen, Jones was on a mission. He had a purpose to roam The City's unnerving graveyard alone. He snaked his way on the path leading down the hill. The top sections were reserved for old bloodline families only. Weaving through the middle, Jones paused and looked at a small headstone beside him. He bent down and rubbed the edges soothingly, a slight tear threatening the corner of his eye.

"Loving wife and mother" marked the spot of Julie's mother. Jones nodded at Cynthia's headstone and leaned in closer.

"Give Julie the strength she needs," he said in a near-whisper before turning away. The sun was setting earlier, the longest day of the year having occurred a few weeks ago. Jones needed to hurry.

He continued down to the very bottom, his feet gradually leaving the inclined path and favoring a flat one. Turning to glance over his shoulder, Jones checked to make sure he was alone. He pushed open the iron-fence gate and closed it with care. This section of the cemetery was reserved for those found guilty of accused crimes and the prison's inmates. They were cornered off in their own section, not to mingle with the assumedly "pure" dead humans and androids resting elsewhere.

Mick admitting that Jeb Taylor was really a time traveled persona of himself horrified Jones. Jones remembered that day in the courtroom, how Jeb tried to flee in desperation when the high judge ruled he would see the death penalty but not for several years. Jeb's frantic eyes grew wide when he reached behind his body and revealed a tiny pocketknife. The room erupted into chaos, humans and androids stampeding out of the room. Jeb rushed for The Supreme with the knife steady in his hand. Jones pleaded with him to stop, to drop the weapon. Jeb didn't listen, and Jones shot him. The bullet was strategically aimed.

Jones had always been a good shot—probably one of the best. During his training at the police academy, he excelled in archery and at the gun range. His skills provided him with a special clearance on the force—the ability to use sniper weapons. Snipers were hardly needed, society remaining mostly violent free since The Resurgence.

But in the last year, insanity spread through The City's inhabitants like an infectious disease running rampant. Using a gun wasn't Jones's preferred method, but now in his career, he had shot and killed a few times: Jeb Taylor and two vigilantes who murdered a posse hominem in the park. Being an android, Jones was supposed to logically understand his duty and not need time to process any feelings as a repercussion of his actions. He couldn't ask for time off—no one was supposed to know how much he truly felt. But each of his kills surged powerfully through him. He would never forget these instances, no matter how hard he tried.

Jeb's gravestone was about one foot high with just his name carved into it. The Taylors didn't have any money; they were strapped for cash. The only way they'd been able to afford a headstone for their excommunicated family member was because Jeb had stored some money away in accounts from his art and illegal drug business.

Knowing the truths behind Jeb Taylor's unsavory acts made Jones shiver. Jeb was responsible for many of the kidnappings of humans who would later become posse hominems. Jeb was also the reason for a largely unregulated party drug ring and the occasional overdose in old bloodline families and those with newer wealth and connections. Mick was really the man behind that madness, which clouded Jones's list of confusing feelings for the man. The list continued growing each day, and Jones knew if he asked Julie for her advice, she'd tell him to back away.

"Jones, you deserve better," she had once said to him late in the night after she woke up from a nightmare and she asked him to distract her with some story. Jones didn't know how to make up stories, so he pulled a memory from their years at The University.

Jones hadn't realized he'd started crying s he told the tale of him, her, and Mick drunkenly getting themselves invited to a house party in The Hill, some very well-connected—but not old bloodline—

family. While they walked along the espionage toward the bridge connecting The River to the rest of The City, Mick bet Jones that he would grow an eleventh toe if he swam across the river. Julie had giggled as Mick stripped down to his underwear and splashed into the water. She yelled Mick's name, and he swam expertly across, waiting for them on the other side. Mick did not win his bet—he remained with only ten toes but did get a strange rash on his leg that took a trip to The University's medical center to subside.

Julie had introduced Mick and Jones to each other. Jones was Julie's friend from growing up—they attended school together, and she trusted him with all her secrets. Mick and Julie were both scientific nerds, hoping they would change the world with their inventions.

Little did they know.

Jones scanned the area to ensure the sun had set enough but that he wasn't trapped in complete blackness. Looking down at his bag, Jones pulled out his device.

"Don't worry, I'm here." Anna's voice startled Jones as she emerged from the shadows cast by a large elm tree.

In her hand, she carried two shovels. Jones extended his hand and grabbed the larger one.

When he had asked Anna to help him with this task, he feared she'd stop showing up right then and there. But Anna constantly surprised Jones: She had only nodded and asked what day and what time. He explained to her the information about time travelers and the invincibility of their bodies. Jones longed to trust Mick on this, and when he confronted Julie, she couldn't answer Jones's questions other than to say when she hit the bottom of the cliff, death pained her. Her end wasn't quick, her eyes flickering out of control, the feeling of several crushed bones around her. Julie's last memory was a sight of Colin, but then her eyes closed and stillness calmed her. When she opened her eyes, she was back in the woods on January 28th, 47 A.R.

"Thank you," he said to Anna.

"I've done a lot of crazy shit with you since we started working together," Anna said with a slight chuckle. "I figured on my last day, I should go out with the craziest bang."

Jones nodded and sliced into the ground. He pushed his foot on the shovel and unearthed the first bit of dirt. Anna was quick to follow suit, her hours at the gym paying off.

They dug.

Six feet felt like an eternity, but eventually, Jones and Anna hit the cheap wooden casket. They stared at each other, the sweat glistening on her skin, a similar excreted substance on his scales. Jones knelt in the dirt.

Anna's heavy labored breaths helped Jones concentrate as he gripped the lid of the casket. He closed his eyes and lifted the lid.

Jones wasn't sure what to expect. If Mick hadn't lied, if Mick was honest, there wouldn't be a body there. And that meant Jones really needed someone to confirm if Colin was time traveling. He'd need a time traveler, and one that he could trust, to confirm that Colin really wasn't dead but hiding. Otherwise, Jones would need to dig up Colin's grave.

Something Julie would never forgive me for if she found out.

"Jones? What do you see down there?" Anna's voice brought him back to reality.

Jones took a deep breath and opened his eyes. He couldn't see much in the darkness, even with the advanced android eyes he possessed. He reached for his device and shined the light forward. But when Jones peered inside the coffin, his biggest fear was confirmed.

It was empty.

Chapter 24
Elsie

<u>July 23rd, 47 A.R.</u>

Elsie ripped apart her apartment, throwing what little belongings she had on the floor. She couldn't find the first note Jeb Taylor had left for her. The second one, the letter from Julie, she always kept safely on her person.

"Where the fuck is it?" Elsie cursed, crumpling to the ground in defeat.

Back when Jeb gave her the note, she thought nothing of it. Why would anyone take interest in a bastard from an outcast old blood-line family? One that fell from society's purview? The note was filled with various riddles, everything written in a neatly typed text, not even handwritten.

Even Jeb averted his eyes from Elsie, unable to look at her head-on. His words felt like a distant memory, a hazy recollection of half-truths. Confirmation that someone had violated her body—that someone invaded the most personal part of her: her brain.

Jeb's appearance made her question her sanity. Sure, Elsie liked to have a good time. But she didn't partake in party drugs. She found her vice to be white wine—which she needed now, immediately. Thinking back, Elsie was lost when Jeb appeared. Understanding why her skin flaked, why headaches plagued her, and why nothing felt right provided a strangely reassuring answer.

I'm not crazy, she remembered thinking as Jeb explained posse hominems.

Jeb told her to keep the second note in a safe place—somewhere that her busybody mother wouldn't find. Elsie immediately placed the envelope in her underwear drawer. Roslyn was a nosy woman, but she dared not venture into her daughter's intimate life.

But the first note. The first note Elsie had wanted to burn. She didn't. She placed the note with the second one—she hadn't touched it then.

So why isn't it there with my ridiculously lacy undergarments? Elsie wondered with agitation.

Tears threatened the corners of her eyes, but she blinked quickly to keep them at bay. She refused to be a pawn in the middle of The Supreme's game. Her intentions of visiting the wretched android were meant for distraction. She could only hope the plan she wove together was strong enough to withstand such seasoned players.

A light knock interrupted Elsie's sulking, and she opened the door to find Julie Walsh's forced but still elegant smile.

"I'd welcome you in, but my place is a mess."

"Well," Julie said, her eyes taking in the disaster zone Elsie had made of her home, "you should see my place. There's half a year's worth of dust collecting on the coffee table. I need to forget about all this bullshit. I need a friend."

Julie took a seat at Elsie's kitchen table and leaned back with closed eyes.

"That I can help with."

Both Julie and Elsie grew up in The Monument, attending high school together. But their paths never really crossed until Colin—and The Supreme. Elsie was a troublemaker growing up, and inversely, Julie was a teacher's pet. Julie was always destined for The University, her intelligence a golden ticket that many nobody children yearned for. Elsie wouldn't have gotten in if it hadn't been her old bloodline lineage or that her mother attended. Not that Elsie wasn't smart—she just didn't care for homework or assignments.

Elsie sauntered into the kitchen and pulled out a bottle of white wine from her fridge. She met Julie at the kitchen table and gestured toward the bottle. Julie shook her head, so Elsie didn't push her.

More to ease my own worries. She brought over a bottle of water for Julie.

"So I'm perpetually surrounded by O'Connors for the rest of my life?" Julie said with a charming smile, nudging Elsie in the side.

"Did Colin tell you?" Elsie asked, taking a long sip of her Chardonnay.

"No, but he left the notarized paperwork and DNA sample to

prove you are his half-sister with the family attorney."

"Jeffries?"

"Yes."

"He reached out. I now own a boat."

"Apparently so." Julie grabbed Elsie's hand and squeezed it tightly. "Why haven't you invited me out on the water yet?"

Elsie laughed liberally, and Julie joined in. The sound was foreign. Elsie didn't remember the sound of Julie's laugh because she never heard it before. Julie was enticing in her yellow-painted kitchen, someone Elsie wanted as her friend.

And Elsie never wanted friends.

Julie and Elsie's lives moved so quickly since Colin's death, and the two hadn't had the time to embrace their odd friendship. Ease shifted through Elsie that Julie tried to relax, that Julie tried to escape her extreme grief with her.

She could have chosen Jones. But she picked me.

When Julie traveled time, she wrote long-winded messages to Elsie. Their friendship grew over loneliness. Julie from being stuck as a captive at Joel Kennsington's home and traveling to fix the antidote, and Elsie from having no friends in The Legislature and being in a new role she wasn't prepared for. Elsie believed Julie to be a posse hominem, another commonality that strung them together. Julie hadn't been forthcoming that her microchip was removed, but Elsie didn't blame Julie for being hesitant in fully trusting her.

"Can I say something inappropriate?" Elsie asked, giddy from her wine and high off the experience of Julie Walsh.

"I don't think if I said no that it would stop you."

Elsie playfully rolled her eyes at Julie. "It was nice to see you at COLI*GO. It suits you well, all the science, the business. I don't know how to explain it. But I felt oddly proud of you."

"That's where I belong," Julie agreed, sipping on her water.

"You look good at Colin's desk, though, too."

Julie's right eye squinted.

"Don Jr. thinks so anyway," Elsie tested.

"I know you said making him the Session speaker would push him out of the way in terms of an election, but I don't want that."

"Even if you're not going to run," Elsie said, taking another long sip of her wine, "I don't want Don Jr. as The Constituency's next governor. At least not yet. He's got his own quirks."

"So I've heard."

Elsie and Julie remained silent for a moment too long, and Elsie feared she'd spoken out of turn. But when Julie eyed the bottle of wine and sighed loudly, Elsie felt a shift in Julie.

"What I would do for a glass of that," Julie said, unscrewing the cap from her water bottle but not touching it. "You'll be a much better aunt than Celine."

Elsie's heart fluttered in her chest, and she grabbed Julie's hand.

"Oh," she said with an upturned brow, "so the rumors are true?"

There were no real rumors except for a rumbling from Don Jr.'s legislative aide. The woman was a catty girl, childish and immature. She had whispered to another representative's legislative aide that Julie was pregnant, and she wouldn't be surprised if it wasn't Colin O'Connor's child, especially considering how Representative Ludewing looked at the new governor.

Elsie had been furious, and a bout of jealousy coursed through her veins. She wasn't supposed to love Don Jr., and her feelings for him were nowhere near that level of intimacy. But she cared for the brute, much to her own feminine dismay.

Julie's head leaned back and gently hit the wall.

"This is such a mess."

Elsie nodded, glancing over at Julie. Her eyes didn't sparkle the same warm blue as normal, a tiredness washing over them. Elsie appreciated the authenticity of Julie's looks. Something nearly any woman in The City could relate to.

"Did Isabella Garcia remove your microchip?" Elsie asked after a few moments of comfortable silence. Julie didn't verbally respond but nodded, her fingertips trailing down her jagged silver scar.

"I can't decide if I hate or love this imperfection," Julie said with a tenderness in her voice. "This scar certainly gives me character. Colin . . . The scar didn't bother him. I feel like he almost loved the rawness of my marking. But that's also why I hate it. It makes me a bit tough, but I'm really not. I'm not ready to be ruthless when I know I must be."

"I know a great guy up a few blocks who does wonderful

tattoos to cover that up after whatever hot mess that is growing inside of you emerges. He went to school with us." Elsie touched her tattoo with a sense of appreciation.

"Joey?"

"Yes, how did you know?"

"He also did mine."

"Wait," Elsie said, loudly placing her wineglass on the wooden table. "Dr. Julie freaking Walsh has a tattoo?"

"It's nothing like yours."

Elsie tilted her head to the right, and her eyes nearly bugged out of her head.

"Julie, you little minx! I never would have known."

Julie stood with enthusiasm and lifted the left corner of her blouse up. An intricate strand of DNA snaked up her ribs with flowers and greenery gushing out. The colorful ink on her skin vibrantly stood out against her milky complexion. The tattoo was small but incredibly fitting.

But Elsie was quickly distracted by the rest of Julie's body: Scars violently littered her stomach.

One . . . two . . . three . . . Elsie rapidly counted to twenty-three.

She didn't mean to gasp, but the markings were truly horrific: a violation, an emotional outrage painted across her. A few weeks ago, Colin confided in Elsie that he took Julie to the woods outside The City and stabbed her. And after The Supreme's gift of the time travel device, Elsie suspected Colin's act against Julie wasn't his first. The names of the women over the past decade and beyond whom Jeb Taylor took the blame for flashed through her: Christine Hoek, Brittany McCarthy, Michelle Tenner, Jennifer O'Brien, Sophia Henderson, Jessica Hacket, Katherine Ryan, Amanda MacDonald, Kendra Washington, and Kathleen Murphy.

Julie Walsh was the only woman who got away—the only one to truly escape the confines of death.

An odd urge vibrated through Elsie, and she reached out toward Julie, her fingers lightly tracing the scars on her stomach.

Julie dropped the fabric of her shirt and backed away, unable to look Elsie in the face.

"It's okay, Julie," Elsie stammered, afraid she intruded on a secret. "Colin told me."

"I'm sorry. It's just that no one else has touched them, especially like that. Besides him."

"How could you forgive him?" Elsie didn't fear the answer Julie would likely provide, but she feared the truth of the urges existing within her, being linked to her half-brother.

"Colin . . . Colin faced many demons. He suffered a difficult trauma in his childhood, one that birthed a coping mechanism in his brain. Another personality. He separated good and evil in those personas. The struggle in his mind . . . I can forgive him for that. I did. I accepted him. All of him."

Elsie's body shook, and she grabbed her glass on the table with shaky hands.

"I have also done some terrible things," Elsie said, looking down and away from Julie. "I killed Paul McGuire when he threatened the safety of posse hominems."

Paul's murder was only two months ago. The sensation of hitting the vile man's head against his desk flashed through her memory. Not only did he believe androids didn't deserve the same rights as humans but also did he eye Elsie like a prized piece of meat the moment she entered his room. As Governor Colin O'Connor's legislative aide and secretary, she was sought after by many men—a reason she accused Don Jr. of several times—men who wanted to be close to power.

Elsie was attractive enough. Tall for a woman, with larger hands and an angled face. Her lean and muscular body was often mistaken for a slight curve under the right outfits. Her smile was charming, persuasive, and even fascinating. But that didn't give any of them an excuse to feel like they owned her. That they could do whatever they wanted to her with no repercussions.

Elbowing Paul in the nose worked wonders, distracting the man while blood burst from his nostrils. Elsie trained in kickboxing and knew a thing or two about self-defense. As Paul McGuire stumbled backward, Elsie reached for the syringe that was filled with the tranquilizer, one that Colin had given her. She jabbed the needle in Paul's neck, pushing down on the plunger with an unnecessary amount of force.

He stumbled to the floor.

Elsie had stared at him for a while, towering over his body with one foot planted firmly on the left side of his waist and the other hovering over his neck. She pushed her high-heeled shoe down against the skin of his throat, the bubbling noises erupting between his unconscious lips. His death was anything but peaceful.

She wasn't sure what possessed her to walk over to his desk and pull out the tiny pocketknife he kept inside the shallow drawer. Stabbing Paul didn't mean anything to her—choking him, making him gasp for air unknowingly, brought a forbidden glee.

"Colin did what he needed to do," Elsie said with newfound confidence. "I have and I will continue to make similar decisions if they are best for society—for The Constituency, for humans, androids, and posse hominems. I want to run, Julie. I want to run for governor."

***

Elsie thought about knocking on Peter's door but picking his lock was too enticing. He lived in an older building in The Bay with large limestone entry steps and intricate crown molding. From the window, a historical church cast its shadows on the building and shops, and restaurants lined the quaint one-way street.

Snooping was one of Elsie's favorite pastimes, and Peter's small apartment provided ample entertainment for this guilty pleasure. His bed was unmade, but the rest of his home was clean and tidy. The refrigerator housed a carton of milk, a wilted bag of spinach, and a package of string cheese—unsurprising, considering his trash can was filled with takeout containers.

Two small vials rested on his nightstand. A metallic tinge to the liquid inside made Elsie pause in a trance. An odd sensation that she was supposed to know what this was overcame her.

I know this isn't the antidote or the toxin. Elsie scratched her head. *Why is this familiar?*

The need to pocket one of the vials and escape without confronting the confusing scientist overwhelmed Elsie, but Peter kept this pharmaceutical tucked away in his bedroom and out of sight for a reason—it was valuable.

The cardstock beside the other vial also looked oddly familiar. Picking it up with her large hands, Elsie flipped it over to find a neatly handwritten message in a script she was all too familiar with.

Dear Peter,

On June 23rd, please bring this box and its contents to 15 Beacon Street. Do not open the box. Do not tell anyone about the box.

You will know what to do. I trust you'll make the correct decision.

"Can I help you, Elsie?" Peter's voice echoed behind her.

Elsie flinched and turned to face him. He was a handsome man, and her mixed feelings from their night together filled her heart. She coughed and gingerly placed the note back on his nightstand.

"I didn't like how the meeting with Governor Walsh went."

"So you decided to break into my home and go through my things?" He raised a brow in her direction and walked to her.

Elsie inched closer to him, the crisp smell of his cologne making her nostrils flare in delight. The sound of her own heart beating rapidly vibrated through her ears, and she reached out to touch Peter but he backed away.

Rejection stung, and Elsie shook her head, trying to snap herself out of these odd feelings. Memories of their passionate embrace raced through her mind and clouded her vision. Elsie's aggressive pursuit of Peter lingered awkwardly like an itchy sunburn, but sleeping with Peter was a mistake. From his physical response to Elsie, he thought their night together was an error, a onetime occurrence.

But why would he change his mind so quickly?

"I should have knocked or called," Elsie admitted, walking away from the dark shadows in Peter's bedroom. "I apologize. But that doesn't give you an excuse to act like I have cooties or something."

Peter rolled his eyes, and his cheeks flushed in bashful desire.

"Look, Elsie," he pleaded, grabbing her shoulder and turning her so that they faced one another. "I'm afraid of you."

His words granted Elise pause—she couldn't understand why.

Normally, anyone claiming they feared her was considered a compliment, but from Peter it felt more like a stab in the heart.

"Why are you afraid of me?"

Peter's eyes grew wide, and he bit his bottom lip. His stance straightened, and worry crossed his big brown eyes.

"You really don't know?"

Elsie shook her head and stomped loudly into the living room. After several moments, Peter met her in the main area of his apartment and combed his fingers through his dirty blonde hair.

"You kill me in the future," Peter said softly, unable to look at her. "But you don't seem like yourself. You were possessed. Acting as if you were someone else."

Peter and Elsie embraced the horrific silence separating them. Elsie swiftly hid her shaking hands behind her back.

"Are you really here to talk about Julie?" Peter finally broke their silence.

"Sort of."

Elsie sat on his couch and pulled out the vial she had stolen and placed in her pocket. Peter lunged for her, but Elsie was quick enough to pull her hand away.

"You can't take that."

"What is it?"

"You really don't know," Peter said as more of a statement than a question. "This is from that metal briefcase with the vials of Dr. Filipe Garcia's drug. You're the one who told me to give it to Isabella and Anna for safekeeping."

Chapter 25
Julie

A loud knock sounded on the governor's office door.

"Julie," Elsie said, peeking her head in. "Representative Ludewing is here. He's being rather . . . persistent."

"Let him in," Julie said and stood to greet her new Session speaker.

Don Jr. wore a stylish navy three-piece suit with a silk tie and intricate brown dress shoes. His smug smile made Julie's breathing unsteady in an alarming manner. There was something about the governor's seat that didn't settle correctly in Julie's bones. She was always on edge. Navigating the rocky waters of COLI*GO's internal politics made sense to her—this was completely foreign.

In her first few weeks as acting governor, she'd only been able to successfully appoint Dr. Isabella Garcia as head of FACERE. No matter how much she pushed The Representatives of The Androids to reach a resolution on the lack of a supreme, no one budged. The Representatives of The People didn't seem to care—they secretly didn't want an android leader, moving along with the status quo of Julie being the only government leader. Some spoke of never appointing another supreme at all—all talks from the Humanizers. The threat of rebellion lingered on android lips while they fluttered through the halls.

Colin would never forgive her if The Resurgence uprising occurred again. And Julie would never forgive herself either if she couldn't help The Constituency find another android leader until the selected FACERE android was of age.

Don was likable compared to his predecessor, Representative Joel Kennsington, but Julie felt the stringent worry that Colin faced in schmoozing the Session speaker. Both were incompetent men who filibustered The Legislature rather than moved it along in a steady course of action.

"Hello, Dr. Walsh," Don said with a bright toothy grin.

"Representative Ludewing, what can I do for you today?" Julie asked, settling back into her seat. Everything tired her lately, both mentally and physically.

Don kicked his one foot across his thigh and settled into the chair opposite her desk.

"I want to know when you'll officially announce that you're not running for the gubernatorial election. And I want to be the first to know who you'll endorse."

Julie tilted her head up and kept her glare confident and proud. The election committee announced earlier in the week that a free and fair election across The Constituency would occur on October 25th, and the new governor would transition into the office by January 28th, 48 A.R.

That particular date unsettled Julie, but she pushed it aside as a daring coincidence. The timing couldn't be any worse. January 28th haunted Julie's mind, the visions of her blood soaking the snow and her legs running clumsily but hurriedly through the barren woods on that same date this year. A one-year anniversary of a horrid day.

And it was also her due date.

"What makes you think I won't run?" Julie asked, her tone solid and slightly brazen. She smiled warmly at the representative, allowing for a small flirtatious sparkle in her eye.

Julie was not ready for love. She wasn't sure she ever would be. Colin meant everything to her—and then when she spent her time with It, she knew for sure that he was her soulmate. But charm helped Colin move things along, and Julie wasn't above taking a page out of his book if it pleased her.

Don Jr. chuckled and scratched at the stubble on his chin. His light and dreamy brown eyes softened, and he leaned closer to the desk.

"You don't like it in his seat. I can tell how uncomfortable you feel. It's spread all across your face, the tightness in your cheeks, the wandering of your eyes."

Julie didn't respond. His claim wasn't incorrect—Julie felt

impossible in this role, only trying her best to honor Colin's wishes and those of The Constituency who believed in her. Humans, androids, and posse hominems.

"I wonder if part of the reason you don't like sitting in Colin's seat has more to do with him than his job as governor." Don's left eyebrow shot up.

He rose from his chair and walked toward the large floor-to-ceiling windows overlooking the courtyard. They were nice features, ones that Julie found herself zoning out to when there was too much clouding her mind. But Don Jr. didn't admire the flora and the greenery. He stared longingly at The Supreme's office across the way. Empty and collecting dust.

"When I was young, I let them play me for a fool once." Don glanced back at Julie, his finger pointing toward the window. "The first time I ran for office, back in 35 A.R., your late husband and I were not on good terms. We hardly spoke to each other."

"Why is that, Representative Ludewing?" Julie asked, curious as to why Colin would hate this man who sympathized with androids.

"I worked for him as a policy researcher in my early twenties and we got into a bit of a disagreement. I'll spare you the messy details, but it stemmed from a particular night out. Reckless, I'm sure. I don't really remember; we were all high on drugs I purchased from Jeb Taylor. I hastily quit my job the moment Colin raised his voice at me the next day. He told me I needed to obey him if I wanted a future in this building. I don't take strongly to controlling and domineering people, especially men."

Julie pushed her chair back and walked over to where Don stood. It'd been a while since she'd studied The Supreme's office. She only ever visited The Supreme at her office in COLI*GO. Colin also held an office there, but he rarely worked on the 101st floor and always insisted on Julie meeting with him here when she asked for his help to get the antidote back in front of Martin Borges and Celine O'Connor.

"I was surprised when Kathleen Murphy requested a meeting for Colin and me with my press secretary at the time." Don paused. "Jennifer O'Brien."

Julie flinched at the woman's name. She was a victim of The

City's serial killer.

Colin . . .

"Granted," Don continued with his cautionary tale, "I hired Jennifer because my father asked me to. I didn't realize she was a staunch Humanizer. It's an odd thing, really, being part of an old bloodline family. We desperately aim to please our parents. They hold so much authority, so much power over our lives because, in an instant, the trust we expected to receive upon their death is suddenly donated in full to charity or granted to a distant cousin. All because we pissed them off."

"Not to be rude," Julie said in a stern tone, "but is this monologue going anywhere? I have a very tight schedule."

Don recoiled from Julie's retort, but his suggestive smile crawled back into the corners of his full lips like a snake ready to devour its prey.

"Apologies, Dr. Walsh," he said, looking down at his hands before placing them in his pockets. "I think you know that Jennifer O'Brien is no longer with us. She was a victim of a gruesome murder. One that was never solved. Her death came from strangulation, but the killer didn't stop there. Oh, no. He stabbed her. Twenty-three times."

Julie's mouth tightened, and images of Colin's swift movements puncturing her own stomach appeared before her eyes. She'd imagined them only; Colin had drugged her before he took her into the woods and stabbed her. Julie had no recollection of that night and never intended to watch that scene before her own eyes through time travel.

"I'm so sorry." The words tasted bitter on Julie's lips. She didn't mean them.

Don Jr. removed his hands from his pockets and grabbed Julie's tiny hands with his own. When he pulled away from her, he left a golden-chain bracelet with tiny pearls behind. The sound of Julie's rapidly beating heart pounded in her ears.

Impossible. She looked down at the trinket, the sick trophy. She'd seen this before. Colin kept all the jewelry from his kills in the drawer in the laundry room. Julie had seen the pieces herself, touching the cool metals and shiny stones out of curiosity.

"You see, when Colin came to The Legislature in February and admitted to killing Kathleen Murphy, he provided the confirmation I needed. I wasn't the only one over the years who was bullied through violence. Joel Kennsington lost his legislative aide to that sick bastard and so did Representative Charlton even though he's now long since retired. We've all made deals with Colin O'Connor, but more importantly, we all made unsavory deals with The Supreme around the same time. Her words still haunt me, the words she spoke after Colin and I made amends and he offered to endorse me in my first election. Right before he killed Jennifer, she said, 'We'll do just about anything in our power to make sure you get a seat in The Legislature.' I was so naïve about what she truly meant. A couple of days after Jennifer's death, an android hand-delivered her bracelet to me with a cryptic note. 'The Supreme sends her regards.' I wasn't sure what that meant, but between her and Colin, killers have sat in these chairs for too long."

"I am not my husband," Julie said, looking up at Representative Ludewing with her large ocean-blue eyes. Her gaze captivated him but quickly dissipated.

"No, you're too kind. You're too likable. And that's an even larger threat. You must support the correct candidate for this role. I am supportive of my old bloodline friends, but . . . not if they're killers."

"I think it's time you leave, Representative Ludewing."

Don chuckled and looked at the bracelet in Julie's hand. "Keep it. It might look good on you, like how that emerald ring does."

***

Julie felt a foreign sensation in Colin's home. She used to long being there, abandoning her expensive studio apartment in The Bay—one that she used all of her sign-on bonus for a down payment on. There had been a warmth in the townhouse that made her feel giddy, and the home always smelled of the wooden, smoky scent of Colin. Julie coveted their time here, the nights she spent with him, the dinners they cooked together, fires they lit in the expansive white brick chimney.

Celine drifted in and out of the house with no rhyme or reason, balancing her life between the O'Connor residence and the one she kept with Martin. The Supreme still hid in the confines of the brownstone, and Julie questioned how the android leader hadn't lost her processor by staying locked inside for weeks on end. Julie had nearly gone mad being a prisoner to Joel Kennsington earlier that winter and spring. Her confinement in Joel's house in The South caused her such pain that she made rash decisions, ones that included traveling to the past.

Julie promised herself she would keep the past as pure as she could, but she couldn't help the escape. She'd travel back in time and watch Colin, watch her father and her sister, Becky, and relive the most wonderful memories she had of her and her mother.

Emilia couldn't time travel. She was truly a captive to the town-home. The Supreme's presence didn't bother Julie, but after a long day, she didn't want to walk through the ostentatious townhome. Elsie gripped Julie's hand tightly when she dropped her off, promising to keep her device by her nightstand if Julie needed her.

The smell of roasted chicken and a meaty steak cascaded from the kitchen and into the entryway. Julie's mouth watered while her stomach simultaneously turned. She followed the scent of a well-cooked meal all the way into the dining room where Celine's presence graced her. Celine sat straight in her chair, and a plate of food was situated in the setting beside her.

"Come," Celine said, pointing with her fork to the empty chair and full plate. "Join me."

Julie paused before making her way to the table. She and Celine hadn't spoken one-on-one since Jeffries shared Colin's will. And Julie had since contested it, sharing her secret with the O'Connor family attorney: She was pregnant, with her and Colin's baby.

An animosity lingered between the two strong-headed women, and Julie ventured that Jeffries informed Celine of Julie's condition.

"Are you experiencing morning sickness?" Celine asked after several moments of silence. Julie's hands held the utensils tightly in place. "I had the worst morning sickness in the very beginning, but it eventually went away."

"That doesn't really seem to bother me too much. I'm more akin to strong smells."

If Celine wants to act like she isn't furious with me, then so be it. Julie eyed the socialite with extreme care and caution. Celine never approved of Julie and Colin's relationship, only putting up with Julie because of her career capabilities. *I was an investment; I helped make her money. That's the only reason she respected me, not because her brother cared about me.*

"I was happy but surprised to hear the news from Jeffries. I'm sorry if you wanted to tell me, but I've been unapproachable. I'm not sure how to deal with all of this." Celine waved her arms around before grabbing Julie's forearm. She squeezed tightly with her fingertips and smiled a bit too brightly.

"I think we all are. Thank you, I was happy when I found out too," Julie stammered and looked back down at her food.

She hadn't been happy when she found out she was pregnant. Julie was equally horrified and terrified. She and Colin had always been careful. He'd asked her once if she thought they would have children of their own someday. Julie had answered yes but otherwise hadn't really thought much about when. Colin was older than her by thirteen years, but he didn't seem to be in a rush, either. Julie's career drove her attention, and there was more she wanted to accomplish before thinking about being a mother.

Being alone, without Colin, petrified her more. A million thoughts ran through her mind when the android nurse told her. Julie was thankful Jones was by her side and held her while she cried. She was pretty sure she screamed too. When she told Jones she didn't think she could do all this alone, he pushed back her bloody, greasy hair and smiled at her.

"You're not alone, Julie. He loves you. He always loved you, and you accepted each other. He's not here anymore, but I am. And so is Elsie. And your father. And, hopefully, one day, you'll make amends with your sister." A flutter of warmth had filled Julie's chest in that moment, her heart exploding.

Maybe life doesn't have to be lonely—maybe I can do this. For me. For Colin. For our child, she had thought. It was the only sense of motivation that got her home, washed and dressed for the rest of that tragic day.

"I'm assuming this changes your outlook on the gubernatorial election?" Celine asked with direct and clear words. Celine was always consistent, and Julie appreciated her no-bullshit attitude.

But there's always a price when it comes to Celine . . . an ulterior motive.

"I hear Don Jr. is vying for the seat," Celine continued, her brow raised as she cut into her steak.

"Yes," Julie said, allowing the lie to slip between her lips. He wouldn't make for a good governor. He was more curious about Julie's support. Men like Don Jr. coasted, they enjoyed exuberating power when they saw fit, but they hardly yearned for the true responsibilities of it.

Celine reached for her wine glass and took a slow sip.

"I know we've had a rocky start. But I do care about you. I think I was grieving in the wrong ways. Colin's death took us all by surprise. I miss him. I was wrong to push you aside. We're O'Connor women; we have to stick together. A united front for the legacy we'll build for our children and this family."

Julie placed her fork and knife down slowly.

"I'd like that very much," she admitted. "I'd like for us to start fresh. Put the past behind us."

The words brought a light flush of pink to Celine's cheeks, and she genuinely smiled.

"I think COLI*GO would be in amazing hands with you at the front of the helm, and COLI*GO's board agrees," Celine said, grabbing Julie's hand. "We've voted for you to be our new CEO. With you as CEO and me as governor, the opportunities are end-less. We can continue the great work Colin and you started."

What Celine failed to realize was that Julie had already played this game. She was interim CEO while Colin was governor, and the opportunities, while brighter and easier, were not endless. They still faced challenges with the Board of Directors and roadblocks in The Legislature for clinical trial approvals.

And Colin worked alongside me. We shared the same goals. He would never backstab me. Celine . . . I'm not certain I can say the same.

"There needs to remain some kind of separation."

Celine's body froze, and a bit of rosy color in her face faded.

"Whatever do you mean?"

"If you're the governor and still a founder on COLI*GO's board, you'll have twice the voting power. This isn't that I don't believe in your guidance or abilities, but in the name of science, you should consider appointing a delegate in your place if you get elected as governor. Might I recommend an android? Or a posse hominem? There is no representation on the board beside the vacant supreme appointment."

Celine's eyes glanced sideways, contemplating the proposal.

"Is that really fair for you to say? Between the stocks you've accumulated over the years and Colin's gift of stocks to you, even when you choose to retire, you'd have enough to remain on the Board of Directors if you please. You're right, it makes sense to shift you out of The Legislature with that in mind, but I need time to consider that proposal. I suggest you bring it up at the first board meeting you lead as CEO." Celine straightened the napkin resting in her lap and looked back at Julie. "I'll make the announcement tomorrow that you will return to your role in a limited capacity on election day, October 25th, and fully transition over by January 28th."

Julie smiled and picked her fork and knife back up. An unforeseen hunger coursed through her. She wanted nothing more than to be back in the CEO position at COLI*GO. She belonged there—Celine might have founded the company, but she didn't understand the culture of biotech anymore. Her lack of knowledge limited her and her credibility to her employees.

"I expect an announcement from your office about the gubernatorial endorsement shortly following COLI*GO's announcement."

"Of course," Julie said, cutting into her vegetables with precision. Her smile shimmered back in a slight reflection of the knife. "I couldn't think of anyone else leading The Constituency besides a woman. And an O'Connor."

Chapter 26
Isabella

<u>July 26th, 47 A.R.</u>

Acquiring more time traveler blood remained the largest risk to Isabella's program. Hers was plenty and easily accessible, but she worried about the cancer coursing through her. She was relieved this was the death of her, rather than death being at the hands of one of The City's infamous time travelers. Knowing when her time came, Isabella didn't mind taking liberal trips to the past to obtain the samples she needed.

One test subject wouldn't suffice for confirming that android silver liquids needed to be eliminated in future iterations of android manufacturing. Colin's blood was perfect. Isabella joked when they were younger that he was a bleeder—the smallest nick and the incision was wrapped multiple times over with gauze to stop the bleeding.

Isabella thought fondly of her time with Colin and sincerely wished she could change the course of their relationship. If she'd been willing to accept his demons, he might not have sought emotional intimacy from Julie. But deciding if or when to change the past wasn't a simple task. At least here in FACERE, Isabella had a purpose. Her mission was straightforward; she knew the outcomes she needed to achieve for success.

Anna puttered around the experimental laboratory and sat beside one of the androids who used to preoccupy the viscous tubes. She had striking features, a thin and jagged jawline with large wings spanning across her back.

"Did you hear?" Anna asked without looking up from her micro-scope. Isabella shifted through the laboratory, her long lab coat too big for her nearly hitting the floor. When Isabella didn't respond, Anna continued, "Celine O'Connor and the Board of Directors at

COLI*GO just voted for Julie to resume the role of CEO after the election. Celine is stepping down."

The news didn't shock Isabella. She'd seen the future—there were dimensions she traveled to where Julie sat at the helm, where Julie made the largest decisions for biotech and tech in The Constituency. The young scientist led with compassion, something Isabella couldn't hate her for. There was an acute accusation that Julie was too kind, making her a phony, but those were quickly squashed by anyone who spent more than an hour with the scientist. She possessed a sharpness, making her relatable.

The Supreme concocted a plan that made Julie the interim CEO before she was ready, and even with a passing year, Julie was young for a prestigious position. But Celine was no fool.

Isabella and Celine puttered around each other at social events, and niceties were paramount for their images. They were pitted against each other: Celine was ruthless and Isabella smart.

But I suppose Celine was once Julie's age.

And Isabella never saw anything wrong with the level of control and power Celine possessed.

Isabella grabbed the control and turned on the large sleek device along the wall. She scrolled a few channels until she found the local news.

A reporter with sweat stains under his arms stood outside The Capitol Building. He was younger than the normal reporter, staying as far away from the steps of The Legislature in fear that something awful, something terrible, would happen like what occurred the day of Colin's assassination.

The camera zoomed in on Julie standing at the podium, which now was encased with bulletproof glass. The new governor appeared confident, without a device or notes to guide her through her press conference. Julie smiled brightly in her black dress with three-quarter-length sleeves, her high-heeled shoes emerald green. They were the only pop of color in her wardrobe.

She must be sweltering in this summer heat.

"I'm here to address the recent news about my appointment from the Board of Directors of COLI*GO. I will be returning to the company this fall and fully assume the role of CEO by the time you have a new governor." Julie looked down at her hands and clasped them together, leaning on the front of the podium in a casual but attractive manner. "The tragic death of my husband, and your beloved governor, has been eye opening. I know how much he loved serving The Constituency. He believed in freedoms for all beings, humans and androids."

She paused and smiled while looking out at the cameras broadcasting her news to everyone safe in the confines of their own homes and workplaces.

"Colin even believed in freedoms for posse hominems. You did not ask for this transformation, but I promise your voice matters inside the Session room of The Capitol Building. I want to ensure that the next person who holds this prestigious seat contains certain qualities. They need to lead with confidence, ready to fight on your behalf. They should work tirelessly, regardless of how insignificant the legislation might feel to some. Knowledge of the ins and outs of what happens behind closed doors in this building is another important competency. This is where I find I'm much better suited in a lab coat on the 101st floor of COLI*GO." Julie chuckled, and the news reporters joined in with her.

Julie truly was charismatic.

Maybe even just as much as Colin was, Isabella decided. She admired the scientist but also didn't mind taking advantage of the past. Using time travel for selfish reasons and then using Colin while she did gave Isabella an invigorating perspective. Taking advantage of a time when Colin loved her, not Julie, didn't make Isabella feel any regret. Times that Colin yearned to feel Isabella's kindness, times that Colin adored her . . . She couldn't give it up.

I will not do that anymore, Isabella promised to herself. *It isn't good for me or Colin.*

But Isabella was terrible at keeping her promises.

Anna sat beside Isabella and crossed her arms. Isabella took a long sip from her coffee mug. The sisters continued watching, waiting for whatever bewitching words Julie would speak next. Julie cast a spell on all of them. They couldn't look away.

"I believe strongly that the minority has served this Legislature for far too long. Society—humans, androids, and posse hominems—deserves a leader who embodies the true representation of this Constituency. That's why I'm endorsing my late husband's half-sister for the gubernatorial seat: Miss Elsie Sullivan O'Connor."

Isabella's mug fell to the floor, shattering loudly upon impact.

***

Mick sat in the chair, his eyes fixated on the screen in front of him. Isabella's sympathy for the time traveler never wavered. Others considered him evil, a coward, even. But she understood his plight.

That's why we work so well together, Isabella thought with an adoring smile. Mick smiled back up at her.

"Are you ready?" Anna asked, goosebumps of anticipation freckling her tan skin.

Sitting opposite Mick was an android who appeared very much like himself. The android scales were less harsh and more muted on this body with the jet-black ink color. Otherwise, the resemblance was uncanny, immaculate, and flawless.

This version of Mick appeared younger, modeling him after a less harsh time in his life. Before traveling dimensions corrupted the elasticity of his skin cells.

Mick nodded in Anna's direction and locked eyes with Isabella. She approached the android slowly and made her delicate incision. Placing her new microchip technology into place only took a matter of minutes. Mick observed her small skilled hands stitch up the scaly skin, without a noticeable mark left behind.

Isabella smiled like a pet performing the perfect trick. She was good at this. She'd done this thousands of times and would do it a thousand more if this worked.

A plastic pouch of Mick's blood scourged and pulsated between them. Grabbing the end of one tube, she glided the hanging bag over to the android test subject. Anna approached with a large syringe in her hand and placed the tip of the needle into the port entrance at the top of the bag. A silvery liquid, one that Martin Borges had developed to help androids suppress their changing, glowing scales when they felt emotions, trickled inside. The blood and strange drug mixed inside, and Isabella set a timer.

Placing both IVs into the hands of the android, the blood began pumping inside him. Color vibrated across his scales, lights shimmering and pronouncing that he was in fact an android, not Mick Taylor. Waiting for his eyes to awaken felt like eons, but once his lashes fluttered upwards, Isabella could barely contain her glee.

The android opened his mouth slightly and looked around the room.

"Hello," Isabella said with a wide grin. His eyes scanned her body, and he nodded in her direction.

"Hello, Dr. Garcia."

Mick and Anna smiled at the android, taking his vitals and recording copious notes. The Constituency spent years developing androids, modeling them after people with various differentiations. And once they created their androids, upgrades were minimal.

No engineer or doctor thought outside the box. None of them dreamt of a type of android that had their own identity, that couldn't get corrupted by mischievous, malevolent leaders. Androids who were distinctly their own—who were allowed to understand humans better. Live their lives and prosper the way humans could.

No one at FACERE had successfully made a version two.

But now I have. I have created my legacy. My work is done.

***

The sun set outside with a golden hue, reminding Isabella of her least favorite android's scales. Thoughts of The Supreme sent shivers down Isabella's spine, and she longed for a day when the weight of her part in The Supreme's tyranny didn't negatively cloud her thoughts. She needed to concentrate on the success of androids version 2.0. She felt like a fantastic physician—one who created life.

A quiet knock sounded on the other side of Isabella's door.

"Come in," she called out and froze in her chair at the sight of Martin Borges. Isabella gripped the edges of the chair's arms at the sight of him.

"It's nice to see you in person again, Dr. Garcia," Martin said with a sly smile.

He was a handsome man, tall and lean with longer-styled hair than most old bloodline men. He wore fitted clothing and didn't look like he'd aged a day from his healthy diet and exercise routine.

"Thank you for sending me the note about the success of my family legacy's retired pharmaceutical in your new android prototype."

Isabella flashed her bright white teeth and gestured for Martin to take a seat beside her at her desk. She and Martin were great friends, a strong point of contention between him and his second wife, Celine O'Connor. Martin might have wronged her father, but he wouldn't have even entertained the ludicrous nature of her father's passion project without influence from Isabella.

Martin's family was one of the founders of FACERE, scientists and researchers who worked in the biotech space for years. They created many drugs and treatments for androids, helping FACERE keep itself intact during turbulent times.

"You're welcome," Isabella said, leaning in closer. "I'm glad you didn't think I was out of my mind when I asked to experiment it with human blood."

Martin stroked his chin and leaned farther back in his chair. "I think what you're doing here is monumental."

His compliment spread like a warmth throughout her entire body, but a hint of grave sadness lingered in his hazel eyes.

"What's wrong?"

Martin looked out the window behind Isabella, in the direction of COLI*GO. He let out a large sigh, one so great Isabella felt the weight of the world was resting on his shoulders.

"There have been quite a few peculiar events in the last year that I can't place my finger on. Most recently, I've discovered that my interim CEO resurfaced your father's pharmaceutical. He's trying to pass it off as a newer researched version of Julie's antidote. But I swear, Isabella, it's exactly the same."

Isabella's face scrunched in discomfort. Anna spoke fondly of the disgruntled scientist, but she'd barely worked with him, hardly knew him. Peter Schneider was abrasive and sometimes pushed too hard when asking questions. He was dangerous—he knew the truth of Isabella's involvement in the lower lab project.

"Peter is rather close with Anna," Isabella said, afraid if she spoke the words out loud she could never take them back. "And Anna idolized my father."

"That drug is dangerous," Martin warned in a soft voice. "It's just as dangerous as the toxin. I'm shutting it down."

"The toxin?" Isabella asked with a raised delicately plucked eyebrow.

Martin shifted his gaze back to her, his eyes taking in hers, her lips, and the small soft spot where her neck met her collarbone. Martin coughed, shaking his head.

"Julie discovered a single-dose injection of her antidote but instead of the drug latching on to the healthy cells, it regenerated the disease, allowing for it to completely take over. She nicknamed it 'the toxin.'"

"When did she have time for such a thing?" Isabella asked, challenging the charming researcher.

"She traveled time." Martin shook his head in disbelief.

"So you are aware of such a capability?" Isabella said, unlocking the top drawer of her desk and pulling out her time travel device.

"It's hard not to when Celine O'Connor is your wife. I didn't think that was possible at first when Julie told me, but then . . . then I remembered some instances that made little sense. And I dug up all the financials of the lower lab account, and low and behold . . . everything was there."

"I won't lie, Martin," Isabella said, unable to look at him, wondering if he was trying to trick her into an admission she wasn't ready to give. Confessing to Colin that she was the surgeon behind the posse hominem experiments was difficult enough. She couldn't relive that experience again so soon. "Time travel is addictive."

"I can imagine," he responded and pressed his forehead into his fist. "Colin visited me. He gave me this journal and said Julie would come for it. She did."

"What was in the journal?"

"I'm not sure. I decided not to read it. The least I could do was respect that one request."

They sat in silence, and Isabella closed her eyes. She allowed her mind to drift to a tempting thought of exposing herself, admitting to all the bad parts of herself.

"I hope you know I regret all of that. I was swept away by The Supreme. I thought it was a noble, innovative cause. This terrible desire to please Celine overtook me. I wanted her to like me so badly, and she never did. For once, I thought she'd see me as more than just a socialite or philanthropist. That she would respect me."

"I need a favor from you," Martin said without malice. "I need you to confiscate the pharmaceutical from Peter. The Supreme will deliver it to him through time travel."

"How? She's an android. She can't travel time."

"I'm not sure," Martin said, "but it's what I know. And it's what already happened."

Isabella bit her lower lip and leaned in closer to Martin. A metal briefcase sat in Anna's office, and the feeling of a memory she did not recently experience whirled through Isabella's mind. The images were fragmented and choppy—an apartment building in The Hill, opposite The Capitol Building, Peter knocking on the door, Anna jumping from her seat to greet him. The metal briefcase.

"I think I know where it is or at least, who can lead me to it."

Martin hugged her. Isabella was tiny in his embrace, his sturdy chest comforting her. She couldn't remember the last time someone held her like this. When she pulled away, she saw how dewy his eyes were. He rubbed them and backed away.

"Do you ever wonder if what we were truly looking for was right in front of us the whole time?" Martin asked. He laughed at himself, straitening his relaxed posture. "Imagine what we could have been, had we both not been so entranced by the O'Connors."

Isabella smiled with a small chuckle escaping between her lips and said, "Unstoppable."

Chapter 27
Elsie

The moment Elsie walked into her condo, she realized she forgot her device at her desk in The Capitol Building. She contemplated leaving it there and enjoying a peaceful night without any technology. But she promised Julie earlier that she'd have her device by her side in case she needed her.

Elsie turned around and walked back to her vehicle parked halfway up the hilly one-way street. Darkness cast sinister shadows along the marble floors, and the sound of her shoes clicking filled the otherwise empty building. Elsie wanted to scream. She felt uncomfortable here, alone at night. An odd sensation, one couldn't place or shake away, wiggled through her body.

She neared the corner of the hallway and paused upon hearing a crashing thump coming from behind the governor's office doors. Elsie held her breath and shook her head, but her imagination hadn't run wild when the sound came again.

The door was slightly ajar, and Elsie peeked her head inside. The color drained from her face as a menacingly tall dark figure hovered over the mahogany desk. He stood wide, his feet planted more than shoulder-width apart. A pair of feminine legs dangled between them, and Elsie's hand flung to her mouth to stop herself from gasping aloud.

The woman's breath gave out in a raspy tone, and her trembling legs went limp. Elsie hadn't stumbled upon an indecent act of passionate lovemaking—she'd just witnessed a strangulation. Elsie stilled her shaking hands and backed away, gripping the edge of the doorframe. The man turned and faced her, the corner of his mouth upward in an attractive, disturbing grin.

"Did you think that you'd seen the last of me?" he asked with a playful, taunting gleam in his eyes.

Colin O'Connor released his hands from around Don Jr.'s legislative's aide's neck. He chuckled a harsh yet familiar sound. The woman's limp body collapsed across the desk with a solid thud. Elsie flinched.

"No," she replied with a sharp inhale, "I never doubted you for a second."

Colin was supposed to be dead. But he also time traveled, and now, Elsie did too. If another time traveler truly killed him, he would really be dead. If he traveled to the future, Elsie could only see him because she traveled time.

But Don's legislative aide doesn't travel time. Elsie gulped and her eyes grew wide. *None of this makes any sense. Unless Colin isn't really dead.*

"Let this be a message to Representative Ludewing that he does not fucking torment an O'Connor's wife." Colin's voice boomed in a loud hiss, and he glanced back over at Elsie. "And that he is not worthy of fucking an O'Connor either."

Elsie approached Colin with a purposeful stride. The blade in his left hand shone elegantly and grotesquely from the bright moonlight seeping through The Capitol Building's large windows. The legislative aide was already dead, but Elsie knew what came next.

She outstretched her arm toward Colin's figure. His eyes flashed with a wild excitement as she approached him.

"Hand me the knife," Elsie said with a sense of newfound confidence.

Colin obeyed and stepped away. The handle of the blade felt sticky in Elsie's grasp, but she tightened her grip and raised the knife high above her head. The warm, sultry blood thickly sprayed across her face. The incisions felt personal, oddly satisfying, and terrifyingly perfect.

Elsie continued, the sharp blade meeting the young woman's soft skin with a vengeance.

All the strange feelings Elsie tucked deep inside herself emerged, blossoming out in a rapid succession with the rhythm of her stabbing motions. She hated how she fell for Don Jr. She hated how he didn't care that his press secretary all those years ago planned on outing him and falsely accusing Colin. She hated how he didn't care that his legislative aide now was planning on spreading a damaging rumor that Julie was pregnant with Don's child, that they had an affair when they never did. She hated knowing deep down inside that Don wouldn't deny it, he would use the rumor to spark his own interests, to place Julie in a corner and go after a seat in the governor's office. Elsie hated everything about how evil, how disturbing, and how disgusting men like Don Jr. truly were.

The knife almost slipped out of Elsie's hands as she stepped away from the bloodied, graphic mess she created. Colin grabbed her shoulders, steadying her trembling body.

The mirror hanging on the back wall behind his desk reflected a horrendous image. Elsie was covered in the woman's blood. Her stomach, bare and raw, ragged and red, resembled fresh meat, and the desk that Julie was supposed to sit at tomorrow was beyond soiled by this unnamed woman's bodily fluids.

Bile rose in Elsie's chest, but the urge to vomit never met up with it. Her hair, pulled back in a ponytail, now had loose strands flying in various directions. Blood splatter covered her face, droplets falling from the edges of her eyelashes. They fell one by one, painting her pale cheeks a crimson red.

Elsie glanced down at the woman and reached for her wrist—a tiny diamond tennis bracelet with blood-crusted jewels gracefully wrapped around it. She ripped the bracelet from the woman's body and placed the trophy in her pocket.

Colin grabbed the knife from Elsie's hands with his gloved ones and pulled out a rag from his briefcase. He affectionately wiped her face clean and looked down at her sodden clothing. Elsie closed her eyes and sobbed as he placed his suit jacket over her shoulders and buttoned it—the difference in their size allowing it to fully button but the similar height they shared only let the suit jacket linger just below her waist.

When she opened her eyes, she was in the back of the vehicle, the garage of the O'Connor townhouse coming into view. Colin's thumb pressed against Elsie's cheek, and his eyes gravitated toward the door. They ascended the steps together, and he led her to the kitchen. Elsie didn't need an invitation; she found the beverage fridge and pulled out a bottle of white wine.

Colin walked to the oversized refrigerator and pulled out a hoppy-looking IPA. The top of the beer bottle popped softly, and he took a long guzzle from the neck of the bottle. He nodded, and they continued their journey. All of this was new to Elsie, but this process was like a pattern to Colin.

A ritual.

They made it to the next landing by the stairs, walking past various paintings on the walls, one of which was a coveted Jeb Taylor mural of a woman bending down to the outline of a pair of shoes. The sadness in the painted woman's face swirled with heavy brush strokes—it was horrific and unrecognizable while, at the same time, terribly beautiful.

Entering the laundry room, Colin opened the washing machine and handed Elsie a bathrobe. He left the room, and she took off her clothes, placing them gently inside. The diamond bracelet glistened in between Elsie's fingertips, but she didn't wash the blood off; she placed it carefully inside the small drawer opposite the machines.

This is where it belongs, she thought, looking at the other jewelry, the pieces so familiar to her.

Tightening the robe, Elsie washed her hair in the laundry room basin, watching the red water seep down the drain like hair dye. The washing machine made a small clicking noise, and the water rushed behind the glass window as the machine zoomed to life.

Exiting the laundry room, Colin joined her again, and they continued up the stairs to the third floor. The floorboards creaked under their weight. Elsie tried to remain quiet, aware that Julie and The Supreme slumbered somewhere inside. Her eyes drifted to a spare bedroom, but Colin tapped her shoulder and pointed to the room on the right. The door was open, and Julie slept soundly, curled in a small ball on the bed.

"This will help," Colin whispered, placing a small pill in the palm of Elsie's hand.

***

A blade, thick coats of deep maroon gore, and the feeling of anguish and release flooded through Elsie's nightmare. A terrible dream of vicious, bloodthirsty murder trickling through The Capitol Building once more.

Elsie woke in a startle, the upper half of her body propelling upward instantaneously away from the pillow. When she opened her eyes, she had no idea where she was.

The room was dark but massive, and the moonlight cast unfamiliar shadows across the large bed. A mirror hung above the headboard, and when Elsie glanced to her right, she nearly jumped at the sight of another body.

Julie lay peacefully asleep beside her. An indescribable need to escape the confines of their shared bedsheets rippled through Elsie, but simultaneously, she wanted to grab Julie's warm, comforting body and draw her into her chest.

How did I get here? How did I end up in The O'Connor townhouse? In Julie and Colin's bed? Elsie's hand slowly gravitated over Julie with curiosity. *Waking her up might prevent scaring her if I accidentally do trying to get out of this room.* Elsie felt heavy with tension and fearful anticipation. *Did I black out? No, I didn't drink. I didn't take any drugs.*

But the image of a pill, swallowing it with a swig from a bottle of white wine sparked across her mind. Elsie's head turned to the night side table, and there, lonely and with no accompanying glass, sat an empty bottle of Chardonnay.

No, she reassured herself. *That was all just a dream. This can't be real.*

A firm, scaly grip tightened around Elsie's left ankle, and she looked out toward the end of the bed. The Supreme held her finger in a quieting motion to her lips, and her amber hue illuminated a bright orange in the midnight light. Elsie looked back and forth from an oblivious, sound-asleep Julie to an intruding Supreme.

Letting go of Elsie's leg, The Supreme stood and tiptoed toward the bedroom door. Elsie followed her, gripping the corners of the bathrobe she wore. The smell of blood coursed through her nostrils, and she looked down at her hands. They were clean, but as she tucked back a loose strand of hair, she found the source of the scent.

My hair. She shook her head in disbelief.

Elsie quietly closed the bedroom door and puttered down the hall toward the study. The Supreme, with her large steps and wide stride, was nearly there. *All of this is so very odd.*

"What's going on? Why am I here and not home?" Elsie whispered, unsure what other ghosts crept within the halls of the historic home.

Ghosts . . . Colin. Elsie had seen him. Colin had been there when she went to The Capitol Building. He wasn't dead; he was time traveling—he wouldn't have been able to touch, to strangle, Don Jr.'s legislative aide otherwise.

The Capitol Building . . . Don Jr.'s legislative aide. The horrid dream came flooding back to her. She stabbed the legislative aide savagely, the woman's blood gushing around her body, staining Elsie's face, her hair. Colin had handed her the knife, and Colin brought her back here, cleaned her up, offered her a pill, and put her to bed.

"Oh god," Elsie whispered, her hands flying up to her face.

Then where is he? And why did he tuck me into the covers beside Julie?

As if reading Elsie's mind, The Supreme smiled wickedly in Elsie's direction and pulled open the bottom drawer of the large mahogany desk.

"It . . . it worked."

"What worked?" Elsie asked, her hands now shaking uncontrollably, subconsciously knowing what she'd done wasn't a nightmare but a suppressed reality.

The Supreme placed a knife, dried with crusty blood on the edges, on the desk.

"You should have cleaned up better after yourself. I hope you didn't leave any incriminating evidence in the governor's office."

Elsie collapsed to the floor. The Supreme crouched down beside Elsie, grabbing Elsie's chin in her scaly hand and lifting her face up to meet hers.

"I killed Don's legislative aide?" Elsie asked, trying to release herself from The Supreme's firm grip.

The Supreme's crooked smile made Elsie's heart stop beating in her chest. Her vision tunneled, darkness encasing the corners.

"Did you bring him back?" Elsie barely said the words aloud. "Did you find him? Is he really not dead?"

"Colin?" The Supreme asked, her head tilted to the side.

"Yes," Elsie cried out in a whisper, her hands covering her face as tears escaped from her eyes. "Colin was there, I walked in on him strangling Don Jr.'s legislative aide, and then I . . . I helped. He brought me back here."

"Oh, my dear," The Supreme said, shaking her head. A laugh so disturbing, so immoral, ruptured through The Supreme's throat. "Colin was never there. That was all inside your pretty little head."

Elsie's eyes narrowed, and she sat up straighter, pulling herself out of The Supreme's grip. She searched for an explanation in The Supreme's ghostly green eyes.

A mocking glee was all Elsie found.

"What do you mean Colin was never there? I saw him with my own two eyes. He time traveled. He must have."

The Supreme shook her head, and Elsie's grasp on reality loosened.

"Colin is dead, Elsie. He did not time travel back and teach you to kill the way he did. Colin despised that part of himself. He worked so hard to keep It contained, locked away. He asked Julie to cure him of It—the reason she pursued perfection in the antidote, especially after unsuccessful tries." The Supreme strode over to a locked wooden case. Her bright gold scales shimmered over the keypad, and she punched in the numbers.

A spot inside alongside various weapons caught Elsie's eye—the holder for the hunting rifle was barren.

"But he's a time traveler . . ." Elsie said, grasping for a way these events made sense. She didn't believe she acted alone. Colin had been so kind, so gentle in guiding her through a dreadful, horrendous process.

"Yes, but a time traveler can kill another time traveler. Unfortunately, I cannot. And while I would have loved to pull the trigger, it wasn't me." The Supreme sighed, turning away from the gun cabinet and back at Elsie. "Celine didn't realize that she'd fatally kill her brother with the double fire of a family heirloom. I withheld the information from her, and Peter Schneider never reached her in time. He was too busy tangled up with someone else." The Supreme's eyes warmed, and her scales hummed inside the study, lighting up the room in an iridescent glow. Elsie shuddered. "She thinks he will come back. Her grief helps convince her of this. I think Julie knows better. She knows Colin is truly gone."

Elsie's mouth opened, and her shoulders pinched upward. The Supreme laughed at her, a rotten, masculine sound.

"This evening was all in your head, Elsie. I put It there. I programmed your microchip that way, emulating Colin and his experiences whenever he killed. That's why you killed Paul McGuire in a near similar fashion." The Supreme walked back over to Elsie, their eyes evenly matched from being the same height.

The Supreme glanced quickly down at a larger device resting on top of the desk before her eyes met back up with Elsie's.

"Now answer me truthfully," she said, her index finger lightly tracing the scaled serpent tattoo on Elsie's neck. "Are you afraid?"

Chapter 28
Commissioner Jones

Representative Don Ludewing Jr. stood to Jones's left, and Julie and Elsie stood to his right. Jones's arms were crossed, Julie kept sneaking glances over at Don Jr., and Elsie stiffened like a statue, staring head-on at the gory mess in the governor's office.

"Are you fucking serious," Jones said quietly under his breath. He looked over at Don with a squint in his eye. Don wasn't capable of such madness. The quick logic of Jones's processor ran the analysis. There were only two people who could be responsible: Colin O'Connor or Elsie Sullivan.

The heat in the musty building made Don's legislative aide's body rot quicker, the decomposition festering in the air alongside them. The stench of death cascaded through Jones's nostrils, and he knew this affected Julie worse because she walked over to the trash can by the door and vigorously vomited.

A hollow look in Elsie's eyes matched the slight trembling of her left hand. Elsie had killed Paul McGuire in a similar style to The City's infamous serial killer, deviating from one distinct and important factor: Paul McGuire was a man. Colin O'Connor killed women connected to important beings. But if Elsie didn't kill Don Jr.'s legislative aide, Jones faced a much more complicated investigation.

After Anna and Jones unearthed Jeb Taylor's empty grave, they looked warily up the cemetery's hill. Where Colin lay.

"Do you think—" Anna started, but Jones had interrupted her.

"No."

"Don't you want to just take a look?"

The idea coursed a wave of fear through Jones's processor. The sun was beginning to rise, the harsh morning light peeking out from behind The City's skyline. He wouldn't disturb Colin, out of respect for the governor himself and out of respect for Julie.

But that means Julie needs to be more forthcoming with me, Jones had thought. Jones shook his head, bringing himself back to the scene in front of him.

"The first day we're without a chief medical examiner," he said with a large sigh.

Anna leaving was something Jones kept pushing to the back of his thoughts. Her timing was terrible, but that's how Anna always was. She put her own needs in front of others, and while good intentions led her, the old bloodline selfishness trickled through.

"Dr. Anna Garcia doesn't work for The City anymore?" Julie asked, her tone wavering from concern to agitation, as if Jones should have thought to tell her.

She's right, he thought, realizing his own stupidity. *I would have told Colin right away.*

"No," Jones answered. "I'll have to contract this out to a local physician."

"It's trivial at this point—we know the answer," Elsie whispered.

"The answer?" Don Jr. asked, stepping back from them. "Please enlighten me, Miss Sullivan."

"I think it's rather convenient for you Don," Elsie responded with an icy glare. "Do you want to tell me how you came into possession of Jennifer O'Brien's missing pearl bracelet? Why you threatened the governor with terrible rumors? Rumors that came directly from your office? Are you trying to send a message or set someone up?"

Jones stiffened, but instead of glancing over at either Don or Elsie, he looked at Julie. Julie's eyes furrowed in frustration, and Jones bowed his head. He investigated The City's original serial killer, eventually coming to the realization the culprit was Colin O'Connor. Digging up that buried mess wasn't on his list to relive. There had been the wrongful admission of Jeb Taylor—or more accurately, the time traveled version of Mick—and then The City felt at ease. Colin's admission to The Legislature about Kathleen helped hide his multiple transgressions, but murder was rare in The City. The media took notice, and citizens sat uncomfortably until the commissioner provided the public with answers. Paul McGuire was easy enough to pin and misdirect. He didn't fit in the parameters.

But this . . . this death is too much like the others.

"I am not in possession of such a thing." Don's words were curt and pointed, his glance shifting toward Julie with an oddly grave grin.

Julie scoffed and walked over to the representative with a sultry glare. Her doe eyes were large and round, observing the representative in a singular stare. Placing a hand on his chest, Julie tilted her head to the side and then walked over to the large desk, pointing down toward the bracelet that lay beside his legislative aide's dead body.

"Then why would you give me such a disturbing gift? Especially so close to your legislative aide's death?" Julie skimmed her stare back over at Jones, with a playful tone softly curling the corners of her accusations against the Session speaker. "You did tell me you felt a certain animosity toward my dead husband. Was it you who broke into my office?"

Don stepped away from Julie, glancing at Commissioner Jones with a pleading look.

"Representative Ludewing, I'd recommend you don't leave The City any time soon and that you alert your lawyer. All of you, please leave the crime scene. I'll take formal statements individually."

"What am I supposed to do with this?" Jones asked in a whisper to Julie once they were out in the hallway, headed toward the meeting rooms in the governor's wing.

Julie cast a glance at Elsie.

"Bury it." The words came from Elsie, but Julie didn't contradict her. Jones waited, wanting desperately for Julie's honest nature to emerge, for her to say that wasn't fair to hide the death of a woman, regardless of her species, regardless of her political beliefs.

"We will not bury this, Elsie. We can't," Julie said sternly. Jones felt a large sigh of relief leave his body. "In your statement, please do not discuss the nature of the death other than it is being treated as an investigation for the time being."

A compromise filled with conflict. That emotion itched through Jones's scales, suffocating his body on a daily basis. Julie followed

Jones to the hallway and pulled him into a small meeting room. The curtains were pulled back, and the smell of fresh flowers from the courtyard wafted inside—a pleasant reprise from the sweltering nasty smell in Julie's office.

"You understand why we can't be as open about this murder investigation?" Julie asked, walking toward the window and taking a seat on the ledge.

"But what if it was Colin time traveling to the future?"

"It is not Colin." The words that left Julie's mouth held a different meaning. They were carefully articulated, pointed directly to Jones in a way for her to express a small lingering doubt. Fear crept into Jones's stomach.

"Then that means this was the work of Elsie."

Julie glanced over to the closed meeting room door, her legislative aide likely lurking behind the thick wooden panels.

"That's not fair to say," Julie protested.

"Are you sure this isn't the work of Colin? Of It?"

"I'm sure," she said, pushing herself off the windowsill and making her way to the corner of the room. "He's dead, Jones. A time traveler killed him. I went back in time to confront him. He knew about this."

"Did he tell you who killed him?" Jones asked, racing over to Julie. She opened her mouth to speak but paused and vomited again in the trash bin.

"I don't know, but please, help me get rid of this mess. You can't rule Don out, either. Let us focus on the gubernatorial election. The person who takes this seat is more important than letting the public get wigged out that a killer is on the loose."

Jones rocked back and forth on his legs. His friend never played these political games. Jones hadn't experienced her persona first-hand at COLI*GO, but knowing Julie for over fifteen years, he didn't want to believe her ability to persuade and manipulate others was used in a similar process conspired by old bloodline families.

"I don't like this either, Jones, but I can't let Elsie take the blame."

"Why?" Jones asked, approaching Julie. "She killed Paul McGuire, the head of finance at FACERE. I was able to cover that up, but this seems like a very similar kill."

"I won't be the governor for very long, and I've already placed my allegiance with Elsie. She'll be a better leader than Celine."

Jones stilled. Julie wasn't happy in this role that Colin bestowed upon her. But she was good at it—strategic enough, liked by humans, androids, and hybrids. Julie simply stating she sought the governor's seat for a full term would guarantee her the win. She wouldn't have to campaign. The public adored the scientist. They believed in her.

*I believe in her. I want to see her as my governor, not the CEO of COLI*GO.*

"Why aren't you running?" Jones grabbed Julie's hands in his and walked her over to the doors leading to the courtyard.

He couldn't stand the confines of this room. They needed an escape from death surrounding the inside of The Capitol Building, an escape from everything. Julie closed her eyes and sat on a small bench in the courtyard.

"Because there are two things I plan to do," Julie said, gripping Jones tighter. "Enact change and create partnerships to advance society and make this a better place for everyone. The Legislature is useless unless there's someone vicious and strong-handed whipping votes. FACERE and COLI*GO have always been head-to-head and competitive with one another for reasons I can't understand other than Celine O'Connor is incompetent at bending the knee every once in a while. I have a strategic partner at FACERE now; imagine what COLI*GO and FACERE could do together?"

Julie glanced over at The Supreme's office. The lights were turned off. No one was anywhere in sight; there hadn't been for a very long time.

"And I'm going to force The Legislature to put an end to no representation for androids in my last few months. There needs to be a supreme, and the supreme needs to be the correct android. That's not something only I believe in, but Colin had his nomination written out and planned. I can't execute that wish if I'm also pursuing the office myself. That needs to be my focus, not running a campaign. I'm afraid whoever gets elected in as governor might persuade The Representatives of The People to keep the status quo until Ethan becomes of age. And by that point, who knows what kind of repressive bullshit the Humanizers will enact?"

Jones felt tears threatening the corners of his eyes. Julie was sympathetic and crafty, choosing this new skill set against those who didn't deserve her kindness or the kindness of society. He couldn't hate her the same way he couldn't hate Colin's choices for bettering society for the greater good.

"This is a game, Jones. If Colin influenced my attitude or my character, those traits are the only aspects he succeeded in changing. He made me a strategic player."

"If that's what you need me to do," Jones said, looking away, "I'll do it. But I still need to investigate who killed Colin, and make sure he didn't try to kill himself and end up in the situation you're in."

"How could he? Colin might shield me of the truth, but It? It didn't lie when he told me this was inevitable," Julie said, tears now coming to her own eyes. "I know he's dead because he wouldn't force me to make the decisions I need to make if he was alive."

"How can you be so sure?" Jones wondered.

Julie placed a hand on her stomach, not showing any indication of the secret she kept there quite yet.

"He would never make me do this alone unless there was a greater plan in play. If The Supreme wasn't still a threat. It doesn't matter that she's out of the spotlight for now. If Colin made a mistake and wasn't able to correct it, and if I wasn't able to guide the future in the right direction before making my own plans, we'd lose."

Chapter 29
Celine

<u>July 28th, 47 A.R.</u>

Fury and rage swept through Celine while watching Julie's press conference. Her grief was already unbearable, and now, she felt betrayed, slighted, and backstabbed. The pieces were all crumbling down around her instead of building her up, helping her shine.

After publicizing that Julie would resume her role as CEO at COLI*GO after the election, Celine made a pointed announcement she would run for her brother's seat. The press release dazzled with the right words—how the family legacy mattered, how her brother would appreciate her in the seat, fulfilling his legislative agenda.

Celine didn't plan on following her brother's policies to a T. She certainly didn't agree with all of them, although she was a Sympathizer like he was. Getting the seat with Julie's endorsement would have been so easy, but now she needed to work for the election if she wanted it.

Old bloodline families were losing influence in The City, and Julie's tasteless words about the governor needing to represent the public outraged Celine. The public did not know what to do; they did not know what they wanted.

And Elsie is old bloodline. Is it because she's a posse hominem? Celine froze in place. *Elsie is a posse hominem, and no one knows. She has yet to reveal that side of herself. She actively hides it with that serpent tattoo.*

Celine ran forward in a sprint like a child on a sugary candy high and then huffed in her seat, a frown spreading across her lips. Elsie would surely disclose this information. Julie was once a posse hominem, and the people loved her for her honesty about the situation.

Henry Jr. wailed from his room in the condo she shared with Martin. Her urgent steps brought her through the modern home, a space not meant for small children, let alone a baby. Picking up her son in her arms, Celine whispered sweet nothings in his ear until he soothed.

"You can still win without Julie's endorsement." Martin's baritone voice made Celine melt a little inside. She thought fondly of her husband, his large hands, how gentle and thoughtful he was.

He always forgave me. He always understood even if it pained him, she thought as he reached for Henry. The baby slept soundly, his almond eyes shaped like his father's. *Old bloodline men, they always take after their fathers.*

"I appreciate your confidence, but Dr. Julie Walsh is a difficult challenger to beat. She nearly ruined all my chances at continuing my family's legacy."

"Why did you give up COLI*GO, Celine?"

She hadn't expected this question from Martin. He placed Henry back into his crib, and they made their way out toward the living space. The floor-to-ceiling windows gave their modern home a luscious view of The City.

Celine loved The City. Ever since she was young, she knew she differed from other girls. She was rowdy but still feminine, enjoying being prim and proper one moment and a complete disaster the next. This back and forth drove her father mad, and getting his attention over Colin's drove her to dig deeper into this persona.

Martin poured a cup of coffee into a mug and handed it over to her. He was waiting for her response, but she knew he already had an accusation ready to spit in retort.

It was a bargaining chip for Julie's endorsement. That's what Emilia insinuated. I did this for Emilia.

The Supreme was another transgression on Celine's long list of dirty laundry against her husband. But if she spoke the words out loud, if she openly claimed a loyalty to her childhood friend, Martin would know. He'd been there during her affair with Amanda. She hated calling the intimacy she shared with her colleague an affair— Amanda was so much more than that. Yet she still pursued Martin, anyway, when Amanda stole her heart.

And that's because I never fully had Amanda's heart, either.

"I've been partnering with Dr. Isabella Garcia," Martin said, taking a seat on the couch. "I haven't told you because I know you don't particularly care for her."

He patted the cushion next to him and smiled up at Celine. She took a seat beside him and leaned into his chest. Martin's breathing soothed her, the small heavy beats of his heart almost putting her exhausted self to sleep.

"Isabella is working on a new version of androids altogether. The microchip technology and silver liquid are a hindrance to the individuality and personal freedom of androids currently. By creating a new bloodlike substance that is coded with individual chips, an android is protected from a virus . . . or the potential of their microchip being altered remotely by the government or hackers."

Celine glanced over toward the hallway, where the third bedroom—used as a home office—held the control panel device Emilia created to track her microchips in posse hominems. Isabella was familiar with this; she monitored patient vitals on the device.

"Emilia is not who you think she is. She will betray you when it suits her right. At least Colin never would." Martin did not say this viciously; he said the words as if he felt sorry for Celine.

And that infuriated her.

Celine lifted herself off his chest and stood from her comfortable position on the couch.

"I'm so sick and tired of everyone treating me like a pawn in their games. I'm the one who gave Emilia the means for time travel research. I'm the one who provided her and Isabella the opportunity to create posse hominems. I promoted Julie even when she wasn't ready. And I shot Colin when he asked me to. He promised he would come back—he promised time travelers were invincible." Celine burst into tears, releasing the suppressed, dark secrets into the room.

"You have to fix this, Celine," Martin pleaded. "Everything has become so convoluted."

"I can't fix this unless I become the governor. What else can I do?"

"Expose The Supreme. Turn her in!" Martin's booming voice startled Celine. She'd never heard him raise his voice this way even after he found out about her affair with Amanda.

"I can't," Celine said, shaking her head. "I love her too much."

***

Emilia and Julie sat on opposite sides of the dining room table with untouched plates of food. Silence and tension sliced through the air the moment Celine returned to the townhouse. With an icy glare, she sat at the head of the table and belligerently cut into her meal. Julie's shoulders dropped, and she pushed her plate back, ready to leave her seat.

"Sit back down," Celine commanded. Julie froze but honored Celine's request.

"Let's not be hostile," Emilia said in an even tone.

"You will not speak another word until I tell you."

A dark golden hue spread across Emilia's body. Threatening Julie and The Supreme came naturally to Celine, but she smirked at how easily they obeyed.

"You," Celine said, pointing her knife in Julie's direction, "I would kick you out of this house if I legally could. What you did was a disgrace to this family."

"I—"

"And you," Celine interrupted, pointing her fork at The Supreme, "you better start being honest with me and forgoing your ridiculous riddles from here on out. We're partners in this, Emilia. You and I had a plan. You do not get to cross me when you feel like it. I don't trust either of you at this point in time, but I still need you."

Julie's eyes softened at the hint of vulnerability Celine was willing to admit. The scientist was an empathetic woman; this would place Julie right into her trap.

"You can endorse whomever you want to endorse. But I am not giving up any of my shares of COLI*GO or allowing a stand-in to honor my voting power on the Board of Directors. Don't expect me to approve of any raises or bonuses for you in the near future, and when it comes to budget planning for next year, you better hope Martin has your back on the projects you plan to endorse or I will make you beg and plead on your fucking hands and knees for my votes."

"Celine, my decision to support Elsie in the election isn't because I don't believe in your ability as a potential governor. It's because there needs to be change," Julie said softly, looking down at her half-eaten plate. "We cannot keep repeating the past over and over again. And if you're in office, that's exactly what will happen."

"I don't care," Celine said, fighting back tears. She needed to remain strong, she needed to instill fear into the naïve woman her brother forced into their lives. "And Emilia, it isn't safe for you here in the townhouse. The risk is too high, especially now that I'm running for office. I'm sending you to The Oceanside estate."

Julie protested, "I'm not sure—"

"No," Celine silenced Julie with a severe glare. "After what you did to me, you do not get a say in that. I do not care that you now own the estate."

Julie nodded slowly, conceding to Celine.

"You're really sending me away?" Emilia asked, heartbreak an obviously new feeling for the android based on her iridescent scales flickering between golden and tangerine.

Celine cut into her steak with the delicately sharp knife and placed a small piece of meat into her mouth. She let out a breathy sigh and closed her eyes, the taste of it savory in her watering mouth.

"It's for your own good," Celine said, opening her eyes and staring longingly at the android she loved, the android she felt so connected to that she would burn any building down for. There was a danger in the fierceness of their love—that was something Emilia should have understood, should have foreseen. They were too intertwined; they would scorch the other in their path to elevate together to the top. "And it's for my own good too."

***

A fire sparked inside Celine, the embers strong and radiating a tremendous heat. The days felt repetitive, but a sense of nostalgia coursed through her and she worked with the same level of feverish passion as she had when building COLI*GO. Campaigning heavily across The City and venturing out to The Outskirts on weekends gave her little time to focus on anything else, and even though her anger toward Julie for her betrayal hadn't subsided, Celine was secretly glad she didn't have to return from her maternity leave to COLI*GO. And with Emilia now safely living in The Oceanside, she could focus her free time on her son and her husband. Martin was right—she could win, but it wouldn't be through these efforts alone. Celine needed ammunition on Elsie, something that could disqualify the young half-blood, but nothing jarring came to mind.

Celine's device buzzed, and the number of The Oceanside burner she'd given Emilia appeared on her screen. Emilia had not reached out to Celine since she shipped her away, and adrenaline coursed through Celine's veins as she opened the message.

Please ship the following to the estate. Thx:
-My collection of Chuck Palahniuk novels (at condo)
-Wooden chessboard on coffee table (at condo)
-Case of Dom Perignon (at condo)
-The control panel (at townhouse)

Celine rolled her eyes at the strange request. She left her campaign headquarters at the bottom of The Hill and waved good-night to her youthful and vibrant staff. Wandering through one-way side streets in The Hill with historic gas lamp lights, bright brick townhomes, and cobblestone streets provided a calmness and helped Celine unwind from her busy day.

Instead of heading toward the townhouse, she made her way up The Hill. The Supreme's abandoned condo came into view, and Celine looked up and down the street to make sure no one saw her.

A slight musty smell filled Celine's nostrils as she entered the dark space. She didn't dare turn on the light, afraid to draw any attention from the outside.

A layer of dust coated the top of the countertops and tables, but Emilia kept a minimalist home. Celine spotted the chessboard, delicately placing the wooden pieces with gold-leaf engravings into her bag and then folding the board in half. She did not feel like lugging around a case of champagne, and sending one with a courier proved more convenient. The collection of novels was stacked pristinely on Emilia's desk, but they had yellowing edges.

Maybe I'll get her new ones for the holidays, Celine thought with a sigh.

Guilt waged war in her mind about the decisions she'd made before Colin's death. Part of her believed that The Supreme could have prevented a true killing, had she told Celine the truth that time travelers could mortally kill another time traveler.

How did Colin not know? Does Julie know? A stubbornness inside Celine wouldn't allow her to confide in the scientist. Admitting the truth to Martin was terrifying enough. She was lucky he understood her, that he believed the truth: She didn't know. Celine thought she was helping Colin by honoring the request.

Colin originally planned to travel back in time and carry out the wicked task himself. But he was a terrible shot. After telling her of his plans, Celine paced back and forth for days, trying to come up with a better solution. But there was none.

"I know you want to do it, but it needs to be me," she had said to him in his study when they formalized their plans before the FACERE raid.

"You're right," Colin had said. "You should be the one to have the honors."

The plan was perfect. Colin would jolt society with a jarring assassination; people and androids would realize how extreme they were and would be forced to come together. Celine would get what she always wanted: the O'Connor family legacy. Colin was tired, he wanted an escape. Her brother had never been as strong willed as she was, as cutthroat when it came to the politics of societal pressures.

Celine now sat in the android leader's vacant condo. *I don't believe Emilia. Colin knew about Julie's pregnancy.*

When they were younger, Colin had always lingered in the shadows. He was incredibly smart, but his aloof personality kept him from thriving or pushing back against their father.

Celine was the one who encouraged Colin to run for the governor's office—she believed if anyone could outsmart the Humanizers and wrangle The Legislature, it was he. But had she not pushed him, she doubted he would have ever run. It wasn't his style.

Colin confided in Celine halfway through his first term that he feared becoming their father—he believed that their father's long hours and constant pressures to right the wrongs in society drove him to the miserable person he was.

"I'd retire from The Capitol Building the day a child of mine graced this earth. And then I'd raise my family here," he had said to her that summer while they visited The Oceanside on the anniversary of their mother's death.

Everything except the secret marriage makes sense now. A heavy sadness weighed on her chest. This deviated from the plan she and Colin had discussed. But Celine didn't know much about the other side of Colin's personality—It. *This side of him didn't trust me. And maybe he was right not to.*

Headlights passed by the large window, illuminating the curio cabinet Emilia had in her sitting room. Inside lay the hunting rifle Celine used to kill her brother. She rose from the couch and slowly approached the cabinet with outstretched hands. Her fingertips brushed the handles ever so slightly, and an idea sparked inside Celine's mind.

The gun, Celine thought with a wicked smile.

Chapter 30
Commissioner Jones

<u>August 1st, 47 A.R.</u>

The police headquarters was swarmed with detectives buzzing around the building like active bees in a hive. The murder investigation into Lily Clark—Don Jr.'s legislative aide—was no longer contained. Jones tried to bury as much about the investigation as he could, but while he wanted to appease Julie, he had his own political games to play—and the autopsy report was just released to Jones and the lead detectives on the case.

Representative Don Ludewing Jr. didn't take kindly to Jones's aggressive approach of touting him around when he came in for questioning. The Representative of The People individually called his office on the daily asking for updates. Android representatives were less intrusive, but a few stopped by his office, expressing their sincere trust in him to find the killer.

"Your raid at FACERE was such an honorable and successful mission," one of the android representatives—a dull-gray-scaled android who went by the name Burns—had said with a certain sparkle in his eye. "We're eyeing you."

Between the representatives and Julie's hint, he believed a nomination for the role of supreme was coming in his direction. Representatives wouldn't nominate themselves—unlike humans, their logic deterred them from self-promotion and overconfidence. This android quality rippled through Jones; he wasn't sure if he wanted the role, but if it was bestowed upon him, he couldn't say no.

FACERE had chosen an android named Ethan to assume the position of the next supreme when he turned the legal age: twenty-five. But he still had ten years. Julie had expressed how selecting an android before the new governor was elected was paramount. Jones was honored that Colin planned on putting Jones's name in the running and that Julie planned to honor Colin's wishes. He suspected his friend believed in his abilities too.

But the responsibility was enormous—and Jones was only just learning how to navigate the political waters of his current role as the commissioner. He couldn't imagine the undertaking and extremes that role entailed for a supreme.

The governor's office was fully swept. Other DNA beyond Lily's was found in Julie's office—Julie's, Elsie's, Don's, a few other representatives' and their legislative aides', and Isabella's—but there were valid reasons for it. She held meetings with these individuals regularly.

Anna's short stature loomed over his desk, and large bags were under her eyes. A twinge of guilt passed through Jones—Anna was busy at FACERE in her new role. Jones hired Anna as a consultant to perform the autopsy; he didn't know anyone else and didn't want to waste time trying to hire a local physician or medical student. Anna had rolled her eyes when he asked, but she respected him and agreed to lend a hand.

"This is the last time I do this, Jones," Anna said, handing over her device with the autopsy report. Jones scanned the document and hung his head.

He suspected either Elsie or Colin the moment he walked into Julie's office. Julie remained persistent that Colin was truly dead and not traveling to the future to torment The City.

"The hands were large, but," Anna said, leaning over and pointing to the notes on her report, "they were nowhere near as large as The City's original serial killer."

Jones sighed, placing the device flat on his desk, leaning back in his chair, and shielding his face with his hands. "So, strangulation killed Lily?"

"Yes. Additionally, the killer was right-handed. The stab wounds from The City's serial killer indicated a left dominant hand."

"You can confirm then that this wasn't Colin?"

"Jones," Anna said, grabbing his hands. "You're one of my closest friends. Hell, I helped you dig up Jeb Taylor's grave to prove that it was really Mick and because Mick travels time, a body would no longer be there."

Jones nodded and gripped Anna's hands back, waiting for her to continue. "There's a 'but,' though, isn't there?"

"Well, I think you're very fixated on Colin's death and believing that because he's a time traveler, he's still around. The suspect pool is small—and none of them would bring me any relief either to know the answer. I know you and Colin grew closer after your promotion, but he wasn't a good guy. Yes, he had good qualities. He wanted to leave society in a better place than how he found it. He believed in freedom, in equality. But that doesn't change the fact that he killed so many women."

Anna's right. A small pang clunked in his chest. *Why do I feel this way? Why is this so complicated for me?*

"Colin is dead, Jones. I don't think you've ever experienced loss in this way, understood all the feelings that you now feel. But we need you to uncover who it was. You're not going to unless you accept he is gone forever."

Jones glanced over to the war zone on his corkboard. Two photos remained: Celine O'Connor and Elsie Sullivan. A sinking feeling spread from his chest, into his shoulders and back. Based on Anna's autopsy report, he knew Elsie murdered Don's legislative aide. There might never be enough evidence to convict her of the crime, but she clearly picked up an uncanny character trait from her half-brother.

And she intends to continue to do so. She killed Paul so easily . . . and now Lily too. Who is next?

Celine's professional headshot stared back. Both women were technically O'Connors. And both women were running for the governor's seat. Celine played a large part in the posse hominem project, somehow scathing her way out of the limelight in any accusations to The Legislature. Both were responsible for death in one way or another.

A sudden anger rose in Jones. *Things never change. Anna is right; I have to figure out who caused Colin's death and bring some type of justice to this miserable society. Because I'm going to have to sell my morality one way or another with one of the O'Connor women. One of them will get elected, and it looks like I'll be running The Legislature alongside whoever that is.*

***

Jones rolled over, put his arm around Mick, and pulled him closer. Stress blocked Jones's ability to power down his processor and sleep comfortably over the last few months. Having Mick back in his life did bring its own sense of peace and comfort from otherwise restless nights. Jones enjoyed watching Mick's calm slumber, and seeing Mick work on projects at COLI*GO and FACERE provided some hope that less time travel occurred in his boyfriend's life.

"Mick," he whispered into the darkness. "Why does Elsie kill the same way Colin did? Is Colin's condition hereditary? Will . . . will Julie's child be affected?"

Mick grumbled, half-awake and half-asleep, and rolled into Jones's embrace.

"Jones, it's two o'clock in the morning."

"I can't sleep."

Mick reached over to the nightstand and turned on the bedside lamp. Being back in The Harbor was quieter than The Bay, with the sounds of boats in the harbor a lulling white noise compared to the shining lights and foot traffic on Commonwealth Avenue's busy street.

"I'm not a medical doctor, so I don't know if it's hereditary or not. I've always been under the impression that It was caused by the original time loop," Mick said in the dim light of the bedroom.

"I worry more than I ever worried before."

"I've noticed," Mick said, pulling Jones into his skinny body. Jones felt Mick's protruding bones and tried to pull away, afraid he would hurt him with his clunky frame and heavy processor. "But even if so, Julie and I are working on the antidote. There's an answer. I know there is."

"She'll succeed?"

"Yes."

The silence should have calmed Jones, but he found his processor racing more, trying to fill the empty void. Mick rubbed circles into Jones's back, and the soothing sensation stilled him. Adjusting his position, Mick reached over and turned the lamp off.

"It's the microchip in Elsie's brain," Mick finally said into the darkness. "It's programmed a certain way, and it can be altered too. That's why what Isabella is doing is so important. I hope The Legislature understands. I hope Julie can help push it through."

Mick shared small bits and pieces of his projects with Jones but nothing in full detail. Their schedules were opposite lately—Mick spending late hours in the lab and Jones rising early to get to the police headquarters. This mirrored the routine Mick and Jones had before they broke up. Jones wasn't sure if they were necessarily back together, but they acted as such: cooking dinners together when schedules allowed, sharing a bed, listening to one another, and offering advice where they could. Jones didn't mind—he missed Mick, and while Mick still wouldn't tell Jones he loved him, Jones sensed their love was never lost.

"I thought microchips had to be taken out to get updated?" Jones asked.

"Well, with some of the new updates FACERE rolled out, like the eye-scanning capabilities, no. You're now keyed into the larger cloud network, and the newer androids being manufactured are too. Isabella discovered the posse hominem microchips were linked to the cloud—that's how she could track movement and vitals after her surgeries. Your microchips are what make you unique, what identify you as you. In humans, the indicators are blood, thumbprints, DNA. If your microchip is connected and unique to your blood, then we can avoid corruption or cloud updates. This makes androids more secure. FACERE pushed the cloud network for a long time. I'm afraid it'll be challenging to persuade the representatives."

"So if we had access to this cloud, we could change Elsie's microchip and make her less aggressive. Change it so she never had the urge to kill?" Hope bubbled up deep within Jones's body. Earlier, the gloom consumed him thinking that if Elsie, someone he once worked so closely with, was elected as governor, he would have to essentially contain a worsened version of Colin O'Connor. But if they could change Elsie, she had the potential to be a moral leader—one who cared for everyone.

"Of course, her microchip could be updated at any point in time," Mick said, "but that's not the issue, Jones. We don't have the control panel, but whoever does holds an extreme sense of power."

Jones twisted his head in the direction of Mick's voice. "The Supreme must have it then."

"Yes, or Celine O'Connor."

Chapter 31
Julie

COLI*GO's large glass doors welcomed Julie. Focusing on science in the wake of her grief helped provide direction in Julie's work, and destroying Peter's false drug and strengthening her antidote and her toxin invigorated her. The awkwardness between Julie and Mick lessened with each passing day, and she was grateful that this version of him remembered her from their time travels. She sensed a shift in Mick's attitude—he was brighter and happier than she remembered—and he was forthcoming with assisting at FACERE and helping the Garcia sisters explore more medical advancements for androids.

Optimism filled the air of the COLI*GO laboratory today. The promise of a permanent return sparked excitement with each pass of a colleague, the smile on every employee's face she passed in the halls. Congratulations were shared with each person and android Julie ran into, and many already requested time on her calendar during the fall and winter months.

The simulations reports for the molecule Peter wanted them to focus on weren't negative, but similar issues projected across the predictive algorithm. Triggers like stress, trauma, or certain anxieties exacerbated the patients' conditions and made the pharmaceutical less effective.

"Why are we wasting our time with this?" Mick asked with a shake of his head and sulked back over to another workbench.

Julie eyed Mick and checked the laboratory doors to ensure they were alone.

"I've recreated the toxin," she said, pushing away from her machine and walking over toward Mick. Holding out a small vial in Mick's direction, Julie smiled at how wide his eyes grew at the sight of it.

The toxin looked like an ordinary subcutaneous drug—a clear liquid inside a COLI*GO logo vial. It matched the original antidote in look, but a full vial was needed for the treatment regimen. The drug that Peter provided Julie and Mick with had a silver tinge to it, and the metallic glistened in the bright laboratory lights.

"What do you plan to do with this?" Mick asked, holding the toxin up toward the light.

"We must stop playing around in simulations. I think staying on the screen is what's truly holding us back." Julie turned on another device and placed security goggles over her eyes. "I couldn't understand why developing the antidote from this has been so challenging until I realized we should go back to the basics."

Mick placed her precious drug down by her belongings, and the small ping of the glass vial against the metal table placed Julie in a slight trance.

"The basics?"

"We need a live subject. By injecting the toxin in an extremely small, negligible dose, we can then extract resulting antibodies from the host's blood. And then hopefully you'll be able to help me evaluate the results—that will create the antidote."

Technological advancements in drug discovery and research and development helped subside these less ideal testing subjects. This proved a safer method, allowed any chance of death or toxicity to be nearly zero, and studied interactions more precisely than more traditional clinical studies. Live subjects weren't brought in until the very end, when confidence in the asset was established.

Julie developed the toxin in COLI*GO's lower lab—and technically in the past—so no studies outside of computer simulations had been performed yet. She and Peter promised one another they wouldn't ever test the toxin—only use the knowledge in its mechanism of action to help aid the development on the new antidote.

"Where would we find a live subject?"

Julie tilted her head back against the wall and closed her eyes. It pained her to say the thoughts that lingered in her mind. Her methods were extremely unethical, but she couldn't think of any other viable options.

"The Supreme switched out some vials of the antidote I used with a placebo when I tried curing Colin last year. I believe she started doing so halfway through his treatment." Julie gripped the sides of the table while an uncontrollable shiver rippled through her.

I know, this is terrible. And this is probably all related somehow in a roundabout, strange way. Another time loop engrained in an even larger time loop. She held her breath, hoping the moment would pass. Mick didn't push her.

"I would travel back in time and inject Colin with a small dose of the toxin, not even anywhere near half the dosage, get a blood sample, and come back. As long as I don't inject him with the toxin until after his last treatment of the antidote is no longer inside him, it should be safe. There won't be anything that could be considered a contraindication. I'm thinking that would be early November."

Mick stilled, then gasped deeply for air.

"That would be a very small test subject, but I fear you're right—it's the only solution we have, especially under these tight timelines. Are you sure it's safe to travel time?" Mick eyed Julie with scrutiny.

"I time traveled while I was unknowingly pregnant. I traveled right after I found out," Julie said with a sigh. "I'm fairly certain this baby was conceived while time traveling. I don't think I could make our situation any worse at this point."

***

"I have an update on the investigation and some questions," Jones said, sitting on the edge of Julie's bed in her one-room studio apartment. She was glad to stay in her apartment in The Bay tonight—the townhouse was stuffy and uncomfortable.

Celine and Julie's relationship was now completely strained, and the niceties they made with one another at COLI*GO were not the same as the snide remarks and lack of respect contained in the confines of the O'Connor townhouse. Being there was next to unbearable because Julie never knew when Celine would grace the historic home with her presence. Julie couldn't escape during the weekends to The Oceanside; she was too busy with the antidote, and with The Supreme there, the risk was even greater.

I wouldn't put it past Celine to expose that Emilia is at the estate, and now since I own the home, it'll be I who takes the fall for hiding her presence from the authorities.

Colin trusted Celine, but It was leery of her allegiances. Julie's decision to support Elsie was more rushed than she would have liked, but she was too unsettled by the closeness between Emilia and Celine. And Don Jr. was not an option—the Session speaker forced Julie's hand and showed his true colors with his threats about Colin.

"The weapon used to kill Colin was registered to him."

"What do you mean?" Julie asked. She didn't know of any guns, Colin never went to the range, and the large gun cabinet in The Oceanside estate was empty.

Jones's scales flashed a stoplight green. "You don't know about all the vintage rifles in the study?"

Julie's thoughts raced to the study, picturing the room in great detail. She'd been in the study countless times. There was the massive desk, a large oriental rug, a comfy leather chair, and book-shelves galore. Some shelves had doors, and Julie never looked inside, assuming they were locked with collectible editions, not guns.

"No," she answered. *But I should have.*

Jeffries had given her a list of all the O'Connor family inheritances between the townhouse and the estate in The Oceanside, but she'd yet to read through the full list. "Things" didn't matter much to Julie, and to feel like Colin was still with her, she hadn't changed his historic townhome or moved a single thing. His clothes still took up more than half of the master bedroom closet, and his snow boots sat in the mudroom, ready for his feet to slide in on a cold, snowy winter day.

"They used to keep some at The Oceanside, but Colin never mentioned they were moved to the townhouse," Julie said, sitting next to Jones.

"It knocked a few people off my list," Jones said, scratching his scaly chin. "Was Peter over at the townhouse when you got back from the raid?"

Julie paused and thought back to that day. So much happened—Joel Kennsington took her to Maggie Rivera, who insisted on opening up Julie's brain at the guidance of The Supreme. Emilia refused to help, claiming she didn't know how the operation was performed. Julie didn't doubt that—Emilia wasn't a surgeon, Isabella was. When Colin and Jones came in with the police force, Julie fled the building and made her way to the townhouse on foot. She wasn't entirely aware of what happened after she left FACERE, but Colin, Elsie, and The Supreme showed up shortly after Julie arrived. Celine was in the townhome already with Henry Jr.

Pain scorched through Julie's body from being punched in the face with the butt of Joel Kennsington's gun. The bruises had taken a while to disappear. Elsie had left the townhouse shortly after arriving. Colin held Julie firmly in his arms the whole night, and she'd snuggled into his chest, the smell of cigars and his smoky cedar scent calming her nerves.

"No. I made it there first, but Elsie, Colin, and The Supreme weren't far behind me. Elsie left shortly after dropping them off, and it was only Celine, Colin, The Supreme, and I for the rest of the evening."

"Are you entirely sure?"

Julie closed her eyes. She nodded.

"And in the morning?"

"Colin and I woke up before The Supreme and headed to The Capitol Building. Elsie met us there."

"And what about Celine? Where was she?" Jones asked, his scales throbbing beside Julie.

She reached out and grabbed his arm, hoping to soothe him. He burned to the touch, and Julie nearly flung her hand away.

"Jones, are you okay?"

"Oh, God," Jones said. "Celine. It was Celine."

PART SEVEN
The Past

Chapter 32
The Governor

<u>November 20th, 46 A.R.</u>

Colin never hated Martin Borges, but he never found himself fond of the man, either. There was something sticky about him—something unclear and wavering. Colin referred to Martin as a spineless man, a jellyfish. Even It agreed with him.

Martin was easily swayed by Celine to leave his wife, Maggie Rivera, and marry her instead. And when Celine pushed hard about waiting for them to start their family, he obeyed. Celine's husband even floundered around society, preaching science while simultaneously embarking on ethical, meditational journeys. Everything about the man seemed like a walking contradiction.

But Martin believed in thoughtful risk-taking. He believed in a strong sense of truth prevailing over all else, and Colin wanted to embrace this. He needed someone whom Julie wouldn't question. Julie trusted Celine's maverick scientist husband. She shared glowing recommendations of him to Colin every chance she had even if Colin rolled his eyes in return.

Julie respected the man because he respected her, and Colin believed he could trust Martin to perform the one simple task that would save him and the woman he loved.

"Colin," Martin said, gripping his beer tightly. "You might want to sit down for this one."

Colin ignored Martin's request. This trip to the past already agitated him. Parts of him hated time travel and preferred to leave the trips to It. Coming back in time, Colin was leaving behind important documents that solidified his ties to Julie. If something happened to him, as It suggested in the dark confines of his mind, then he needed to be prepared. Julie needed to be prepared.

After forging Julie's signature onto different documentation than he originally provided to her, they were officially married. Seeing Elsie's wide eyes from reading the paperwork before she notarized it cemented the truth in that no one suspected he and Julie were an item at all.

Celine knew the truth, or at least, she knew he loved her interim CEO. The notion that Colin found love didn't bother his sister—it was with whom. The list of Julie's faults in Celine's mind was minuscule but impactful: Julie wasn't of old bloodline descent.

I hope I'm making the right decision here, Colin thought, studying his brother-in-law a bit closer. Martin always let his hair grow out long and often ruffled it back in a nervous twitch. His deep almond-shaped eyes showcased hazel green irises, and his lean body showed that he treated himself well, cared about his health.

"Okay," Martin said, taking a deep breath. "I have reason to believe that Celine is tied up with The Supreme in trying to overthrow the government."

Colin laughed, his verbose chuckle emerging from deep within his belly.

His sister craved power, and she loved money—Colin wouldn't deny either of those facts—but tyranny? The claim sounded ridiculous. The Supreme was capable of these accusations, but Celine was only a piece on Colin's and Emilia's board.

Martin's eyes furrowed in anger. He didn't like being the butt of Colin's jokes, something Colin insisted upon for years.

"I'm serious, and I think you should listen to me."

Colin's laughter stopped, and he grabbed a beer. He rarely drank beer, leaving the hoppy substance to It for indulgent purposes. His perception of Martin Borges changed the moment he handed over his device. The contents looked strikingly familiar to the words of Julie's accusations, ones she left in a note for him that he used with The Legislature after traveling back in time to give him. The very letter would occupy the drawer in his study until he turned himself in this upcoming winter to The Legislature for Kathleen's death.

But Celine's involvement seemed likely, but not this invasive. Julie insinuated Celine's knowledge but not outright assistance.

Why?

"There have been missing funds. I've been working on capturing them all with Dr. Julie Walsh," Martin started.

The confirmation Colin needed. He never questioned how Julie collected the astounding amount of evidence against The Supreme and her wrongdoings in the lower lab at COLI*GO. Julie was meticulous, and as a trained researcher, she excelled in the skill of observation. But being the CEO and managing the hostile climate of a cutthroat biotech company was time consuming. She had access to the documentation needed, the files hidden, and the financial accounts, but Martin knew exactly where to look.

And who warned him?

"Julie has shared the same concerns." The words escaped Colin's mouth before he could stop them.

"She has?" Martin asked, backing away from the kitchen island and leaning against the countertop.

"Don't be so bashful, Martin. We don't have time to play these games."

"I won't lie," Martin admitted, taking a long sip of his beer. "I was surprised when she approached me. I was already looking into the accounts on my own after Isabella warned me that COLI*GO would be a sinking ship if I didn't act fast."

Isabella? Colin's shoulders stiffened.

"What makes you think Celine is involved? Julie's accusations seem to lie with The Supreme," Colin noted, hoping to move the conversation back to the real reason he needed Martin and Martin needed him.

Martin's hands shuffled in his pant pockets, and he pulled out a second device. This one was about the same size as his personal one, but the screen was sleeker.

"I think they're doing research into some kind of microchip. I thought FACERE handled android microchips, and while Celine always has had a personal vendetta against FACERE, I never imagined she'd want to invest COLI*GO funds in this type of innovation."

Martin unlocked the screen and shared it with Colin. Being a time traveler provided Colin with a great advantage and the opportunity to use this information against The Supreme when the time was right. A darker truth unfurled from the brightly illuminated screen—the microchips were trackable remotely, providing insights from biometrics to tracking locations.

"From what I gather, if these microchips are connected to a network, they can be updated and changed at any point. I could basically say, 'Hey, I want this android to actually be a bit more like my broody brother-in-law,' and adjust his understanding of emotions just like that." Martin snapped his fingers. "Essentially, they could make any android or any of these hybrids do whatever they wanted. Like revolt."

A sinister chill rushed through Colin's body.

"We've just finally recovered from the most severe impacts of The Resurgence."

"I know," Martin said, sliding his finger across the device once again. "But there's one in particular that bothers me. A microchip that's blank."

"Why does that bother you?" Colin asked, studying the different lines on the screen.

"Because it means they could upload any android microchip to that blank microchip."

Martin eyed Colin with curiosity.

"Who possesses that microchip?" Colin asked. Martin averted his gaze and paced around the kitchen. The nervous energy surging off the man's body caused small beads of anticipating sweat to ripple on Colin's forehead.

"Julie."

The insistence in my head wasn't wrong. He felt guilt for all the pain and hurt he caused Julie with the betrayal that night in the future in the woods. Colin fretted over the difficult decision for nearly a month after It visited him to confirm Julie was a posse hominem. But Colin never pushed back when he should have, which Julie pointed out in her letter to him. Wondering why he didn't fight harder plagued his sleepless nights in the future. Now, Colin could blame time travel.

Time travel was a twisty, strange technology, affecting time travelers in ways that even Mick Taylor didn't understand—especially the brain. Neuroscience was Julie's specialty, and hematology was Mick's. Dreams and memories intertwined in strange ways.

Colin couldn't trust his own mind to begin with, and time travel worsened his sureness too.

Closing his eyes, Colin asked the question he feared most. "And it's Celine who had possession of this tracking device, not The Supreme?"

Martin nodded slowly. "I love her. She means so much to me. There have obviously been infidelities, indiscretions," Martin said, looking out the kitchen window above the sink. "But we always come back to each other. I just find it hard to believe that she would go this far. Especially now that we have Henry Jr."

Colin wanted to say something reassuring but couldn't think of anything. He wanted to believe that Celine would fall in step with him over Emilia, but with how far they took the lower lab project, Colin's confidence wavered.

"I want you to talk to her. She will listen to you." Martin stared at Colin intensely and grabbed his hands. "I don't want anything bad to happen to her."

"I understand," Colin answered. He didn't want Celine tied up in whatever nonsense Emilia had filled in her head, but as the mountain of Julie's and Martin's evidence coagulated together, Colin's heart slowed with a heavy realization.

He spent his whole life pitted against the android leader. They shared similar interests in their youth, and while that sparked a kinship, it also birthed a competitive nature between them. Their continuous games were out of hand, their desires to outplay one another extended. Everything Emilia did was in reaction to Colin, and his downfalls, his demons, were reactionary to Emilia's actions.

"I'm glad to hear that you and Julie are working together on this," Colin said, shifting up from the barstool and standing confidently beside Martin. "I know Julie was looking for more concrete records. Once I have those, I will go to The Legislature and turn in Emilia. But there's a chance all of this goes awry. If everything crumbles in The Legislature, I want Julie to have this."

Colin pulled out a thick brown leather journal from his briefcase. Mick Taylor had given this to him, and while the contents scorched Colin's heart for many reasons—the threads of Mick, Julie, and his mother tied ominously together—Julie needed these insights to knock Emilia's king off the board once and for all.

Martin eyed the novelty of such an old-fashioned formality with an oddly wistful grin. Gripping the jagged edges and crème pages, Colin stopped Martin before he had a chance to flip through them.

"Please don't read it. That's all I ask of you."

Martin nodded and clutched the journal between his two hands. "When should I expect her?"

"January 28th," Colin answered, walking over toward the beverage fridge once more. He pulled out a second beer and took a long gulp of the inhibiting liquid. "I'll shield Celine from this as much as I can."

Chapter 33
Julie

<u>November 3rd, 46 A.R.</u>

Being back in the fall of 46 A.R. gave Julie a different perspective. At the time, Julie was the interim CEO, and she was busy working with Martin on uncovering the missing financials at COLI*GO. And she and Colin were excited. He'd finished his treatment of the antidote—or what Julie thought was a full treatment of the antidote—in October. They had celebrated how It would never come back, that It would never hurt them.

And now knowing It . . . Julie wished to pretend to be this dimension's version of herself, but now she possessed a dead giveaway—her ugly scar. She hated this scar for many reasons. Isabella promised that she had tried her best when removing her microchip but was unsuccessful.

When she awoke in the woods, a small puncture in her neck protruded a sliver of blood into the snow. Without understanding why, Julie's nightmare—which wasn't really a nightmare but a memory of her posse hominem surgery—flooded instantly into her mind while she lay there, bleeding out in the snow. With pure instinct running through her veins mixed with the high of adrenaline and the bitter cold air, Julie plunged her finger into the incision and felt for the threads attached to the microchip. Her curiosity was what caused the scar. She wouldn't have thought to stupidly reach into her body and rip up her wound further if it hadn't been there at all.

It adored her scar, and his acceptance of her battered history helped Julie feel less subconscious about it. But Colin didn't know this Julie—and Colin couldn't know this Julie. She was tempted to spend another long night with him and decided if she could get away with this journey undetected, then maybe she would come back again, despite her best efforts to stop time traveling.

The full moon glowed in the sky, making the shadow of stars impossible with its brightness. The townhouse was mostly dark except for the entryway. In complete darkness, Julie climbed the grand staircase to the third floor and slowly opened the master bedroom door. Colin was nowhere to be found.

Confusion furrowed Julie's brow, and she made her way back downstairs and tiptoed to the front of the townhouse. A small fire crackled in the living room, and curled into the large comfortable sofa was Colin. He was fast asleep, a slight snore disrupting the otherwise quiet townhouse. Julie crawled under the large blanket he had wrapped himself up in, searching for warmth.

A glass with a half-melted ice cube sat on the coffee table, and Julie held in a frustrated sigh—she loathed Colin's fondness for whiskey and Scotch, how he abused the substance to help him sleep on particularly reckless nights. But she was thankful for the deep slumber this inhibitor put him in tonight.

Holding her breath in with fear and anticipation, Julie uncapped the tiny syringe she held in her hand and injected the tiny, thin needle into Colin's arm. A few units of the toxin excreted into his arm and she slowly pulled the needle back out. Colin didn't even flinch at the intrusion.

Julie soundlessly let out a sigh of relief and placed the safety cap back on the needle. Fidgeting in her pocket, Julie pulled out a small tube similar to what Mick used to store his time travel samples. With a sterile, second needle, Julie took a sample of Colin's blood. He bled a bit more than she expected and she nearly swore, but with a light touch, the bleeding subsided.

Having felt her presence, Colin rolled over in his slumber and spooned against Julie's body. She froze, afraid he'd wake up and her cover would be blown. A faint scratch from Colin's five o'clock shadow scraped against Julie's soft skin as he settled into her familiar body. Julie held back tears—she desperately wanted to turn around and kiss him. She wanted to hold him in her arms and see his smile.

I can't. I can't. I can't. She fisted her hands into tight balls and pressed her nails into her palms.

Colin buried his face into her hair and inhaled deeply, stirring a bit more restlessly. Turning so she faced him, Julie kissed his lips before he opened his eyes.

"Shh," she soothed, running her fingers up and down his back the way he liked. "Go back to sleep. I didn't mean to wake you."

With a tiny grunt, Colin pulled her in closer, wrapping her in a tighter embrace. Tears burst from the corner of Julie's eyes, and she held in her cry. This trip to the past was more difficult than she anticipated—burning a small hole in her already shattered heart.

But I have to do this. I couldn't save my mother. I couldn't save Colin. But if I get the antidote right, I could save someone else's mother, someone else's daughter, someone's partner, husband, or wife.

His breathing grew heavy again after a few moments passed, and his shoulders relaxed, loosening the grip he held her in. Julie paused, the idea of leaving him a sharp, furious pain in her chest. But the longer she waited, the more she risked getting caught.

Crawling carefully out of his embrace, Julie navigated to the back of the townhouse. She eyed the carriage house across the courtyard with intrigue. She'd spent many nights there, watching Colin and watching It. The small converted space contained an efficient miniature kitchen with an open area for a loveseat and a chair and a small bed in the back.

The carriage house lulled Julie toward it, and she climbed the steps to the top, pulled the key out from under the mat, and unlocked the door. Mick also used this space when he time traveled, considering it his safe space from others.

Movement from the back of the room made Julie stop in her tracks.

"Julie?"

Mick's stalking figure emerged from the shadows. His skin was smoother, his eyes brighter, and his build a bit stockier. With a less sickly appearance, Mick resembled more of the friend she knew from her years at The University over the old man she spent day in and day out within COLI*GO's lab. His eyes gravitated from her face, grew wide at the sight of her ghastly neck scar, and finally settled on the tube of Colin's blood that she clenched in her hand.

Instinct forced Julie to step away from him as he lunged toward her. He chased her through the small space, knocking her to the ground with a small thud.

This is not Mick. This is a different version of Mick.

Julie's feet lashed violently as Mick held on to her ankle, and she heard the crunch of Mick's glasses. With the release of Mick's grip on her, Julie stood and ran, holding on to her prized possession with all her might. Mick's figure followed her, but Julie knew this part of The Hill better than him. She cut through an alleyway and popped out on Charles Street, making a quick right turn and keeping her pace until she reached the public garden. In the darkness and beneath the trees, Julie lost Mick.

Dropping to her knees, Julie finally let out the loud cries she'd held in since she arrived. The bitter air constricted her lungs, forcing her to rest in order to catch her breath.

That's it, Julie swore, ripping out the time travel glasses and chrome box. She placed her blood on the slide and selected the date in September, 47 A.R. *I will never time travel again.*

Chapter 34
Celine

May 18th, 18 A.R.

The townhouse was quiet. Colin was locked in his room with a book, and her father was hiding out in his study. He strode past Celine in the kitchen an hour ago without saying a word and stomped upstairs. A bad day in The Legislature. Her father grew more miserable over the last year. While he and Filipe were up to no good when it came to her brother, her father backed off, and there were fewer trips to the carriage house to untangle Colin from his confinements. Celine suspected a woman captured his interest for a bit but now was most likely gone.

Emilia sat on the living room couch with her device, typing up a report for school. In her typical impatient manner, Celine shoved Emilia's device out of the way.

"What?" Emilia's vibrant scales flickered briefly before dulling to their normal shade.

Celine liked when Emilia's scales changed colors and shimmered in the light. Feelings weren't supposed to occur often with androids, and Emilia was no exception. The rarity of her display of emotions was an indulgent treat Celine wanted more of.

"Let's do something fun," Celine taunted with excitement in her voice. "Let's sneak out. I heard that the Borges brothers are throwing a party while their parents are out of town."

Emilia rolled her eyes, but her scales flickered again. Celine smiled wider. She touched Emilia's arm, the coolness of her scales sending a shiver down Celine's spine.

"They're reckless, dumb boys." Emilia's monotone response wasn't what Celine wanted to hear.

"They aren't boys. They're going to be sophomores next semester at The University."

"Then you're a reckless, dumb girl." Emilia eyed Celine, challenging her by insulting her.

"I'm sixteen! I'm hardly a girl anymore." Celine pouted, proving the immaturity Emilia accused her of. Sitting in the townhouse all bored Celine; she thirsted for wild excitement.

"Why do you want to go anyways?" Emilia asked, crossing her arms against her chest.

"I heard they have beer, and I would like to try some."

"If you want beer that badly, I doubt your father would notice a bottle missing from the fridge." Emilia pointed toward the kitchen.

Celine sighed. She wanted a sense of adventure this evening. School was only a week away from summer recess. She'd already finished her finals and only had one more exam before a summer spent entirely down at The Oceanside, away from all the opportunities that The City offered.

Freedom in The City tasted good on Celine's lips, and she wanted more of it before her miserable father drank himself to sleep and required her to take care of all the matters of scheduling dinners and parties at their summer estate. And they were only about a month away from the sixth anniversary of her mother's disappearance. Colin sulked, and Henry disappeared in himself. Celine wished to feel something different from the monotonous life she lived. She wanted to escape, to have something so incredibly distracting that she didn't have to worry about anyone else for a few hours.

"So you're not going to come with me?" Celine asked, her lips plump from pouting.

Emilia glanced away and shook her head. "I'm going to stay here. Colin owes me the final match in our game of chess. We're tied. I can't let up on my winning streak."

"You're such a bore these days, Emilia."

Celine climbed out of her window on the third floor of the townhouse an hour later. The lattice and green vines were strong and sturdy, easily holding her thin frame. Celine wandered up The Hill a bit closer toward The Capitol Building. The Borges family lived on the backside of The Hill with a beautiful view of The River neighborhood. Construction projects littered The River's skyline, new buildings and tall skyscrapers that would be ready someday soon for new tech and pharmaceutical companies.

No one recognized Celine as she passed through the busy streets, everyone was distracted by their devices or engaged in conversation with their companions. It was late but still far early for anyone looking to go out for a good time.

When Celine reached the Borgeses' residence, her finger hovered near the doorbell. This probably wasn't the right way to enter the house. She had never been to a house party before and while Celine liked to think of herself as mature, there was still an innocence and a greenness raging through her.

The door opened before Celine had to decide, and a beautiful woman with thick dark curly hair stepped outside. She squinted at Celine with a questionable look in her eyes, but Celine darted inside before the girl could recognize her. The thumping beat of music lingered from the basement level of the brownstone, and Celine followed the captivating rhythm.

Several of her old bloodline peers congregated around a beer pong table. Matthew Borges pounded his chest, cheering as his partner's pong ball sloshed in the red plastic cup. Marta McKenna lingered beside Matthew, her fingers delicately holding on to the belt loop of his jeans. Celine stole a glass from someone's hand and took a large gulp. Beer buzzed in her mouth and against her tongue, like pop rocks tasting of dirt. She didn't like the flavor or the feeling.

Why is everyone so obsessed with this? she wondered and placed the now-empty container down on a side table.

Her eyes took in the full room, observing each guest with intrigue. Most were old bloodline, a few were newer, rich money— people Martin and Matthew met at The University. There were no androids here, and Celine was relieved that Emilia did not accompany her. The intoxicating liquid she pounded back would have made her stare inappropriately at Emilia's scales, hoping they'd shine the autumn colors. Her secret desires to touch them with the tip of her tongue was not socially acceptable. Movement from the far corner of the room caught her attention—Martin Borges settled in by himself on the couch.

He was the quieter of the twins. Martin kept his hair longer and slicked back with a little gel. Celine found this style dangerous and fun. She sat beside him and tapped his muscular arm.

"So how much does The University actually suck?" she asked.

Martin eyed her for a moment, trying to place the girl he obviously knew with hazy, half-drunken eyes.

"I actually don't mind it. I know I want to be a scientist. Matthew, on the other hand, he can tell you how much he hates assignments. He has no idea what he wants to do."

"A scientist?" Celine asked, her charming smile spreading widely. She shifted her gaze over to Matthew and boldly placed her hand on his thigh.

The twins were identical and equally attractive, but Matthew was full of himself, a player. Martin was calmer, more aloof. She sensed a chase with Matthew . . . and Celine didn't like to chase anyone. For once, she wanted to be chased.

"Yes," he said and leaned into her ear. "How did you get invited to our party?"

Celine grabbed the cup from Martin's hand and took a long sip. She really hated the taste of beer, but she desperately wanted to fit in and the alcohol made her more comfortable.

"Your brother."

"Ah, well, he can never say no to a pretty girl."

Celine smiled at the compliment, and the effects of the alcohol gave her a giddy confidence. She kissed Martin Borges, allowing her hands to liberally explore his chest. He kissed her back after a moment of confused hesitation.

Celine had only kissed one other boy before, but she'd read plenty of romance books. Her previous act had been with a nobody in her class and it surely pissed off her father. Henry sat beside his daughter in the principal's office after school, ushering her off and into her room when they made it back to the townhouse. She thought her choice of a nobody had angered her father, but she was wrong.

"I just wanted your attention," Celine had huffed from the one side of the door. She felt her father's weight on the other side.

"I don't care if you kiss an old bloodline or if you kiss a nobody. Keep your mouth to yourself—you don't want to fall in love with anyone, Celine. It'll only hurt you," he had said. His heavy footsteps walked away, and when she pulled down on the doorknob, she realized he had locked the door.

Celine didn't know what she was doing when it came to boys and allowed Martin to lead her. In the movies and shows, men always took advantage of women when they kissed them. Martin didn't. Celine felt like the aggressor with curious hands and a vivacious tongue. She wondered if she was belligerent with her personality . . . if she needed a calm, soothing presence to keep her from being too pugnacious.

Celine's device vibrated in her pocket, and she ignored it. After several minutes of nonstop calls, Celine pulled away from Martin's embrace and looked at the screen.

Emilia had called her, sent her multiple messages, and left voice notes. Celine sighed, the words "come home now" and "SOS" lighting up her screen.

"Are you in trouble?" Martin asked playfully, a characteristic she hadn't expected from the nerdy University student. His fingers threaded through her hair.

"I'm always in trouble." Celine smirked, kissing him one last time before escaping out the back door. She left the party and hurried back home.

Filipe Garcia's vehicle was parked in the garage beside her father's, and she groaned. There was something uncomfortable about the psychologist and his insistence that her brother's broody nature was twisted but curable.

Celine had spent years watching the man torture her brother and her father saying nothing about it. Henry pushed back in the beginning, but he also seemed desperate. Colin didn't like to talk to anyone; he grew agitated and upset quickly. But he was never violent.

Not until Filipe started tying him up, making him swallow all those pills, and giving him all those shots.

Celine didn't bother going into the townhouse and wandered out to the courtyard. The buzz of the alcohol coursing through her veins made her clumsy and noisy. She paused and peered into the carriage house.

Filipe and Henry argued, the two men nearly hitting one another. Colin wasn't there.

She detoured back to the townhouse and rushed inside. Colin and Emilia sat wide eyed on the living room floor. Emilia bandaged Colin's wrists, applying an ointment to them.

"What happened?" Celine asked, breathless.

Colin looked up at his sister with his large steely gray eyes. An icy stare cast through them, one that startled her. But Emilia looked calm, unbothered by the devious glare consuming Colin.

"He told Father I'd grow up to be a monster. That he wouldn't be surprised if I became a cold-blooded killer. That I have a personality disorder."

Celine looked over at Emilia, seeking verification of the interaction. Emilia nodded and said, "Then Henry punched Filipe."

Celine's eyes widened. Her father was a miserable bastard, but he wasn't physically violent. He never placed a finger on her. He never placed a finger on Emilia. The only physical hurt he caused was helping restrain Colin sometimes.

"It snapped, and Father snapped too."

The slumped feeling of Celine's drunken buzz ventured its way up her throat. She felt the vomit rising but kept pushing it back down. In a blind fury, she raced to the carriage house and burst through the door.

"Don't think you'll expose me, Dr. Garcia." Henry's booming voice echoed loudly. "What do you think the media will say when I tell them you worsened my son's condition with your homemade, non-approved drugs? That you threatened to make him into this monster?"

Dr. Garcia held a bloody rag to his nose, broken and shifted to the right side of his face. The clanking of a needle scattered across the tiled floor, landing close to Celine's feet. Both men paused, looking directly at the young lady in the kitchen.

"Colin isn't a monster!" she yelled, the vomit from too much beer finally escaping her body.

Henry rushed toward his daughter, pulling her hair away from her face and wiping the corners of her mouth with his sleeve.

"Get out, Filipe!" he shouted, his eyes back on the psychologist. "And I never want to see you ever again. Don't you dare ever come anywhere close to me or my children."

Dr. Garcia stammered out of the carriage house, and the sound of his heavy boots against the iron steps rang in timed unison.

"Celine," Henry said, looking at his daughter with crisp, alert eyes. "Are you drunk?"

She pursed her lips together and shook her head.

"Don't lie to me." His voice was stern and intimidating.

"Yes, Father."

"How much did you hear?"

"Just that Dr. Garcia was planning on using something you didn't want him to use on Colin."

Henry stilled and picked the needle up off the floor. He looked at the liquid inside and placed it carefully on the kitchen countertop.

"Go get your brother for me."

"But Father—"

Henry closed his eyes and gripped the edges of the marble tightly. "I said go."

Celine obeyed.

Chapter 35
Elsie

<u>April 1ˢᵗ, 47 A.R.</u>

Springtime in The City was damp and chilly with gray clouds and misty, wet streets. The café near the prison and police headquarters was filled with more androids than humans, so Elsie took a seat in the far back corner.

Jimmy's scales were neon and bright compared to the dreary day, and an alertness shot through Elsie's consciousness when gazing upon him. A slight tremor wavered through Jimmy's right hand, and his left held it, steadying himself.

Elsie moved her warm latte to the side and placed a small device on the table. Waiting for instructions from her, Jimmy didn't move a muscle, but his eyes glanced back and forth between Elsie and the device.

"You know Representative Joel Kennsington, correct?" Elsie asked, taking a long foamy sip of her drink.

"Yes."

Her brow raised, waiting for him to say more than his simple response.

"He and many other representatives employ me as a driver some-times."

Elsie held back a scoff. With self-driving cars, the idea was antiquated, but The Supreme also used Jimmy as a driver. The move was more a showcase of power or wealth, not a necessity, and certainly not a legitimate requirement or need.

"I completely understand," she said evenly. Tapping the screen with her pointer finger, the light illuminated off the table and her stare-off with Jimmy continued. "Representative Kennsington has someone in his possession who is very valuable to me."

Jimmy gulped, reaching for his black coffee, and a look of

acknowledgment flickered in his otherwise robotic eyes. He hovered closer to the table and leaned in, his face mere inches away from Elsie's.

"The missing COLI*GO CEO?"

"Yes."

Relaxing back into the booth, Jimmy closed his eyes. "I don't know if I'm capable of assisting with a kidnapping."

The idea brought a zealous smile to Elsie's lips. She wished this was what she'd ask Jimmy to do instead, but Julie had her reasons for staying at Joel Kennsington's home in The South and the scientist needed to remain hidden from the public for a little while longer.

"I'm not asking you to kidnap her," Elsie said. Jimmy noted her smirk and tilted his head to the side, his processor running different scenarios. "I need you to get this to her without Kennsington seeing."

Elsie pushed the device closer to Jimmy's side of the table. With a small flickering of his illustrious scales, Jimmy scooped up the device and placed it in his pocket, looking around the café to make sure no one had seen.

"Is Commissioner Jones aware?"

"Yes. This was partially his idea." The lie came easily for Elsie. Jones and she discussed ways to get to Julie once they pieced together her location.

The City's detectives had been searching for the scientist for a long time. Her device was found in her office at COLI*GO, giving them no way to track her location. With not much else to go on, Jones studied any other visitors through the police's ability to track device locations when within city limits. Julie's device took an interesting adventure, its last pinging location on the edges of The City near the last stop on the red subway line, back to her apartment in The Bay, and finally ending at COLI*GO the morning of January 29th. Representative Joel Kennsington had entered the COLI*GO building on January 29th early in the morning. Records showed he came in for a meeting on the 101st floor, but his host's name was not recorded.

The assumption was easy for Jones and Elsie to make— Kennsington was the last one to see Julie Walsh before she "disappeared," and with her known hatred of the representative, and Colin's distaste for the man, where else could she go where no one could expect to find her?

Jones knew something else in this; Elsie could physically feel him holding back a dark, disturbing truth that didn't belong. They were supposed to work together for Colin's sake even though Elsie hadn't officially started her new role yet.

The role of the governor's legislative aide and secretary was a prestigious position, and when the high judge nudged Elsie to put her name in the running, she initially hesitated. The idea that someone as young and inexperienced as her—at least, within The Legislature—would qualify baffled Elsie. But she was surprised when Joel Kennsington himself called her on behalf of The Legislature and asked her to come in for an interview.

Her old bloodline name carried some weight, and the representatives, both people and androids, highly respected her mother. That Elsie was only considered because of her lineage annoyed her, but Kennsington wasn't the fool everyone made him out to be. There were other highly qualified candidates—legislative aides of other representatives, a former political campaign manager, and even Martin Borges's executive assistant at COLI*GO, to name a few. Elsie was naïve and green in Kennsington's eyes, and she surely believed he convinced the other Humanizer representatives that they could sway her and ultimately influence their governor.

"Is she expecting this?" Jimmy asked, finishing the last of his harsh and bitter-looking beverage.

Elsie shook her head and placed her coffee cup down. "No. Tell her we send our regards."

***

The Port neighborhood was newer and glamorous, with various bars, restaurants, and nightclubs. The price tag to live in this trendy part of time would hurt even the rich's budget, but it was a price they were willing to pay for proximity.

Elsie enjoyed going out in The Port with her friends and coworkers. The drinks were overpriced and watered down, but the music was deafening enough to make anyone forget their woes for a few hours. And accessing some ridiculous old bloodline man or woman willing to share their black-market pharmaceuticals if one touched their leg the right way or danced suggestively came easily enough.

The Grand sparkled in bright lights, and the android bouncer let Elsie inside with a quick scan of her eyes and recognition that she belonged to an elite family in society. Elsie normally didn't care that she was a Sullivan, but in situations like these, she used her name for all the worth it was left.

Androids and humans crowded the club, and the music vibrated loudly. The bass shook the room with a full dance floor. They danced to the music together in scandalous outfits. Elsie herself wore a lacy top and a short skirt, but she beelined for the restroom the moment she stepped into the club. She pulled out a tight neon backless dress from her bag. The dress did what it could for her thin frame—thanks to frequent time travel—and Elsie opted for flat shoes to conceal her height as best she could.

Stepping out of the stall, Elsie approached the sink and stared at her reflection in the mirror. She would do just about anything at this point for this mission to save society, to keep The City safe, and was grateful for the microchip in her brain. The microchip allowed her to disengage, and she felt less guilt and indulged in various unsavory acts. Sex didn't mean anything to Elsie as long as it was a good time. Joel Kennsington was trash, a dirty Humanizer. But at least he was attractive and known as a good romp in the sheets.

The purple hair dye in her bag settled in at the tips of her blonde wig's strands as she put on a full face of makeup and green contact lenses in her eyes. She smiled in the mirror. Before her stood a newly transformed woman—one she barely even recognized.

As she made her way across the dancefloor, random hands stretched out, touching her skin and tempting her with a good time. Nightclubs were some of the few places where society deemed it socially acceptable for cross-beings to engage in such behaviors. Strobe lights flashed, and drinks were passed from various bartenders to patrons on the floor. Cozying up at the bar, Elsie observed her surroundings, waiting for Joel and Julie to arrive. With all the bodies pushed up against one another, Elsie needed a drink to cool down.

"Can I buy you a drink?" a familiar voice shouted over the music and in her ear.

Peter fucking Schneider, Elsie cursed in her mind as she turned in the direction of his voice. His flushed face and large pupils gave away Peter's level of intoxication. Elsie smiled, flashing her pearly whites and placing her large hand on his forearm.

"I'll have a Jameson on the rocks with a splash of soda," Elsie said to the bartender with a nod in Peter's direction.

Peter drove Elsie wild in the present, between their back-and-forth at COLI*GO and The Capitol Building. Here, he was different, less affected by the whims of Celine's subtle pushing and Anna Garcia's brazenness. His betrayals pained Elsie, but nothing compared to what they would do to Julie in the future. Her boss worked hand-in-hand with Peter to develop her toxin, and in a desperate grab for control and power, Peter ruined it all for an out-dated therapeutic that never made it to market.

He would make a nice addition to my list, Elsie thought deviously, her fingers tightening around the edge of the bar in a manner that she imagined them tightening around the handle of a sharp blade. Colin's sharp blade.

Paul McGuire differed from Don's legislative aide but felt better. After killing Lily Clark, Elsie vowed to never use her dark side against women ever again. Disappointment flooded through Julie at the realization it was Elsie who used someone's life as a bargaining chip in the same fashion Colin once did.

She expects better of me and so do I.

A chill crept through Elsie's otherwise overheated body. Julie and Joel entered the club. Joel was dressed in his daytime suit and tie, obviously wanting everyone in his presence to know that he was a representative. Julie wore a leather jacket and a simple black dress.

Have I ever seen her in any other color?

The two made their way across the room—heading directly to the bar.

"Meet me by the private booths," Elsie whispered into Peter's ear, feverishly needing him far away from her. As much as Elsie secretly enjoyed Peter's company, distracting Joel was her number-one priority for the evening. Peter eyed her up and down and obeyed, grabbing her drink for her and heading into the crowded dancefloor.

Julie and Joel found a small open spot at the bar on the other end, and Elsie took a deep breath and straightened her shoulders and chest. With confidence, she strode over to them and leaned up against the other side of Joel, careful to let her fingers quickly nip his belt loop and allow her eyelashes to flutter in his direction. The bartender placed two drinks on the bar—a vodka soda for Julie and a whiskey for Joel—and Elsie smiled, captivating Joel's attention. Joel gravitated toward her, his hand lingering too low on her back.

"I'll go sit in one of those booths on the back wall. Come get me when we're leaving," Julie yelled over to Joel. Elsie watched Julie make her way to the other side of the room, and Elsie continued shamelessly flirting with the piggish man they all hated.

A small part of her felt disappointed that Joel didn't recognize her even with the disguise. He'd spent days grilling her in interviews for Colin's legislative aide and secretary position.

Am I really that unnoticeable?

"Is that your girlfriend?" Elsie asked in a high-pitched tone.

Joel nearly choked on his drink at the sound of her ridiculous question. "No."

"Good, then send her away. Focus on me, so then later, I can focus all on you," Elsie said, her fingers trailing down the buttons of Joel's shirt. She was slightly disgusted with herself. She felt whorish, a bit evil. But the façade was needed—getting Julie the device was more important.

Joel pulled out his own device and scrolled through his contacts. A bright smile flashed on Elsie's face as Jimmy's name appeared on the screen.

Checkmate.

Chapter 36
Julie

<u>January 28th, 47 A.R.</u>

A chill from both adrenaline and the harsh winter weather ran through Julie's body as she took off the time travel glasses. Celine's condo differed greatly from the O'Connor townhouse. The decorations were modern, and the glass structure was harsh with cold colors that allowed all the light from The City into the living space.

Martin sat cross-legged on a yoga mat on the floor, his floppy brown hair and olive skin radiating in the dim lamplight. He was an odd man, very logical and scientific, but he believed strongly in a unique lifestyle of meditation and clean eating. Julie had never seen him hold an alcoholic beverage in his hand.

"Dr. Julie Walsh," Martin said without opening his eyes. He turned his palms upward and took a deep inhale. "I've been expecting you."

A second yoga mat sat squarely beside him with candles burning on the corners. Julie sat down next to him and crossed her legs. Awkwardness hung in the air, and she refused to close her eyes.

Martin looked over at her with one eye open and warmly smiled before reaching behind his back and outstretching his hands toward her. Martin possessed Mick's journal.

"You've come looking for answers," Martin said, his eyes wide with a still fear. "I never imagined being a part of this mess, but I suppose the moment I agreed to help Celine, I didn't really have a choice. I tried to warn Colin, but he won't do anything about his knowledge. He will always protect his sister. The responsibility falls on me and you."

The leather-bound journal made Julie's heart skip a few beats as she flipped through the pages. Mick's scraggly handwriting consumed most of the journal, followed by the perfectly legible handwriting of Jones. Julie recognized the next script as her own. She remembered most of these entries but not the last one. Entry seventeen stared back at her with a gaping reality. Her pulse quickened as she came across letters from Melanie O'Connor, a goodbye entry from her fair-weather friend, Mick, and a final entry from Colin.

"How did you know I was coming here?" Julie asked Martin, finally breaking away from her transfixed stare at messy, rambling riddles.

"Colin told me."

Julie closed the journal. There were no answers here; she would need to make her own choices based on what she knew now.

Martin looked up from the ground and nodded. The sounds of Henry Jr. crying in the background escalated, and Martin motioned to find and comfort his son. Gripping the journal tightly in her arms, Julie ran out the door and pulled her device out to request a ride. She was already running behind.

The warmth of the vehicle welcomed Julie, but she still shivered in the backseat. She held on to the journal but affectionately felt for the two important syringes she kept in her pocket. Relief flooded through her knowing they were safe and sound in her puffy jacket.

The driver took them through the heart of The City, neglecting the underground tunnel system and remaining on the open surface roads. While it was a chilly night, Julie smiled softly at the people and androids wandering into restaurants and bars and leaving some small shops closing up for the night. They reached the highway and quickly exited into The Outskirts. The presence of triple-decker-style homes eased into houses with small yards and a bit of space between.

With a sharp transition, the vehicle approached the woods, and trees climbed high into the sky, thickly nestled together. The driver pulled over to a parking lot.

One recognizable vehicle was parked at the farthermost edge, and Julie rushed out of the car, slamming the door with emphasis and confidence.

The path was well marked, and old footprints guided her in what she hoped was the right direction. Everything was so dark, and the lights from The City weren't visible in the deepness of the woods. Looking up above, a blank sky stared back down, the stars hiding. Julie's breath surrounded her, the cool air freezing her face and making her exposed hands dry and itchy.

She pulled her puffer coat closer to her body. A clearing ahead made Julie pause. Sharp vibrations ricocheted through her body. Another time traveler.

There are too many of us now. This has gotten out of control.

"Which version of you am I speaking to?" Julie asked, and a familiar face turned around to greet her.

Mick pushed his glasses up the bridge of his nose. He smiled lightly at Julie, his eyes lingering on the jagged scar on her neck. With instinct, Julie pulled back.

"Are you the same Julie who went to The Island with me?" Mick asked.

Julie squinted. This was a time travel version of Mick not from her present, not from the fall of 47 A.R. This Mick came from before. Wrapping her arms around herself, she shifted on her feet, trying to hide her slightly protruding stomach from this version of Mick.

But it was too late. He looked from her stomach to her eyes, and an odd smile curled on his lips.

***

Julie continued up the hill, optimistic when the view of The City started meeting the skyline. This was a night full of regret, misery, and mistakes.

And now, I must fix them.

The outline of a figure ahead made the blood course louder in Julie's ears, her heart picking up its pace. She expected to find this version of Mick the first time around, and having run into an earlier version of him made her nervous. Goosebumps prickled her skin as she approached this Mick.

The right Mick.

"Julie," Mick said, extending out his arms for a hug. Julie

embraced him, tears trickling down her face.

"Mick, the journal. You need to give it to Jones." She handed him the leather-bound book, but Mick's eyes wandered down to the two syringes she held in her hand. Julie gripped them tighter and placed them safely back inside her jacket pocket.

"Julie . . ." The sound of her name brought her back to the cold winter woods, and she noticed Mick trembled with eyes wide and full of fear. Mick continued backing away slowly, his mouth open in awe and terror.

Julie turned around and gasped.

"I have to stop them."

Colin's devilish figure appeared down in the clearing, but this wasn't the Colin who killed her in the woods that night. This was a time traveler visiting from another dimension, his face a bit more sunken in. This was It.

Beside him stood a woman Julie faintly recognized. She was dressed in inappropriate clothing for the weather, a flowy sundress with a light cardigan and sandals. They hovered over a body bleeding out in the snow.

My body.

Melanie and It threatened the time loop. Julie needed to make it back to the townhouse, Mick needed to find this body, and he needed to save this version of herself or . . .

No. The time loop. This is the answer to solving the time loop.

Julie sprang into action.

PART EIGHT
Mick's Journal

"Let my enemies devour each other."
—*Salvador Dali*

Entry Eighteen:

November 22nd, 2 A.R.

Dear Melanie,

I'd like to introduce myself. My name is Mick Taylor, and I'm a time traveler. I know, that sounds absolutely insane. I promise I am not—although maybe insanity would be better. You've done so much in such little time for families like mine across The Constituency. I grew up out in The Countryside, where life is a bit different compared to the hustle and bustle of The City. I don't know which I prefer anymore. I used to hate my life in The Countryside. Everything centered on our family farm. There was no room to explore my own hobbies, to pursue science. I had to leave them. I had to say goodbye to family and accept a new life here in The City, alone. I felt like such an outsider. But I had science, and I was ready to pursue my studies in hematology.

I admire you. You also left your life behind for Henry O'Connor. This fascinates me. I'm sure most people would say you landed in heaven, being swept up into the life of a rich old bloodline family. And I see the way you are with him and how he is with you. I like this version of the man very much. This man, I would vote for him without a second guess. But you still entered a new life, a life of unknowns. Fitting in must have been hard. I see how much of a game old bloodlines make of every-thing. I wonder why. Are they bored? There's so much they can do, so much influence they have, and yet they don't.

Please don't give up on your charitable endeavors. They make such an impact. I look forward to the day that I time travel with you.

Best,
Mick

Entry Nineteen:

December 1st, 2 A.R.

Dear Mick,

Thank you for your letter. I try to write back to everyone who reaches out, whatever the method. I will say, a traditional handwritten note threw me for a loop. I can't remember the last time I didn't use a device to communicate with my family, my friends, or my constituents.

You must be a time traveler from the past, then? There's so much history about our city that I wish I knew, and I would like to pick your brain. History repeats itself over and over again. I want to see a place that learns from its mistakes—a group of people willing to admit their wrongs and work to make them right.

Normally, I would say I don't believe in abstract concepts like time travel. But you speak to me as if I someday time travel—that intrigues me, Mick. Do you really think I make this much of an impact on the lives of those around me? That's all I've ever wanted. You're right about Henry. He is a good man. He's passionate—when he loves, he loves, but when he hurts, he feels that immensely.

I hope I never hurt him. I can't bear the thought that I could ever be the source of his pain. Tell me something about the future? If you've ever been past this date, that is.

I look forward to more of your letters and anticipate a day in which I time travel with you too.

Sincerely,
Melanie

Entry Twenty:
December 28th, 2 A.R.

Dear Melanie,

I am glad you don't consider me a lunatic. That you believe in me. Or at least, entertain me enough to make me feel believed. Lately, I feel so alone.

I'm in love with an android. I know I shouldn't be. But I'm convinced he is my soulmate. Do you think he and I will ever find peace and acceptance in society? My desire for us to express our love without repercussions has caused a lot of conflict in my life. I've made mistakes.

I lost my best friend. I'm trying to gain back her trust, but I betrayed her. Have you ever betrayed anyone? It's the worst feeling. I'm hoping for forgiveness even though I might not deserve it. Do you think you could ever forgive someone who tried doing the right thing but ended up betraying you?

I'll tell you a wonderful thing about the future. Your children are impressive. Your daughter is a brilliant businesswoman on a quest to save society through innovation and technology, and your son follows in your husband's footsteps, helping people as the governor. Do not take this offensively, but your son is a better, stronger leader than your husband. The people call him the most beloved governor of our time. You should be proud. Both your children find happiness even if the road is messy and unpredictable.

And most importantly, you've positively impacted their lives. Your genuine love for them reminds them, especially when they feel so alone, that there are beings in their lives who accept them, who choose them over other superfluous desires.

I feel obligated to tell you that your son time travels and makes a decision that will torment him forever—and I ask that you consider an opportunity. For your last time travel trip, I'd ask you to use his blood sample to travel to January 28th, 47 A.R. It will all make sense once you get there.

I'd like to tell you something about the past, but that's difficult for me. I travel from the future, not the past, as you think. And time travel is through blood. I'd have to find a very old person to get back in time to where anything interesting (in a good way, not a chaotic way) happened.

My best friend, the one I lied to, she's also a time traveler. I'd like for you to meet her someday. You remind me of her in some ways.

Best,
Mick

Entry Twenty-One:
January 18th, 3 A.R.

Dear Mick,

I'm a sucker for a tragic love story. Maybe because I've lived one. Your words are kind. I think one day there will be more acceptance in our society. We need kindness, we need recognition, and we need forgiveness. These attributes will bring us forward, unite us as one.

Unity is of the utmost importance—without it, we crumble. We fail.

I'm slightly disappointed you can't tell me any facts from history. If I hadn't needed to take a job making money after school, I would have gone and studied history. I love learning, and I hope my children love learning too. I'm glad to hear the next child of mine will be a son. Henry will be excited (but I won't tell him. I don't think he'd take too kindly to me writing letters with a time traveler). Old bloodline families have such an odd affinity to their firstborn sons.

Whatever happened to daughters? Why are they not just as important? I can already tell that Celine will be a vibrant young woman when she's grown. I've never thought a baby could require so much energy on so little sleep.

I hope I get to meet my son soon.

Will I ever get to meet you? I'd really like to make sure I haven't gone crazy—or who knows, maybe I am getting these letters from a man who walks the future as you say.

Give your friend time. Time heals all wounds. I'm an optimist at heart, but I truly believe we all forgive. I can't imagine thinking anyone filled with so much malice that they do not feel regret would not be willing to accept the words "I'm sorry."

Sincerely,
Melanie

288   LEE S. HANNON

but I truly believe we all forgive. I can't imagine thinking anyone filled with so much malice that they do not feel regret would not be willing to accept the words "I'm sorry."

Sincerely,
Melanie

Entry Twenty-Two:

October 25ᵗʰ, 47 A.R.

Dear Julie,

You will make the correct choice. I believe in you. We deserved so much more for one another. I never wanted things to end more perfectly than they do this way. I do not deserve your forgiveness. I do not deserve Colin's. I forced all the horrible things in your life on you. But I also like to think about how this experience has changed us all for the better. I miss the naïve nature of our friendship, when we first met. I like lying in a public garden with this journal, closing my eyes to the warm sun, and allowing my mind to tread down the possibility that if I travel back in time and destroy the device, then this would all be over.

But the device isn't one of the time travel glasses and accompanying chrome box. I've realized the device is me. I need to end, or I'll keep destroying everything around me. You must make the final blow in this dimension and then travel back and start anew. Give us all hope, give us all a chance.

The Supreme wins in this one, Julie. I know this. And there's no way she can't. We've fallen for her fool's mate. The game will always fall in her favor with how the pieces are laid out on the board.

If you go back—if you truly take all the knowledge you have and close this time loop, there's a chance at salvation.

But that means you need to kill me. Can you do that, Julie?

With regret,
Mick

Entry Twenty-Three:

June 23rd, 47 A.R.

Dear Julie,

I don't know if you'll ever forgive me—but I must do this. I've played this game long enough to know that anyone who wants the victory so badly is a liar, a cheater, a murderer, and someone willing to create chaos. And they don't deserve it. I will give you a taste, so you understand. But I will not allow The Legislature to consume you.

The roughness of this life took my father away, and I saw it slowly doing the same to me. I'd like to blame Mick's discovery of time travel on all of this, but we're all creations of our own demons, our own desires.

I'd appreciate a great rest. To forget all about the pain and suffering I've endured and the tremendous amount of pain and suffering I've put on others. And I think once you're given the journal, you'll be ready for one too. I believe in you. I believe in everything you've written to me here.

You accepted me. You even went so far as to tell me I didn't need to take the antidote once it was fixed if I didn't want to. Do you understand the power of that choice? And that you trusted me enough to make the right decision for me, for you, for us.

I hope to see you on the other side of this. There's no one else I trust to perform the task of killing me than my sister so we can be together. Yes, she's not perfect. She is selfish. She craves power. She longs for our family legacy to be hers.

Let Celine suffer in the toxicity of this game, the crooked legacy my family passed down for generations. I tried to warn her, but she refuses to listen to me. She's my sister and I swore to watch out for her, but I cannot continue wading into darkness for her. One day, she must venture to fight her own fight.

Let her and The Supreme implode, scratch at the surface, and take each other down while claiming to love the other. They can take the final blows on the board. I don't care anymore.

Have you ever noticed that most executions are not performed by kings but by queens?

Let them have it, Julie.

We only need each other and our family.

Love,
Colin

PART NINE
The Present

"The world might indeed be a cursed circle; the snake swallowed its tail and there could be no end, only an eternal ruination and endless devouring."
—*Silvia Moreno-Garcia*

Chapter 37
Celine

Commissioner Jones paced back and forth beside Elsie's desk at The Capitol Building. Celine steadied herself and hid the smile that threatened to spread across her angular face. He called her here, asking if she had a moment to verify the weapon that had been found stashed in a closet in Elsie's office in the governor's wing.

The plan folded perfectly in Celine's lap when she was at The Supreme's condo. Elsie threatened the legitimacy of the O'Connor family name, but her slight lead in the gubernatorial election posed a larger threat. Elsie was a time traveler, and Celine was too. While Celine refused to travel to the future for her own selfish reasons—she did not want to age her body or threaten her perfect skin with wrinkles—she never believed the future was set. Changes in the present would affect the results of the future. She didn't need to be a scientist to understand that logic.

"Hello, Commissioner Jones," Celine said in as even a tone she could muster.

This thrill of setting Elsie up for Colin's death reminded Celine of her youthful years, when she played members of The Legislature to vote and approve clinical trials, when she founded COLI*GO and scoured the crème de le crème of society for investments.

"Ms. O'Connor." He said her name with a flash of emerald illuminating off his scales. One of Jones's detectives held her father's hunting rifle in gloved hands. The gun was beautiful, a treasure, and a sought-after collectible with its long barrel and perfect scope.

"You found the family rifle, I see."

Jones crossed his arms and stared at Celine. The stand-off caused a small bead of sweat to trickle down the back of Celine's neck, settling on the collar of her blazer.

He knows, she realized. While Jones was an android, the feeling vibrated off him. His knowledge, somehow, that she was the one who pulled the trigger, vibrant like a watercolor in the room with them.

"Thank you for confirming this is the O'Connor rifle," he said, looking away. Celine felt a rush of relief in her body now that his gaze landed somewhere beyond her. "We're going to bring it in for testing. I do, however, need to also bring you into the station."

"Whatever for?" Celine asked, a small tremble in her voice.

Stay strong. Do not allow this android to push fear into you when he doesn't understand fear himself.

"We believe you might know the whereabouts of The Supreme based on some new evidence. Representative Don Ludewing Jr. has requested me to bring you in for an interrogation on the matter. Hiding a fugitive is a serious crime."

You bastard. Jones was the one who helped free Emilia from FACERE. He was intricately involved in all of Colin's plans to help her escape. They made a pact—they would shield and protect one another to keep The Supreme safe until a new android came into power. *Until Emilia could transfer her microchip into a new host.*

"I don't know . . ."

"I'd like to remind you," Jones said, staring directly into Celine's steely blue-gray eyes, "that you have the right to remain silent. Anything you say can and will be used against you in the high judge's court of law."

"You're arresting me?" Celine yelped, stepping away from the detective who approached her from behind Jones.

Jones stepped between her and the detective and leaned in close to Celine's ear. A shiver crept down her spine at how close his pulsing green scales were to her body.

"You forgot to turn off your device before you went into The Supreme's condo," Jones whispered into Celine's ear. "I'm afraid to also uncover any gunpowder residue there that matches this particular rifle in her home. I can make a play for The Supreme being Colin's assassin. It fits nice into the narrative. But you need to figure out a great way to explain why you were there."

Jones stepped back away from Celine and nodded to his detective, who gave Celine enough respect to not restrain her as he led her down the hallway and out into the entrance of The Capitol Building.

***

Martin sat on the other side of the partition, a look of annoyance spread across his face. They hadn't shared any deep conversations since their argument, Celine too busy with her campaigns and him watching Henry Jr. while managing his role at COLI*GO. The police headquarters gave a chill to the air with the metal fixtures and gray tile floor. The monochrome made Celine's head spin, and with the lack of windows, she wasn't sure what time of day it was or how much time had passed since Jones took her here.

"This is insane," Celine said, wrapping her arms around Martin's stiff shoulders when he entered the room.

"Is it?" he asked with a raised brow and tired lines across his forehead. He backed away from her with a scrunched-up nose.

"Of course it is. I have no idea where The Supreme is. Yes, I went back to her condo, but she and I were friends—everyone knows that. It isn't suspicious at all."

Celine couldn't believe she'd been so stupid to forget to turn off her device, but the days blended together and the campaign tired her out. There was too much on her plate, but Celine would eat it all, shovel the food into her mouth until she could physically not lift another forkful. That's how she'd always been; she didn't see a need for change.

"I spoke to the commissioner," Martin said in a low voice, crossing his arms and leaning against the door. "If you admit to helping Emilia leave The City—you don't need to admit to knowing where she went—then you'll only face a few fines from the high judge and he will request that you donate a five-million-dollar bond to a low-income education project sponsoring android and nobody children to attend The University. The commissioner promised to not leak any of your crimes to the news. Your reputation will be saved. But there's one more condition: You have to bow out of the election."

Celine's heart dropped. Anger flushed through her system, and her brain raced, hoping to find some solution, some way out of this mess where she could still get everything she wanted: the gubernatorial seat, her shares at COLI*GO, and the O'Connor family legacy all for herself. Her mind ran dry, unable to validate any kind of path forward that included it all.

"You can't be serious."

"Deadly," Martin said with a raised brow. "This is probably for the best. Maybe stepping back will be good for you, for us, for our son. After the dust settles in a few years, there could be other opportunities."

"No." Celine sharply turned away from her husband, afraid to cry in front of him. The notion was entirely ridiculous—Martin had seen Celine in her lowest lows and her highest highs. He knew her better than this. She couldn't sit still; she needed to create an opportunity for Emilia to come back, especially if Colin couldn't.

"Celine." Martin's voice was sharp while pleading. "It's over. You must accept this."

The disappointment reminded her of how her father always said her name when he couldn't deal with her, when she exhausted him to the point of him not wanting to parent her or guide her any further. The sting of the situation spread enormously through Celine's veins, like a poison slowly wreaking havoc on her organs, shutting her body down. Celine's knees hit the floor with a tremendous boom, and wails escaped her body.

"It isn't fair," she screamed into the air. Martin approached her, his feet slowly coming into view. Celine refused to look up, reaching for him and wrapping her arms around his lower legs.

The horrible painting her father purchased, the one hanging in the townhouse created by that awful artist Jeb Taylor, flashed before her eyes. The woman begging, defeated, and kicked to the ground, bending to the whim of men.

"I'll concede," Celine said, standing to face her husband in the eye. She didn't loathe him; it wasn't his fault all her plans went awry. But he symbolized the parts of society, the way old bloodlines and The City would always be. "But this won't be my last fight. There's always another match. And I'll be even more ruthless, even more ready for it when the time is right."

Martin lifted Celine up by her chin and kissed her lips lightly. "That's why I love you."

Chapter 38
Isabella

<u>October 5th, 47 A.R.</u>

"I'm glad you could make it over to FACERE, Governor Walsh," Isabella said, extending her hand to shake Julie's. "I wanted to speak with you before the next scheduled Session to discuss my advancements for androids."

"Mick Taylor has said that you've been awfully busy," Julie responded with a bright smile as they made their way through the downstairs lobby.

"The election has been fascinating to watch." Isabella's brow rose with suspicion, testing how much she could poke Julie for information.

Isabella was always clashing with Celine O'Connor, and seeing someone else finally speak against her and not do as she said provided her with a giddy feeling.

Elsie Sullivan—and apparently half an O'Connor—was doing well in the polls, but Celine wasn't far behind. The race was too close to call. Elsie had yet to reveal her truth of being a posse hominem, and Isabella couldn't figure out why.

"I will support whatever decision the voters make at the polls on election day." Julie's response was diplomatic but honest.

Isabella held open the door to her office for Julie and glanced at her up and down. Don Jr.'s office spread rumors that Julie was with child, but it was difficult to gauge in Julie's black loose-fitted dress.

Still wearing the colors of mourning. An odd pang of jealousy ripped through Isabella at the accusation. She wanted desperately to be a mother, but Colin had always pushed the issue aside, claiming they had plenty of time and should get married first. *But he never rose to that occasion either.*

Anna already sat in a chair in Isabella's office but stood to shake

Julie's hand when they entered.

"Dr. Garcia," Julie said with a twinkle in her eyes, "it's so good to see you again."

"It's nice to see you as well, Dr. Walsh," Anna responded politely.

They huddled in the center of the room. Anna and Julie had gotten off to a rough start, but Isabella hoped their differences were put aside, considering how close Julie and she had become.

"The Session next week will be incredibly important," Julie said, refusing to take a seat. The small stress marks on Julie's face were only apparent in the harsh hallway lights. Here, she looked more angelic even with her scar. "You'll be showcasing this product road map that I'm excited to hear about, and The Legislature and I will be voting on a new supreme. I'd like your support. Your relationship with the future governor and the future supreme sets a precedent."

"Who is receiving the nomination?" Isabella asked with a curl of her lips.

Isabella never imagined being in a role that held so much political sway, but Julie reminded her how much power she held in this coveted seat at FACERE.

"Commissioner Jones," Julie said with a thoughtful, appropriately sized smile even though Jones was her friend. Anna straightened, and a bit of hope spread across her face. "This was Colin's wish. I want to respect it. I also believe Jones has earned the role. He's a thoughtful android and has proven his rational capabilities with The Legislature ever since he began investigating Kendra Washington's death back in 43 A.R. And his work in uncovering the corrupt groups at FACERE and implementing a successful plan sealed the deal."

Isabella nodded. She hardly knew Jones, but Anna worked well with the android and spoke fondly of him. With Anna holding a position of power at FACERE, this seemed like the best of both worlds.

"I look forward to working with Commissioner Jones again—especially not at the police headquarters," Anna said and uncrossed her arms. "Should we show you the developments we've made?"

Julie nodded and listened carefully as Anna explained the android version 2.0 renewal. Nervousness consumed Isabella's mind. She wanted Julie's support and appreciated how a scientist would perceive the medical advancements she proposed. This was a rarity in The Legislature—these representatives made the most important decisions without typically having any medical or scientific backgrounds. The once-in-a-lifetime opportunity of Julie sitting in the most coveted seat provided a chance Isabella couldn't let go to waste.

"I've wanted to correct my wrongs from the very beginning. This role has empowered me to highlight that I am more than just a socialite, that I'm a skilled surgeon. This will help create a better society. I don't have much time left here. I've unfortunately been diagnosed with an aggressive form of acute monocytic leukemia, and I've chosen not to pursue aggressive treatments."

Julie's eyes grew wide, and she grabbed Isabella's hands.

"I hope this medical advancement for androids will be the positive mark I leave on society. I hope it somewhat makes up for all the atrocities I helped Celine O'Connor and The Supreme accomplish."

"This is truly incredible," Julie finally said. Her smile beamed in the room as she dotted away the tears from her eyes. "You really took something and made it your own. This is an astonishing legacy to provide an optimistic future. I do have some questions."

"I would have been surprised if you didn't." Isabella smiled.

***

Peter's office in COLI*GO was no longer in the right-wing corner of the 101st floor—he now kept a smaller office on that level of the building.

"How is the progress going on my father's asset?" Isabella asked, tapping her perfectly manicured nail against the table. Peter's eyes followed Isabella's nails. He looked horrid, thin, and tired.

He is resembling Mick Taylor more and more each day, Isabella thought with a twinge of sorrow. Mick Taylor became dependent on the sensation as much as his addiction depended on the answers he constantly searched for. Large dark bags loomed under Peter's eyes, and his skin sagged from muscle loss.

"Terribly," he admitted, ruffling his hair with a sweeping motion of his hand. "At least it's been keeping Mick Taylor and me busy. It's a political disaster trying to use it in the lab. Martin is suspicious, and Anna keeps pinging me to see if there are any updates because she cares too much about it. Frankly, I don't know what to do anymore other than just try to push it through at the next board meeting."

With a slight nod, Isabella hid the smile on her face. Her eyes gravitated toward the metal briefcase—one that resembled the same case in her odd memory-dream flashback. Peter followed Isabella's gaze, and his eyes rose to the briefcase.

"I still don't understand why this was sent to me," Peter said, his fingers brushing against the cool metal with affection. "Are you still working with her?"

Isabella drew in a sharp breath and exhaled with emphasis. Separating herself from The Supreme hadn't been easy, especially with the fear she evoked in those who partnered themselves with her.

"No, I'm not." Isabella stood from the chair, suddenly infuriated by the conversation. "I think it's best I take the asset with me if you're struggling with it. It's hard to create without the correct equipment, and if Martin shuts down this program—like it's rumored he will—then I want to make sure this is safe and sound."

"And where will that be?"

"That's none of your concern." Isabella grabbed the metal case from his hands, breaking it free with ease.

Desperation and loneliness spread across Peter's face. She almost pitied the man, but she found it incredibly difficult to feel sorrow for someone who sided with Celine O'Connor at the drop of a pin. She was a great deceiver, even worse than The Supreme.

Peter had little time left in this city, his demise as sharp and quick as the slice of Colin's blade. Isabella sensed this deep in her bones, the sensation vibrating across her with the same level of pain as when another time traveler graced their presence nearby.

Time travel might make us somewhat inevitable, but that security really highlights the rawness of death too.

Isabella left COLI*GO for the last time.

***

The halls of the governor's wing were bustling with people and androids, legislative aides and policy researchers, all vying for Governor Walsh's time. While Elsie currently ran for the position, she still served as Julie's legislative aide and secretary.

Isabella hardly knew Elsie, but she was Julie's gatekeeper. Needing the governor in her pocket for the last few months, she tried to treat Elsie with warmth and respect.

"Hello, Elsie," Isabella said, placing the heavy metal briefcase down on the floor beside her feet. "I was hoping to pop in and see Dr. Walsh before the Session today. There are a few quick outstanding items I need her perspective on. I also would like to leave this with her." Isabella gestured toward the container on the floor.

If Martin's accusations were correct, Peter was trying to use her father's technology and pass it off as his own. Isabella felt a fondness for her father's antiquated drug. Destroying the contents violated her familial loyalty, but with Julie, there was hope that someday the scientist would utilize whatever knowledge this could bring to future research.

Elsie poked her head to the side and glanced down at the metal briefcase. Her eyebrows scrunched together, and she glanced over at the monitor on her desk.

"I'm afraid Julie is with your cousin, Representative Ludewing, at the moment. And you're first on the agenda for the Session today. You'll need to be over there in the next twenty minutes or so." Elsie studied Isabella's demeanor and reached for the heavy briefcase. Dragging it under her desk, she reached for a piece of paper and a pen. "Why don't you write her a quick note and I'll make sure she gets this after the Session today. I can schedule you time with her early next week if you'd like."

Isabella sighed and looked down at the watch on her wrist. Elsie was correct—she didn't have much time before she needed to head to the Session room and set up her presentation on the new versions of androids. And she needed to meet with Anna too.

"Okay," Isabella said and hastily scribbled her father's name on the piece of paper, followed by a quick explanation that he tried accomplishing a similar solution to psychological conditions as she had with her antidote. Elsie smiled softly and folded the paper, taping it to the top of the briefcase under her desk.

Picking up her pace, Isabella headed to the other side of The Capitol Building. She passed through one of the newer wings, resurrected after The Resurgence when the original burned down in a riot. The building was historical otherwise, but the newness of this section taped itself together and attempted to match the rest of the décor with replica patterns in the marble and columns a tad too crystal and white.

When she reached the Session room, dozens of sets of eyes watched Isabella cross the gold-leaf-designed carpet toward the center of the room. Nearly half of the representatives were already seated, waiting for the meeting to start. Anna sat at the table, and beside her was Commissioner Jones. First on the agenda was Isabella and Anna's presentation on the new androids they proposed adding to the production line, followed by a new supreme appointment, and then a final vote on both FACERE's topic and the supreme nomination.

Anna grabbed Isabella's hand under the table and squeezed it tightly while the rest of the representatives filtered in. Their cousin's smooth honey-brown eyes met theirs, and he gave them a slight nod. Julie entered behind Don, choosing to sit on the lower level instead of in the governor and supreme galley a few stories up.

Don cleared his throat and banged a light gavel on his desk.

Thump. Thump. Thump.

Silence followed suit.

"We are here today in Session to hear from FACERE and The Representatives of the Androids, championed by Governor Walsh, in the selection and nomination of a new supreme. All rise, and we shall begin."

Everyone in the room stood as The Constituency's anthem played lightly in the background. Once the chorale music subsided, the rustling of wooden chairs and bodies sounded through the room. With a motion of Don's hand, he introduced his cousins and sat back down.

"Good afternoon, Representatives," Isabella said, looking down at her hands for a moment. Anna lightly cleared her throat, distracting Isabella from her silence. "I'm here to present exciting medical advancements and protections to the rights of androids in the future."

The screen highlighted the security risks of cloud technology currently used at FACERE to create microchips. Notes based on COLI*GO's forbidden lower lab project of posse hominems appeared on the left side of the screen. Everything about the proposal for personalized blood in androids provided sound, logical reasoning. Various representatives stilled in their seats. The unknown terrified them all—something Isabella sympathized with them. To her surprise, an android representative with dusty pale pink scales clapped her hands. The rest followed her action, and Don Jr. started clapping as well.

"Please settle down," he said after a few moments. "There is much to consider in this proposal, but I think we can unanimously agree that something along these lines is the correct path forward."

Julie agreed, "Yes, I propose we schedule a specific Session in November to go through more data in greater detail and discuss implementation into the next wave of android manufacturing. It's only fair that the new supreme has a say in this as well."

The rumblings in the room agreed with their governor.

"And to that note, let us discuss the next agenda topic. The appointment."

The room quieted, and Isabella smiled at Anna and Jones. An android representative with gray and silver scales stood, and all eyes directed their attention toward him.

"We've been interviewing various candidates for a supreme replacement, and the time has come that we decide. On behalf of The Representatives of The Androids, I would like us to vote in and verify the appointment of supreme to Commissioner Jones."

Murmurs escaped across the room, and the representatives sat in their seats to cast their votes. With wide eyes, Isabella watched the board in the front of the Session room explode with Yay and Nay votes. The measure needed seventy Yay votes to pass. The suspense intensified around the room, so palpable that Isabella reached for Jones's hands, rubbing small circles into his scaly palm to help calm his scales from glowing any brighter.

Cheers erupted across the room as seventy-nine Yay votes, twenty-one Nay votes, and zero abstained votes appeared on the screen.

"Congratulations, Commissioner Jones," Isabella said, her bright red lips smiling wide.

"Yes," Anna chimed in, placing her arm around Jones's stiff, terrified shoulders, "congratulations, Supreme Jones!"

Chapter 39
Mick

<u>October 24th, 47 A.R.</u>

Mick studied the antibodies in Colin's blood for days and days on end. Antibodies swirled within the blood, and Mick carefully extracted them, placing them into the simulation machine with continuous copying to provide more samples for testing.

Julie's eyes grew wide with excitement while she worked on injecting these properties in with her antidote origination. With hours spent testing different levels of the antibodies and various data sets observed, they believed they found the correct formulation. The antidote felt more special than previously, now that Mick's expertise and Julie's knowledge were used to create it. He couldn't wait to package up the data and present it.

A fitting ending. Mick relaxed knowing what his fate looked like. Correcting his wrongs with Jones, avoiding the temptations of The Supreme and her empty promises, and finally reconnecting with Julie. *I can leave this world, this dimension, and know that forgiveness will provide the ultimate winning move in this sadistic game of chess.*

"How's it looking, Mick?" Julie asked, walking through COLI*GO's laboratory doors.

She grabbed a pair of safety glasses and put on a long stained lab coat. They were waiting on the last set of simulation results to see if the artificial intelligence models predicted efficacy and would likely meet clinical program endpoints. The features of her face were glowing even in the harsh lights, and Mick couldn't help but smile in her direction.

"I was about to message you and tell you that the results are in. I haven't looked at them yet. I wanted you to be the first to see them."

Julie picked up her pace and placed her delicate hands on Mick's shoulders, leaning in to look at the screen. Mick double-clicked on the machine, and the results uploaded, the spinning circle on the screen causing anxiety and anticipation in the pit of Mick's stomach.

Data sets exploded across the screen—all pointing toward a successful single-dose antidote that worked not only for Alzheimer's patients but also predicted meeting the endpoints for patients suffering from bipolar disorders and dementia.

Julie yelped in excitement, wrapping her arms around Mick's gangly body and squeezing him tight into her chest. She kissed his cheek and pointed at the screen.

"It looks like it will work—the antidote will really work!"

Mick turned on his stool and pulled her in close, giving her a welcoming hug.

"I have to type up the reports and get this over to Martin and the rest of the board."

"Julie," Mick started, grabbing her by the shoulders and steadying her, "take a minute, take a deep breath."

Her breathing stilled a bit, but her breaths were heavy and she trembled slightly in Mick's weak grasp. This moment was monumental for her. After a decade of researching this drug, the cure for those suffering from some of the most excruciating and saddening neurological and psychological conditions was finally developed. Julie started working on her antidote in her years at The University, fought to present her findings to COLI*GO's board, spent countless hours of her own personal time in the advanced laboratories to continue her research, and finally received funding, resources, and a team to make this dream a reality. With all the setbacks, the hardships, and long frustrating days and nights—the antidote was real.

"You're right," Julie said, struggling to hold back her tears of joy.

"First, let's make some samples. I think you deserve to physically hold the antidote in your hands."

"Then we'll get back to work afterwards. This is only the beginning. There's still so much to do." Julie left Mick's station and started working on her own, transferring files and setting up machines to produce the sample drug.

Mick shook his head and chuckled. She was a racehorse,

determined and powerful.

Now that we have the antidote, we can destroy this dimension once and for all. The laboratory buzzed to life and both Julie and Mick watched as advanced machinery and tools zipped and spun, creating the molecules on the screen into a physical reality.

With a small beep, the latch opened, and Julie looked at Mick before reaching in with her gloved hand and pulling out a glass vial with clear liquid inside. The COLI*GO logo was stamped along the side, and Julie reached for a black marker and filled in the line:

COL23—AntidoteV2

***

The answers were finally laid out, the simulations promising, and the antidote an actual reality.

Mick's life was intertwined with time travel in the same way Julie's identity was woven into her antidote, both passion projects turned into much more. The stakes were always high in science and innovation, but knowing that they solved this giant puzzle together, that Julie could now help the man she loved and prevent families from losing their loved ones to madness, made all the pain and suffering worth it. Just as Julie would face an uncertainty of what obstacle in pharmaceuticals to take on next, Mick had to say goodbye to time travel.

After pulling an all-nighter and creating a few sample batches in the lab, Mick and Julie made their way back to the townhouse to celebrate. Colin's study was quiet except for the humming sound of the heater kicking on for the first time this fall.

Mick looked up at Julie and raised his glass of apple cider to meet hers. The clinking sound erupted throughout the room, and Julie leaned back in Colin's seat with a relaxed grin.

"What are you going to do now?"

Julie blinked rapidly, taken aback by Mick's question. The emptiness that came after drug discovery was one that neither of them understood but particularly not Julie. There had always been another project, some other asset COLI*GO needed for its success. The antidote and the toxin were Julie's first drugs she created from scratch and led all the way through to perfection.

"We must terminate all information about the toxin from electronic files. The implications of someone using this to hurt society are too great. Dr. Garcia's false drug championed through Peter was a good lesson of that," Julie said, looking straight into Mick's eyes. "But I'm not sure who stole the documentation on the toxin from Peter. He never should have brought it to the present with him when we were working on the asset in the past. Now, I have to find the culprit and destroy the information they possess. But, Mick, I'm so tired. I'm so, so tired, I don't know if I have the strength."

"You're right; that was dangerous of him," Mick said, his hands shifting in his pockets. He pulled out a small flash drive and placed it on the mahogany desk between him and Julie. "Luckily, I'm the one who took it and kept it for safekeeping."

Julie's eyes widened, grasping the small drive between her tiny fingers.

"I hope that this proves to you I was never out to hurt you," Mick said, looking down and away from Julie. Tears burst from his eyes. "I made many mistakes. Maybe I am not worthy of your forgiveness. Maybe I am not worthy of anyone's. But regardless, I did correct my course, and I've protected the right pieces on the board—most importantly, you. I couldn't save Colin, but I sure as hell fought to make things as difficult as possible for The Supreme."

"I know so much now," Julie said, grabbing Mick's dry, fragile hands in hers. "And that information is valuable. I wouldn't be here without you. You saved me. You gave me a fighting chance, but now I don't know how to correct all the wrongs or how to truly eliminate The Supreme for good."

He was a disaster, the bones popping out of his shoulders, his collarbone a ghastly sight. The pain coursing through his body was too much to bear, the messed-up components of his blood from Isabella's tests and trials wreaking havoc on him.

But Mick had played his part. He was done with this world, ready for a sense of stillness and reconciliation he hadn't known since before he invented time travel.

Mick's lips trembled, and he released Julie's hands.

"The Supreme needs a counter. It will always be that for her. It is her inverse, her constant back and forth. That's what she uses as Colin's weak spot. If you think about it, the only way to fix any of this is to go back. And at that point, you might as well go all the way back to when Colin attempted to kill you. Take the antidote with you and then destroy It."

"But changing the past has created all these issues. These time loops are convoluted," Julie said.

This is the only way to ensure peace. Destroy The Supreme. Take away the pieces on the board she uses against one another. Leave her with almost nothing to play her games with.

"Think about going back. There's a reason I've run into you in the woods so many times on that night. Rescuing you was the time loop that ignited this fire. Put it out before it can even start, and with your knowledge, you'll be able to properly prepare for battle with Emilia. And you can be with Colin, raise your child together."

Julie paced beside Mick. Wrapping her arms around him, she carefully pulled in her friend. They stood behind the desk, staring out the window into the skyline view of The River, the carriage house in direct view. The gloomy fall clouds made the sky gray, and raindrops left pinpricks on the river separating The Hill neighborhood. The sun rose, fighting its way out of the horizon.

"I forgive you, Mick."

Mick looked down at Julie before putting his face in his hands. He cried, the sorrows of all his sins washing out of his mind. Freeing him, freeing them.

"This is perfect, Julie. Absolutely perfect."

"What do you mean?" she asked, her brow raised.

"Take this with you," he said, handing her the toxin and the files containing its blueprint. "Destroy it. And please, go back and don't come back. Get rid of the time travel device too and give me the journal. I believe that version of me will listen. Do you promise me? End this madness."

Julie grabbed the toxin's roadmap and the sample syringe and placed them securely in a small bag with the single-dose injection of the antidote. Mick coughed, and Julie looked back up. In his other hand, outstretched, was Colin's knife. The color drained from Julie's face, and she shook her head violently.

"Only another time traveler can kill another time traveler. I've killed myself hundreds of times at this point, so I can't do it again," Mick said with a trembling lower lip. "I always end up back to the moment of my death. And I'm not sure how I'm supposed to feel about that."

"Mick . . ." Julie said slowly. "Where is that moment? When is that moment?"

Mick stalked over to Julie slowly, a smile spreading across his face. Julie's eyes followed his hands as he wrapped his lanky, bony fingers around her wrists, slipping the handle of the cool blade into her palms. Colin's knife trembled in her hands.

"Now."

With all his strength, Mick yanked down. The knife dove into his chest as Julie screamed in terror. Her grip loosened from the knife, but Mick's remained firm on her wrists. The pain shattered him, an overpowering sensation snaking its way through his body. Lights flickered in his vision. The view felt out of body, the sight of terror on Julie's otherwise pristine face.

"I'm sorry, Julie, I'm so terribly sorry." His knees hit the ground, crimson blood spilling from the left corner of his mouth. Mick's fingers relaxed, and she knelt next to him, stroking his cheek.

"I'm sorry, too, Mick. We deserved better versions of ourselves. I'll make sure that happens."

Mick's vision tunneled, but he felt peace in the arms of his best friend. She forgave him—and she gave them a chance to start over again.

Rebirth.

Chapter 40
Julie

<u>October 25th, 47 A.R.</u>

Julie watched Mick take his final breath by her side, and she held him for a while longer, waiting to see if he would reemerge, if he would come back.

He didn't.

Julie stumbled over to the desk and sat in Colin's large leather chair, still gripping the handle of the knife. With her other hand, Julie traced each scar slowly, her fingers lingering on her abdomen.

Mick was correct, she thought. The decision wasn't difficult anymore. *I'm glad we could make amends before I make this one last, final journey.*

Julie swore she'd never fully corrupt the present by traveling to the past, but she wanted a better world. A world where life could blossom, thrive.

They all deserved a real chance.

Ending the antidote program was the most difficult moment in Julie's professional career. The answers were finally laid out; the simulations proved a promise, a glimmer of hope for patients suffering from the most excruciating mental agony.

Martin could have ended this program a long time ago if he wanted—but he knew from the journal, he knew how impactful this would be for COLI*GO. He knew Julie could find the answer, and Mick believed even if Julie traveled back to the past and started over, she'd find it again. But now she didn't have to. The hard work paid off.

Julie cleaned Colin's knife with antiseptic and toweled it dry before placing it back in the bottom left-hand drawer of his desk. She pulled Mick's flash drive out of her bag and walked over to the fireplace. With the flicker of a match, Julie watched the small storage device melt away, the plans to her toxin along with it. She placed her bag with a syringe filled with the toxin and a syringe filled with the antidote into the bottom drawer beside the knife and locked it.

The carriage house appeared dark across the courtyard, and Julie eyed Mick's journal one last time. She paused, considering writing one last entry in the confines of the diary but decided the memory of today would be enough for her—and while she wanted to trust Mick and his own belief that he'd change his tune once he read the entries already logged inside the journal, Julie didn't trust time travel enough to provide the answers so blatantly and left the leather-bound notebook hidden in the secure container as it was.

The COLI*GO building came into sight after a few moments of Colin's vehicle driving through the windy streets of The City. The morning was young, but Martin was an early riser, enjoying his morning routine of meditation in his office before heading down to the laboratory to assist with researchers on the various projects and pipeline assets COLI*GO was developing. With a slight knock on his door, Julie entered without asking for permission.

"Martin," she said with a small smile. He was seated on the floor on his yoga mat and opened his eyes at the sound of his name.

"Julie," he said with a wide beaming smile, "I saw the memo you left me but hadn't had a chance to read through it all." He stood and approached her at the entrance of his office. "Is it true?"

"Yes," Julie answered, unable to contain the giddy smile that painted her freckled face. "The antidote is now viable."

She handed him several of the vials she and Mick created over the night. Martin looked at the clear liquid promising a reprise of normalcy to millions of people throughout The Constituency.

"We'll get started on all the applications for The Legislature right away," Martin said with a newfound pep in his step. He flickered on his device, typing furiously.

"Of course," Julie said. She paused, realizing this wouldn't be the last time she'd give this news to Martin. The promise of a repeat of this memory sparked hope inside Julie—a feeling she hadn't experienced in a long time. "I'm going to take some time today. I have a few things to do at The Capitol Building, and then I'll probably take a nap. Last night's discovery exhausted me. If you can't reach me for the rest of the day, that's why."

Martin nodded. "I'll get started on everything. Take some time and relax. You deserve it."

Julie hugged him tightly before exiting the prestigious glass skyscraper. When she reached the garage, she leaned back in the car's leather seat and closed her eyes. She was tired, but there was still one more being she needed to see.

"Take me to The Oceanside," Julie said to the voice-activated vehicle.

Chapter 41
The Supreme

<u>October 25th, 47 A.R.</u>

The waves crashed along the cliffs with the premonition of a terrible storm. The early afternoon clouds threatened another set of rain clouds, and Emilia roamed the abandoned halls once again. While the O'Connor estate offered more space than the townhouse, the memories of her childhood here stained any chance for finding comfort in these halls.

Emilia had grown up alongside the O'Connor siblings, and they spent many summer months here, even after Melanie O'Connor's disappearance. An android's processor contained all memories, making it virtually impossible for them to forget anything—a blessing and a curse.

One memory came into the forefront of Emilia's processor as she passed by the bedroom that had once been hers. In the summer of 13 A.R., one year after Melanie's death, Celine snuck across the grand hall, darting in and out of the lights to reach the room Emilia slept in on the other side of the home. She'd nearly jump into the covers beside Emilia and pull the blankets up over her eyes.

"What is it?" Emilia asked, afraid that if she spoke too loudly, Henry would hear and yell at the girls for their reckless behavior. Emilia was only accused of inattentive actions when she spent too much time influenced by Celine.

"I swear I saw my mother. Her ghost haunts this place."

Emilia had rolled her eyes back then. She thought Celine was silly, speckled by a desire to see her mother again mixed with a wild imagination. But now, as an adult, Emilia knew better that time travel was real and that some illusions were actually realities.

Did Melanie O'Connor travel time? she wondered. Mick spoke fondly of the woman, claiming he watched her when he traveled to the past to understand the dynamics of all the players. Back when he first began working for The Supreme, he was a loyal subject, telling her of his observations, his research, and his findings. As time passed, he drifted away, more so after the death of his uncle Jeb.

Mick betrayed Emilia—but she figured he would. His allegiance to Julie was difficult to barter against, and his devotion to his android lover made him too weak and vulnerable. But Emilia didn't need Mick anymore. He wasn't a key piece on the board. She kept him around long enough, and now she was ready to relieve him of his duties.

The sound of the mountainous front door echoed across the marble floors. The estate was purely ostentatious and only charming because the O'Connor siblings had kept the style intact from their childhood memories. They made minor modifications and updates, keeping it as original as possible in homage to their mother.

Dr. Julie Walsh strode into the grand hall, her shoes clicking against the stone floors. The Supreme let out a sigh of relief she hadn't realized she held in. Emilia was still a fugitive, a woman with a large bounty on her head.

"Dr. Walsh." Emilia motioned to the scientist.

"Hello, Madam Supreme."

"I hear you shouldn't be calling me by that name anymore. Didn't your dear friend Commissioner Jones just steal that post from me?" A smile as curvy as a snake mirrored across The Supreme's face.

To pass the time, she watched the news, read her books, and strolled the secluded grounds. The same segments played over and over again on the large screen in the living room. Isabella Garcia discovered an advancement for androids, one that The Legislature and FACERE didn't reveal in full. Isabella was a strange pet, one that The Supreme wished she had treated differently. Her harshness pushed the surgeon away, and had she understood or felt the emotion of empathy, Emilia might have held on to the beautiful woman's attention a bit longer.

"That is correct," Julie said with a large smirk. "Jones is now The Constituency's supreme."

Emilia nodded slowly. "So then, why did you come visit me?"

Julie stalked over to where Emilia stood and tilted her head up to meet Emilia's gaze. Julie wasn't a short woman, but even with average height, The Supreme towered over her.

"I came to say goodbye."

"You're not banishing me away somewhere new now either, are you?"

"No," Julie said with a pause. "I'm leaving. And I don't plan on coming back."

Time travel, The Supreme thought suspiciously. *The scientist thinks she can run away from the tragedies of this dimension by going back to an older one.*

Emilia walked over to the couch and settled into the large cushions. Opening the coffee table, she revealed her treasured wooden chess set. She was glad Celine had the decency to mail it to The Oceanside estate. It was one of her most prized belongings. Henry O'Connor had gifted the board to her as a congratulations present when she graduated from The University. Her graduation represented many new beginnings—she could no longer live in the home she grew up in, in the townhouse. She was moved to her own condo and studied exclusively under the wing of Edward, the supreme before her. The parting gift was beautiful, and it symbolized the gratitude she held for the wretched O'Connor man and everything he had taught her.

"Why don't we play a game?" Emilia said, temptation itching in Julie's outstretched fingers. The scientist made her way over and sat opposite The Supreme while she set up the board.

"I'm not much of a player," Julie admitted, lining up her pieces with care and precision.

"Oh, Dr. Walsh, give yourself a little bit more credit." Emilia chuckled. "Did Colin never teach you?"

"I know how to play; I just haven't since my childhood. This was not the kind of game Colin and I played together."

When the pieces were laid out, Emilia gestured toward Julie to let her start the game.

"The art of chess is really in distraction," Emilia said, pushing her first pawn forward. "It's about making your opponent think a certain piece is after their king when it isn't."

Julie advanced her own pawn forward and eyed The Supreme with silence. The two continued taking turns back and forth, stealing pawns from one another with ease.

"It's about making your opponent feel a sense of excitement and desire when they finally take that piece they've been eyeing for so long," The Supreme said with a smile, snatching one of Julie's knights with her queen. "You must capture your opponent's attention by any means possible. Each piece plays a part in that."

Julie's next move caught Emilia off guard, and the scientist's delicate fingers stole The Supreme's rook.

"Ahh . . . Mick Taylor. Now you have him back—I should have known better than to think Mick would forever hold the fort down for me. Luckily, I have a few other pieces left on the board." The Supreme advanced her bishop.

Julie eyed the board for a moment and grabbed her queen.

"I think caring about winning so ferociously is a distraction all on its own," Julie said, looking up at The Supreme with her lips turned upwards in a seductive smile.

The Supreme glanced back down at the board, and her scales flickered uncontrollably to the colors of an autumn tree turning its leaves. A loud thumping noise echoed in Emilia's ears, the sound of her silver liquid android version of blood whooshing around her body.

Damiano's Mate.

Julie tapped Emilia's king with her queen. "Checkmate."

"Well done, Dr. Walsh," The Supreme said with an extended hand and a shimmering smirk pressing between her lips. "Until next time."

Chapter 42
Supreme Jones

<u>October 25th, 47 A.R.</u>

Jones watched the election results pour in quickly on the screen. After Celine O'Connor dropped out of the race, claiming her true place was with her husband and her child, Elsie won. The back-end deal Jones made with Martin Borges worked in his favor. He wanted to keep a good relationship with COLI*GO, and even with Julie sitting at the helm as CEO, if Jones learned anything lately, it was that as many allies as possible would serve him well.

Becoming the next supreme wasn't ever originally in Jones's fate, but with time travel and greed, the tables had turned. He believed in himself, but doubt crept into his processor. His desire to make sure he served his fellow androids would lead him in the right direction. Julie's endorsement and kind words after the announcement a couple weeks back provided Jones with the public's astounding approval.

He worked diligently with Anna Garcia and Isabella at FACERE, ensuring he and the android representatives were heavily involved in the studies of this new medical advancement that promised androids more autonomy. The City faced extreme turmoil for far too long, and a bit of optimism flushed through Jones's processor with each passing day.

Maybe we will all be okay, he thought, looking out the window of his new office in The Capitol Building. The room was brighter than his office in the police headquarters, and Jones enjoyed the views of the courtyard with its tall flowers and crisscrossed green vines flourishing even in the chillier fall weather due to the greenhouse that kept them safe.

Elsie still bothered Jones, but he desperately hoped they could fall in step together. A little tension was required, a necessary evil to make sure they kept one another in line. But Elsie's distance since she started campaigning nagged in his processor. She hadn't informed the public that she was a posse hominem, and this strange omission settled poorly in his stomach.

A slight knock on his door echoed, and Jones called in his visitor. The half-Sullivan, half-O'Connor, half-human, half-android appeared in his doorway. Elsie's frame had thinned over the summer and into the fall, the giveaway that she kept one of Mick's time travel devices and qualified Jones's suspicion that she was another time traveler.

"Well, I'll be swearing you in later this evening on live television," Jones said with a smile. He stood and shook Elsie's hand. "Congratulations, Governor Sullivan-O'Connor."

"Thank you. I really look forward to working together again. I think we were great partners in the past, don't you?"

Jones nodded slowly and took a seat in his comfortable chair. He decided to keep the desk—the inscription and carvings of androids toppling statues, fighting off guards in riot gear. The piece originally belonged to the first supreme, Edward, which he commissioned, and Emilia had kept it like an odd android family heirloom.

Emilia desperately wanted to be an old bloodline even if she wouldn't admit this truth. Jones blamed her childhood impressions and being raised in Henry O'Connor's home. Her greed was not inherent, but it was a learned behavior.

"Some things never change, do they?" Elsie asked, glancing around the room with a nostalgic gaze. She settled into the comfortable velvet chair that Jones had yet to get rid of—a piece of Emilia's that didn't match his style.

"What do you mean?" Jones inquired, finding comfort in the sound of Elsie's smooth voice.

"An O'Connor in the governor's office and an android who understands too many emotions in the supreme's office."

Jones cocked his head to the side and allowed her astute accusation to marinate. He never told Elsie of his true abilities, and Julie had never betrayed Jones in this way.

How does she know?

In a sharp movement, Elsie's hand shot up to her head like a migraine overwhelmingly controlled her. She let out a small cry of frustration and violently shook her head with rapidly blinking eyes.

"Elsie? Are you all right?" Jones asked, leaning in and placing his scaly hand on top of hers. Elsie closed her eyes and stilled herself before looking back up at him.

"Yes, Supreme Jones," she said. A scoff escaped between her lips.

Jones raised a brow and hesitantly backed away from her, the episode subsiding and mellowing out.

"I'm sorry," Elsie continued. "It's just so strange to address you by a name that once meant so much to me."

Chapter 43
Julie

<u>October 25th, 47 A.R.</u>

Once back at the townhouse, Julie made her way up the wooden staircase and settled into the townhouse's study. She turned on the small lamp sitting on Colin's desk and felt her hands shake in anticipation. She was going to the past, but she didn't know how. If she killed herself, she'd end up back in the woods, where she needed to go, but then risked leaving the time travel device unattended in the wrong dimension.

Julie twisted the tiny key that locked the bottom drawer of the desk. The knife greeted her again, a shiny, taunting toy once stained with her own blood, among many others.

Behind the weapon were various bottles of dangerous pills Colin used to help himself sleep or keep him awake when the stresses of being the governor were too much. She'd studied all these drugs back at The University; she knew which cocktail to make herself but would still need almost a full bottle of Scotch from the cabinet across the room.

She looked down. *I can't,* she thought, fully aware she was invincible to death in this current state. *I need to listen to Mick.*

Julie picked up the knife and twirled the sharp blade in between her fingertips. The time travel glasses and chrome box sat on the desk. A sharp pain pierced her fingertip, the poke coming from the knife. Crimson blood bubbled up quickly. With a flick of her wrist, Julie grabbed the two syringes and placed them securely in her thick, puffy winter coat. The glasses fit uncomfortably as they always did on her face, and her nose scrunched, her ears wiggling to accommodate the extra weight.

"Goodbye, Colin." Her voice echoed quietly in the empty room. "Goodbye for now."

***

She flung the glasses toward Mick as the bitter cold snow seeped into her shoes. The decision was made, and it tasted sweet. Julie was giving up her only way back to the present she knew. Surrendering to the darkness, to the complete unknown, never felt so promising.

Finally giving up time travel.

With a dropped jaw and color draining from her face, she crashed to her knees at the sight of It and Melanie, staring at one another, shocked they met again. It ventured closer, and Melanie backed away. Both appeared shocked to meet like this again, but instead of on the cliffs at The Oceanside, they stood deep in the woods on a hill facing The City.

"Now!" Mick yelled. "You don't have much time."

"I'm sorry, I want you to know this was never my intention." The words came from It, but Julie tried to stay hidden, not wanting to further distract the pair. Julie saw the torment spread across the face of the man she loved, but she didn't blame his mother for backing away. The diversion needed so that she could pass by them and make her way to her other body.

"All I ever wanted was for you to be happy," Melanie said, finally allowing herself to stop placing more distance between them. "And I see that you were. I was at least able to watch you and Celine grow up through the gift of time travel. I don't know if we'll ever find salvation for society, Colin, but don't let your desire to save society eat you alive inside as it did your father. If you get a second chance, find salvation for yourself, for your family. I forgive you."

Tears stung in the corner of Julie's eyes as she watched him hug Melanie. Colin regretted not getting to say goodbye to his mother—and It regretted the unknowing urge to push her off the ledge of the cliffs.

With their backs finally facing her, Julie approached the dying version of herself. Another version of Mick—realizing now that there were three of them here—would look for her. Her soiled body stained the snow beneath it a bright, flirtatious red.

Vomit rose in Julie's throat, a too-familiar feeling, as the bile uncontrollably flung from her mouth, coating her lips. She gulped, testing her body and praying her wave of sickness was over.

There could not be two versions of her. This version would survive if Mick found her; this version would go on and try to help Colin, to help The City. But The Supreme would win if this version of Julie lived.

In the end, no time traveler is morally better than Mick, Julie thought desperately as she picked up the mess that was her past self.

Colin's stab wounds were shallow, but blood still rapidly escaped them, bleeding out like a flooded river, creating new inlets in as many nooks and crannies as possible. Carrying her body took a bit of effort, but she half-dragged herself through the woods, away from Mick, away from Melanie, and away from It.

When she made it to the bottom of the trail, tears escaped her eyes. The moonlight reflected off the still water of the pond. She took off her warm winter jacket and waded into the water. A tremble slipped through her, a chill cascading throughout her entire body. But Julie persisted until her shoulders were covered and she came face-to-face with a thick, sheer coat of ice.

Her other body she carried remained limp when she let go of it, drifting underneath the water until it was trapped beneath the ice. An odd pain crept through Julie's body, similar to the sensation of a time traveler entering the universe, but the silence of the air provided comfort that wasn't the case. It was the final goodbye for that version of Julie.

Back on shore, Julie stripped off her wet, cold clothes and put back on her pants and the warm jacket. The dim lights illuminating the clearing where she had left Mick, It, and Melanie behind made her pause. Their bodies were collapsed on top of the snow, crimson disintegrating pixels surrounding them, bursting vividly in the air.

Julie stepped back in awe and shock—a mix of fear and enchantment at the scene occurring in front of her.

My body, the rescue of my body, really was the time loop that sparked the future dimension I come from. By destroying myself, I really did close the loop, not allowing it to be a continuous circle. Mick was right.

She placed her hand on her lower abdomen and stroked the small bump finally beginning to show. *Thank you,* she thought. *And now, I can resume in this dimension. I can take her place.*

The walk took her almost an hour, and her fingers and toes went completely numb. The ends of her hair froze, icicle-like condensation forming along her eyelashes. When the subway station appeared, Julie smiled.

No one bothered giving a second glance at the nearly frostbitten woman sitting next to them on the red line. Everyone minded their own business at this hour of night. Eventually, The City's high skyscrapers came into view and the heat in the subway car finally warmed Julie. Wiggling her toes and fingers, she checked her pockets again. Much like the first time Julie took this route after returning to this point in time, she waited until Park Street to exit the subway.

Her favorite green space in The City appeared when she made her way up from underground. Even in the nighttime, the park was lit up brightly, and Julie felt safe here. Instead of heading southwest toward The Bay and her apartment, Julie moved directly west toward The Hill. The Capitol Building came into view, the golden dome eyeing her suspiciously in the evening light. It was only a matter of minutes before the O'Connor townhouse appeared.

Colin's vehicle was in the garage, and Julie heard the washing machine from the laundry room. The house still smelled of the pasta she remembered them cooking together that evening. A slight purple ring hugged the table runner on the dining room table where a missing bottle of wine once stood.

The sound of Colin's heavy footsteps upstairs startled her, but Julie remained stealthy as she rushed to the staircase. Few lights were on, but the sound of rustling in the study solidified a perfect opportunity.

Julie darted for the master bedroom and paused at the bottle of pills on the nightstand, her college sweatshirt tossed on the floor next to her socks. She advanced to the bathroom, hoping there she could hide long enough to catch Colin by surprise. The light shone brightly, and she held her breath.

His advancing footsteps sounded in the master bedroom. Only one set—she wasn't dealing with a time traveler version of him too. The tall, looming, recognizable shadow appeared across the tiled bathroom floors.

He stilled, and they stared at one another with wide eyes. Her body was unrecognizable to him in this form, and he wasn't expecting to see the woman he recently left bleeding in the woods standing unharmed in his bathroom.

"Julie?" he asked.

She looked down at her trembling hands and the two syringes: the antidote and the toxin. Going back and forth on the decision before time traveling did her no good. Either choice had its own consequences. But she needed to decide, and she had to decide quickly.

"This must be done."

Julie instinctually dropped the syringe in her right hand, her dominant hand, and it bounced on the floor with a small ping. The cap of the other syringe in her left hand flicked off the needle, and she swiftly turned, colliding with him and injecting the drug into his arm. Julie pushed down on the plunger, the contents of the single-dose injection entering his body.

He didn't flinch. He didn't move.

As if he expected this.

PART TEN
The Future

"This part I will do alone, leaving you behind. Don't follow. I'm well beyond
you now, and traveling very fast."
—Jeff VanderMeer

<u>Epilogue</u>

<u>June 23rd, 50 A.R.</u>

He walked over to the balcony's ledge, gripping the stone barrier tightly. The sun shone brightly, no clouds painting the sky above and the salty air filled his nose. A small smile crept across his face as he looked back toward the crumpled sheets on the bed, Julie's college sweatshirt thrown haphazardly in the corner. The smell of coffee wafted up the stairs.

He climbed down and smiled seeing the French doors left open out to the patio, enticing him to wander outside. The morning dew on the green lawn felt slippery on his feet. This summer promised glorious weather, few storms, and a serenity along the coastline. He couldn't wait to buckle down here, leaving The City out of sight and out of mind when Julie took a few weeks in a row off from COLI*GO.

The sounds of harsh waves breaking against the cliffs drew his attention toward the steps leading down the rocks to a beachy, secluded spot. Julie's sandals rested at the top of the wooden staircase, and he heard her indistinguishable laughter carried up by the wind. Carefully descending the steps, he leaped after the sound of Julie's voice.

This part of the beach was safer and calmer, a small pool letting in the possibility of an afternoon swim if the water wasn't too cool. They needed a few more weeks of warm weather and then venturing in past the knees would be welcoming after sunbathing in the warm rays of sunshine. As he reached the sandy beach, a tingle edged across the skin of his bare feet. The tide waded out slowly, its vengeance subsided for now.

Joy consumed him at the sight of Julie and the toddler hugging against her hips, kissing her cheek, and squealing in youthful delight.

Julie turned around and smiled wide in his direction. She waved and kissed the top of their child's head. She waded back to the edge of the shoreline until only sand cascaded around her feet. The toddler kicked with eager legs, and Julie placed her down into the sand.

Excitement and thrill flung across her wildly thrown arms and big steely-blue eyes. Innocence in its truest form, a gift he'd always treasure. One he'd always protect.

It crouched down and spread his arms wide, ready to embrace his daughter. But she ran straight past him and his open arms.

Acknowledgements

Writing REVIRESCO was one of the most challenging creative experiences I've encountered. I knew how this story would unfold, I thoughtfully planned the wrap-ups for Jones, Mick, Celine, Elsie, and The Supreme. But It, Colin and Julie—that last sentence haunted me for months on end. I told my beta-readers and my editor that I wasn't sure if I would keep the last sentence or not. I did not tell anyone what I ended up deciding but I hope you understand why I kept the last sentence. Ultimately, I believe the essence of this story—no matter how much I love the complex, dark and twisted understanding relationship between It and Julie—required an ambiguous ending fitting to the UNITAS universe.

First, as always, thank you to my readers. As always, I can't believe I created a world and characters that people not only believe in, but enjoy. The UNITAS story wouldn't be here if it weren't for all of you.

Thank you to my dad, Geoff Smith. Because of him, I am a huge sci-fi book lover, and getting to share all of the theories, rabbit holes, and oddly intellectual conversations that make zero sense to anyone eavesdropping in is years of memories I will cherish forever.

Second, thank you to my mom, Linda Smith. The industry says your parents shouldn't be considered beta-readers but honestly, you're the best beta reader—and she's willing to read my stories over and over again. My parents are my number one supporters and I love you. Thank you for everything.

A sincere and heartfelt thank you to my cover artist and one of my closest friends, Tori Mulhern. I almost gave up on this series and I'm forever grateful that you talked me out of giving up. Our friendship makes holding physical copies of these beautiful books so much more special knowing you're an integral part of them.

A special shout out to some of my "OG" beta-readers: Barbara, Cathy, Kira, and Kirstie.

This story wouldn't be where it is today without my amazing editor, Jenny. Thank you so much for all your hard work, catching the mistakes and making them beautiful—I'm so glad to have you through this process. Your comments make me laugh, and I'll never forget your note about my dangerous last sentence! Jenny is one of the rare gems who champions writers and I couldn't be luckier.

Thank you to my fantastic graphic designer, Keir DuBois. Without him we wouldn't have the map that everyone loves! It is truly stunning and I'm forever grateful that you helped visually build the world of the UNITAS Series.

I took various creative liberties while writing about specific topics but would like to acknowledge the research, studies and papers that enlightened and educated me in areas where I'm not a subject matter expert.

Thank you to my grandmother, Idella White. I miss her so much. She is truly the inspiration for my publishing company and its namesake. Thank you to my grandfather, James White for the unconditional love and support.

Thank you to my friends, family, co-workers, and BookTok friends/community who have listened to me talk about my writing journey (probably too much) and have been huge cheerleaders regardless. In no particular order, rhyme or reason: Rachel, Jonathan, Emily, Jessie, Joshua, Holly, Anu, Ranga, Josh, Andrea, Rachel, just to name a few.

Lastly, thank you to everyone who relates to someone in this story. I see you, I believe in you, and I accept you.

I know this is the end of the UNITAS Series, but I hope to see you on the other side of my upcoming story, *The Demon's Prometheus*. I can't wait.

Sincerely,
Lee S. Hannon

About Lee S. Hannon

While not a time traveler yet, Lee S. Hannon works in the biotech & pharmaceutical industry, helping launch and sustain novel therapies within rare diseases.

She writes fantasy, speculative & science fiction.

Lee S. Hannon resides in Boston, the city inspiring the world of the UNITAS Series. Her passion for crafting thought-provoking stories with her background in biotech inspired her ideas on time travel through blood and a cutting-edge world desperately wishing it was better than our own.

When not working or writing, Lee S. Hannon can be found at a spin class, trying a new recipe in her kitchen, or adventuring to a new coffee shop.

Lee S. Hannon loves hearing from readers. Please reach out at sleehannon@gmail.com or follow her on social media platforms: Instagram, TikTok, Twitter, and Facebook (@LeeSHannonBooks).